Lessons in Chemistry

LESSONS

IN

CHEMISTRY

·········· ········ ·········

Bonnie Garmus

DOUBLEDAY

New York

Copyright © 2022 by Bonnie Garmus

All rights reserved. Published in the United States by Doubleday, a division of Penguin Random House LLC, New York.

www.doubleday.com

DOUBLEDAY and the portrayal of an anchor with a dolphin are registered trademarks of Penguin Random House LLC.

Book design by Maria Carella
Jacket design and illustration by Jim Tierney
Back-of-jacket images: (oars) © marina_ua/Shutterstock; (dog) asmakar/iStock/Getty Images

Library of Congress Cataloging-in-Publication Data
Names: Garmus, Bonnie, author.
Title: Lessons in chemistry : a novel / Bonnie Garmus.
Description: First edition. | New York : Doubleday, [2022]
Identifiers: LCCN 2021008194 (print) | LCCN 2021008195 (ebook) |
ISBN 9780385547345 (hardcover) | ISBN 9780385547376 (ebook)
Subjects: LCSH: Women scientists—Fiction. | Single mothers—Fiction. |
Television cooking shows—Fiction. | Sex role—Fiction.
Classification: LCC PS3607.A756 L47 2022 (print) |
LCC PS3607.A756 (ebook) | DDC 813/.6—dc23
LC record available at https://lccn.loc.gov/2021008194
LC ebook record available at https://lccn.loc.gov/2021008195

MANUFACTURED IN THE UNITED STATES OF AMERICA
16 18 20 19 17
First Edition

For my mother, Mary Swallow Garmus

LESSONS IN CHEMISTRY

CHAPTER 1

November 1961

Back in 1961, when women wore shirtwaist dresses and joined garden clubs and drove legions of children around in seatbeltless cars without giving it a second thought; back before anyone knew there'd even be a sixties movement, much less one that its participants would spend the next sixty years chronicling; back when the big wars were over and the secret wars had just begun and people were starting to think fresh and believe everything was possible, the thirty-year-old mother of Madeline Zott rose before dawn every morning and felt certain of just one thing: her life was over.

Despite that certainty, she made her way to the lab to pack her daughter's lunch.

Fuel for learning, Elizabeth Zott wrote on a small slip of paper before tucking it into her daughter's lunch box. Then she paused, her pencil in midair, as if reconsidering. *Play sports at recess but do not automatically let the boys win,* she wrote on another slip. Then she paused again, tapping her pencil against the table. *It is not your imagination,* she wrote on a third. *Most people are awful.* She placed the last two on top.

Most young children can't read, and if they can, it's mostly words like "dog" and "go." But Madeline had been reading since age three and, now, at age five, was already through most of Dickens.

Madeline was *that* kind of child—the kind who could hum a Bach concerto but couldn't tie her own shoes; who could explain the earth's rotation but stumbled at tic-tac-toe. And that was the problem. Because while musical prodigies are always celebrated, early readers aren't. And that's because early readers are only good at something others will eventually be good at, too. So being first isn't special—it's just annoying.

Madeline understood this. That's why she made it a point each morning—after her mother had left and while her baby-sitter neighbor, Harriet, was busy—to extract the notes from the lunch box, read them, then store them with all the other notes that she kept in a shoebox in the back of her closet. Once at school she pretended to be like all the other kids: basically illiterate. To Madeline, fitting in mattered more than anything. And her proof was irrefutable: her mother had never fit in and look what happened to her.

It was there, in the Southern Californian town of Commons, where the weather was mostly warm, but not too warm, and the sky was mostly blue, but not too blue, and the air was clean because air just was back then, that she lay in her bed, eyes closed, and waited. Soon she knew there'd be a gentle kiss on her forehead, a careful tuck of covers about her shoulders, a murmuring of "Seize the day" in her ear. In another minute, she'd hear the start of a car engine, a crunch of tires as the Plymouth backed down the drive, a clunky shift from reverse to first. And then her permanently depressed mother would set off for the television studio where she would don an apron and walk out onto a set.

The show was called *Supper at Six,* and Elizabeth Zott was its indisputable star.

CHAPTER 2

Pine

Once a research chemist, Elizabeth Zott was a woman with flaw-less skin and an unmistakable demeanor of someone who was not average and never would be.

She was, as all good stars are, discovered. Although in Eliza-beth's case, there was no malt shop, no accidental bench sight-ing, no lucky introduction. Instead, it was theft—specifically food theft—that led to her discovery.

The story was simple: a child named Amanda Pine, who enjoyed food in a way some therapists consider significant, was eating Madeline's lunch. This was because Madeline's lunch was not average. While all the other children gummed their peanut butter and jelly sandwiches, Madeline opened her lunch box to find a thick slice of leftover lasagna, a side helping of buttery zuc-chini, an exotic kiwi cut into quarters, five pearly round cherry tomatoes, a tiny Morton salt shaker, two still-warm chocolate chip cookies, and a red plaid thermos full of ice-cold milk.

These contents were why everyone wanted Madeline's lunch, Madeline included. But Madeline offered it to Amanda because friendship requires sacrifice, but also because Amanda was the only one in the entire school who didn't make fun of the odd child Madeline already knew she was.

It wasn't until Elizabeth noticed that Madeline's clothes began to hang on her bony frame like bad drapes that she began to wonder what was going on. According to her calculations, Madeline's daily intake was exactly what her daughter required for optimal development, making weight loss scientifically inconceivable. A growth spurt, then? No. She'd accounted for growth in her calculations. Early onset food disorder? Not likely. Madeline ate like a horse at dinner. Leukemia? Definitely not. Elizabeth wasn't an alarmist—she wasn't the type who lay awake at night imagining her daughter was plagued by incurable disease. As a scientist, she always sought a sensible explanation, and the moment she met Amanda Pine, her little lips stained a pomodoro-sauce red, she knew she'd found it.

"Mr. Pine," Elizabeth said, sweeping into the local television studio and past a secretary on a Wednesday afternoon, "I've been calling you for three days, and not once have you managed the courtesy of a return call. My name is Elizabeth Zott. I am Madeline Zott's mother—our children attend Woody Elementary together—and I'm here to tell you that your daughter is offering my daughter friendship under false pretenses." And because he looked confused, she added, "Your daughter is eating my daughter's lunch."

"L-lunch?" Walter Pine managed, as he took in the woman who stood resplendent before him, her white lab coat casting an aura of holy light save for one detail: the initials "E.Z." emblazoned in red just above the pocket.

"Your daughter, Amanda," Elizabeth charged again, "eats my daughter's lunch. Apparently, it's been going on for months."

Walter could only stare. Tall and angular, with hair the color of burnt buttered toast pulled back and secured with a pencil, she stood, hands on hips, her lips unapologetically red, her skin luminous, her nose straight. She looked down at him like a battlefield medic assessing whether or not he was worth saving.

"And the fact that she pretends to be Madeline's friend to get her lunch," she continued, "is absolutely reprehensible."

"Wh-who are you again?" stammered Walter.

"Elizabeth Zott!" she barked back. "Madeline Zott's mother!"

Walter nodded, trying to understand. As a longtime producer of afternoon television, he knew drama. But this? He continued to stare. She was stunning. He was literally *stunned* by her. Was she auditioning for something?

"I'm sorry," he finally said. "But all the nurse roles have been cast."

"I beg your pardon?" she snapped.

There was a long pause.

"Amanda Pine," she repeated.

He blinked. "My daughter? Oh," he said, suddenly nervous. "What about her? Are you a doctor? Are you from the school?" He leapt to his feet.

"Good god, no," Elizabeth replied. "I'm a chemist. I've come all the way over here from Hastings on my lunch hour because you've failed to return my calls." And when he continued to look baffled, she clarified. "Hastings Research Institute? Where Groundbreaking Research Breaks Ground?" She exhaled at the vacuous tagline. "The point is, I put a great amount of effort into making a nutritious lunch for Madeline—something that I'm sure you also strive to do for your child." And when he continued to stare at her blankly, she added, "Because you care about Amanda's cognitive and physical development. Because you know such development is reliant on offering the correct balance of vitamins and minerals."

"The thing is, Mrs. Pine is—"

"Yes, I know. Missing in action. I tried to contact her but was told she lives in New York."

"We're divorced."

"Sorry to hear, but divorce has little to do with lunch."

"It might seem that way, but—"

"A man *can* make lunch, Mr. Pine. It is not biologically impossible."

"Absolutely," he agreed, fumbling with a chair. "Please, Mrs. Zott, please sit."

"I have something in the cyclotron," she said irritably, glancing at her watch. "Do we have an understanding or not?"

"Cyclo—"

"Subatomic particle accelerator."

Elizabeth glanced at the walls. They were filled with framed posters advertising melodramatic soap operas and gimmicky game shows.

"My work," Walter said, suddenly embarrassed by their crassness. "Maybe you've seen one?"

She turned back to face him. "Mr. Pine," she said in a more conciliatory manner, "I'm sorry I don't have the time or resources to make your daughter lunch. We both know food is the catalyst that unlocks our brains, binds our families, and determines our futures. And yet . . ." She trailed off, her eyes growing narrow as she took in a soap opera poster featuring a nurse giving a patient some unusual care. "Does anyone have the time to teach the entire nation to make food that matters? I wish I did, but I don't. Do you?"

As she turned to leave, Pine, not wanting her to go or fully understanding what he was about to hatch, said quickly, "Wait, please just stop—*please*. What—what was that thing you just said? About teaching the whole nation how to make food that—that *matters*?"

Supper at Six debuted four weeks later. And while Elizabeth wasn't entirely keen on the idea—she was a research chemist—she took the job for the usual reasons: it paid more and she had a child to support.

From the first day Elizabeth donned an apron and walked onto the set, it was obvious: she had "it," the "it" being that elusive, entirely watchable quality. But she was also a person of substance—someone so forthright, so no-nonsense that people didn't know what to make of her. While other cooking shows featured good-natured chefs gleefully tipping back the sherry, Elizabeth Zott was serious. She never smiled. She never made jokes. And her dishes were as honest and down-to-earth as she was.

Within six months, Elizabeth's show was a rising star. Within a year, an institution. And within two years, it had proven its uncanny power not only to unite parents with their children, but citizens with their country. It is not an exaggeration to say that when Elizabeth Zott finished cooking, an entire nation sat down to eat.

Even Vice President Lyndon Johnson watched her show. "You want to know what I *think*?" he said as he waved off a persistent reporter. "I think you ought to write less and watch TV more. Start with *Supper at Six*—that Zott, she knows what she's doing."

And she did. You'd never find Elizabeth Zott explaining how to make tiny cucumber sandwiches or delicate soufflés. Her recipes were hearty: stews, casseroles, things made in big metal pans. She stressed the four food groups. She believed in decent portions. And she insisted that any dish worth making was worth making in under an hour. She ended every show with her signature line: "Children, set the table. Your mother needs a moment to herself."

But then a prominent reporter wrote an article entitled "Why We'll Eat Whatever She Dishes Out" and, in passing, referred to her as "Luscious Lizzie," a nickname that, because it was both apt and alliterative, stuck to her as quickly as it did the paper it was printed on. From that day forward, strangers called her Luscious, but her daughter, Madeline, called her Mom, and although she was just a child, Madeline could already see that the nickname belittled her mother's talents. She was a chemist, not a TV cook. And Elizabeth, self-conscious in front of her only child, felt ashamed.

Sometimes Elizabeth lay in bed at night and wondered how her life had come to this. But the wonder never lasted long because she already knew.

His name was Calvin Evans.

CHAPTER 3

Hastings Research Institute

Calvin Evans also worked at Hastings Research Institute, but unlike Elizabeth, who worked in crowded conditions, he had a large lab all to himself.

Based on his track record, maybe he deserved the lab. By age nineteen, he had already contributed critical research that helped famed British chemist Frederick Sanger clinch the Nobel Prize; at twenty-two, he discovered a faster way to synthesize simple proteins; at twenty-four, his breakthrough concerning the reactivity of dibenzoselenophene put him on the cover of *Chemistry Today*. In addition, he'd authored sixteen scientific papers, received invitations to ten international conferences, and had been offered a fellowship at Harvard. Twice. Which he turned down. Twice. Partly because Harvard had rejected his freshman application years earlier, and partly because—well, actually, there was no other reason. Calvin was a brilliant man, but if he had one flaw, it was his ability to hold a grudge.

On top of his grudge holding, he had a reputation for impatience. Like so many brilliant people, Calvin just couldn't understand how no one else *got it*. He was also an introvert, which isn't really a flaw but often manifests itself as standoffishness. Worst of all, he was a rower.

As any non-rower can tell you, rowers are not fun. This is because rowers only ever want to talk about rowing. Get two or more rowers in a room and the conversation goes from normal topics like work or weather to long, pointless stories about boats, blisters, oars, grips, ergs, feathers, workouts, catches, releases, recoveries, splits, seats, strokes, slides, starts, settles, sprints, and whether the water was really "flat" or not. From there, it usually progresses to what went wrong on the last row, what might go wrong on the next row, and whose fault it was and/or will be. At some point the rowers will hold out their hands and compare calluses. If you're really unlucky, this could be followed by several minutes of head-bowing reverence as one of them recounts the perfect row where it all felt easy.

Other than chemistry, rowing was the only thing Calvin had true passion for. In fact, rowing is why Calvin applied to Harvard in the first place: to row for Harvard was, in 1945, to row for the best. Or actually *second* best. University of Washington was *the* best, but University of Washington was in Seattle and Seattle had a reputation for rain. Calvin hated rain. Therefore, he looked further afield—to the other Cambridge, the one in England, thus exposing one of the biggest myths about scientists: that they're any good at research.

   The first day Calvin rowed on the Cam, it rained. The second day it rained. Third day: same. "Does it rain like this *all* the time?" Calvin complained as he and his teammates hoisted the heavy wooden boat to their shoulders and lumbered out to the dock. "Oh never," they reassured him, "Cambridge is usually quite balmy." And then they looked at one another as if to confirm what they had already long suspected: Americans were idiots.

Unfortunately, his idiocy also extended to dating—a big problem since Calvin very much wanted to fall in love. During all six lonely years he spent in Cambridge, he managed to ask out five women, and of those five, only one consented to a second date, and that was only because she'd thought he was someone else when she answered the phone. His main issue was inexperience. He was like a dog who, after years of trying, catches a squirrel and then has absolutely no idea what to do with it.

"Hello—uh," he'd said, his heart pounding, his hands moist, his mind suddenly completely blank as his date opened the door. "Debbie?"

"It's *Deirdre*," his date sighed, taking the first of what would be many glances at her watch.

At dinner, the conversation lurched between the molecular breakdown of aromatic acids (Calvin), to what movie might be playing (Deirdre), to the synthesis of nonreactive proteins (Calvin), to whether or not he liked to dance (Deirdre), to look at the time, it was already eight thirty p.m. and he had to row in the morning so he would be taking her straight home (Calvin).

It goes without saying that there was very little sex after these dates. Actually, there was none.

"I can't believe you're having trouble," his Cambridge teammates would tell him. "Girls *love* rowers." Which wasn't true. "And even though you're an American, you're not bad looking." Which was also not true.

Part of the problem was Calvin's posture. He was six feet four inches tall, lanky and long, but he slouched to the right—probably a by-product of always rowing stroke side. But the bigger issue was his face. He had a lonesome look about him, like a child who'd had to raise himself, with large gray eyes and messy blondish hair and purplish lips, the latter of which were nearly always swollen because he tended to chew on them. His was the kind of face that some might call forgettable, a below-average composition that gave no hint of the longing or intelligence that lay behind, save for one critical feature—his teeth—which were straight and white, and which redeemed his entire facial landscape whenever he smiled. Fortunately, especially after falling in love with Elizabeth Zott, Calvin smiled all the time.

They first met—or rather, exchanged words—on a Tuesday morning at Hastings Research Institute, the sunny Southern Californian private research lab where Calvin, having graduated from Cambridge with a PhD in record time and with forty-three employment offers to weigh, accepted a position partly because of reputation, but mostly because of precipitation. It didn't rain much in Commons. Elizabeth, on the other hand, accepted Hastings's offer because it was the only one she received.

As she stood outside Calvin Evans's lab, she noted a number of large warning signs:

DO NOT ENTER
EXPERIMENT IN PROGRESS
NO ADMITTANCE
KEEP OUT

Then she opened the door.

"Hello," she called over Frank Sinatra, who was blasting from a hi-fi that sat incongruously in the middle of the room. "I need to speak to whoever is in charge."

Calvin, surprised to hear a voice, poked his head out from behind a large centrifuge.

"Excuse me, miss," he called, irritated, a large pair of goggles shielding his eyes from whatever was bubbling off to his right, "but this area is off-limits. Didn't you see the signs?"

"I *did*," Elizabeth yelled back, ignoring his tone as she made her way across the lab to switch off the music. "There. Now we can hear each other."

Calvin chewed his lips and pointed. "You can't be in here," he said. "The *signs*."

"Yes, well, I was told that your lab has a surplus of beakers and we're short downstairs. It's all here," she said, thrusting a piece of paper at him. "It's been cleared by the inventory manager."

"I didn't hear anything about it," Calvin said, examining the paper. "And I'm sorry, but no. I need every beaker. Maybe I'd better speak with a chemist down there. You tell your boss to call me." He turned back to his work, flipping the hi-fi back on as he did.

Elizabeth didn't move. "You want to speak to a chemist? Someone other than ME?" she yelled over Frank.

"Yes," he answered. And then he softened slightly. "Look, I know it's not your fault, but they shouldn't send a secretary up here to do their dirty work. Now I know this might be hard for you to understand, but I'm in the middle of something important. Please. Just tell your boss to call me."

Elizabeth's eyes narrowed. She did not care for people who made assumptions based on what she felt were long-outdated visual clues, and she also didn't care for men who believed, even if she had been a secretary, that being a secretary meant she was incapable of understanding words beyond "Type this up in triplicate."

"What a coincidence," she shouted as she went straight over to a shelf and helped herself to a large box of beakers. "I'm busy too." Then she marched out.

More than three thousand people worked at Hastings Research Institute—that's why it took Calvin over a week to track her down—and when he did finally find her, she seemed not to remember him.

"Yes?" she said, turning to see who had entered her lab, a large pair of safety glasses magnifying her eyes, her hands and forearms wrapped in large rubber mitts.

"Hello," he said. "It's me."

"Me?" she asked. "Could you be more specific?" She turned back to her work.

"Me," Calvin said. "Five floors up? You took my beakers?"

"You might want to stand back behind that curtain," she said, tossing her head to the left. "We had a little accident in here last week."

"You're hard to track down."

"Do you mind?" she asked. "Now *I'm* in the middle of something important."

He waited patiently while she finished her measurements, made notations in her book, reexamined yesterday's test results, and went to the restroom.

"You're still here?" she asked, coming back. "Don't you have work to do?"

"Tons."

"You can't have your beakers back."

"So, you do remember me."

"Yes. But not fondly."

"I came to apologize."

"No need."

"How about lunch?"

"No."

"Dinner?"

"No."

"Coffee?"

"Listen," Elizabeth said, her large mitts resting on her hipbones, "you should know you're starting to annoy me."

Calvin looked away, embarrassed. "I sincerely beg your pardon," he said. "I'll go."

"Was that Calvin *Evans*?" a lab tech asked as he watched Calvin weave his way through fifteen scientists working elbow to elbow in a space a quarter the size of Calvin's private lab. "What was he doing down here?"

"Minor beaker ownership issue," Elizabeth said.

"Beakers?" He hesitated. "Wait." He picked up one of the

new beakers. "That big box of beakers you said you found last week. They were *his*?"

"I never said I found beakers. I said I *acquired* beakers."

"From Calvin Evans?" he said. "Are you crazy?"

"Not technically."

"Did he say you could take his beakers?"

"Not technically. But I had a form."

"What form? You know you have to go through me. You know ordering supplies is my job."

"I understand. But I've been waiting for more than three months. I've asked you four times, I've filled out five requisition orders, I've spoken to Dr. Donatti about it. Honestly, I didn't know what else to do. My research depends on getting these supplies. *They're just beakers.*"

The lab tech closed his eyes. "Listen," he said, slowly reopening them as if to dramatize her stupidity. "I've been here a lot longer than you and I know things. You know what Calvin Evans is famous for, don't you? Besides chemistry?"

"Yes. Having an excess of equipment."

"No," he said. "He's famous for holding a grudge. A grudge!"

"Really?" she said taking interest.

Elizabeth Zott held grudges too. Except her grudges were mainly reserved for a patriarchal society founded on the idea that women were less. Less capable. Less intelligent. Less inventive. A society that believed men went to work and did important things—discovered planets, developed products, created laws—and women stayed at home and raised children. She didn't want children—she knew this about herself—but she also knew that plenty of other women *did* want children *and* a career. And what was wrong with that? Nothing. It was exactly what men got.

She'd recently read about some country where both parents worked *and* took part in raising the children. Where was that, again? Sweden? She couldn't remember. But the upshot was, it functioned very well. Productivity was higher; families were stronger. She saw herself living in such a society. A place that didn't always automatically mistake her for a secretary, a place where, when she presented her findings in a meeting, she didn't have to brace herself for the men who would invariably talk over her, or worse, take credit for her work. Elizabeth shook her head. When it came to equality, 1952 was a real disappointment.

"You have to apologize to him," the lab tech was insisting. "When you take the damn beakers back, grovel. You put our entire lab at risk, and you made me look bad."

"It'll be fine," Elizabeth said. "They're beakers."

But by the next morning, the beakers were gone, replaced by dirty looks from a few of her fellow chemists who now also believed she'd put them in jeopardy of Calvin Evans's legendary grudge holding. She tried to talk with them, but each gave her the cold shoulder in their own way, and later, as she was walking by the lounge, she overheard the same few grousing about her— about how she took herself so seriously, how she thought she was better than any of them, how she'd refused dates from all of them, even the single men. And how the only way she could have possibly gotten her master's from UCLA in organic chemistry was the *hard* way—the word "hard" being accompanied by rude gestures and tight laughter. Who did she think she was anyway?

"Someone ought to put her in her place," said one.

"She's not even that smart," insisted another.

"She's a cunt," declared a familiar voice. Her boss, Donatti.

Elizabeth, accustomed to the first words but stunned by the last, pressed herself against the wall, overcome by a wave of nausea. This was the second time she'd been called that word. The first time—the first horrible time—had been at UCLA.

It had happened nearly two years ago. A master's candidate with only ten days left before graduation, she was still in the lab at nine p.m., certain she'd found a problem with the test protocol.

As she tapped a freshly sharpened number-two pencil against the paper, weighing her hunch, she heard the door open.

"Hello?" she called. She wasn't expecting anyone.

"You're still here," said a voice free of surprise. Her advisor.

"Oh. Hello, Dr. Meyers," she said, looking up. "Yes. Just going over the test protocol for tomorrow. I think I found a problem."

He opened the door a little wider, stepping inside. "I didn't ask you to do that," he said, his voice edgy with irritation. "I told you it was all set."

"I know," she said. "But I wanted to give it one last look." The one-last-look approach wasn't something Elizabeth liked to do—it was something she knew she *had* to do to maintain her position on Meyers's all-male research team. Not that she really cared about his research: his was safe stuff, not at all groundbreaking. Despite a notable lack of creativity paired with an alarming absence of new discoveries, Meyers was considered one of the top DNA researchers in the United States.

Elizabeth didn't like Meyers; no one did. Except, possibly, UCLA, who loved him because the man published more papers than anyone in the field. Meyers's secret? He didn't write the papers—his graduate students did. But he always took full credit for every word, sometimes only changing the title and a few phrases here and there before passing it off as an entirely different paper, which he could do because who reads a scientific paper all the way through? No one. Thus his papers grew in number, and with them, his reputation. That's how Meyers became a top DNA researcher: quantity.

Besides his talent for superfluous papers, Meyers was also famous for being a lecher. There weren't many women in the science departments at UCLA, but the few there were—mostly secretaries—became the focus of his unwanted attention. They usually left after six months, their confidence shaken, their eyes swollen, citing personal reasons. But Elizabeth did not leave— she couldn't, she needed the master's. So she endured the day-to-day degradations—the touches, the lewd comments, the rank suggestions—while making it clear she had no interest. Until the day he called her into his office, ostensibly to talk about her admittance to his doctoral program, but instead shoving his hand up her skirt. Furious, she forcibly removed it, then threatened to report him.

"To whom?" he laughed. Then he admonished her for being "no fun" and swatted her bottom, demanding that she go fetch his coat from his office closet, knowing that when she opened the door she would find it lined with pictures of topless women, a few splayed, expressionless, on their hands and knees, a man's shoe resting triumphantly on their backs.

"It's here," she said to Dr. Meyers. "Step ninety-one on page two thirty-two. The temperature. I'm fairly certain it's too high, which means the enzyme will be rendered inactive, skewing the results."

Dr. Meyers watched her from the door. "Did you show this to anyone else?"

"No," she said. "I just noticed it."

"So, you haven't talked with Phillip." Phillip was Meyers's top research assistant.

"No," she said. "He just left. I'm sure I could still catch him—"

"No need," he interrupted. "Is anyone else here?"

"Not that I know of."

"The protocol is right," he said sharply. "You're not the expert. Stop questioning my authority. And don't mention this to anyone else. Do you understand?"

"I was only trying to help, Dr. Meyers."

He looked at her, as if weighing the veracity of her offer. "And I need your help," he said. And then he turned back toward the door and locked it.

His first blow was an open-handed slap that spun her head to the left like a well-hit tetherball. She gasped in shock, then managed to right herself, her mouth bleeding, her eyes wide with disbelief. He grimaced as if unsatisfied with his results, then hit her again, this time knocking her off the stool. Meyers was a big man— nearly 250 pounds—his strength a product of density, not fitness. He bent down to where she lay on the floor and, grabbing her by the hips, hoisted her up like a crane lifting a sloppy load of lumber, plunking her back down on the stool like a rag doll. Then he flipped her over, and kicking the stool away, slammed her face and chest against the stainless-steel counter. "Hold still, cunt," he demanded as she struggled, his fat fingers clawing beneath her skirt.

Elizabeth gasped, the taste of metal filling her mouth as he mauled her, one hand pulling her skirt up past her waist, the other twisting the skin of her inner thighs. With her face flat against the table, she could barely breathe, let alone scream. She kicked back furiously like an animal caught in a trap, but her refusal to concede only infuriated him more.

"Don't fight me," he warned, as sweat dripped from his stomach onto the backs of her thighs. But as he moved, her arm regained freedom. "Hold *still*," he demanded, enraged, as she twisted back and forth, gasping in shock, his bulbous torso flattening her body like a pancake. In a final effort to remind her who was in charge he gripped her hair and yanked. Then he shoved himself inside her like a sloppy drunk, moaning with satisfaction until it was cut short by a shriek of pain.

"Fuck!" Meyers yelled, pulling his weight from her. "Jesus, fuck! What was that?" He shoved her away, confused by a blaze of misery springing from the right side of his body. He looked down at his blubbery waist, trying to make sense of the pain, but all he saw was a small pink eraser sticking out from his right iliac region. It was encircled by a narrow moat of blood.

The number-two pencil. With her free hand, Elizabeth had found it, gripped it, and driven it straight into his side. Not just part of it—all of it. Its sharply pointed lead, its friendly yellow wood, its shiny gold band—all seven inches of it versus all seven inches of him. And in doing so, she pierced not only his large and small intestine, but her academic career as well.

"Do you *really* go here?" the campus police officer said after an ambulance had taken Dr. Meyers away. "I need to see some student ID."

Elizabeth, her clothes torn, her hands shaking, a large bruise beginning to bloom on her forehead, looked back, incredulous.

"It's a valid question," the officer said. "What would a woman be doing in a lab this time of night?"

"I'm a gr-graduate student," she stuttered, feeling like she might be sick. "In chemistry."

The officer exhaled as if he didn't have time for this sort of nonsense, then took out a small notepad. "Why don't you tell me what you *think* happened."

Elizabeth supplied him with the details, her voice dulled by shock. He looked as if he was jotting it down, but when he turned away to tell another officer he "had it all under control," she noticed that the notepad was blank.

"Please. I . . . I need a doctor."

He flipped his notepad shut. "Would you like to make a statement of regret?" Then he gave her skirt a glance as if the fabric alone was an obvious invitation. "You stabbed the man. It'll go better for you if you show some remorse."

She looked back at him, hollow eyed. "You . . . you misunderstand, Officer. He attacked me. I . . . I defended myself. I need a doctor."

The officer exhaled. "No statement of regret, then?" he said, clicking his pen shut.

She stared at him, her mouth slightly open, her body trembling. She looked down at her thigh where Meyers's handprint was outlined in a light purple. She choked back the urge to vomit.

She looked up in time to see him checking his watch. That small movement was all it took. She reached out and snatched her ID card back from between his fingers. "Yes, Officer," she said, her voice as taut as prison wire. "Now that I think about it, I do have one regret."

"Much better," he said. "Now we're getting somewhere." He clicked his pen back open. "Let's hear it."

"Pencils," she said.

"Pencils," he repeated, writing it down.

She raised her head to meet his eyes, a rivulet of blood coursing from her temple. "I regret not having more of them."

The attack, or "unfortunate event," as the admissions committee called it just before they formally rescinded her admittance to the doctoral program, had been her doing. Dr. Meyers had caught her cheating. She'd tried to change a test protocol to skew the experiment's results—he had the proof right here—and when he'd confronted her, she'd thrown herself at him, offering sex. When that didn't work, a physical fight ensued and before he knew it, he had a pencil in his gut. He was lucky to be alive.

Almost no one bought this story. Dr. Meyers had a reputation. But he was also important, and UCLA had no intention of losing someone of his stature. Elizabeth was out. Her master's was complete. Her bruises would heal. Someone would write her a recommendation. Go.

That's how she'd ended up at Hastings Research Institute. And now here she was, outside the Hastings lounge, her back pressed against a wall, sick to her stomach.

She looked up to find the lab tech peering at her. "You all right, Zott?" he asked. "You look kind of funny."

She didn't reply.

"My fault, Zott," he admitted. "I shouldn't have made such a big deal about the beakers. As for them," he said, tipping his head toward lounge—it was clear he'd overheard the conversation—"they're just being fellas. Ignore 'em."

But she couldn't ignore them. In fact, the very next day, her boss, Dr. Donatti—the one who'd called her a cunt—reassigned her to a new project. "It'll be a lot easier," he said. "More your intellectual speed."

"Why, Dr. Donatti?" she asked. "Was there something wrong with my work?" She'd been the driving force behind her current group research project and as a result, they were close to publishing results. But Donatti pointed to the door. The next day, she was assigned to a low-level amino acid study.

The lab tech, noting her growing dissatisfaction, asked her why she wanted to be a scientist anyway.

"I don't want to be a scientist," she snapped. "I *am* a scientist!" And in her mind, she was not going to let some fat man at UCLA, or her boss, or a handful of small-minded colleagues keep her from achieving her goals. She'd faced tough things before. She would weather what came.

But weathering is called weathering for a reason: it erodes. As the months went by, her fortitude was tested again and again. The only thing that gave her any respite at all was the theater, and even that sometimes disappointed.

It was a Saturday night, about two weeks after the beaker incident. She'd bought a ticket to *The Mikado,* a supposedly funny operetta. Although she had long looked forward to it, as the story unfolded, she realized she didn't find it funny at all. The lyrics were racist, the actors were white, and it was blatantly obvious that the female lead was going to be blamed for everyone else's misdeeds. The whole thing reminded her of work. She decided to cut her losses and leave at intermission.

As luck would have it, Calvin Evans was also there that night, and had he been able to pay attention, he might have shared all

Elizabeth's opinions. But instead he was on a first date with a secretary from the Biology Division, *and* he was sick to his stomach. The former was a mistake: the secretary had asked him to the operetta only because she believed his fame meant he was rich, and he, reacting to her eye-watering perfume, had blinked several times, which she thought meant "I'd love to."

The queasiness started in act 1, but by the end of act 2, it had escalated to a roiling boil. "I'm sorry," he whispered, "but I don't feel well. I'm leaving."

"What do you mean?" she said suspiciously. "You look fine to me."

"Sick to my stomach," he murmured.

"Well, excuse me, but I bought this dress special for tonight," she said, "and I'm not leaving till I've worn it the full four hours."

Calvin thrust some cab money in the general direction of her astonished face, then rushed himself out to the lobby, one hand on his abdomen as he headed straight toward the bathroom, careful not to jounce his hair-trigger stomach.

As luck would also have it, Elizabeth had reached the lobby at the same moment, and like Calvin, she too was making her way to the bathroom. But when she saw the long line, she whirled away in frustration, and in doing so, slammed directly into Calvin, who instantly vomited on her.

"Oh god," he said, between retches, "oh Jesus."

Stunned at first, Elizabeth gathered herself and, ignoring the mess he'd just made of her dress, put a comforting hand on the bent torso. "This man is sick," Elizabeth called to the bathroom line, not yet realizing who it was. "Could someone call a doctor?"

But no one did. All the theater bathroom goers, reacting to the stench and the sound of violent illness, vacated the area immediately.

"Oh my god," Calvin said over and over again, holding his stomach, *"oh my god."*

"I'll get you a paper towel," Elizabeth said gently. "And a

cab." And then she took a good look at his face and said, "Say, don't I know you?"

Twenty minutes later, she was helping him into his house. "I think we can rule out the aerosol dispersion of diphenylaminearsine," she said. "Since no one else was affected."

"Chemical warfare?" he gasped, holding his stomach. "I hope so."

"It was probably just something you ate," she said. "Food poisoning."

"Oh," he moaned. "I'm so embarrassed. I'm *so* sorry. Your dress. I'll pay for the cleaning."

"It's fine," she said. "It's only a splatter." She helped him onto his sofa, where he collapsed into a large heap.

"I . . . I can't remember the last time I vomited. Much less in *public*."

"It happens."

"I was on a date," he said. "Can you imagine? I left her there."

"No," she said, trying to remember the last time she'd even had a date.

They were silent for a few minutes, then he closed his eyes. She took this as her cue to leave.

"Again, so sorry," he whispered, as he heard her make her way to the door.

"Please. There's no need to apologize. It was a reaction, a chemical incompatibility. We're scientists. We understand these things."

"No, no," he said weakly, wanting to clarify. "I mean about assuming you were a secretary that day—about telling you to have your boss call me," he said. "I am so *sorry*."

To this she had no response.

"We've never been formally introduced," he said. "I'm Calvin Evans."

"Elizabeth Zott," she answered, gathering her things.

"Well, Elizabeth Zott," he said, managing a small smile, "you're a lifesaver."

But it was clear she hadn't heard.

"My DNA research focused on polyphosphoric acids as condensing agents," she told Calvin over coffee in the cafeteria the following week. "And it's been going well up until now. As of last month, I've been reassigned. To an amino acid study."

"But why?"

"Donatti—don't you work for him, too? Anyway, he decided my work was unnecessary."

"But condensing agent research is critical to further understanding of DNA—"

"Yes, I know, I *know*," she agreed. "It was what I'd planned to pursue in my doctorate. Although what I'm really interested in is abiogenesis."

"Abiogenesis? The theory that life arose from simplistic, non-life forms? Fascinating. But you're not a PhD."

"No."

"But abiogenesis is PhD territory."

"I have a master's in chemistry. From UCLA."

"Academia," he nodded sympathetically. "It got old. You wanted out."

"Not exactly."

A long moment of uncomfortable silence followed.

"Look," she started up again, taking a deep breath, "my hypothesis of polyphosphoric acids is as follows."

Before she knew it, she'd talked to him for more than an hour, Calvin nodding as he made notes, occasionally interrupting with elaborate questions, which she easily fielded.

"I would be further," she said, "but as I mentioned, I was 'reallocated.' And before that, getting the basic supplies to continue my real work proved nearly impossible." That's why, she explained, she'd been reduced to stealing equipment and supplies from other labs.

"But why was it so hard to get supplies?" Calvin asked. "Hastings has plenty of money."

Elizabeth looked at him as if he'd just asked how, with all those rice paddies, there could possibly be starving children in China. "Sex discrimination," she answered, taking the number-two pencil she always wore either behind her ear or in her hair and tapping it with emphasis on the table. "But also, politics, favoritism, inequality, and general unfairness."

He chewed on his lips.

"But mostly sex discrimination," she said.

"What sex discrimination?" he asked innocently. "Why wouldn't we want women in science? That makes no sense. We need all the scientists we can get."

Elizabeth looked at him, astonished. She had been under the impression that Calvin Evans was a smart man, but now she realized he was one of those people who might only be smart in one narrow way. She studied him more closely, as if assessing what it might take to get through. Gathering her hair in both hands, she wound it twice before placing it in a knot on top of her head. Then she secured it with her pencil. "When you were at Cambridge," she said carefully, placing her hands back on the table, "how many women scientists did you know?"

"None. But my college was all-male."

"Oh, I see," she said. "But surely, women had the same opportunities elsewhere, correct? So how many women scientists do you know? Do not say Madame Curie."

He looked back at her, sensing trouble.

"The problem, Calvin," she asserted, "is that half the population is being wasted. It's not just that I can't get the supplies I need to complete my work, it's that women can't get the education they need to do what *they're* meant to do. And even if they do attend college, it will never be a place like Cambridge. Which means they won't be offered the same opportunities nor afforded the same respect. They'll start at the bottom and stay there. Don't even get me started on pay. And all because they didn't attend a school that wouldn't admit them in the first place."

"You're saying," he said slowly, "that more women actually want to be in science."

She widened her eyes. "*Of course we do.* In science, in medicine, in business, in music, in math. Pick an area." And then she paused, because the truth was, she'd only known a handful of women who'd wanted to be in science or any other area for that matter. Most of the women she'd met in college claimed they were only there to get their MRS. It was disconcerting, as if they'd all drunk something that had rendered them temporarily insane.

"But instead," she continued, "women are at home, making babies and cleaning rugs. It's legalized slavery. Even the women who wish to be homemakers find their work completely misunderstood. Men seem to think the average mother of five's biggest decision of the day is what color to paint her nails."

Calvin pictured five children and shuddered.

"About your work," he said, trying to redirect the battle. "I think I can fix it."

"I don't need you to fix anything," she said. "I'm perfectly capable of fixing my own situation."

"No, you're not."

"Excuse me?"

"You can't fix it because the world doesn't work that way. Life isn't fair."

This infuriated her—that *he* would tell *her* about unfairness. He wouldn't know the first thing about it. She started to say something, but he cut her off.

"Look," he said, "life has never been fair, and yet you continue to operate as if it is—as if once you get a few wrongs straightened out, everything else will fall into place. They won't. You want my advice?" And before she could say no, he added, "Don't work the system. Outsmart it."

She sat silently, weighing his words. They made annoying sense in a terribly unfair way.

"Now here's a lucky coincidence: I've been trying to rethink polyphosphoric acids for the last year and I'm getting nowhere. Your research could change that. If I tell Donatti I need to work with your findings, you'll be back on it tomorrow. And even if I didn't need your work—which I do—I owe you. Once for the secretarial remark, and again for the vomit."

Elizabeth continued to sit silently. Against her better judgment, she felt herself warming to the idea. She didn't want to: she didn't like the notion that systems had to be outsmarted. Why couldn't they just be smart in the first place? And she certainly didn't like favors. Favors smacked of cheating. And yet she had goals, and dammit, why should she just sit by? Sitting by never got anyone anywhere.

"Look," she said pointedly, as she brushed a strand of hair off her face. "I hope you won't think I'm jumping to conclusions, but I've had trouble in the past and I want to be clear: I'm not dating you. This is work, nothing more. I am not interested in a relationship of any kind."

"Nor am I," he insisted. "This is work. That's it."

"That's it."

And then they gathered their cups and saucers and went off in opposite directions, each desperately hoping the other didn't mean it.

CHAPTER 4

Introduction to Chemistry

About three weeks later, Calvin and Elizabeth were walking out to the parking lot, their voices raised.

"Your idea is completely misguided," she said. "You're overlooking the fundamental nature of protein synthesis."

"On the contrary," he said, thinking that no one had ever called any of his ideas misguided and now that somehow had, he didn't particularly like it, "I can't believe how you completely ignore the molecular struc—"

"I'm *not* ignoring—"

"You're forgetting the two covalent—"

"It's *three* covalent bonds—"

"Yes, but only when—"

"Look," she interrupted sharply as they stopped in front of her car. "This is a problem."

"What's a problem?"

"*You,*" she said firmly, pointing both hands at him. "You're the problem."

"Because we disagree?"

"That's not the problem," she said.

"Well then, *what?*"

"It's . . ." She waved her hand uncertainly, then looked off into the distance.

Calvin exhaled, and laying his hand on the roof of her old blue Plymouth, waited for the rebuff he knew was coming.

In the last few weeks, he and Elizabeth had met six times—twice for lunch and four times for coffee—and each time it had been both the high and low point of his day. The high point because she was the most intelligent, insightful, intriguing—and yes—the most alarmingly attractive woman he'd ever met in his life. The low point: she always seemed in a hurry to leave. And whenever she did, he felt desperate and depressed for the rest of the day.

"The recent silkworm findings," she was saying. "In the latest issue of *Science Journal*. That's what I meant by the complicated part."

He nodded as if he understood, but he didn't and not just about the silkworms. Each time they'd met, he'd gone out of his way to prove that he had absolutely no interest in her beyond a professional capacity. He hadn't offered to buy her coffee, he hadn't volunteered to carry her lunch tray, he hadn't even opened a door for her—including that time when her arms were so full of books he couldn't even see her head. Nor did he faint when she accidentally backed into him at the sink and he caught a whiff of her hair. He didn't even know hair could smell like that—as if it had been washed in a basin of flowers. Was she to give him no credit for his work-and-nothing-more behavior? The whole thing was infuriating.

"The part about bombykol," she said. "In silkworms."

"Sure," he answered dully, thinking of how stupid he'd been the first time he'd met her. Called her a secretary. Kicked her out of his lab. And then what about later? He'd thrown up on her. She said it didn't matter, but had she ever worn that yellow dress again? No. It was obvious to him that even though she said she didn't hold a grudge, she did. As a champion grudge holder himself, he knew how it worked.

"It's a chemical messenger," she said. "In female silkworms."

"Worms," he said sarcastically. "Great."

She took a step back, surprised by his flippancy. "You're not interested," she said, the tips of her ears reddening.

"Not at all."

Elizabeth took a short breath in and busied herself by searching in her purse for her keys.

What a huge disappointment. She'd finally met someone she could actually talk to—someone she found infinitely intelligent, insightful, intriguing (and alarmingly attractive whenever he smiled)—and he had no interest in her. None. They'd met six times in the last few weeks, and each time she'd kept it all business and so had he—although his was almost to the point of rudeness. That day when she couldn't even see the door because her arms were full of books? He couldn't be bothered to help. And yet each time they were together, she felt this practically irresistible urge to kiss him. Which was *extremely* unlike her. And yet after each meeting—which she ended as soon as she could because she was afraid she *would* kiss him—she felt desperate and depressed for the rest of the day.

"I need to go," she said.

"Business as usual," he retorted. But neither of them moved, instead turning their heads in opposite directions as if looking for the person they'd actually meant to meet in the parking lot even though it was almost seven o'clock on a Friday night and the south lot now contained only two cars: hers and his.

"Big plans for the weekend?" he finally ventured.

"Yes," she lied.

"Enjoy," he snapped. Then he turned and walked away.

She watched him for a moment, then got in her car and closed her eyes. Calvin wasn't stupid. He read *Science Journal*. He must have known what she was implying when she mentioned bombykol, the pheromone released by female silkworms to attract male mates. *Worms,* he'd said almost cruelly. What a jerk. And what a fool she'd been—so blatantly broaching the subject of love in a parking lot, only to get rejected.

You're not interested, she'd said.

Not at all, he'd replied.

She opened her eyes and shoved the key in the ignition. He probably assumed she was only after more lab equipment anyway. Because in a man's mind, why else would a woman mention bombykol on a Friday evening in an empty parking lot when the soft breeze was coming out of the west carrying the scent of her extremely expensive shampoo directly into his nasal cavity unless it was all part of a plot to get more beakers? She couldn't think of another reason. Except for the real one. She was falling in love with him.

Just then there was a sharp rap to her left. She looked up to find Calvin motioning for her to roll down her window.

"I'm not after your damn lab equipment!" she barked as she lowered the pane that separated them.

"And I'm not the problem," he snapped as he bent down to face her straight on.

Elizabeth looked back at him, fuming. How *dare* he?

Calvin looked back at her. How dare *she*?

And then that feeling came over her again, the one she had every time she was with him, but this time she acted on it, reaching out with both hands to draw his face to hers, their first kiss cementing a permanent bond that even chemistry could not explain.

CHAPTER 5

Family Values

Her lab mates assumed Elizabeth was dating Calvin Evans for one reason only: his fame. With Calvin in her back pocket, she was untouchable. But the reason was much simpler: "Because I love him," she would have said if someone asked. But no one asked.

It was the same for him. Had anyone asked him, Calvin would have said Elizabeth Zott was what he treasured most in the world, and not because she was pretty, and not because she was smart, but because she loved him and he loved her with a certain kind of fullness, of conviction, of faith, that underscored their devotion to each other. They were more than friends, more than confidants, more than allies, and more than lovers. If relationships are a puzzle, then theirs was solved from the get-go—as if someone shook out the box and watched from above as each separate piece landed exactly right, slipping one into the other, fully interlocked, into a picture that made perfect sense. They made other couples sick.

At night, after they made love, they would always lie in the same position on their backs, his leg slung over hers, her arm atop his thigh, his head tipped down toward hers, and they would talk: sometimes about their challenges, other times about their future, always about their work. Despite their postcoital fatigue, their conversations often lasted long into the early morning hours, and whenever it was about a certain finding or formula, eventually, invariably, one of them would finally have to get up and take a few notes. While some couples' togetherness tends to affect their work in a negative way, it was just the opposite for Elizabeth and Calvin. They were working even when they *weren't* working—fueling each other's creativity and inventiveness with a new point of view—and while the scientific community would later marvel at their productivity, they probably would have marveled even more had they realized most of it was done naked.

"Still awake?" Calvin whispered hesitantly one night as they lay in bed. "Because I wanted to run something by you. It's about Thanksgiving."

"What about it?"

"Well, it's coming up and I wondered if you were going home, and if you were, if you were going to invite me to tag along and"—he paused, then rushed ahead—"meetyourfamily."

"*What?*" Elizabeth whispered back. "*Home?* No. I'm not going home. I thought we might have Thanksgiving here. Together. Unless. Well. Were *you* planning on going home?"

"Absolutely not," he said.

In the past few months, Calvin and Elizabeth had talked about almost everything—books, careers, beliefs, aspirations, movies, politics, even allergies. There was only one obvious exception: family. It wasn't intentional—not at first, anyway—but after months of never bringing it up, it became clear it might never come up.

It's not to say they were incurious of each other's roots. Who didn't want to dip into the deep end of someone else's childhood and meet all the usual suspects—the strict parent, the competitive siblings, the crazy aunt? Not them.

Thus the topic of family was like a cordoned-off room on a historic home tour. One could still tip a head in to get a vague sense that Calvin had grown up somewhere (Massachusetts?) and that Elizabeth had brothers (or was it sisters?)—but there was no opportunity to step inside and sneak a peek at the medicine cabinet. Until Calvin brought up Thanksgiving.

"I can't believe I'm asking this," he finally ventured in the thick silence. "But I realize I don't know where you're from."

"Oh," Elizabeth said. "Well. Oregon, mostly. You?"

"Iowa."

"Really?" she asked. "I thought you were from Boston."

"No," he said quickly. "Any brothers? Sisters?"

"A brother," she said. "You?"

"None." His voice was flat.

She lay very still, taking in his tone. "Was it lonely?" she asked.

"Yes," he said bluntly.

"I'm sorry," she said, taking his hand under the sheets. "Your parents didn't want another child?"

"Hard to say," he said, his voice reedy. "It's not really the kind of thing a kid asks a parent, is it? But probably. Certainly."

"But then—"

"They died when I was five. My mother was eight months pregnant at the time."

"Oh my god. I'm so sorry, Calvin," Elizabeth said, bolting upright. "What *happened*?"

"Train," he said matter-of-factly. "Hit them."

"Calvin, I'm so sorry. I had no idea."

"It's okay," he said. "It was a long time ago. I don't really remember them."

"But—"

"Your turn," he said abruptly.

"No wait, wait, Calvin, who *raised* you?"

"My aunt. But then she died, too."

"What? *How?*"

"We were in the car and she had a heart attack. The car jumped the curb and slammed into a tree."

"God."

"Call it a family tradition. Dying in accidents."

"That's not funny."

"I wasn't trying to be funny."

"How old were you?" Elizabeth pressed.

"Six."

She squeezed her eyes shut. "And then you were put in a . . ." Her voice trailed off.

"A Catholic boys home."

"And . . . ," she prompted him, hating herself for doing so. "What was that like?"

He paused as if trying to find an honest answer to this obscenely simple question. "Rough," he finally said, his voice so low she barely heard him.

A quarter mile away, a train whistled and Elizabeth cringed. How many nights had Calvin lain there and heard that whistle and thought about his dead parents and his almost sibling and never said a word? Unless, perhaps, he never thought about them—he'd said he could barely remember them. But then who *did* he remember? And what *had* they been like? And when he'd said, "Rough," what did that *mean* exactly? She wanted to ask, but his tone—so dark and low and strange—warned her to go no further. And what about his later life? How did he ever learn to row in the middle of Iowa, much less make his way to Cambridge to row there? And college? Who'd paid for it? And his earlier education? A boys home in Iowa didn't sound like it provided much in the way of learning. It's one thing to be brilliant, but to be brilliant without opportunity—that was something else. If Mozart had been born to a poor family in Bombay instead of a cultured one in Salzburg, would he have composed Symphony no. 36 in C? Not a chance. How, then, had Calvin come from nothing to become one of the most highly respected scientists in the world?

"You were saying," he said, his voice wooden, as he pulled her back down next to him. "Oregon."

"Yes," she said, dreading the telling of her own story.

"How often do you visit?" he asked.

"Never."

"But *why*?" Calvin almost shouted, shocked that she could throw away a perfectly good family. One that was still alive anyway.

"Religious reasons."

Calvin paused, as if he might have missed something.

"My father was a . . . a type of religious expert," she explained.

"A what?"

"A sort of God salesman."

"I'm not following—"

"Someone who preaches gloom and doom to make money. You know," she said, her voice filling with embarrassment, "the kind who rants about how the end is near but has a solution—say a specialized baptism or a pricey amulet—that will keep Judgment Day off just a bit longer."

"There's a living in that?"

She turned her head toward his. "Oh yes."

He lay silent, trying to imagine it.

"Anyway," she said, "we had to move a lot because of it. You can't keep telling everyone the end is near if the end never comes."

"What about your mother?"

"She made the amulets."

"No, I mean, was she also very religious?"

Elizabeth hesitated. "Only if you count greed as a religion. There's lots of competition in this area, Calvin—it's extremely lucrative. But my father was especially gifted and the new Cadillac he got every year proved it. But when it comes down to it, I think my father's talent for spontaneous combustion really made him stand out."

"Wait. *What?*"

"It's really hard to ignore someone who shouts, 'Give me a sign,' and then something bursts into flame."

"Wait. Are you saying—"

"Calvin," she said, reverting to her standard scientific tone, "did you know pistachios are naturally flammable? It's because of their high fat content. Normally pistachios are stored under fairly rigid conditions of humidity, temperature, and pressure, but should those conditions be altered, the pistachio's fat-cleaving enzymes produce free fatty acids that are broken down when the seed takes in oxygen and sheds carbon dioxide. Result? Fire. I will credit my father for two things: he could conjure a spontaneous combustion whenever he needed a convenient sign from God." She shook her head. "Boy, did we go through the pistachios."

"And the other?" he asked in wonder.

"He was the one who introduced me to chemistry." She exhaled. "I should thank him for that, I guess," she said bitterly. "But I don't."

Calvin turned his head to the left, trying to disguise his disappointment. In that moment, he realized how much he'd wanted to meet her family—how much he'd hoped to sit at a Thanksgiving table, surrounded by people who would finally be his because he was hers.

"Where's your brother?" he asked.

"Dead." Her voice was hard. "Suicide."

"Suicide?" Air left his chest. "How?"

"He hanged himself."

"But . . . but why?"

"Because my father told him God hated him."

"But . . . but . . ."

"Like I said, my father was very convincing. If my father said God wanted something, God usually got it. God being my father."

Calvin's stomach tensed.

"Were . . . were you and he close?"

She took a deep breath. "Yes.

"But I don't understand," he persisted. "Why would your father do such a thing?" He turned his attention to the dark ceiling. He'd not had much experience with families, but he'd always assumed that being part of one was important: a prerequisite for

stability, what one relied on to get through the hard times. He'd
never really considered that a family could actually *be* the hard
times.

"John—my brother—was a homosexual," Elizabeth said.

"Oh," he said, as if now he understood. "I'm sorry."

She propped herself up on one elbow and peered at him in the
darkness. "What is *that* supposed to mean?" she shot back.

"Well, but—how did you know? Surely he didn't tell you
he was."

"I'm a scientist, Calvin, remember? I *knew*. Anyway, there's
nothing wrong with homosexuality; it's completely normal—
a basic fact of human biology. I have no idea why people don't
know this. Does no one read Margaret Mead anymore? The point
is, I knew John was a homosexual, and he knew I knew. We
talked about it. He didn't choose it; it was simply part of who
he was. The best part was," she said wistfully, "he knew about
me, too."

"Knew you were—"

"*A scientist!*" Elizabeth snapped. "Look, I realize this may be
hard for you to fathom given your own terrible circumstances,
but while we may be born into families, it doesn't necessarily
mean we belong to them."

"But we do—"

"No. You need to understand this, Calvin. People like my
father preach love but are filled with hate. Anyone who threat-
ens their narrow beliefs cannot be tolerated. The day my mother
caught my brother holding hands with another boy, that was
it. After a year of hearing that he was an aberration and didn't
deserve to live, he went out to the shed with a rope."

She said it in a too-high voice, the way one does when one
is trying very hard not to cry. He reached for her and she let him
take her in his arms.

"How old were you?" he asked.

"Ten," she said. "John was seventeen."

"Tell me more about him," he coaxed. "What was he like?"

"Oh, you know," she mumbled. "Kind. Protective. John was the one who read to me every night, bandaged my skinned knees, taught me how to read and write. We moved a lot and I never really got any good at making friends, but I had John. We spent most of our time at the library. It became our sanctuary—the only thing we could count on from town to town. Sort of funny now that I think about it."

"What do you mean?"

"Because my parents were in the sanctuary *business*."

He nodded.

"One thing I've learned, Calvin: people will always yearn for a simple solution to their complicated problems. It's a lot easier to have faith in something you can't see, can't touch, can't explain, and can't change, rather than to have faith in something you actually can." She sighed. "One's self, I mean." She tensed her stomach.

They lay silently, both wading in the misery of their pasts.

"Where are your parents now?"

"My father's in prison. One of his signs from God ended up killing three people. As for my mother, she divorced, remarried, and moved to Brazil. No extradition laws there. Did I mention my parents never paid taxes?"

Calvin let loose a long, low whistle. When one is raised on a steady diet of sorrow, it's hard to imagine that others might have had an even larger serving.

"So after your brother . . . died . . . it was just you and your parents—"

"No," she interrupted. "Just me. My parents were often gone for weeks at a time, and without John I had to become self-sufficient. So I did. I taught myself to cook and do small house repairs."

"And school?"

"I already told you—I went to the library."

"That's it?"

She turned toward him. "That's it."

They lay together like felled trees. From several blocks away, a church bell tolled.

"When I was a kid," Calvin said quietly, "I used to tell myself every day was new. That anything could happen."

She took his hand again. "Did it help?"

His mouth sagged as he remembered what the bishop at the boys home had revealed to him about his father. "I guess I'm just saying we shouldn't let ourselves get stuck in the past."

She nodded, imagining a newly orphaned boy trying to convince himself of a brighter future. That had to be a special brand of bravery, for a child to endure the worst, and despite every law in the universe and all evidence to the contrary, decide the next day might be better.

"Every day is new," Calvin repeated as if he were still that child. But the memory of what he'd learned about his father still proved too much for him and he stopped. "Look, I'm tired. Let's call it a day."

"We should get some sleep," she said, not yawning.

"We can talk about this another time," he said, depressed.

"Maybe tomorrow," she lied.

CHAPTER 6

The Hastings Cafeteria

There's nothing more irritating than witnessing someone else's unfair share of happiness, and to some of their colleagues at Hastings Research Institute, Elizabeth and Calvin had an unfair share. He, because he was brilliant; she, because she was beautiful. When they became a couple, their unfair shares automatically doubled, making it really unfair.

The worst part, according to these people, was that they hadn't earned their shares—they'd simply been born that way, meaning their unfair share of happiness arose, not from hard work, but from genetic luck. And the fact that the duo decided to combine their unearned gifts into one loving and probably highly sexual relationship, which the rest of them had to witness at lunch every day, just made it that much worse.

"Here they come," said a geologist from the seventh floor. "Batman and Robin."

"I heard they're shacking up together—did you know that?" asked his lab mate.

"*Everyone* knows that."

"I didn't know that," a third named Eddie said grimly.

The three geologists watched as Elizabeth and Calvin chose

an empty table in the middle of the cafeteria, the clash of trays and silverware *rat-a-tat-tat*-ing around them like gunfire. As the stink of cafeteria stroganoff threatened to asphyxiate the rest of the room, Calvin and Elizabeth placed a set of open Tupperware containers on the table. Chicken parmesan. Au gratin potatoes. Some sort of salad.

"Oh, I see," said one of the geologists. "So the food here isn't good enough for them."

"My cat eats better than this," the other geologist said, shoving his tray away.

"Hi, fellas!" chirped Miss Frask, a too-cheerful, wide-bottomed secretary from Personnel. Frask set down her tray, then cleared her throat as she waited for Eddie, a geology lab tech, to pull out her chair. Frask had been dating Eddie for three months, and while she would have liked to report it was all going very well, it wasn't. Eddie was immature with boorish tendencies. He chewed with his mouth open, guffawed at jokes that weren't funny, said things like "va-va-va-voom." Still, Eddie had one important thing going for him: he was single. "Well, thank you, Eddie," she said as he leaned over and yanked her chair out for her. "So sweet!"

"Proceed at your own risk," one of the geologists warned, tipping his head in Calvin and Elizabeth's general direction.

"Why?" she said. "What are we looking at?" She spun in her chair to follow their gaze. "Jeez Louise," she said, spying the happy couple. *"Again?"*

The four of them watched in silence as Elizabeth pulled out a notebook and passed it to Calvin. Calvin studied the page, then made some comment. Elizabeth shook her head, then pointed at something specific. Calvin nodded and, cocking his head to the side, slowly started to chew his lips.

"He is *so* unattractive," Frask said in disgust. But because she was in Personnel and Personnel never comments on an employee's physical appearance, she added, "And by that I only mean that blue is not his color."

One of the geologists took a bite of stroganoff, then set down his fork in resignation. "Hear the latest? Evans was nominated for the Nobel again."

The whole table issued a collective sigh.

"Well, that's meaningless," one of the geologists said. "Anyone can be nominated."

"Oh really? Have you ever been nominated?"

They continued to watch, transfixed, as a few minutes later Elizabeth reached down and pulled out a package wrapped in wax paper.

"What do you think that is?" one of the geologists asked.

"Baked goods," Eddie said, his voice filled with awe. "She *bakes,* too."

They watched as she offered Calvin brownies.

"Oh good god," Frask said, exasperated. "What do you mean, 'too'? Anyone can bake."

"I don't understand her," one of the geologists said. "She's got Evans. Why's she still here?" He paused as if weighing all possibilities. "Unless," he said, "Evans doesn't *want* to marry her."

"Why buy the cow when you can get the milk for free?" the other geologist suggested.

"I grew up on a farm," Eddie contributed. "Cows are a lot of work."

Frask glanced at him sideways. It irritated her that he continued to crane his neck toward Zott like a plant to sunlight.

"I'm a specialist in human behavior," she said. "At one point I was pursuing a PhD in psychology." She looked at her lunch mates, hoping they'd ask her about her academic aspirations, but no one seemed even slightly interested. "Anyway, that's why I can say with confidence: it's *she* who's using *him.*"

From across the room, Elizabeth straightened her papers, then rose. "Sorry to cut this short, Calvin, but I have a meeting."

"A meeting?" Calvin said, as if she'd just announced she was attending an execution. "If you worked in my lab, you'd never have to go to meetings."

"But I don't work in your lab."

"But you *could*."

She sighed, busying herself with the Tupperware. Of course, she'd love to work in his lab, but it wasn't possible. She was an entry-level chemist. She had to make her own way. Try to understand, she'd told him more than once.

"But we live together. This is just the next logical step." When it came to Elizabeth, he knew logic ruled the day.

"That was an economic decision," she reminded him. Which, on the surface, it was. Calvin had initiated the idea, saying that because they spent most of their free time together, it made financial sense to share living quarters. Still, it was also 1952, and in 1952 an unmarried woman did not move in with a man. So he was a bit surprised when Elizabeth didn't hesitate. "I'll pay half," she'd said.

She removed the pencil from her hair and tapped it on the table awaiting his response. She hadn't actually meant she'd pay half. Paying half was impossible. Her paycheck hovered just above ridiculous; half was out of the question. Anyway, the house was in his name—only he would receive the tax benefit. Therefore, half wouldn't be fair. She'd give him a moment to do the math. Half was outrageous.

"Half," he mused, as if considering it.

He already knew she couldn't pay half. She couldn't even pay a quarter. This was because Hastings paid her a penurious wage—about half what a man in her position made—a fact he'd encountered in her personnel file, which he'd peeked at illegally. Anyway, he didn't have a mortgage. He'd paid off his tiny bungalow last year with the proceeds from a chemistry prize and had instantly regretted it. You know how people say, "Never put all your eggs in one basket?" He had.

"Or," she'd said, brightening, "perhaps we could work out a trade agreement. You know, like nations do."

"A trade?"

"Rent for services rendered."

Calvin froze. He'd overheard all the gossip regarding the free milk.

"Dinner," she said. "Four nights a week." And before he could reply she said, "Fine. *Five.* But that's my final offer. I'm a good cook, Calvin. Cooking is serious science. In fact, it's chemistry."

So they'd moved in together and it had all worked out. But the lab idea? She refused even to consider it.

"You were just nominated for a Nobel, Calvin," she reminded him as she snapped the Tupperware lid closed on the remaining potatoes. "Your third nomination in five years. I want to be judged on my own work—not work people think you did for me."

"Anyone who knows you would never think that."

She burped the Tupperware, then turned to look at him. "That's the problem. No one knows me."

She'd felt this way her entire life. She'd been defined not by what she did, but by what others had done. In the past she was either the offspring of an arsonist, the daughter of a serial wife, the sister of a hanged homosexual, or the graduate student of a renowned lecher. Now she was the girlfriend of a famous chemist. But she was never just Elizabeth Zott.

And on those rare occasions when she wasn't defined by others' actions, then she was dismissed out of hand as either a lightweight or a gold digger based on the thing she hated most about herself. How she looked. Which happened to be just like her father.

He was the reason she didn't smile much anymore. Before becoming an evangelist, her father had wanted to be an actor. He had both the charisma and the teeth—the latter, professionally capped. The only thing missing? Talent. So when it became clear that acting was out, he took his skills to revival tents where his fake smile sold people on the end of the world. That's why, at age ten, Elizabeth stopped smiling. The resemblance faded.

It wasn't until Calvin Evans came along that her smile re-emerged. The first time was that night at the theater when he'd vomited all over her dress. She hadn't recognized him at first, but when she did and despite the mess, she bent over to get a better look at his face. Calvin Evans! True, she'd been a little rude to him after he'd been rude to her—the beakers—but between the two of them there'd been immediate, irresistible pull.

"Still working on that?" she asked, pointing at a nearly empty container.

"No," he said, "you eat it. You could use the extra fuel."

Actually, he'd planned to eat it, but he was willing to forgo the extra calories if only she would stay. Like Elizabeth, he'd never been much of a people person; in fact, it wasn't until he'd found rowing that he'd made any real kind of connection with others. Physical suffering, he'd long ago learned, bonds people in a way that everyday life can't. He still kept in contact with his eight Cambridge teammates—had even seen one of them just last month when he'd been in New York for a conference. Four Seat—they still called one another by their seat names—had become a neurologist.

"You have a what?" Four Seat had said, surprised. "A *girlfriend*? Well, good for you, Six!" he said, slapping him on the back. "About bloody time!"

Calvin had nodded excitedly, explaining in detail Elizabeth's work and habits and laugh and everything else he loved about her. But in a more somber tone, he also explained that although he and Elizabeth spent all of their free time together—they lived together, they ate together, they drove back and forth to work together—it didn't feel like enough. It wasn't that he couldn't function without her, he told Four Seat, but rather that he didn't see the *point* of functioning without her. "I don't know what to call it," he'd confided following a full examination. "Am I addicted to her? Am I dependent in some sick sort of way? Could I have a brain tumor?"

"Jesus, Six, it's called happiness," Four Seat explained. "When's the wedding?"

But that was the problem. Elizabeth had made it clear that she had no interest in getting married. "It's not that I disapprove of marriage, Calvin," she'd told him more than once, "although I do disapprove of all of the people who disapprove of us for not being married. Don't you?"

"I do," Calvin agreed, thinking how much he would like to say those words to her in front of an altar. But when she looked at him expecting more, he added quickly, "I do think we're lucky." And then she smiled at him so earnestly that something inside his brain went haywire. As soon as they parted, he drove to a local jeweler, scanning the selections until he found the biggest small diamond he could afford. Sick with excitement, he kept the tiny box in his pocket for three months waiting for exactly the right moment.

"Calvin?" Elizabeth said, gathering the last of her things from the cafeteria table. "Are you listening? I said I'm going to a wedding tomorrow. Actually, I'm *in* the wedding if you can believe that." She gave a nervous shrug. "So we should probably discuss that acid study tonight if that works."

"Who's getting married?"

"My friend Margaret—the Physics secretary? That's who I'm meeting in fifteen minutes. For a fitting."

"Wait. You have a *friend*?" He thought Elizabeth only had

workmates—fellow scientists who recognized her skill and under-mined her results.

Elizabeth felt a flush of embarrassment. "Well, yes," she said awkwardly. "Margaret and I nod to each other in the hallways. We've spoken several times at the coffee urn."

Calvin willed his face to look as if this were a reasonable description of friendship.

"It's very last-minute. One of her bridesmaids is sick and Margaret says it's important to have an even ratio of bridesmaids to ushers." Although as soon as she said it, she realized what Margaret really needed: a size 6 without weekend plans.

The truth was, she wasn't good at making friends. She'd told herself it was because she'd moved so much, had bad parents, lost her brother. But she knew others had experienced hardships and they didn't have this issue. If anything, some of them seemed *better* at making friends—as if the specter of constant change or profound sorrow had revealed to them the importance of making connections wherever and whenever they landed. What was wrong with her?

And then there was the illogical art of female friendship itself, the way it seemed to demand an ability to both keep and reveal secrets using precise timing. Whenever she moved to a new town, girls would take her aside at Sunday school and breathlessly confide their crushes on certain boys. She listened to these confessions, faithfully promising she would never tell. And she didn't. Which was all wrong because it turned out she was *supposed* to tell. Her job as confidante was to break that confidence by telling Boy X that Girl Y thought he was cute, thus initiating a chain reaction of interest between the two parties. "Why don't *you* just tell him yourself?" she'd say to these would-be friends. "He's right *there*." The girls would draw back in horror.

"Elizabeth," Calvin said. "Elizabeth?" He leaned over the table and tapped her hand. "Sorry," he said as she startled. "I think I lost you there for a moment. Anyway, I was just saying, I love weddings. I'll go with you."

Actually, he hated weddings. For years, they'd reminded him that he was still unloved. But now he had her and tomorrow she'd be in close proximity to an altar and he hypothesized such proximity could revise her perception of marriage. This theory even had a scientific name: associative interference.

"No," she said quickly. "I don't have an extra invite, and besides, the fewer people who see me in this dress the better."

"Come on," he said, reaching one long arm across the span that separated them, pulling her back down. "Margaret can't expect you to go alone. And as for the dress, I'm sure it's not that bad."

"Oh, no, it *is*," she said, reverting to her sensible tone of scientific certainty. "Bridesmaids' dresses are designed to make the women in them look unappealing; that way the bride looks better than usual. It's an accepted practice, a basic defensive strategy with biological roots. You see this sort of thing in nature all the time."

Calvin thought back to the weddings he'd attended and realized she might be right: not once had he ever had the urge to ask a bridesmaid to dance. Could a dress really have that much power? He looked across the table at Elizabeth, her firm hands moving through space as she described the gown: extra padding at the hips, sloppy gathering at the waist and chest, fat bow spanning the buttocks. He thought about the people who designed these dresses; how, like bomb manufacturers or pornography stars, they had to remain vague about the way they made their livings.

"Well, it's nice of you to help out. But I thought you didn't like weddings."

"No, it's only marriage I don't like. We've talked about it, Calvin; you know where I stand. But I'm happy for Margaret. Mostly."

"Mostly?"

"Well," she said, "she keeps repeating how by Saturday night, she'll finally be Mrs. Peter Dickman. As if changing her name is the finish line for a race she's been in since she was six."

"She's marrying *Dickman?*" he said. "From Cellular Biology?" He didn't like Dickman.

"Exactly," she said. "I've never understood why when women marry, they're expected to trade in their old names like used cars, losing their last and sometimes even their first—Mrs. *John* Adams! Mrs. *Abe* Lincoln!—as if their previous identities had just been twenty-odd-year placeholders before they became actual people. Mrs. Peter Dickman. It's a life sentence."

Elizabeth Evans, on the other hand, Calvin thought to himself, *was perfect.* Before he could stop himself, he felt around in his pocket for the small blue box, and without hesitation, placed it in front of her. "Maybe this could help improve the dress," he said, his heart at full gallop.

"Ring box," announced one of the geologists. "Brace yourself, kids: engagement in process." But there was something about Elizabeth's face that didn't read right.

Elizabeth looked down at the box and then looked back up at Calvin, her eyes wide with terror.

"I know your position on marriage," Calvin said in a rush. "But I've been giving it a lot of thought and I think you and I would have a different kind of marriage. It would be very unaverage. Fun, even."

"Calvin—"

"There are also practical reasons to get married. Lower taxes, for instance."

"Calvin—"

"At least look at the ring," he begged. "I've been carrying it around for months. Please."

"I can't," she said, looking away. "It'll just make it harder to say no."

Her mother had always insisted that the measure of a woman was how well she married. "I *could* have married Billy Graham," she'd often claimed. "Don't think he wasn't interested. By the way, Elizabeth, when you do get engaged, insist on the biggest rock possible. That way, if the marriage doesn't work out, you can hock it." As it turned out, her mother was speaking from experience. When her parents filed for divorce, it was revealed she'd been married three times before.

"I'm not going to marry," Elizabeth told her. "I'm going to be a scientist. Successful women scientists don't marry."

"Oh really?" Her mother laughed. "I see. So you think you're going to marry your work like the nuns marry Jesus? Although say what you want about nuns—at least they know their husband won't snore." She pinched Elizabeth's arm. "No woman says no to marriage, Elizabeth. You won't either."

Calvin opened his eyes wide. "You're saying *no*?"

"Yes."

"Elizabeth!"

"Calvin," she said carefully, reaching across the table for his hands while taking in his deflated face. "I thought we'd agreed on this. As a scientist yourself, I know you understand why marriage for me is out of the question."

But his expression indicated no such understanding.

"Because I can't risk having my scientific contributions submerged beneath your name," she clarified.

"Right," he said. "Of course. Obviously. So it's a work conflict."

"More of a societal conflict."

"Well that is AWFUL!" he shouted, causing any table that

wasn't already watching to turn their full attention to the unhappy couple in the middle.

"*Calvin,*" Elizabeth said. "We've discussed this."

"Yes, I know. You disapprove of the name change. But have I ever suggested that I wanted your name to change?" he protested. "No, in fact, I *expected* you to keep your name." Which wasn't completely true. He'd assumed she'd take his name. Nevertheless, he said, "But in any case, our future happiness should not depend on whether a handful of people might mistakenly call you Mrs. Evans. We'll correct those people." This seemed like the wrong time to tell her he'd already added her name to the deed on his tiny bungalow—Elizabeth Evans, that's the name he'd given the county clerk. He made a mental note to call the clerk as soon as he was back in his lab.

Elizabeth shook her head. "Our future happiness does not depend on whether or not we're married, Calvin—at least not to me. I'm fully committed to you; marriage will not change that. As for who thinks what, it's not just a handful of people: it's society—particularly the society of scientific research. Everything I do will suddenly be in your name, as if you'd done it. In fact, most people will *assume* you've done it simply because you're a man, but especially because you're Calvin Evans. I don't want to be another Mileva Einstein or Esther Lederberg, Calvin; I refuse. And even if we took all the proper legal steps to ensure my name won't change, it will still change. Everyone will call me Mrs. Calvin Evans; I will *become* Mrs. Calvin Evans. Every Christmas card, every bank statement, every notice from the Bureau of Internal Revenue will all come to Mr. and Mrs. Calvin Evans. Elizabeth Zott, as we know her, will cease to exist."

"And being Mrs. Calvin Evans is absolutely the worst thing that could ever happen to you," he said, his face collapsed in misery.

"I want to be Elizabeth Zott," she said. "It's important to me."

They sat for a minute in uncomfortable silence, the hateful little blue box plopped between them like a bad referee at a tight
match. Against her will, she found herself wondering what the
ring looked like.

"I really am sorry," she repeated.

"Not a problem," he said stiffly.

She looked away.

"They're breaking up!" Eddie hissed to the others. "They're going
straight down the tubes!"

Shit, Frask thought. *Zott's back on the market.*

Except Calvin couldn't let it go. Thirty seconds later, completely
oblivious to the dozens of pairs of eyes resting upon them, he
said in a voice far louder than he'd intended, "For the love of *god,*
Elizabeth. It's just a *name.* It doesn't matter. You're *you*—that's
what matters."

"I wish that were true."

"It *is* true," he insisted. "What's in a name? Nothing!"

She looked up with sudden hope. "Nothing? Well in that
case, what about changing your name?"

"To what?"

"To mine. To Zott."

He looked at her in astonishment, then rolled his eyes. "Very
funny," he said.

"Well, why not?" Her voice had an edge.

"You already know why not. Men don't do that. Anyway,
there's my work, my reputation. I'm . . ." He hesitated.

"What?"

"I'm . . . I'm . . ."

"Say it."

"Fine. I'm *famous,* Elizabeth. I can't just *change* my name."

"Oh," she said. "But if you weren't famous, *then* changing your name to mine would be fine. Is that what you mean?"

"Look," he said, grabbing the small blue box. "I get it. I didn't make this tradition; it's just the way things are. When women get married, they take their husband's name, and ninety-nine point nine percent of them are fine with it."

"And you have some sort of study to back up this assertion," she said.

"What?"

"That ninety-nine point nine percent of women are fine with it."

"Well, no. But I've never heard any complaints before."

"And the reason why you can't change your name is because you're famous. Although ninety-nine point nine percent of men who aren't famous also happen to keep their names."

"Again," he said, stuffing the small box in his pocket with such force that the fabric gave way at the corner. "I didn't create the tradition. And as I stated earlier, I am—*was*—in full support of you keeping your name."

"Was."

"I don't want to marry you anymore."

Elizabeth sat back hard.

"Game, set, match!" crowed one of the geologists. "Box is back in the pocket!"

Calvin sat fuming. It had already been a tough day. Just that morning, he'd gotten a bunch of new crank letters, most from people purporting to be long-lost relatives. This wasn't unusual; ever since he'd gotten a little famous, the flimflam artists wrote en masse. A "great uncle" wanted Calvin to invest in his alchemy scheme; a "sad mother" claimed she was his biological mother and wanted to give *him* money; a so-called cousin needed cash. There were also two letters from women claiming they'd had his baby and he needed to pay up now. This was despite the fact that the only woman he'd ever slept with was Elizabeth Zott. Would this ever end?

"Elizabeth," he implored, as he raked his fingers through his hair. "Please understand. I want us to be a family—a *real* family. It's important to me, maybe because I lost my family—I don't know. What I do know is that ever since I met you, I've felt there should be three of us. You, me, and a . . . a . . ."

Elizabeth's eyes grew wide in horror. "Calvin," she said in alarm, "I thought we agreed about that, too."

"Well. We've never really talked about it."

"No, we have," she pressed. "We *definitely* have."

"Just that once," he said, "and it wasn't really a talk. Not really."

"I don't know how you can say that," she said, panicked. "We absolutely agreed: no children. I can't believe you're talking like this. What's happened to you?"

"Right, but I was thinking we could—"

"I was clear—"

"I know," he interrupted, "but I was thinking—"

"You can't just change your mind on this one."

"For Pete's sake, Elizabeth," he said, getting mad. "If you'd just let me finish—"

"Go ahead," she snapped. "Finish!"

He looked at her, frustrated.

"I was only thinking that we could get a dog."

Relief flooded her face. "A dog?" she said. "A dog!"

"Goddammit," Frask commented quietly as Calvin leaned over to kiss Elizabeth. The entire cafeteria instantly echoed her sentiment. From every direction, silverware fell to trays in resigned clatters, chairs were kicked back in moody defeat, napkins were wadded in dirty little balls. It was the noxious noise of profound jealousy, the kind that never results in a happy ending.

CHAPTER 7

Six-Thirty

Many people go to breeders to find a dog, and others to the pound, but sometimes, especially when it's really meant to be, the right dog finds you.

It was a Saturday evening, about a month later, and Elizabeth had run down to the local deli to get something for dinner. As she left the store, her arms laden with a large salami and a bag of groceries, a mangy, smelly dog, hidden in the shadows of the alley, watched her walk by. Although the dog hadn't moved in five hours, he took one look at her, pulled himself up, and followed.

Calvin happened to be at the window when he saw Elizabeth strolling toward the house, a dog following a respectful five paces behind, and as he watched her walk, a strange shudder swept through his body. "Elizabeth Zott, you're going to change the world," he heard himself say. And the moment he said it, he knew it was true. She was going to do something so revolutionary, so necessary, that her name—despite a never-ending legion of naysayers—would be immortalized. And as if to prove that point, today she had her first follower.

"Who's your friend?" he called out to her, shaking off the odd feeling.

"It's six thirty," she called back after glancing at her wrist.

Six-Thirty was badly in need of a bath. Tall, gray, thin, and covered with barbed-wire-like fur that made him look as if he'd barely survived electrocution, he stood very still as they shampooed him, his gaze fixed on Elizabeth.

"I guess we should try to find his owner," Elizabeth said reluctantly. "I'm sure someone is worried to death."

"This dog doesn't have an owner," Calvin assured her, and he was right. Later calls to the pound and listings in the newspaper's lost and found column turned up nothing. But even if it had, Six-Thirty had already made his intentions clear: to stay.

In fact, "stay" was the first word he learned, although within weeks, he also learned at least five others. That was what surprised Elizabeth most—Six-Thirty's ability to learn.

"Do you think he's unusual?" she asked Calvin more than once. "He seems to pick things up so quickly."

"He's grateful," Calvin said. "He wants to please us."

But Elizabeth was right: Six-Thirty had been trained to pick things up quickly.

Bombs, specifically.

Before he'd ended up in that alley, he'd been a canine bomb-sniffer trainee at Camp Pendleton, the local marine base. Unfortunately, he'd failed miserably. Not only could he never seem to sniff out the bomb in time, but he also had to endure the praise heaped upon the smug German shepherds who always did. He was eventually discharged—not honorably—by his angry handler, who drove him out to the highway and dumped him in the middle of nowhere. Two weeks later he found his way to that alley. Two weeks and five hours later, he was being shampooed by Elizabeth and she was calling him Six-Thirty.

"Are you sure we can take him to Hastings?" Elizabeth asked when Calvin loaded him into the car on Monday morning.

"Sure, why not?"

"Because I've never seen another dog at work. Besides the labs aren't really that safe."

"We'll keep a close eye on him," Calvin said. "It's not healthy for a dog to be left alone all day. He needs stimulation."

This time it was Calvin who was right. Six-Thirty had loved Camp Pendleton, partly because he was never alone, but mostly because it had given him something he'd never had before: purpose. But there'd been a problem.

A bomb-sniffing dog had two choices: find the bomb in time to allow disarmament (preferred), or throw himself on the bomb, making the ultimate sacrifice to save the unit (not preferred, although it did come with a posthumous medal). In training, the bombs were only ever fake, so if a dog did throw himself upon it, the most he might get was a noisy explosion followed by a huge burst of red paint.

It was the noise; it scared Six-Thirty to death. So each day, when his handler commanded him to "Find it," he would immediately take off to the east, even though his nose had already informed him that the bomb was fifty yards to the west, poking his nose at various rocks while he waited for one of the other, braver dogs to finally find the damn thing and receive his reward biscuit. Unless the dog was too late or too rough and the bomb exploded; then the dog only got a bath.

"You can't have a dog here, Dr. Evans," Miss Frask explained to Calvin. "We've gotten complaints."

"No one's complained to me," Calvin said, shrugging, even though he knew no one would dare.

Frask backed off immediately.

Within a few weeks, Six-Thirty made a full inventory of the Hastings campus, memorizing every floor, room, and exit, like a firefighter preparing for catastrophe. When it came to Elizabeth Zott, he was on high alert. She'd suffered in her past—he could sense it—and he was determined she should never suffer again.

It was the same for Elizabeth. She sensed that Six-Thirty had also suffered beyond the usual dog-left-by-the-roadside neglect, and she, too, felt the need to protect him. In fact, it was she who insisted that he sleep next to their bed even though Calvin had suggested he might be better off in the kitchen. But Elizabeth won out and he stayed, completely content, except for those times when Calvin and Elizabeth locked their limbs in a messy tangle, their clumsy movements punctuated with panting noises. Animals did this too, but with far more efficiency. Humans, Six-Thirty noticed, had a tendency to overcomplicate.

If these encounters took place in the early morning, Elizabeth would rise soon after to go make breakfast. Although she'd originally agreed to cook dinner five nights a week in exchange for rent, she also added breakfast, then lunch. For Elizabeth, cooking wasn't some preordained feminine duty. As she'd told Calvin, cooking was chemistry. That's because cooking actually *is* chemistry.

@200° C/35 min = loss of one H_2O per mol. sucrose; total 4 in 55 min = $C_{24}H_{36}O_{18}$ she wrote in a notebook. "So that's why the biscuit batter is off." She tapped her pencil against the countertop. "Still too many water molecules."

"How's it going?" Calvin called from the next room.

"Almost lost an atom in the isomerization process," she called back. "I think I'll make something else. Are you watching Jack?"

She meant Jack LaLanne, the famous TV fitness guru, a self-made health aficionado who encouraged people to take better care of their bodies. She didn't really have to ask—she could hear Jack shouting "Up down up down" like a human yo-yo.

"I am," Calvin called back, breathless, as Jack demanded ten more. "Join us?"

"I'm denaturing protein," she shouted.

"And now, running in place," urged Jack.

Despite what Jack said, running in place was the one thing Calvin would not do. Instead he did extra sit-ups while Jack ran in place in what very much looked like ballet slippers. Calvin didn't see the point of running indoors in ballet slippers; instead, he always did his running outside in tennis shoes. This made him an early jogger, meaning that he jogged long before jogging was popular, long before it was even called jogging. Unfortunately, because others were unfamiliar with this jogging concept, the police precinct received a steady stream of calls regarding a barely clad man running through neighborhoods blowing short, hard bursts of air out between his purplish lips. Since Calvin always ran the same four or five routes, police soon became accustomed to these calls. "That's not a criminal," they'd say. "That's just Calvin. He doesn't like to run in place in ballet slippers."

"Elizabeth?" he called again. "Where's Six-Thirty? Happy's on."

Happy was Jack LaLanne's dog. Sometimes he was on the show, sometimes he wasn't, but when he was, Six-Thirty always left the room. Elizabeth sensed there was something about the German shepherd that made Six-Thirty unhappy.

"He's with me," she called back.

Holding an egg in the palm of her hand, she turned to him. "Here's a tip, Six-Thirty: never crack eggs on the side of a bowl—it increases the chance of shell fragments. Better to bring a sharp, thin knife down on the egg as if you're cracking a whip. See?" she said, as the egg's contents slipped into the bowl.

Six-Thirty watched without blinking.

"Now I'm disrupting the egg's internal bonds in order to elongate the amino acid chain," she told him as she whisked, "which will allow the freed atoms to bond with other similarly freed atoms. Then I'll reconstitute the mix into a loose whole, laying it on a surface of iron-carbon alloy, where I'll subject it to precision heat, continually agitating the mix until it reaches a stage of near coagulation."

"LaLanne is an animal," Calvin announced as he wandered into the kitchen, his T-shirt damp.

"Agreed," Elizabeth said as she took the frying pan off the flame and placed the eggs on two plates. "Because humans *are* animals. Technically. Although sometimes I think the animals we consider animals are far more advanced than the animals we are but don't consider ourselves to be." She looked to Six-Thirty for confirmation, but even he couldn't parse that one.

"Well, Jack gave me an idea," Calvin said, lowering his large frame into a chair, "and I think you're going to love it. I'm going to teach you to row."

"Pass the sodium chloride."

"You'll love it. We can row a pair together, maybe a double. We'll watch the sun rise on the water."

"Not really interested."

"We can start tomorrow."

Calvin still rowed three days a week, but only in a single. That wasn't uncommon for elite rowers: once in a boat oared by teammates who seemed to know one another at a cellular level, they sometimes struggled to row with others. Elizabeth knew how much he missed his Cambridge boat. Still, she had no interest in rowing.

"I don't want to. Besides, you row at four thirty in the morning."

"I row at five o'clock," he said as if this made it so much more reasonable. "I only leave the house at four thirty."

"No."

"Why?"

"*No.*"

"But why?"

"Because that's when I sleep."

"Easily solved. We'll go to bed early."

"No."

"First I'll introduce you to the rowing machine—we call it the erg. They have some at the boathouse, but I'm going to build one for home use. Then we'll move to a boat—a shell. By April we'll be skimming across the bay, watching the sun rise, our long strokes clicking along in perfect unison."

But even as he said it, Calvin knew the rowing part wasn't possible. First, no one learns to row in a month. Most people, even with expert instruction, can't row well within a year, or sometimes three years, or for many, ever. As for the skimming part—there is no skimming. To get to the point where rowing might resemble skimming, you've probably reached the Olympic level and the look on your face as you fly down the racecourse is not one of calm satisfaction but controlled agony. This is sometimes accompanied by a look of determination—usually one that indicates that right after this race is over, you plan to find a new sport. Still, once he'd hatched the idea, he loved it. Rowing a pair with Elizabeth. How glorious!

"No."

"But *why*?"

"Because. Women don't row." But as soon as she'd said it, she regretted it.

"Elizabeth Zott," he said, surprised. "Are you actually saying women *can't* row?"

That sealed it.

The next morning they left their bungalow in the dark, Calvin in his old T-shirt and sweatpants, Elizabeth in whatever she could find that looked remotely sporty. As they pulled up to the boathouse, both Six-Thirty and Elizabeth looked out the car window to see a few bodies on a slick dock doing calisthenics.

"Shouldn't they be doing that inside?" she asked. "It's still dark."

"On a morning like this?" It was foggy.

"I thought you didn't like rain."

"This isn't rain."

For at least the fortieth time, Elizabeth found herself doubting this plan.

"We'll start off easy," Calvin said as he led her and Six-Thirty into the boathouse, a cavernous building that smelled of mildew and sweat. As they walked past rows of long wooden rowing shells layered to the ceiling like well-stacked toothpicks, Calvin nodded at a bedraggled-looking person who yawned and nodded back, conversation not yet possible. He stopped when he found what he was looking for—a rowing machine, the erg—which had been tucked in a corner. He pulled it out, positioning it in the middle of the bay between the stacks of boats.

"First things first," he said. "Technique." He sat down, then started to pull, his breaths quickly becoming a series of short torturous bursts that seemed neither easy nor fun. "The trick is to keep your wrists flat," he huffed, "your knees down, your stomach muscles engaged, your—" But whatever else he said was lost in his urgency to breathe and within a few minutes, he seemed to forget Elizabeth was even there.

She slipped away, Six-Thirty at her side, and went to explore the boathouse, pausing in front of a rack holding a forest of oars so impossibly tall, it looked as if giants played here. Off to its side sat a large trophy case, the early morning light just beginning to reveal its stash of silver cups and old rowing uniforms, each a testament to those who had proven faster or more efficient or more indomitable, or possibly all three. Brave people, according to Calvin, who'd shown the kind of focus that put them first over the finish.

Alongside the uniforms were photographs of strapping young men with gargantuan oars, but there was one other person, too: a jockey-sized man who looked as serious as he was small, his

mouth fixed in a firm, grim line. The coxswain, Calvin had told
her, the one who told the rowers what to do and when to do it:
take up the rate, make a turn, challenge another boat, go faster.
She liked that a diminutive person held the reins to eight wild
horses, his voice, their command; his hands, their rudder; his
encouragements, their fuel.

She turned to watch as other rowers began to file in, each
of them nodding in deference to Calvin as he continued to erg
on the noisy machine, a few revealing a trace of envy as he took
up the stroke rate with such obvious smoothness that even Elizabeth could recognize it as a sign of natural athleticism.

"When are you going to row with us, Evans?" said one of
them, clapping him on the shoulder. "We'll put that energy to
good use!" But if Calvin heard or felt anything, he didn't react.
He kept his eyes forward, his body steady.

So, she thought, he was a legend here, too. It was obvious, not
only in their deference, but in the obsequious manner in which
they tried to work around him and his ridiculous position—
Calvin had placed the rowing machine right in the middle of
the boathouse floor. The coxswain, clearly annoyed, assessed the
situation.

"Hands on!" he called to his eight rowers, causing them to
jump into position on one side of their shell, their bodies braced
to pick up the heavy boat. "Slide it out," he commanded. "In
two, up to shoulders."

But it was obvious they weren't going anywhere—not with
Calvin in the middle.

"Calvin," Elizabeth whispered urgently, scuttling up behind
him. "You're in the way. You need to move." But he just kept
erging.

"Jesus," said the coxswain, blowing air out between his lips.
"*This* guy." He glanced at Elizabeth, then thumbed her sharply
out of the way, taking up a crouched position directly behind
Calvin's left ear.

"Atta boy, Cal," he growled, "keep the length, you son of

a bitch. We've got five hundred to go and you're not done yet. Oxford is coming up on starboard and they're starting to walk."

Elizabeth looked at him, astonished. "*Excuse me,* but—" she started.

"I know this ain't all you got, Evans," he snarled, cutting her off. "Don't hold out on me, you fucking machine; in two I'm calling for a power twenty, in *two,* on *my* call, you're gonna put these Oxford sons of bitches to bed; you're gonna make these boys wish they were already dead; you're gonna kill 'em, Evans, wind it up, brother, we're at a thirty-two on our way to *fucking forty,* on my call: there's one, there's two, take it up, POWER TWENTY YOU MOTHERFUCKER!" he screamed. "RIGHT NOW!"

Elizabeth didn't know what was more shocking: the little man's language or the intensity with which Calvin reacted to that language. Within moments of hearing the words "you fucking machine" and "sons of bitches," Calvin's face took on a crazed look usually not seen outside of low-budget zombie films. He pulled harder and faster, his exhales so loud, he sounded like a runaway train, and yet the little man was not satisfied; he kept yelling at Calvin, demanding more and getting more as he counted down the strokes like an angry stopwatch: Twenty! Fifteen! Ten! Five! And then the count evaporated and all that was left were two simple words that Elizabeth couldn't agree with more.

"Way enough," the coxswain said. Upon which Calvin slumped heavily forward as if he'd been shot in the back.

"Calvin!" Elizabeth cried, rushing to his side. "My god!"

"He's fine," the coxswain said. "Aren't you, Cal? Now move this fucking machine out of our fucking way."

And Calvin nodded, sucking in oxygen. "Sure . . . thing . . . Sam," he panted between gulps of air, "and . . . thanks. . . . But . . . first . . . I'd . . . like . . . you . . . to meet . . . Eliz . . . Eliz . . . Elizabeth Zott. My . . . new . . . pair . . . partner."

Immediately Elizabeth felt all eyes in the boathouse upon her.

"A pair with Evans," one of the rowers said, his eyes wide. "What'd you do? Win a gold medal in the Olympics?"

"What?"

"You've rowed on a women's team, then?" the coxswain asked, taking interest.

"Well, no, I've never really—" And then she stopped. "There are *women's* teams?"

"She's learning," Calvin explained as he began to catch his breath. "But she already has what it takes." He inhaled deeply, then got off the machine and started to drag it out of the way. "By summer we'll be wiping the bay with all of you."

Elizabeth wasn't sure what that meant exactly. Wiping the bay? He didn't actually mean compete, did he? What happened to watching the sunrise?

"Well," she said quietly, turning toward the coxswain, as Calvin went to towel off. "I'm not sure this is really my—"

"It is," the coxswain interrupted before she could finish. "Evans would never ask anyone to be in a boat with him if they couldn't hold their own." And then he closed one eye and squinted. "Yeah. I see it too."

"What?" she said, surprised. But he'd already turned away, barking out orders for the boat to be walked down to the dock. "One foot in," she heard him yell, "and down." And within moments, the boat disappeared into a thick fog, the men's faces oddly eager despite the first fat drops of a cold rain warning of the discomfort that was yet to come.

CHAPTER 8

Overreaching

The first day on the water, she and Calvin flipped the pair and fell in the water. Second day, flipped. Third day, flipped.

"What am I doing wrong?" she gasped, her teeth chattering as they pushed the long, thin shell toward the dock. She had neglected to tell Calvin one little fact about herself. She couldn't swim.

"Everything," he sighed.

"As I've mentioned before," he said ten minutes later as he pointed at the rowing machine, indicating that, despite her wet clothes, she should sit, "rowing requires perfect technique."

While she adjusted the foot stretchers, he explained that rowers usually erged when the water was too rough, or they had to be timed, or when the coach was in a really bad mood. And, when done right, especially during a fitness test, there was vomiting. Then he mentioned that erging had a way of making the worst day on the water seem pretty good.

And yet, that is exactly what they continued to have: the worst of days. The very next morning they were back in the water. And it was all because Calvin continued to omit one simple truth: the pair is the hardest boat to row. It's like trying to learn to fly by starting out in a B-52. But what choice did he have? He knew the men weren't going to let her row with them in a bigger boat like an eight; besides being female, her lack of experience meant she'd ruin the row. Worse, she'd probably catch a crab and crack a few ribs. He hadn't mentioned crabs yet. For obvious reasons.

They righted the boat and crawled back in.

"The problem is that you're not patient enough up the slide. You need to slow the hell down, Elizabeth."

"I am going slow."

"No, you're rushing. It's one of the worst mistakes a rower can make. Every time you rush the slide, you know what happens? God kills a kitten."

"Oh, for god's sake, Calvin."

"And your catch is too slow. The object is to go fast, remember?"

"Well *that* certainly clears things up," she snapped from the stern. "Go slow to go fast."

He clapped her on the shoulder as if she was finally getting it. "Exactly."

Shivering, she tightened her grip on the oar. What a stupid sport. For the next thirty minutes she tried to heed his contradictory commands: *Raise your hands; no, lower them! Lean out; god not that far! Jesus, you're slouching, you're skying, you're rushing, you're late, you're early!* Until the boat itself seemed sick of the whole thing and pitched them back into the water.

"Maybe this is a bad idea," Calvin said as they marched back to the boathouse, the heavy rowing shell biting into their sodden shoulders.

"What's my main issue?" she said, bracing herself for the worst as they lowered the boat onto the rack. Calvin had always insisted that rowing required the highest level of teamwork—a problem since, according to her boss, she also wasn't a team player. "Just tell me. Don't hold back."

"Physics," Calvin said.

"Physics," she said, relieved. "Thank god."

"I get it," she said, skimming a physics textbook later that day at work. "Rowing is a simple matter of kinetic energy versus boat drag and center of mass." She jotted down a few formulas. "And gravity," she added, "and buoyancy, ratio, speed, balance, gearing, oar length, blade type—" The more she read, the more she wrote, the nuances of rowing slowly revealing themselves in complicated algorithms. "Oh for heaven's sake," she said, sitting back. "Rowing isn't *that* hard."

"Jesus!" Calvin exclaimed two days later as their boat sped unimpeded through the water. "Who *are* you?" She said nothing, replaying the formulas in her head. As they passed a men's eight sitting at rest, every rower turned to watch them go by.

"Did you see that?" the coxswain shouted angrily at his crew. "Did you see how she gets length *without* overreaching?"

And yet about a month later, her boss, Dr. Donatti, accused her of exactly that. "You're overreaching, Miss Zott," he said, pausing to squeeze the top of her shoulder. "Abiogenesis is more of a PhD-university-this-topic-is-so-boring-no-one-cares sort of thing. And don't take this the wrong way, but it exceeds your intellectual grasp."

"And exactly what way am I *supposed* to take that?" She shrugged his hand off.

"What happened here?" he said, ignoring her tone as he took her bandaged fingers in his hands. "If you're struggling with the lab equipment, you know you can ask one of the fellas to help you."

"I'm learning to row," she said, snatching her fingers back. Despite her recent gains, the next several rows had been complete failures.

"Rowing, eh?" Donatti said, rolling his eyes. *Evans.*

Donatti had been a rower too, and at Harvard, no less, where he'd had the incredible misfortune to row just once against Evans and his precious Cambridge boat at the fucking Henley. Their catastrophic loss (seven boat lengths), witnessed only by a handful of people who'd managed to glimpse it over a sea of impossibly big hats, was carefully blamed on some fish and chips they'd ingested the night before, instead of the tonnage of beer that had washed it down.

In other words, they were all still drunk at the start.

After the race, their coach had told them to go over and congratulate the la-di-dah Cambridge crew. That's when Donatti had first learned one of the Cambridge boys was an American—an American who held some sort of grudge against Harvard. As he shook Evans's hand, Donatti managed "Good row," but instead of responding in kind, Evans said, *"Jesus, are you drunk?"*

Donatti took an instant dislike to him, a dislike that tripled when he found out that Evans was not only studying chemistry as he was, but he was *that* Evans—*Calvin* Evans—the guy who'd already made a major mark in the chemistry world.

Was it any surprise that, years later, when Evans accepted the incredibly insulting Hastings offer Donatti himself had crafted, Donatti wasn't overly enthusiastic? First, Evans didn't remember him—rude. Second, Evans appeared to have maintained his fitness—annoying. Third, Evans told *Chemistry Today* that he took the position, not based on Hastings's sterling reputation, but because *he liked the fucking weather.* Seriously—the man was an asshole. However, there was one consolation. He, Donatti, was director of Chemistry, and not just because his father played golf with the CEO, or because he happened to be the man's godson, and certainly not because he'd married the man's daughter. Bottom line, the great Evans would be reporting to *him*.

To enforce that pecking order, he called a meeting with the

blowhard, then purposely showed up twenty minutes late. Unfortunately, to an empty conference room, because Evans hadn't shown up at all. "Sorry, Dino," Evans later informed him. "I don't really like meetings."

"It's *Donatti*."

And now? Elizabeth Zott. He didn't like Zott. She was pushy, smart, opinionated. Worse, she had terrible taste in men. Unlike so many others, though, he did not find Zott attractive. He glanced down at a silver-framed photograph of his family: three big-eared boys bracketed by the sharp-beaked Edith and himself. He and Edith were a team the way couples were meant to be a team—not by sharing hobbies like *rowing* for fuck's sake—but in the way their sexes deemed socially and physically appropriate. He brought home the bacon; she pumped out the babies. It was a normal, productive, God-approved marriage. Did he sleep with other women? What a question. Didn't everyone?

"—my underlying hypothesis—" Zott was saying.

Underlying hypothesis his ass. This was the other thing he hated about Zott: she was tireless. Stiff. Didn't know when to quit. Standard rower attributes, now that he thought about it. He hadn't rowed in years. Was there really a women's team in town? Obviously, she couldn't possibly be rowing *with* Evans. An elite rower like Evans would never deign to get in a boat with a novice, even if they were sleeping together. Scratch that; *especially* if they were sleeping together. Evans probably signed her up for some beginner crew, and Zott, wanting to prove that she could hold her own—*per usual*—went along with it. He shuddered at the thought of a bunch of struggling rowers, their blades hitting the water like out-of-control spatulas.

"—I'm determined to see this through, Dr. Donatti—" Zott asserted.

Yes, yes, there it was. Women like her always used the word

"determined." Well, he was determined, too. Just last night he'd come up with a new way to deal with Zott. He was going to steal her away from Evans. What better way to fix the big man's wagon? Then, once he'd made the Evans–Zott romance a crash scene with no survivors, he'd dump her and return to his once-again pregnant housewife and impossibly loud children, no harm done.

His plan was simple: first, attack Zott's self-esteem. Women were so easily crushed.

"Like I said," Donatti emphasized as he stood, sucking in his gut as he shooed her toward the door. "You're just not smart enough."

Elizabeth stalked down the hallway, her heels hitting the tile in a dangerous staccato. She tried to calm herself by taking a deep breath in, but it came rushing back out at hurricane speed. Stopping abruptly, she slammed her fist against the wall, then took a moment to review her options.

Replead case.

Quit.

Set fire to the building.

She didn't want to admit it, but his words were like fresh fuel to her ever-growing pyre of self-doubt. She had neither the education nor the experience of the others. She not only lacked their credentials but their papers, peer support, financial backing, and awards. And yet, she knew—she *knew*—she was onto something. Some people were born to things; she was one of those people. She pressed her hand on her forehead as if that might keep her head from exploding.

"Miss Zott? Excuse me. Miss Zott?"

The voice seemed to come from out of nowhere.

"Miss Zott!"

From just around the next corner peeked a thin-haired man with a sheaf of papers. It was Dr. Boryweitz, a lab mate who often sought her help, as most of the others did, when no one else was looking.

"I was wondering if you could take a look at this," he said in a low voice as he motioned her off to the side, his forehead rutted with anxiety. "My latest test results." He thrust a sheet of paper into her hands. "I'd call this a breakthrough, wouldn't you?" His hands trembled. "Something new?"

He wore his normal expression—frightened, as if he'd just seen a ghost. It was a mystery to most how Dr. Boryweitz had ever gotten a PhD in chemistry, much less a job at Hastings. He often seemed just as mystified.

"Do you think your young man might be interested in this?" Boryweitz asked. "Maybe you could show it to him. Is that where you were headed? His lab? Maybe I could tag along." He reached out, grasping her forearm as if she were a life buoy, something he could cling to until the big rescue ship in the form of Calvin Evans pulled up.

Elizabeth carefully pulled the papers from his grip. Despite his neediness, she liked Boryweitz. He was polite, professional. And they had something in common: they were both in the wrong place at the wrong time, albeit for entirely different reasons.

"The thing is, Dr. Boryweitz," she said, trying to put aside her own troubles as she studied his work, "this is a macromolecule with repeating units linked by amide bonds."

"Right, right."

"In other words, it's a polyamide."

"A poly—" His face fell. Even he knew polyamides had been around forever. "I think you might be mistaken," he said. "Look again."

"It's not a bad finding," she said gently. "It's just that it's already been proven."

He shook his head in defeat. "So I shouldn't show this to Donatti."

"You've basically rediscovered nylon."

"Really," he said, looking down at his results. "Darn." His

head submerged. An uncomfortable silence followed. Then he glanced at his watch as if there might be an answer there. "What's all this?" he finally said, pointing to her bandaged fingers.

"Oh. I'm a rower. Trying to be."

"Are you any good?"

"No."

"Then why are you doing it?"

"I'm not sure."

He shook his head. "Boy, do I get that."

"How's your project going?" Calvin asked Elizabeth a few weeks later as they sat together at lunch. He took a bite of his turkey sandwich, chewing vigorously to disguise the fact that he already knew. Everybody knew.

"Fine," she said.

"No problems?"

"None." She sipped her water.

"You know if you ever need my help—"

"—I don't need your help."

Calvin sighed, frustrated. It was a form of naïveté, he thought, the way she continued to believe that all it took to get through life was grit. Sure, grit was critical, but it also took luck, and if luck wasn't available, then help. *Everyone* needed help. But maybe because she'd never been offered any, she refused to believe in it. How many times had she asserted that if she did her best, her best would win? He'd lost count. And this was despite significant evidence to the contrary. Especially at Hastings.

As he finished their lunch—she barely touched hers—he promised himself he would not intervene on her behalf. It was important to respect her wishes. She wanted to handle this on her own. He would *not* get involved.

"What's your problem, Donatti?" he roared approximately ten minutes later as he burst into his boss's office. "Is it an origin of life issue? Pressure from the religious community? Abiogenesis is just more proof that there actually is no God and you're worried this might not play well in Kansas? Is that why you're canceling Zott's project? And you dare to call yourself a scientist."

"Cal," Donatti had said, his arms stretched casually behind his head. "As much as I love our little chats, I'm kind of busy right now."

"Because the only other viable explanation," Calvin accused, shoving his hands in the front pockets of his voluminous khakis, "is that you don't *understand* her work."

Donatti rolled his eyes as a puff of stale air escaped his lips. Why were brilliant people so dumb? If Evans had any brains at all, he'd accuse him of attempting to horn in on his good-looking girlfriend.

"Actually, Cal," Donatti said, stubbing out a cigarette, "I was trying to give her career a little boost. Giving her a chance to work with me directly on a very important project. Help her grow in other areas."

There, Donatti thought. *Grow in other areas—how obvious could he be?* But Calvin started in on her latest test results as if they were still talking about work. The guy was clueless.

"I get offers every week," Calvin threatened. "Hastings isn't the only place I can conduct my research!"

This again. How many times had Donatti heard it? Sure, Evans was a hot ticket in the research world, and yes, much of their funding was based on his mere presence. But that was only because funders erroneously believed that Evans's name attracted other big-brained talent. Hadn't happened. Anyway, he didn't want Evans to leave; he only wanted Evans to fail—to become so unhinged by love lost that he self-destructed, ruining his reputation and tanking all research opportunities going forward. Once that happened, *then* he could leave.

"Like I said," Donatti replied in a measured voice, "I was only trying to give Miss Zott a chance for personal growth—I'm trying to help her career."

"She can take care of her own career."

Donatti laughed. "Really. And yet here *you* are."

But what Donatti didn't tell Calvin was that a huge fly had recently landed in his get-rid-of-Evans-via-Zott ointment. A donor with impossibly deep pockets.

The man had appeared, out of the blue, two days ago, with a blank check and an insistence to fund—of all things—abiogenesis. Donatti mounted a polite argument. What about lipid metabolism, he suggested. Or cell division? But the man insisted: abiogenesis or nothing. So Donatti had no choice: he put Zott back on her ridiculous mission to Mars.

Truth was, he wasn't making much headway with her anyway. She'd steadily refused to yield to his repeated "you're not smart" put-downs. No matter how many times he said it, she hadn't once responded in the proper fashion. Where was the low self-esteem? Where were the tears? If she wasn't restating her boring case for abiogenesis in a professional way, then she was saying, "Touch me again and live to regret it." What the hell did Evans see in this woman? He could keep her. He'd have to find some other way to fix the big man's wagon.

"Calvin," Elizabeth said, rushing into his lab later that afternoon. "I have great news. I've been keeping something from you and I apologize, but it was only because I didn't want you to get involved. Donatti canceled my project a few weeks back and I've been fighting to get it back. Today that fight paid off. He reversed his decision—said he'd reviewed my work and decided it was too important not to move forward."

Calvin smiled broadly in what he hoped was the appropriate expression of surprise—he'd left Donatti's office less than an hour ago. "Wait? Really?" he said, clapping her on the back. "He tried to cancel abiogenesis? Well that must have been a mistake from the start."

"I'm sorry I didn't tell you about it. I wanted to handle it on my own and now I'm glad I did. I feel like it's a real vote of confidence in my work—in me."

"Definitely."

She looked at him more closely, then took a step back. "I *did* get this on my own. You had *nothing* to do with it."

"First time I've heard about it."

"You *never* talked to Donatti," she pressed, "you *never* got involved."

"I swear," he lied.

After she left, Calvin clasped his hands together in a silent fit of glee and flipped on the hi-fi, dropping the needle on "Sunny Side of the Street." For a second time, he'd saved the person he loved the most, and the best part was, she didn't know.

He grabbed a stool, opened a notebook, and began to write. He'd been keeping journals since age seven or so, jotting down the facts and fears of his life between lines of chemical equations. Even today his lab was full of these nearly illegible notebooks. It was one of the reasons everyone assumed he was getting a lot done. Volume.

"Your handwriting is hard to read here," Elizabeth had noted on several occasions. "What's that say?" She'd pointed to an RNA-related theory he'd been toying with for months.

"A hypothesis about enzymatic adaptation," he answered.

"And this?" She pointed farther down the page. Something he'd written about her.

"More of the same," he said, tossing the notebook aside.

It wasn't that he was writing anything terrible about her—just the opposite. Rather, it was more that he couldn't risk having her discover that he was obsessed with the notion that she might die.

He'd long ago decided that he was a jinx and he had solid proof: every person he'd ever loved had died, always in a freak accident. The only way to put an end to this deadly pattern was to put an end to love. And he had. But then he'd met Elizabeth and, without meaning to, had stupidly and selfishly gone on to love again. Now here she was, standing directly in line of his jinx fire.

As a chemist, he realized his fixation on jinxes was not at all scientific; it was superstitious. Well, so be it. Life wasn't a hypothesis one could test and retest without consequence—something always crashed eventually. Thus he was constantly on the lookout for things that posed a threat to her, and as of this morning, that thing was rowing.

They'd flipped the pair yet again—his fault—and for the very first time, they'd ended up in the water on the same side of the boat and he'd made a terrifying discovery: she couldn't swim. By the looks of her panicked dog paddle, she'd never had a swim lesson in her life.

That's why, while Elizabeth was off in the bathroom at the boathouse, he and Six-Thirty had approached the men's team captain, Dr. Mason. It was bad-weather season: if he and Elizabeth were going to continue to row—she actually wanted to—it was best to be in an eight. Safer. Plus, if the eight did flip—unlikely—there'd be that many more people to save her. Anyway, Mason had been trying to recruit him for more than three years; it was worth a shot.

"What do you think?" he'd asked Mason. "You'd have to take both of us, though."

"A *woman* in a men's eight?" Dr. Mason had said, readjusting his cap over his crew cut. He'd been a marine and hated it. But he'd kept the hairstyle.

"She's good," Calvin said. "Very tough."

Mason nodded. These days he was an obstetrician. He already knew how tough women could be. Still, a woman? How could that possibly work?

"Hey, guess what," Calvin told Elizabeth a minute later. "The men's team really wants both of us to row in their eight today."

"Really?" Her goal had always been to join an eight. The eights rarely seemed to flip. She'd never told Calvin she couldn't swim. Why worry him?

"The team captain approached me just now. He's seen you row," he said. "He knows talent when he sees it."

From below, Six-Thirty exhaled. *Lies, lies, and more lies.*

"When do we start?"

"Now."

"Now?" She felt a jolt of panic. While she'd wanted to row in an eight, she also knew the eight required a level of synchronization she had not yet mastered. When a boat succeeds, it's because the people in the boat have managed to set aside their petty differences and physical discrepancies and row as one. Perfect harmony—that was the goal. She'd once overheard Calvin telling someone at the boathouse that his Cambridge coach insisted that they even blink at the same time. To her surprise the guy nodded. "We had to file our toenails to the same length. Made a huge difference."

"You'll be rowing two seat," he said.

"Great," she said, hoping he didn't notice the violent shake in her hands.

"The coxswain will call out commands; you'll be fine. Just watch the blade in front of you. And whatever you do, don't look out of the boat."

"Wait. How can I watch the blade in front of me if I don't look out of the boat?"

"Just don't do it," he warned. "Throws off the set."

"But—"

"And relax."

"I—"

"Hands on!" yelled the coxswain.

"Don't worry," Calvin said. "You'll be fine."

Elizabeth once read that 98 percent of the things people worry about never come true. But what, she wondered, about the 2 percent that do? And who came up with that figure? Two percent seemed suspiciously low. She'd believe 10 percent—even 20. In her own life it was probably closer to 50. She really didn't want to worry about this row, but she was. Fifty percent chance she was going to blow it.

As they carried the boat to the dock in the dark, the man in front of her glanced over his shoulder as if to try to understand why the guy who usually rowed two seat seemed smaller.

"Elizabeth Zott," she said.

"No talking!" shouted the coxswain.

"Who?" asked the man suspiciously.

"I'm rowing two seat today."

"Quiet back there!" the coxswain yelled.

"Two seat?" the man whispered incredulously. "*You're* rowing two seat?"

"Is there a *problem*?" Elizabeth hissed back.

"You were great!" Calvin shouted two hours later, pounding on the car's steering wheel with such excitement that Six-Thirty worried they might crash before they reached home. "Everyone thought so!"

"Who's everyone?" Elizabeth said. "No one said a single word to me."

"Oh, well, you only hear from the other rowers when they're pissed. The point is, we're in the lineup for Wednesday." He smiled, triumphant. Saved her again—first at work and now this.

Maybe this was the way one ended a jinx—by taking secret but sensible precautions.

Elizabeth turned and looked out the window. Could the sport of rowing really be that egalitarian? Or was this just the usual fear from the usual suspects—rowers, like scientists, were afraid of Calvin's legendary grudge holding.

As they drove along the coast toward home, the sunrise illuminating a dozen or so surfers, their longboards pointed at the shore, their heads turned, hoping to catch a few waves before work, it suddenly occurred to her that she'd never seen this supposed grudge holding in action.

"Calvin," she said, turning back toward him, "why does everyone say you hold a grudge?"

"What's that?" he said, unable to stop smiling. Secret, sensible precautions. The solution to life's problems!

"You know what I mean," she said. "There's an undertone at work—people say if they disagree with you, you'll ruin them."

"Oh that," he said cheerfully. "Rumors. Gossip. Jealousy. There are people I don't like, certainly, but would I go out of my way to ruin them? Of course not."

"Right," she said. "But I'm still curious. Is there anyone in your life you'll never forgive?"

"No one comes to mind," he answered gaily. "You? Anyone you plan to hate the rest of your life?" He turned to look at her, her face still flushed from the row, her hair damp with ocean spray, her expression serious. She held out her fingers, as if counting.

CHAPTER 9

The Grudge

When Calvin claimed he held no grudges and hated no one, he only meant it in that way that some people say they forget to eat. Meaning he was lying. No matter how hard he tried to pretend he'd left the past behind, it was right there, gnawing at his heart. Plenty of people had wronged him, but there was only one man he could not forgive. Only one man he swore to hate until his dying day.

He'd first glimpsed this man when he was ten. A long limo had pulled up to the gates of the boys home and the man had gotten out. He was tall, elegant, carefully dressed in a tailored suit and silver cuff links, none of which fit with the Iowan landscape. With the other boys, Calvin crowded the fence. A movie star, they guessed. Maybe a professional baseball player.

They were used to this. About twice a year, famous people came to the home, reporters in tow, to get their pictures taken with a few of the boys. Occasionally these visits resulted in a couple of baseball gloves or autographed headshots. But this man only had a briefcase. They all turned away.

But about a month after the man's visit, all sorts of things started to arrive: science textbooks, math games, chemistry sets. And unlike the headshots or baseball gloves, there was enough to go around.

"The Lord doth provide," the priest said, handing out a stack of brand-new biology books. "Which means you meek shall shut up and sit the hell still. You boys in the back, sit still, I mean it!" He slammed a ruler on a nearby desk, causing everyone to jump.

"Excuse me, Father," Calvin said, leafing through his copy, "but there's a problem with mine. Some of the pages are missing."

"They're not *missing,* Calvin," the priest said. "They've been removed."

"Why?"

"Because they're wrong, that's why. Now open your books to page one hundred nineteen, boys. We'll start with—"

"Evolution's missing," Calvin persisted, riffling through the pages.

"That's enough, Calvin."

"But—"

The ruler cracked down hard against his knuckles.

"Calvin," the bishop said wearily. "What's wrong with you? This is the fourth time you've been sent to me this week. And that doesn't count the complaints I've received from our librarian about your lies."

"What librarian?" Calvin asked, surprised. Surely the bishop couldn't mean the drunk priest who often holed up in the small closet that housed the home's pathetic book collection.

"Father Amos says you claim to have read everything in our stacks. Lying is a sin, but brag-lying? There's nothing worse."

"But I *have* read—"

"Silence!" he shouted, looming over the boy. "Some people are born bad apples," he continued. "The result of parents who were bad themselves. But in your case, I don't know where it comes from."

"What do you mean?"

"I mean," he said, leaning forward, "that I suspect you were born good but went bad. Rotted," he said, "through a series of bad choices. Are you familiar with the idea that beauty comes from within?"

"Yes."

"Well, your insides match your outward ugliness."

Calvin touched his swollen knuckles, trying not to cry.

"Why can't you be grateful for what you've got?" the bishop said. "Half the pages in a biology book are better than none, aren't they? Lord, I knew this would be a problem." He pushed away from his desk and plodded about his office. "Science books, chemistry sets. What we have to accept just to get cash for the coffers." He turned to Calvin, angry. "Even *that's* your fault," he said. "We wouldn't be in this position if it weren't for your father—"

Calvin jerked his head up.

"Never mind." The bishop retreated to his desk, picking at papers.

"You can't talk about my father," Calvin said, heat rising to his face. "You didn't even know him!"

"I get to talk about whomever I like, Evans," the bishop scowled. "And anyway, I don't mean your father who died in the train wreck. I mean," he said, "your *actual* father; the idiot who's saddled us with all these damn science books. He came here about a month ago in a big limo searching for a ten-year-old whose adoptive parents got hit by a train, whose aunt wrapped her car around a tree, a young boy who 'might be,' the man said, 'very tall?' I went straight to the cabinet and pulled your file. Thought maybe he'd come to reclaim you like a misplaced suitcase— happens all the time in adoptions. But when I showed him your photograph, he lost interest."

Calvin's eyes widened, taking in the news. He'd been adopted? That wasn't possible. His parents were still his parents, dead or not. He fought back tears, thinking of how happy he used to be, his hand tucked into the safety of his father's bigger one, his head resting against his mother's warm chest. The bishop was *wrong*. He was *lying*. The boys were always being told stories about how and why they ended up at All Saints: their mothers died in childbirth and their fathers couldn't cope; they were a problem to raise; there were already too many mouths to feed. This was just one more.

"Just so you know," the bishop said as if selecting from a list, "your real mother died in childbirth, and your real father couldn't cope."

"I don't believe you!"

"I see," the bishop said dryly as he withdrew two pieces of paper from Calvin's file: an adoption certificate and a woman's death certificate. "The budding scientist demands proof."

Calvin stared down at the documents through a cloud of tears. He couldn't make out a single word.

"All righty then," the bishop said, clapping his hands together. "I'm sure this all comes as a shock, Calvin, but look on the bright side. You *do* have a father and he *is* looking out for you—or for your education at least. That's far more than the other boys get. Try not to be so selfish about this. You've been lucky. First you had nice adoptive parents; now you have a rich father. Think of his gift"—he hesitated—"as a remembrance. As a tribute to your mother. A memorial."

"But if he's my real father," Calvin said, still not believing him, "he would take me away from here. He would want me with him."

The bishop looked down at Calvin, his eyes open with surprise. "What? No. I told you: your mother died in childbirth and your father couldn't cope. No, we both agreed—especially after he'd read your file—that you're better off staying here. A boy like you needs a moral environment, lots of discipline. Plenty of rich people send their kids to boarding school; All Saints isn't that different." He sniffed, taking in the sour smells from the kitchen. "Although he did insist that we swell our educational offerings. Which I found presumptuous," he added, as he picked some cat hair off his sleeve. "Telling us—professional educators—how to educate." He rose, turning his back on Calvin to look out the window at the roof that sagged on the west side of the building. "The good news is, he did leave us a nice chunk of change—not just for you, but for the other boys, too. Very generous. Or would have been if he hadn't earmarked all of it for science and sports. God, rich people. They always think they know best."

"He's . . . he's a scientist?"

"Did I *say* he was a scientist?" the bishop said. "Look. He came, he made inquiries, he left. Left a check, too. Far more than what most deadbeat fathers do."

"But when's he coming back?" Calvin begged, wanting more than anything to escape the home, even if it was with a man he didn't know.

"We'll have to wait and see," the bishop said, turning away to look out the leaded window. "He didn't say."

Calvin trudged slowly back to his classroom, thinking about the man—thinking of ways to make him come back. He *had* to come back. But the only things that ever showed up were more science books.

Still, he was a child, and as children do, he held on to his hope long after the hope should have expired. He read all the books his new-to-the-scene father had sent—devoured them as if they were love, stocking his broken heart with theories and algorithms, determined to uncover the chemistry he and his father shared, the unbreakable bond that linked them for life. But what he realized through his self-study was that the complexity of chemistry went well beyond birthright, that it twisted and turned in sometimes heartless ways. And thus he had to live with the knowledge that not only had this other father discarded him—without even *meeting* him—but that chemistry itself had spawned the grudge he could neither hide nor outgrow.

CHAPTER 10

The Leash

Elizabeth hadn't had a pet before and she wasn't sure she had one now. Six-Thirty wasn't human, but he seemed to possess a humanity that far surpassed what she'd found in most people.

That's why she didn't buy him a leash—it seemed wrong. Insulting, even. He rarely strayed far from her side, never crossed the street without looking, didn't chase cats. In fact, the only time he'd ever bolted was on the Fourth of July when a firecracker exploded right in front of him. After hours of worried searching, she and Calvin finally found him tucked behind some trash cans in an alleyway, shaking in shame.

But when the city passed its very first leash law, she found herself reconsidering the idea, although for more complicated reasons. As her attachment to the dog grew, so too grew the idea of attaching the dog to her.

So she bought a leash and hung it on the coatrack in their hallway and waited for Calvin to notice. But after a week, he still hadn't.

"I got Six-Thirty a leash," she finally announced.

"Why?" Calvin asked.

"It's the law," she explained.

"What law?"

She described the new law and he laughed. "Oh—that. Well,

that doesn't apply to us. It's for people who don't have a dog like Six-Thirty."

"No, it's for everyone. It's new. I'm pretty sure they mean business."

He smiled. "Don't worry. Six-Thirty and I pass the precinct almost every day. The police know us."

"But that's about to change," she insisted. "Probably because there's been a surge in pet deaths. A lot more dogs and cats are getting hit by cars." She didn't know if this was factually true, but it seemed like it certainly could be. "Anyway, yesterday I took Six-Thirty out on a walk and used the leash. He liked it."

"I can't run with a leash," Calvin said, glancing up. "I hate feeling tethered. Besides, he always stays right with me."

"Something could happen."

"What could happen?"

"He could run out into the street. He could get hit. Remember the firecracker? It's not you I'm worried about," she said. "It's him."

Calvin smiled to himself. It was a side of Elizabeth he'd never seen before: a mothering instinct.

"By the way," he said, "there's lightning in the forecast. Dr. Mason called—rowing's been canceled the rest of the week."

"Oh, that's too bad," she said, trying not to sound relieved. She'd rowed in the men's eight four times now, and each time it had left her more exhausted than she cared to admit. "Did he say anything else?" She didn't want to sound like she was fishing for a compliment, but she was. Dr. Mason seemed like a decent man; he always spoke to her as an equal. Calvin had mentioned he was an obstetrician.

"He mentioned we're in the lineup for next week," Calvin said. "And that he'd like us to consider a regatta in the spring."

"You mean a race?"

"You'll love it. It's fun."

Actually, Calvin was pretty sure she might not love it. Racing was stressful. The fear of losing was bad enough, but there was also that knowledge that the row itself was going to hurt, that once the word "Attention!" was called, the rower would risk heart attack, cracked ribs, lung donation—whatever it took—just to earn that dime-store medal at the end. Coming in second? Please. It wasn't called first loser for nothing.

"Sounds interesting," she lied.

"It really is," he lied back.

"Rowing was canceled, remember?" Calvin said two days later, surprised to sense Elizabeth getting dressed in the dark. He reached for his alarm clock. "It's four a.m. Come back to bed."

"I can't sleep," she said. "I think I'll go into work early."

"No," he begged. "Stay with me." He pulled at the covers and motioned her back in.

"I'll put that potato dish in the oven on low," she said, slipping on some shoes. "It'll make a good breakfast for you."

"Look, if you're going, I'm going," he said, yawning. "Just give me a few minutes."

"No, no," she said. "You sleep."

He woke an hour later to find himself alone.

"Elizabeth?" he called.

He padded his way to the kitchen, where a pair of oven mitts sat on the counter. *Enjoy the potatoes,* she'd written. *See you soon xoxoxo E.*

"Let's run to work this morning," he called to Six-Thirty. He didn't actually feel like going on a run, but that way they could all ride home together in one car. It wasn't because he cared about saving gas; it was because he couldn't stand the thought of Elizabeth driving home alone. There were trees out there. And trains.

She'd hate it if she knew how much he worried and fussed, so he kept it to himself. But how could he not fuss over the person he loved more than anything, more than seemed even possible?

Besides, she fussed over him too—making sure he ate, constantly suggesting he run indoors with Jack, buying a leash, of all things.

Out of the corner of his eye he spied some bills and made a mental note to file the latest crop of flimflam correspondence. He'd gotten yet another letter from the woman claiming to be his mother—*They told me you'd died,* she always wrote. He'd also gotten one from an illiterate who claimed Calvin had stolen all his ideas, and another from a so-called long-lost brother who wanted money. Oddly, no one had ever written pretending to be his father. Maybe because his father was still out there, pretending he'd never had a son.

Since he'd left the boys home, the only other person, besides the bishop, to whom he'd ever admitted his father grudge, was—of all people—a pen pal. He'd never met the man but they'd managed to establish a strong friendship. Maybe because, like confession, they both found it easier to talk to someone they couldn't see. But when the subject of fathers came up—this was after a year of steady no-holds-barred correspondence—everything changed. Calvin had let it drop that he hoped his father was dead, and his pen pal, apparently shocked, reacted in a way Calvin hadn't expected. He stopped writing back.

Calvin assumed he'd crossed a line—the man was religious and he was not; maybe hoping your father was dead wasn't something one admitted in ecclesiastical circles. But whatever the reason, their tête-à-tête was over. He felt depressed for months.

That's why he'd decided not to mention the fact of his undead father to Elizabeth. He deeply worried that she'd either react like his ex-friend had and drop him, or suddenly wake up to what the bishop had once described as his fatal flaw: an innate unlovability. Calvin Evans, ugly both inside and out. She *had* turned down his marriage proposal.

Anyway, if he told her now, she might question why he hadn't told her before. And that was dangerous because she might ask herself what *else* had he left out?

No, some things were better left unsaid. Besides, she'd kept her work troubles to herself, hadn't she? Having a few secrets in a close relationship was normal.

He pulled on his old track pants, then rummaged in their shared sock drawer, his mood lifting as he caught a whiff of her perfume. He'd never been one for self-improvement—never even gotten through Dale Carnegie's book about making friends and influencing people because ten pages in he realized he didn't care what anyone else thought. But that was before Elizabeth—before he realized that making her happy made him happy. Which, he thought, as he grabbed his tennis shoes, had to be the very definition of love. To actually *want* to change for someone else.

As he bent down to tie his laces, his chest filled with something new. Was it gratitude? He, the early orphaned, never-before-loved, unattractive Calvin Evans, had, by hook or by crook, found this woman, this dog, this research, this row, this run, Jack. It was all so much more than he'd ever expected, so much more than he ever deserved.

He looked at his watch: 5:18 a.m. Elizabeth was sitting on a stool, her centrifuges on full spin. He whistled for Six-Thirty to come meet him at the front door. It was a little over five miles to work, and running together, they could be there in forty-two minutes. But as he opened the door, Six-Thirty hesitated. It was dark and drizzly.

"Come on, boy," Calvin said. "What's wrong?"

Then he remembered. He turned back, grabbed the leash, bent down, and clipped it to Six-Thirty's collar. Securely connected to the dog for the very first time, Calvin turned and locked the door behind him.

He was dead thirty-seven minutes later.

CHAPTER 11

Budget Cuts

"Come on, boy," Calvin said to Six-Thirty, "let's pick it up." Six-Thirty moved to his place five paces in front of Calvin, then glanced back every so often as if to make sure Calvin was still there. As they turned right, they passed a newsstand. "CITY BUDGETS HIT ROCK BOTTOM," screamed a headline, "POLICE AND FIRE SERVICES AT RISK."

Calvin put pressure on the leash, directing Six-Thirty to turn left into an older neighborhood filled with big houses and oceanic lawns. "Someday we'll live here," Calvin assured him as they jogged along. "Maybe after I win the Nobel," which Six-Thirty knew he would win because Elizabeth said he would.

As they took another turn, Calvin almost slipped on moss before regaining his stride. "Close one," he huffed as they neared the police station. Six-Thirty looked ahead at the squad cars lined up like soldiers awaiting inspection.

But the cars hadn't been inspected. This was because the police department had suffered yet another budget cut—their third in four years. All three cuts had fallen under the Do More with Less! initiative, the slogan dreamed up by some middle manager in the city's PR department. What it actually meant this time was that their jobs were on the line. Salaries had already been docked. Raises were extinct. Layoffs were next.

So the officers did whatever they could to keep the layoffs at bay; they took the latest Do More with Less! initiative and stuck it where it belonged: out in the parking lot with the patrol cars. Let the black-and-whites bear the budget-cut brunt this time. No more tune-ups, oil changes, brake relining, retreads, lightbulb changes, nothing.

Six-Thirty didn't like the police parking lot, especially the way the police backed out in such a sloppy hurry. He didn't even like the friendly policemen who sometimes waved to them as he and Calvin jogged by, their slow trudge in sharp contrast to Calvin's vigor. They seemed depressed in Six-Thirty's opinion, shackled by low pay, bored by routine, unchallenged by the endless minor emergencies that never called upon the lifesaving training they'd learned at the police academy.

As he and Calvin approached, Six-Thirty sniffed the air. It was still dark. The sun would rise in about ten more—

CRACK!

From the darkness came a hideous popping sound. It was like a firecracker—sharp, loud, mean. Six-Thirty bucked in fright— *What was that?* He bolted, or tried to, but he was yanked back by the leash that connected him to Calvin. Calvin, too, reacted— *Were those gunshots?*—and bolted in exactly the opposite direction. *POW, POW, POW!* The explosions stuttered like a machine gun. In response, Calvin lifted his foot and lurched forward, yanking Six-Thirty *this way,* while Six-Thirty, wild-eyed, lifted his front paws and yanked back as if to say, *No, this way!* And the leash, taut like a tightrope, left no room for compromise. Calvin brought his foot down in a slick of motor oil, slipping forward like a clumsy ice skater, the pavement coming up fast like an old friend who couldn't wait to say hello.

BAM.

As a thin trail of red created a dark halo around Calvin's head, Six-Thirty turned to help, but something bore down upon them—a huge ship of a thing that moved with such force, it snapped the leash in two, flinging him off to the side.

He managed to lift his head just in time to see the wheels of a patrol car bump up over Calvin's body.

"Jesus, what was *that?*" the patrolman said to his partner. They were accustomed to their cars' constant backfires, but this was something else. They jumped out, startled to see a tall man lying on the ground, his gray eyes wide open, his head wound quickly soaking the sidewalk. He blinked twice at the policeman standing over him.

"Oh my god, did we hit him? Oh my god. Sir—can you hear me? Sir? Jimmy, call an ambulance."

Calvin lay there, his skull fractured, his arm snapped in two by the force of the police car. Around his wrist dangled the remnant of the leash.

"Six-Thirty?" he whispered.

"What was that? What did he say, Jimmy? Oh my god."

"Six-Thirty?" Calvin whispered again.

"No sir," the policeman said bending down beside him. "It's almost six but not quite. Actually, it's about five fifty. That's five five oh. Now we're going to get you out of here—we're going to get you fixed up, don't you worry, sir, there's nothing to worry about."

Behind him, police poured out of the building. In the distance, an ambulance screamed its intent of getting there soon.

"Oh, that's a shame," one of them said as air pressed out of Calvin's lungs. "Isn't that the guy everyone always calls about—the guy who runs?"

From ten feet away, Six-Thirty, his shoulder wrenched from its socket, the other half of the leash dangling from his whiplashed neck, watched. He wanted more than anything to go to Calvin's side, to dip his face close to his nostrils, to lick his wounds, to stop everything from going any further than it already had. But he knew. Even from ten feet, he knew. Calvin's eyes drifted shut. His chest stopped moving.

He watched as they loaded Calvin in the ambulance, a sheet over his body, his right hand hanging off the side of the gurney, the snapped leash still wrapped tight around his wrist. Six-Thirty turned away, sick with sorrow. With his head down, he turned and went to give Elizabeth the bad news.

CHAPTER 12

Calvin's Parting Gift

When Elizabeth was eight, her brother, John, dared her to jump off a cliff and she'd done it. There was an aquamarine water-filled quarry below; she'd hit it like a missile. Her toes touched bottom and she pushed up, surprised when she broke through the surface that her brother was already there. He'd jumped in right after her. *What the hell were you thinking, Elizabeth?* he shouted, his voice full of anguish as he dragged her to the side. *I was only kidding! You could've been killed!*

Now, sitting rigidly on her stool in the lab, she could hear a policeman talking about someone who'd died and someone else insisting she take his handkerchief and still another saying something about a vet, but all she could think about was that moment long ago when her toes had touched bottom, the soft, silky mud inviting her to stay. Knowing what she knew now, she could only think one thing: *I should have.*

It was her fault. This was what she tried to explain to the policeman. The leash. She'd bought it. But no matter how often she said it, he didn't seem to understand, and because of it, she thought there was a chance she'd imagined the whole thing. Calvin wasn't dead. He was rowing. He was on a trip. He was five floors up, writing in his notebook.

Someone said go home.

For the next few days, she and Six-Thirty lay on her unmade bed, sleep impossible, food out of the question, the ceiling their only vista, waiting for him to walk back through the door. The only thing that disturbed them was a ringing phone. Every time it was the same whiney voice—a mortician of all people—demanding that "decisions *must* be made!" A suit was needed for someone's coffin. "Whose coffin?" she said. "Who is this?" After too many of these calls, Six-Thirty, seemingly exhausted by her confusion, nudged her toward the closet and pawed open the door. And that's when she saw it: his shirts swaying like long-dead corpses at a hanging. And that's when she knew: Calvin was gone.

Just like after her brother's suicide and Meyers's attack, she could not cry. An army of tears lay just behind her eyes, but they refused to decamp. It was as if the wind had been knocked out of her: no matter how many deep breaths she took her lungs refused to fill. When she was a kid, she'd remembered overhearing a one-legged man tell the librarian someone was boiling water somewhere in the stacks. It was dangerous, he explained; she should do something. The librarian tried to assure him no one was boiling any water—it was a one-room library, she could see everyone—but he was insistent and shouted at her, and because of it two men had to remove him, one of them explaining that the poor guy was still suffering from shell shock. He'd probably never recover.

The problem was, now she heard the boiling water, too.

To stop the ringing phone, she had to find a suit. Calvin didn't own one, so she gathered what she felt he would have wanted: his rowing clothes. Then she took the small bundle to the funeral home and handed it to the funeral director. "Here," she said.

Long practiced in the art of dealing with the bereaved, the solemn man accepted the assortment with a courteous nod. But right after she left, he handed it to his assistant and said, "The stiff in room four is about a forty-six extra long." The assistant took the bundle and threw it into an unmarked closet where it joined a small mountain of other inappropriate outfits family members, in their grief-stricken state, had brought over the years. The assistant proceeded to a large wardrobe, grabbed a 46 extra long, shook the pants, blew lightly at the dust that grayed the shoulders, and headed for room 4.

Before Elizabeth was even ten blocks away, he'd successfully stuffed Calvin's rigid body within the suit's confines, shoving the hands that had once held her down dark sleeves; cramming the legs that once wrapped around her through woolen cylinders. Then he buttoned the shirt, buckled the belt, adjusted the tie, and knotted the laces, all the while brushing the dust that was so much a part of death from one end of the suit to the other. He stepped back to admire his work, then adjusted a lapel. He reached for a comb; reconsidered. He closed the door and walked down the hall to retrieve his brown-bag lunch, pausing only to give instructions to a woman who sat behind a large adding machine in a small office.

Before Elizabeth had made it twelve blocks, the dirty suit had been added to her bill.

The funeral was packed. A few rowers, one reporter, maybe fifty Hastings employees, a handful of whom, despite their bowed heads and somber clothing, weren't at Calvin's funeral to grieve, but to gloat. *Ding dong,* they cheered silently. *The king is dead.*

As the scientists milled about, several noticed Zott way off in the distance, the dog by her side. Once again, the damn dog wasn't on lead—this despite the city's new leash law, and notwith-standing the signs that encircled the entire cemetery prohibiting dogs from entering in the first place. Same old, same old. Even in death, Zott and Evans acted as if the rules didn't apply to them.

From a distance, Elizabeth shielded her eyes to take in the crowd. A well-dressed nosy couple stood apart at a separate grave site, watching the proceedings as if it were a fifty-car pileup. She rested one hand on Six-Thirty's bandages and considered how to proceed. The truth was, she was afraid to get close to the coffin because she knew she would try to pry it open and climb in and bury herself with him, and that meant dealing with all the people who would try to stop her, and she did not want to be stopped.

Six-Thirty sensed her death wish, and because of it, had been on suicide watch all week. The only problem was, he wanted to die himself. Worse, he suspected she was in the same position— that despite her own deathly desires, she felt beholden to keep *him* alive. What a mess devotion was.

Just then someone behind them said, "Well, at least Evans got a good day for it," as if bad weather would have put a damper on the otherwise festive funeral. Six-Thirty looked up to see a strong-jawed skinny man holding a small pad of paper.

"Sorry to disturb you," the man said to Elizabeth, "but I saw you sitting all by yourself over here and I thought you might be able to help. I'm writing a story about Evans, was wondering if I could ask you a few questions—only if you wouldn't mind— I mean, I know he was a famous scientist, but that's all I know. Could you tell me how you knew him? Maybe supply an anecdote? Did you know him long?"

"No," she said, avoiding his stare.

"No . . . you . . . ?"

"No, I didn't know him long. Definitely not long enough."

"Oh, right," he said, nodding, "I understand. That's why you're over here—not a close friend but still wanted to pay your respects; gotcha. Was he your neighbor? Maybe you could point out his parents. Siblings? Cousins? I'd love to get some background. I've heard a lot of things about him; some say he was a real jerk. Can you comment on that? I know he wasn't married, but did he date?" And when she continued to stare off into the distance, he added, lowering his voice, "By the way, I'm not sure you saw the signs, but dogs aren't allowed in the cemetery. I mean, not at all. The groundskeeper is supposedly a stickler about this one. Unless, I don't know, you need a dog, a Seeing Eye dog, because you're . . . well, you know—"

"I am."

The reporter took a step back. "Oh gee, really?" he said apologetically. "You're— Oh, I'm so sorry. It's just that you don't look—"

"I am," she repeated.

"And it's permanent?"

"Yes."

"That's a shame," he said, curious. "Disease?"

"Leash."

He took another step back.

"Well that's a shame," he repeated, slightly waving his hand in front of her face to see if she would react. And sure enough. Nothing.

Just off in the distance, a minister appeared.

"Looks like the party's starting," he said, telling her what he could see. "People are taking seats, the minister is opening the Bible, and"—he leaned way back to see if more people were coming from the parking lot—"and yet no family. Where's the family? There's not a single soul in the front row. So maybe he really was a jerk." He glanced back to get a response, surprised to see Elizabeth standing. "Lady?" he said. "You don't have to go all the way over there; people understand a situation like yours." She ignored him, feeling for her purse. "Well, if you're really going, you better let me help you." He reached for her elbow, but the second he touched her arm, Six-Thirty growled. "Geez," he said. "I was only trying to help."

"He *wasn't* a jerk," Elizabeth said through gritted teeth.

"Oh," he said, embarrassed. "No. Of course not. I'm sorry.

I was only repeating what I'd heard. You know—gossip. I apologize. Although I thought you said you didn't know him that well."

"That's not what I said."

"I think you—"

"I said I didn't know him *long enough,*" she quavered.

"That's what I said," he replied soothingly, reaching for her elbow again. "You didn't know him very long."

"Don't touch me." She wrested her elbow from his grip and with Six-Thirty at her side made her way across the uneven lawn, expertly avoiding stone angels and exhausted flowers as only one with twenty-twenty vision can do and, embracing the loneliness of the front row, selected a chair directly opposite his long, black box.

What followed was the usual refrain: the sad looks, the dirty shovel, the boring verse, the preposterous prayers. But when the first clods of dirt hit the coffin, Elizabeth interrupted the minister's final tribute by announcing, "I need to walk." And then she turned, and with Six-Thirty, walked away.

It was a long walk home: six miles, in heels, in black, just the two of them. And it was curious: both the route, which took them through as many bad sections as good, and the contrast, a colorless woman and injured dog planted against the conflict of an early spring. Everywhere they walked, even in the drabbest of neighborhoods, blooms poked their way up between sidewalk cracks and flower beds, shouting and boasting and calling attention to themselves, mingling their scents in hopes of creating complex perfumes. And there they were in the thick of it, the only living dead things.

The funeral car followed her for the first mile or so, the driver pleading for her to get in, informing her she'd last no more than fifteen minutes in those heels, reminding her that she'd already paid for the ride, and apologizing that while he wasn't able to take the dog, he was certain someone from another car would. But she was as deaf to his pleas as she had been blind to the reporter's nosiness, and eventually he and everyone else gave up and Elizabeth and Six-Thirty did the only thing that made sense: they just kept walking.

The following day, not able to be in her home, and with nowhere else to go, they went back to work.

This was a problem for her coworkers. They had already exhausted their full complement of things to say. *I'm so sorry. If there's ever anything you need. What a tragedy. I'm sure he didn't suffer. I'm there for you. He's in God's hands now.* So they avoided her.

"Take all the time you need," Donatti had said to her at the funeral, putting his hand on her shoulder while at the same time noting with surprise that black really wasn't her color. "I'm there for you." But when he saw her sitting on her stool in the lab in a daze, he avoided her, too. Later, after it was clear that everyone was only going to "be there" for her as long as she was "not there," she took Donatti's advice and went away.

The only place left to go was Calvin's lab.

"This might kill me," she whispered to Six-Thirty as they stood in front of Calvin's door. The dog pressed his head into her thigh, begging her to go no farther, but she opened the door anyway, and they both stepped through. The scent of cleaning fluid hit them like a locomotive.

Humans were strange, Six-Thirty thought, the way they constantly battled dirt in their aboveground world, but after death willingly entombed themselves in it. At the funeral, he couldn't believe the amount of dirt needed to cover Calvin's coffin, and when he saw the size of the shovel, he'd wondered if he should offer the help of his back legs to fill the hole. And now dirt was again the issue, but in the wrong direction. Every last trace of Calvin had been scrubbed away. He watched as she stood in the middle of the room, her face blank with shock.

His notebooks were gone. Boxed up and already stored while Hastings management waited nervously to see if a next-of-kin type might come forward and try to claim them. It went without saying that she, who knew and understood his research better than anyone, and whose kinship with him far surpassed the meaning of "kin," would not qualify.

There was only one thing left; a crate where they'd tossed his personal effects: a snapshot of her, some Frank Sinatra records, a few throat lozenges, a tennis ball, dog treats, and at the very bottom, his lunch box—which she realized, with a heavy heart, probably still contained the sandwich she'd made him nine days before.

But when she opened it, her heart nearly stopped. Inside was a small blue box. And inside that, the biggest small diamond she had ever seen.

Just then, Miss Frask poked her head in. "There you are, Miss Zott," she said, her rhinestone cat-eye glasses dangling like a sloppy noose from a chain around her neck. "I'm Miss Frask? From Personnel?" She paused. "I don't mean to disturb you," she said, pushing the door open a bit wider, "but—" Then she noticed Elizabeth going through the box. "Oh Miss Zott, you can't do that. Those things were his personal belongings, and while I know and recognize the—well—unusual relationship you and Mr. Evans enjoyed, we have to—by law—just wait a teeny bit longer to see if someone else—a brother, a nephew, *blood*—might step forward to claim those things. You understand. It's nothing against you or your personal—well, proclivities; I'm not making a moral judgment. But without some sort of document that says he actually meant to leave you his things, I'm afraid we have to follow the letter of the law. We have taken steps to secure his actual work. It's already under lock and key." She stopped short, giving

Elizabeth the once-over. "Are you okay, Miss Zott? You look like you might faint." And when Elizabeth slumped forward slightly, Miss Frask pushed the door all the way open and came in.

After that day in the cafeteria—when Eddie looked at Zott in a way he'd never once looked at her—Frask found Zott hateable.

"I was in the elevator today," Eddie had swooned, "and Miss Zott got in. We rode four whole floors together."

"Did you and she have a nice chat?" Frask said, her molars clenched. "Find out what her favorite color is?"

"No," he said. "But I'll definitely ask next time. Geez, she's something else."

Frask had gone on to hear about exactly *how* Zott was something else at least twice a week since then. With Eddie it was always Zott this and Zott that; he talked about her nonstop—but then, everyone did. Zott, Zott, Zott. She was so fucking *sick* of Zott.

"I'm sure I don't have to tell you," Frask said, placing a dimpled hand on Zott's back, "that it's too soon for you to be at work—especially here," she said, tipping her head at the room that had once held Calvin. "It's not good for you. You're still in shock and you need your rest." Her hand moved up and down in a clumsy pat. "Now I *know* what people are saying," she said, implying her role as ground zero when it came to Hastings gossip, "and I know *you* know what people are saying," she continued, fairly confident Elizabeth did not, "but in my opinion whether or not Mr. Evans was getting the milk for free doesn't mean his untimely death hurts you any less. In fact, in my opinion, it is *your* milk and if *you* choose to spoil it, that is *your* right."

There, she thought, satisfied. *Now* Zott knew what people were saying.

Elizabeth looked up at Frask, stunned. She supposed it took

a certain type of skill to be able to say exactly the wrong thing at exactly the wrong time. Maybe that was a prerequisite for a position in Personnel—a certain clunky, cheerful cluelessness that gave one the ability to insult the bereaved.

"I've been trying to track you down for several reasons," Frask was saying, "the first being the issue of Mr. Evans's dog. Him," she said, pointing a finger at Six-Thirty, who stared back grimly. "Unfortunately, he can't be here any longer. You understand. Hastings Research Institute absolutely venerated Mr. Evans and, because of it, overindulged his quirky tendencies. But now that Mr. Evans has left us, I'm afraid the dog must leave as well. As I understand it, the dog was really his dog anyway." She looked to Elizabeth for confirmation.

"No, he's *our* dog," she managed. "*My* dog."

"I see," she said. "But from now on, he'll need to stay at home."

From the corner, Six-Thirty lifted his head.

"I can't be here without him," Elizabeth said. "I just can't."

Frask blinked as if the room was too bright, and then from out of nowhere produced a clipboard on which she made a few notes. "Of course," she said without looking up, "I like dogs, too," although she didn't, "but as I said, we made allowances for Mr. Evans. He was quite important to us. But at some point," she said as she put one hand back on Elizabeth's shoulder and started patting again, "you have to realize, the coattails only go so far."

Elizabeth's expression changed. "Coattails?"

Frask looked up at her from the clipboard, trying to seem professional. "I think we know."

"I never rode his coattails."

"I never said you did," Frask said with mock surprise. Then she lowered her voice as if confiding a secret. "Can I just say something?" She took a short breath in. "There will be other men, Miss Zott. Maybe not as famous or as influential as Mr. Evans, but men all the same. I studied psychology—I know about these things. You chose Evans, he was famous, he was single, maybe he could help your career, who could blame you? But it didn't work. And now he's gone and you're sad—*of course you're sad*. But look on the bright side: you're free again. And there are lots of nice men, *good-looking* men. One of them is sure to put a ring on your finger."

She paused, remembering ugly Evans just before she pictured pretty Zott back in the dating pool, men teeming about her like frothy bubbles in a bathtub. "And once you find one," she said, "maybe a lawyer," she specified, "then you can stop all this science nonsense and go home and have lots of babies."

"That's not what I want."

Frask straightened up. "Well, aren't we the little renegade," she said. She hated Zott, she really did.

"There's just one more thing then," she continued, tapping her pen against the board, "and that is your bereavement leave. Hastings has awarded you three extra days. That's five days total. Unheard of for a non–family member—very, very generous, Miss Zott—and again an indication of how important Mr. Evans was to us. This is why I want to assure you that you can and should go home and stay there. With the dog. You have my permission."

Elizabeth wasn't sure if it was the cruelty of Frask's words or the foreign feel of the small, cold ring she'd buried in her fist just before Frask walked in, but before she could stop herself, she turned to retch into the sink.

"Normal," Frask said as she darted across the room to collect a wad of paper towels. "You're still in shock." But as she placed a second towel on Elizabeth's forehead, she adjusted her cat-eye glasses and took a much closer look. "Oh," she sighed judgmentally, drawing her head back. "Oh. I see."

"What?" Elizabeth murmured.

"Come on, now," Frask said disapprovingly. "What did you expect?" And then she tsked just loud enough to make Zott understand *she* knew. But when Zott didn't acknowledge that she knew she knew, Frask wondered if there was an outside chance

Zott actually *didn't* know. That's how it was with some scientists. They believe in science right up until it happens to them.

"Oh, I almost forgot," Frask said, withdrawing a newspaper from under the crook of her arm. "I wanted to make sure you'd seen this. It's a nice photo, don't you think?" And there it was, the article from the reporter who'd attended the funeral. "The Brilliance He Buried," claimed the headline, followed by a story that implied that Evans's difficult personality may have kept him from reaching his full scientific potential. And to prove that point, just to the right was a photo of Elizabeth and Six-Thirty standing in front of his coffin, with the caption "Actually, Love *Isn't* Blind," accompanied by a short summary of how even his girlfriend said she barely knew him.

"What a horrible thing to write," Elizabeth whispered, clutching her stomach.

"You're not going to be sick again, are you?" Frask scolded as she held out more paper towels. "I know you're a chemist, Miss Zott, but *surely* you expected this. Surely you've studied biology."

Elizabeth looked up, her face gray, her eyes empty, and for one tiny moment Frask found herself almost feeling sorry for this woman and her ugly dog and the vomit and all the problems that were to come. Despite her brains and beauty and her incredibly slutty approach to men, Zott wasn't any better off than the rest of them.

"Expected *what?*" Elizabeth said. "What are you getting at?"

"*Biology!*" Frask roared as she tapped her pen against Elizabeth's stomach. "Zott, please! We're women! You know very well Evans left you *something*!"

And Elizabeth, eyes suddenly wide with recognition, was sick all over again.

CHAPTER 13

Idiots

Hastings Research Institute management had a big problem. With their star scientist dead, and a newspaper article implying that his lousy personality had kept him from accomplishing anything worthwhile, Hastings's benefactors—the army, the navy, several pharmaceutical companies, a few private investors, and a handful of foundations—were already making noises about "reexamining Hastings's existing projects" and "rethinking future grants." That's how it is with research—it's at the mercy of those who pay for it.

Which is why Hastings management was determined to lay this ridiculous story to rest. Evans *had* been making good progress, hadn't he? His office was overflowing with notebooks and strange little equations written in an indecipherable script and punctuated by exclamation marks and thick underlines like the kind one makes when one is on the brink of something. In fact, he was scheduled to present a paper on his progress in Geneva in just another month. Or would have if he hadn't been backed over by a police car because he insisted on running outdoors in the rain instead of indoors in ballet slippers like everybody else.

Scientists. They just *had* to be different.

That was also part of the problem. Most of the Hastings scientists weren't different—or at least not different enough. They were normal, average, at best slightly above average. Not stupid, but not genius either. They were the kind of people who make up the majority of every company—normal people who do normal work, and who occasionally get promoted into management with uninspiring results. People who weren't going to change the world, but neither were they accidentally going to blow it up.

No, management had to rely on its innovators, and with Evans gone, that left a very small pool of true talent. Not all of them were in lofty positions like Calvin's; in fact, a few of them probably didn't realize they were regarded as true innovators. But Hastings management knew it was from them that nearly every big idea and breakthrough came.

The only real issue with these people, besides the occasional hygiene challenge, was that they always seemed to embrace failure as a positive outcome. "I have not failed," they'd endlessly quote Edison, "I've just found ten thousand ways that won't work." Which may be an acceptable thing to say in science but is absolutely the wrong thing to say to a roomful of investors looking for an immediate, high-ticket, chronic treatment for cancer. God save them from actual cures. Much harder to make money off someone who doesn't have a problem anymore. For that reason, Hastings did whatever it could to keep these people away from the press, unless it was the scientific press, which was fine because no one read that. But now? Dead Evans was on page eleven of the *LA Times,* and there next to his coffin? Zott and the damn dog.

That was management's third problem. Zott.

She was one of their innovators. Unrecognized, of course, but she acted as if she knew. Not a week went by when they didn't get some complaint about her—the way she voiced her opinion, insisted her name appear on her own papers, refused to make coffee; the list was endless. And yet her progress—or was it Calvin's?—was undeniable.

Her project, abiogenesis, had only been approved because a fat-cat investor had dropped from the heavens and insisted on funding, of all things, abiogenesis. What were the *odds*? Although this was exactly the sort of weird thing multimillionaires did:

fund useless pie-in-the-sky projects. The rich man had said he'd read a paper by an E. Zott—something old out of UCLA—and had been fascinated by its expansion possibilities. He'd been trying to track down Zott ever since.

"Zott? But Mr. Zott works here!" they'd told him before they could stop themselves.

The rich man had seemed genuinely surprised. "I'm only in town for a day, but I'd very much like to meet with Mr. Zott," he'd said.

And they hemmed and hawed. *Meet with Zott,* they thought. And find out *he* was a *she*? His check was as good as gone.

"Unfortunately, that won't be possible," they'd said. "Mr. Zott is in Europe. At a conference."

"What a pity," the rich man said. "Perhaps next time." And then he went on to say that he'd only be checking in on the project's progress about once every few years. Because he understood science was slow. Because he knew it required time and distance and patience.

Time. Distance. Patience. Was this man for *real*? "Very wise," they'd told him as they fought the urge to do backflips across the office. "Thanks for your trust." And before he was settled into his limo, they'd already carved up the bulk of his largesse to fund more promising research areas. They'd even given a bit of it to Evans.

But then—Evans. After they'd so graciously reinvested in his no-real-idea-what-the-guy-was-actually-doing research, he'd stormed into their offices saying if they didn't find a way to fund his pretty girlfriend, he'd leave and take all his toys and ideas and Nobel Prize nominations with him. They'd begged him to be reasonable; make them actually fund abiogenesis? Come on. But he refused to budge, went as far as to assert that her ideas might even be better than his own. At the time, they wrote it off to the ramblings of a man who'd hit the jackpot, sexwise. But now?

Her theories, unlike the theories of all the Edison "I'm not *really* a failure" quoters, appeared—at least according to Evans—to be dead-on. Darwin had long ago proposed that life sprang from a single-celled bacterium, which then went on to diversify into a complex planet of people, plants, and animals. Zott? She was like a bloodhound on the trail of where that first *cell* had come from. In other words, she was out to solve one of the greatest chemical mysteries of all time, and if her findings continued apace, there was no question that she would do just that. According to *Evans,* at least. The only issue was, it would probably take ninety years. Ninety completely unaffordable years. The fat-cat investor would surely be dead in far less. More to the point, so would they.

And there was one other minor detail. Management had just learned Zott was pregnant. As in *unwed* and pregnant.

Could their day get any worse?

Obviously, she had to go; no question about it. Hastings Research Institute had standards.

But if she were to go, where did that leave them on the innovation front? With a handful of people making poky-pony progress, that's where. And poky ponies didn't inspire much in the way of big-ticket grants.

Fortunately, Zott did work with three others. Hastings management had sent for them straightaway; they needed assurance that Zott's so-called critical research could limp along without Zott—whatever it would take to make it seem as if the money it never actually got was being put to good use. But as soon as the three PhDs were in the room, Hastings management knew they were in trouble. Two reluctantly conceded that Zott was the main driver, essential to any forward progress. The third—a man named Boryweitz—went the other route. Claimed *he'd* actually done it all. But when he couldn't back up any of his assertions with meaningful scientific explanation, they realized they were in the presence of a scientific idiot. Hastings was rife with them. No surprise. Idiots make it into every company. They tend to interview well.

The chemist sitting in front of them now? He couldn't even spell abiogenesis.

And then Miss Frask from Personnel—the one who'd first sounded the alarm regarding Zott's condition? She'd used her limited talents to spread the Zott's-knocked-up rumor, ensuring that all of Hastings knew of Zott's plight by noon. Which scared the hell out of them. The rumor's wildfire effect meant it was only a matter of time before the institute's big investors knew, and investors—as anyone knew—hated scandals. Plus, there was the problem of Zott's rich man-fan. The multimillionaire who'd written them a virtual blank check on behalf of abiogenesis— who'd claimed to have read *Mr.* Zott's old paper. How would he feel when he learned that Zott was not only a woman, but a knocked-up, unwed woman at that? God. They could picture that big limo swinging back round the drive, the chauffeur keeping the motor running as the man strode in and demanded his check back. "I was funding a professional slut?" he'd probably shout. Trouble. They had to do something about Zott immediately.

"I'm afraid you've put us in a terrible, terrible position, Miss Zott," scolded Dr. Donatti a week later as he pushed a termination notice across the table in her direction.

"You're *firing* me?" Elizabeth said, confused.

"I'd like to get through this as civilly as possible."

"Why am I being fired? On what grounds?"

"I think you know."

"Enlighten me," she said, leaning forward, her hands clasped together in a tight mass, her number-two pencil behind her left ear glinting in the light. She wasn't sure from where her composure came, but she knew she must keep it.

He glanced at Miss Frask, who was busy taking notes.

"You're with child," Donatti said. "Don't try and deny it."

"Yes, I'm pregnant. That is correct."

"That is correct?" he choked. "That is *correct*?"

"Again. Correct. I am pregnant. What does that have to do with my work?"

"Please!"

"I'm not contagious," she said, unfolding her hands. "I do not have cholera. No one will catch having a baby from me."

"You have a lot of nerve," Donatti said. "You know very well women do not continue to work when pregnant. But you— you're not only with child, you're unwed. It's disgraceful."

"Pregnancy is a normal condition. It is not disgraceful. It is how every human being starts."

"How *dare* you," he said, his voice rising. "A woman telling *me* what pregnancy is. Who do you think you are?"

She seemed surprised by the question. "A woman," she said.

"Miss Zott," Miss Frask stated, "our code of conduct does not allow for this sort of thing and you know it. You need to sign this paper, and then you need to clean out your desk. We have standards."

But Elizabeth didn't flinch. "I'm confused," she said. "You're firing me on the basis of being pregnant and unwed. What about the man?"

"What man? You mean Evans?" Donatti asked.

"Any man. When a woman gets pregnant outside of marriage, does the man who made her pregnant get fired, too?"

"What? What are you talking about?"

"Would you have fired Calvin, for instance?"

"Of course not!"

"If not, then, technically, you have no grounds to fire me."

Donatti looked confused. *What?* "Of course, I do," he stumbled. "Of course, I do! You're the woman! You're the one who got knocked up!"

"That's generally how it works. But you do realize that a pregnancy requires a man's sperm."

"Miss Zott, I'm warning you. *Watch your language.*"

"You're saying that if an unmarried man makes an unmarried woman pregnant, there is no consequence for him. His life goes on. Business as usual."

"This is *not* our fault," Frask interrupted. "You were trying to trap Evans into marriage. It's obvious."

"What I know," she said, pushing a stray hair away from her forehead, "is that Calvin and I did not want to have children. I also know that we took every precaution to ensure that outcome. This pregnancy is a failure of contraception, not morality. It's also none of your business."

"You've made it our business!" Donatti suddenly shouted. "And in case you weren't aware, there is a surefire way *not* to get pregnant and it starts with an 'A'! We have rules, Miss Zott! Rules!"

"Not on this you don't," Elizabeth said calmly. "I've read the employee manual front to back."

"It's an unwritten rule!"

"And thus not legally binding."

Donatti glowered at her. "Evans would be very, very ashamed of you."

"No," Elizabeth said simply, her voice empty but calm. "He would not."

The room fell silent. It was the way she kept disagreeing—without embarrassment, without melodrama—as if she would have the last say, as if she knew she'd win in the end. This is *exactly* the kind of attitude her coworkers had complained of. And the way she implied that hers and Calvin's relationship was at some higher level—as if it had been crafted from nondissolvable material that survived everything, even his death. Annoying.

As Elizabeth waited for them to come to their senses, she laid her hands flat on the table. Losing a loved one has a way of revealing a too-simple truth: that time, as people often claimed but never heeded, really was precious. She had work to do; it was all she had left. And yet here she sat with self-appointed guardians of moral conduct, smug judges who lacked judgment, one of

whom seemed unclear on the process of conception and one who
went along because she, like so many other women, assumed that
downgrading someone of her own sex would somehow lift her in
the estimation of her male superiors. Worse, these illogical conversations were all taking place in a building devoted to science.

"Are we done here?" she said, rising.

Donatti blanched. That was *it*. Zott needed to go right now
and take her bastard baby, cutting-edge research, and death-
defying romantic relationship with her. As for her rich investor,
they'd deal with him later.

"Sign it," he demanded, as Frask tossed Elizabeth a pen. "We
want you out of the building no later than noon. Salary ends Friday. You're not allowed to speak to anyone regarding the reasons
for your dismissal."

"Health benefits also end Friday," Frask chirped, tapping her
nail against her ever-present clipboard. "Tick tock."

"I hope this might teach you to start being accountable for
your outrageous behavior," Donatti added as he held out his hand
for the signed termination notice. "And stop blaming others. Like
Evans," he continued, "after he forced us to fund you. After he
stood in front of Hastings management and threatened to leave if
we didn't."

Elizabeth looked as if she'd been slapped. "Calvin did what?"

"You know very well," Donatti said, opening the door.

"Out by noon," Frask repeated as she tucked her clipboard
under her arm.

"References could be a problem," he added, stepping out into
the hall.

"Coattails," Frask whispered.

CHAPTER 14

Grief

The thing Six-Thirty hated most about going to the cemetery was the way it took him past the place where Calvin had died. He'd once heard someone say it was important to be reminded of one's failures, but he didn't know why. Failures, by their very nature, had a way of being unforgettable.

As he neared the cemetery, he kept an eye out for the enemy groundskeeper. Seeing no one, he pressed himself under the back gate and scooted through the rows, nabbing a clutch of fresh daffodils from one tombstone before laying it here:

> *Calvin Evans*
> *1927–1955*
> *Brilliant chemist, rower, friend, lover.*
> *Your days are numbered.*

The tombstone was supposed to have read, "Your days are numbered. Use them to throw open the windows of your soul to the sun," a quote from Marcus Aurelius, but the tombstone was small and the engraver had made the first part too big and had run out of room.

Six-Thirty stared at the words. He knew they were words because Elizabeth was trying to teach him words. Not commands. Words.

"How many words does science tell us dogs can learn?" she'd asked Calvin one evening.

"About fifty," Calvin said, not looking up from his book.

"Fifty?" she'd said, scrunching her lips together. "Well, that's wrong."

"Maybe a hundred," he said, still engrossed in his book.

"A hundred?" she'd answered just as incredulously. "How can that be? He already knows a hundred."

Calvin looked up. "Excuse me?"

"I'm wondering," she said. "Is it possible to teach a dog a human language? I mean the whole thing. English for example."

"No."

"Why?"

"Well," Calvin said, slowly, realizing that this might be one of those things she simply didn't accept—there were so many of those things. "Because interspecies communication is limited by brain size." He closed his book. "How do you know he knows a hundred words?"

"He knows one hundred and three," she said, consulting her notebook. "I'm keeping track."

"And you've taught him these words."

"I'm using the receptive learning technique—object identification. Like a child, he's automatically more receptive to memorizing objects he's interested in."

"And he's interested in—"

"Food." She got up from the table and started gathering books. "But I'm sure he has lots of other interests."

Calvin looked back at her in disbelief.

So that's how their word quest had started: he and Elizabeth on the floor, flipping through big children's books.

"Sun," she'd instructed, pointing at a picture. "Child," she'd read in turn, pointing at a little girl named Gretel eating a candied house shutter. That a child would eat a shutter did not surprise Six-Thirty. In the park, children ate everything. This included whatever they could find up their nose.

From off to the left, the groundskeeper shuffled into view, a rifle resting on his shoulder—a strange thing, in Six-Thirty's opinion, to carry in a place of the already dead. Crouching, he waited for the man to leave, then relaxed his body down the length of the casket buried below. *Hello, Calvin.*

This is how he communicated with humans on the other side. Maybe it worked; maybe it didn't. He used the same technique with the creature growing inside Elizabeth. *Hello, Creature,* he transmitted as he pressed his ear into Elizabeth's belly. *It's me, Six-Thirty. I'm the dog.*

Whenever he initiated contact, he always reintroduced himself. From his own lessons, he knew repetition was important. The key was not to overdo the repetition—not to make it so tiresome that it actually had an inverse result and caused the student to forget. That was called boredom. According to Elizabeth, boredom was what was wrong with education today.

Creature, he'd communicated last week, *Six-Thirty here.* He waited for a response. Sometimes the creature extended a small fist, which he found thrilling; other times he heard singing. But yesterday he'd broken the news—*There's something you should know about your father*—and it began to cry.

He pressed his nose deep into the grass. *Calvin,* he communicated. *We need to talk about Elizabeth.*

At two a.m., about three months after Calvin's death, Six-Thirty found Elizabeth in the kitchen, in her nightgown, wearing galoshes, all the lights blazing. In her hand was a sledgehammer.

Much to his surprise, she drew back and swung the sledgehammer directly into a wall of cupboards. She paused as if to assess the carnage, then swung again, bigger this time, like she was trying to hit a home run. Then she kept batting for two more hours. Sixty-Thirty watched from under the table as she felled the kitchen like a forest, her violent blitz broken only by surgical attacks on hinges and nails, the old floor filling with piles of hardware and boards as plaster dust sifted over the scene like an unexpected snowfall. Then she picked it all up and hauled it out to the backyard in the dark.

"This is where we'll put the shelves," she said to him, pointing at the pockmarked walls. "And over there is where we'll put the centrifuge." She produced a tape measure, and gesturing him out from under the table, inserted one end in his mouth while pointing to the other end of the kitchen. "Take it just down there, Six-Thirty. A little farther. A little farther. Good. Hold it right there."

She jotted some numbers in a notebook.

By eight a.m. she'd sketched out a rough plan; by ten, a shopping list; by eleven, they were in the car and headed to the lumberyard.

People often underestimate what a pregnant woman is capable of, but people always underestimate what a grieving pregnant woman is capable of. The man at the lumberyard eyed her curiously.

"Your husband doing some remodeling?" he asked, noticing her small bump. "Getting ready for the baby?"

"I'm building a laboratory."

"You mean a nursery."

"I don't."

He glanced up from her sketch.

"Is there a problem?" she asked.

The materials were delivered later that same day, and armed with a library-obtained set of *Popular Mechanics* magazines, she set to work.

"Tenpenny nail," she said. Six-Thirty had no idea what a tenpenny nail was; nevertheless, he followed the nod of her head to an array of small boxes that lay close by, selected something, then put it in her open palm. "Three-inch screw," she'd ask a minute later, and he'd dig into another box. "That's a lag bolt," she said. "Try again."

This work would continue all day and often into the night, broken only by their word lessons and the ringing of the doorbell.

About two weeks after she'd been fired, Dr. Boryweitz had dropped by, ostensibly to say hello, but really because he was having trouble interpreting some test results. "It'll only take a quick sec," he promised, but it took two hours. The next day the same thing happened, but this time it was another chemist from the lab. The third time, yet another.

That's when it came to her. She would charge. Cash only. If anyone had the gall to suggest payment was unnecessary because they were simply "keeping her in the loop," she would charge double. An offhand remark about Calvin: triple. Any reference to her pregnancy—the glow, the miracle—quadruple. That was how she made a living. By doing other people's work without any credit. It was exactly like working at Hastings, but without the tax liability.

"Coming up the walk I thought I heard banging," one of them said.

"I'm building a lab."

"You can't be serious."

"I'm always serious."

"But you're going to be a mother," he said, tutting.

"A mother and a scientist," she said, brushing sawdust off her sleeve. "You're a father, aren't you? A father and a scientist."

"Yes, but I have a *PhD*," he emphasized as proof of his superiority. Then he pointed to a set of test protocols that had confounded him for weeks.

She looked at him, perplexed. "You have two problems," she said, tapping the paper. "This temperature is too high. Lower it by fifteen degrees."

"I see. And the other?"

She cocked her head to the side, taking in his blank expression. "Unsolvable."

The transformation of kitchen into laboratory took about four months, and when it was done, she and Six-Thirty stood back to admire their work.

The shelves, which spanned the length of the kitchen, were freshly lined with a wide array of laboratory materials: chemicals, flasks, beakers, pipettes, siphon bottles, empty mayonnaise jars, a set of nail files, a stack of litmus paper, a box of medicine droppers, assorted glass rods, the hose from the backyard, and some unused tubing she'd found in the trash bin in the alley behind the local phlebotomy lab. Drawers that once stored utensils were now taken up by acid- and puncture-resistant mitts and goggles. She'd also installed metal pans under all the burners to aid in alcohol denaturation, purchased a used centrifuge, cut up a window screen to create a set of 4 x 4 wire flats, dumped out the last of her favorite perfume to create an alcohol burner—including cutting one of her lipstick containers, which she then stuck into Calvin's old thermos bottle cork, creating the stopper—made test tube holders out of wire hangers, and converted a spice rack into a suspension structure for various liquids.

The friendly Formica countertop was gone too, as was the old ceramic sink. In their place, she'd crafted a countertop template using the plywood she'd purchased from the lumberyard, a template that she'd then taken in pieces to a metal fabrication company, which had created an exact stainless-steel replica, bending and cutting the metal to ensure a perfect fit.

Now atop these gleaming countertops sat one microscope and two used Bunsen burners, one courtesy of Cambridge—the uni-

versity had given it to Calvin as a memento of his time there—
and the other from a high school chem lab that was shedding
equipment due to a lack of student interest. Just above the new
double sinks were two carefully hand-lettered signs. WASTE ONLY
read one. H₂O SOURCE read the other.

Last but not least was the fume hood.

"This will be your responsibility," she told Six-Thirty. "I'll
need you to pull on the chain when my hands are full. You'll also
need to learn how to press this big button."

Cal, Six-Thirty explained to the body below on a later trip to the
graveyard. *She never sleeps. When she isn't working on the lab, or doing
other people's work, or reading to me, she's erging. And when she isn't
erging, she's sitting on a stool staring off into space. This can't be good for
the creature.*

He remembered how Calvin often stared off into space. "It's
how I focus," he'd explained to Six-Thirty. But others had complained about the staring too, grousing that on any given day at
any given hour, one could find Calvin Evans sitting in a big fancy
lab surrounded by the very best equipment, music blaring, doing
absolutely nothing. Worse, he was getting paid to do absolutely
nothing. Even worse, he won a lot of awards this way.

But her staring is different, Six-Thirty tried to communicate. *It's
more of a death stare. A lethargy. I don't know what to do,* he confessed
to the bones below. *And on top of everything else, she's still trying to
teach me words.*

Which was awful because he was unable to give her any hope
for the future using these words. Besides, even if he knew every
word in the English language, he still wouldn't have any idea
what to say. Because what does one say to someone who's lost
everything?

She needs hope, Calvin, he thought, pressing hard against the
grass in case that made a difference.

As if in reply, he heard the click of a safety being released.

He looked up to see the cemetery groundskeeper pointing a rifle at him.

"Ya damn dog," the groundskeeper said, lining Six-Thirty up in his sights. "Ya come in here, ya mess up my grass, ya think ya own the place."

Six-Thirty froze. His heart pounding, he saw the aftermath: Elizabeth in shock, the creature confused; more blood, more tears, more heartache. Another failure on his part.

He sprang forward, knocking the man hard to the ground as a bullet sailed past his ear and plowed into Calvin's tombstone. The man cried out and reached for his gun, but Six-Thirty bared his teeth and took a step closer.

Humans. Some of them didn't seem to grasp their actual status within the animal kingdom. He sized up the old man's neck. One bite to the throat and it would all be over. The man looked up at him, terrified. He'd hit the ground pretty hard; there was a small pool of blood now forming just to the left of his ear. He remembered Calvin's own pool of blood, how large it had been, how it had gone from a simple ooze to a little pond to a big lake in a matter of moments. Reluctantly, he propped himself up against the side of the man's head to stanch the flow. Then he barked until people came.

The first on the scene was that same reporter—the one who'd covered Calvin's funeral—the one who was *still* covering funerals because his desk editor didn't think he was capable of much more.

"You!" the reporter said, instantly recognizing Six-Thirty as the non–Seeing Eye dog, the one who'd led the pretty nonblind widow—scratch that, girlfriend—through the sea of crosses to this very grave site. As others ran up and made hurried plans for an ambulance, the reporter took photographs, composing the story in his head as he posed the dog here, then there. Then he heaved the bloodied animal into his arms, carried him to his car, and drove him to the address listed on his tag.

"Relax, relax, he's not injured," the reporter assured Elizabeth as she swung open the door, crying out at the sight of a blood-matted Six-Thirty in the arms of a vaguely familiar man. "It's not his blood. But your dog's a hero, lady. At least that's the way I plan to spin it."

The next day, a still-shaken Elizabeth opened the newspaper to find Six-Thirty on page eleven, sitting in exactly the same spot he'd sat seven months ago: on Calvin's grave.

"Dog Mourns Master and Saves Man's Life," she read out loud. "Cemetery Dog Ban Lifted."

According to the article, people had long complained about the groundskeeper and his gun, including several who reported he'd shot at squirrels and birds right in the middle of funerals. The man would be replaced immediately, the article promised, as would the grave marker.

She peered at the close-up of Six-Thirty and Calvin's ruined tombstone, which, thanks to the bullet's impact, had lost about a third of its inscription.

"Oh my god," Elizabeth said, taking in the chipped remains.

Calvin E
1927–19
Brilliant che
Your days are nu

Her face changed ever so slightly.

"Your days are *nu*," she read. *"Nu."* She flushed, thinking of the sad night Calvin had shared with her his childhood mantra. Every day. New.

She looked back at the photograph, stunned.

CHAPTER 15

Unsolicited Advice

"Your life is about to change."

"Excuse me?"

"Your life. It's about to change." A woman just ahead of Elizabeth in line at the bank had turned to point at Elizabeth's stomach. Her face was grim.

"Change?" Elizabeth said innocently as she cast her eye down upon her round form as if noticing it for the first time. "Whatever do you mean?"

It was the seventh time that week someone felt compelled to inform her that her life was about to change and she was sick of it. She'd lost her job, her research, bladder control, a clear view of her toes, restful sleep, normal skin, a pain-free back, not to mention all the little assorted freedoms everyone else who is not pregnant takes for granted—like being able to fit behind a steering wheel. The only thing she'd gained? Weight.

"I've been meaning to get this checked," she said, laying a hand on her stomach. "What do you think it could be? Not a tumor, I hope."

For a split second, the woman's eyes widened in shock, then instantly narrowed. "No one likes a smart-aleck, missy," she gruffed.

"You think you're tired now," a wiry-haired woman commented an hour later as Elizabeth yawned in a grocery store checkout line, shaking her head as if Elizabeth were already showing signs of personal weakness. "Just you wait." Then she launched into a dramatic description of the terrible twos, the tiresome threes, the filthy fours, and the fearsome fives, barely taking a breath before piling into the angsty adolescents, the pimply pubescents, and especially, especially, oh lord, the troubled teens, noting always that boys were harder than girls, or girls were harder than boys, and on and on and on until her groceries were bagged and loaded and she was forced to get back into her faux-wood-paneled station wagon and return home to her own personal set of ingrates.

"You're carrying high," the man at the gas station observed. "Definitely a boy."

"You're carrying high," the librarian commented. "Definitely a girl."

"God has given you a gift," said a priest who'd noticed Elizabeth standing alone in front of an odd gravestone at the cemetery later that same week. "Glory be to God!"

"It wasn't God," Elizabeth said, pointing at a new tombstone. "It was Calvin."

She waited until he walked away, then bent down and ran her finger over the complex engraving.

Calvin Evans
1927–1955

$$
\begin{array}{l}
\qquad\qquad\qquad\quad C_6H_4OH \qquad\qquad C_2\text{-}H_5 \\
\qquad\quad NH_2 \;\; O \qquad\quad CH_2 \;\; O \qquad\quad CH\text{-}CH_3 \\
CH_2 - CH - C - NH - CH - C - NH - CH \\
\;S \qquad\qquad\qquad\qquad\qquad\qquad\qquad\quad C{=}O \\
\;S \qquad\qquad\qquad\qquad O \qquad\qquad\qquad O \;\; NH \\
CH_2 - CH - NH - C - CH - NH - C - CH - (CH_2)_2 - CONH_2 \\
\qquad\quad C{=}O \qquad\qquad\quad CH_2 \\
CH_2 - N \qquad\qquad O \quad CONH_2 \;\; O \\
CH_2 - CH_2 \qquad CH - C - NH - CH - C - NH\,CH_2 - CONH_2 \\
\qquad\qquad\qquad\qquad\qquad\quad CH_2 \\
\qquad\qquad\qquad\qquad\qquad\quad CH(CH_3)_2
\end{array}
$$

"To make up for what happened," cemetery management had told her, "we'll not only provide a new tombstone, we'll also make sure it includes the whole quote this time." But Elizabeth had decided against a second round with Marcus Aurelius, opting instead for a chemical response that resulted in happiness. No one else recognized it, but after what she'd been through, no one questioned it either.

"I'm finally going to see someone about this, Calvin," she said, pointing to her bump. "Dr. Mason, the rower, the one who let me row in the men's eight. Remember?" She stared at the inscription as if awaiting a reply.

Twenty-five minutes later, as she pressed a button in a narrow elevator, her only companion a fat man in a straw hat, she braced herself for more unsolicited advice. And sure enough, he reached out his hand and placed it on her belly as if she were a hands-on exhibit at the Natural History Museum. "I bet eating for two is fun," he admonished, patting her, "but remember: one of them is just a baby!"

"Remove your hand," she said, "or live to regret it."

"Bada bada bada!" he sang, thumping her stomach like a bongo drum.

"Bada bada *boom,*" she rejoined, swinging her handbag directly into his crotch, the impact of which was compounded by a heavy stone mortar she'd picked up earlier that day from Chemical Supply. The man gasped, then doubled over in pain. The doors slid open.

"Have a bad day," she said. She stomped down the hallway, encountering a seven-foot-tall stork wearing bifocals and a baseball hat. In its beak hung two bundles: one pink, one blue.

"Elizabeth Zott," she said, moving past the stork to the receptionist. "For Dr. Mason."

"You're late," the receptionist said icily.

"I'm five minutes early," Elizabeth corrected, checking her watch.

"There's paperwork," the woman informed her, handing over a clipboard. Husband's place of work. Husband's telephone number. Husband's insurance. Husband's age. Husband's bank account number.

"Who's having the baby here?" she asked.

"Room five," the receptionist said. "Down the hallway, second door on the left. Disrobe. Put on the gown. Finish the paperwork."

"Room five," Elizabeth repeated, clipboard in hand. "Just one question: Why the stork?"

"Excuse me?"

"Your stork. Why, in an obstetrician's office? It's almost as if you're promoting the competition."

"It's meant to be charming," the receptionist said. "Room five."

"And since every patient of yours is one hundred percent aware that a stork isn't going to spare them the pain of labor," she continued, "why perpetuate the myth at all?"

"Dr. Mason," the receptionist said, as a man in a white coat approached. "This is your four o'clock. She's late. I tried to send her to room five."

"Not late," Elizabeth Zott corrected. "On time." She turned to the doctor. "Dr. Mason, you probably don't remember me—"

"Calvin Evans's wife," he said, drawing back in surprise. "Or no, I apologize," he said, dropping his voice, "his widow." Then he paused, as if trying to decide what to say next. "I'm so very sorry for your loss, Mrs. Evans," he said, covering her hands with his and giving them a few shakes as if mixing a small cocktail. "Your husband was a good man. A good man and a good rower."

"It's Elizabeth Zott," Elizabeth said. "Calvin and I weren't married." She paused, awaiting the receptionist's tsk and Mason's dismissal, but instead the doctor clicked a pen and tapped it into his breast pocket, then took her by the elbow and led her down the hallway. "You and Evans rowed in my eight a few times—do you remember? About seven months ago. Good rows, too. But then you never came back. Why was that?"

She looked at him, surprised.

"Oh, forgive me," Dr. Mason said in a rush. "I'm so sorry. Of course. Evans. Evans died. I apologize." Shaking his head in embarrassment, he pushed open the door to room 5. "Please. Come in." He pointed to a chair. "And are you still rowing? No, what am I saying, of course not, not in your condition." He took her hands and turned them over. "But this is unusual. You still have the calluses."

"I'm erging."

"Good god."

"Is that bad? Calvin built an erg."

"*Why?*"

"He just did. It's all right, isn't it?"

"Well, yes," he said, "certainly. It's just that I've never heard of anyone erging on purpose. Especially not a pregnant woman. Although now that I think about it, erging is good preparation for childbirth. In terms of suffering, I mean. Actually, both pain and suffering." But then he realized pain and suffering had probably been a constant in her life since Evans died and he turned away to hide his latest gaffe. "Shall we take a quick look under the hood?" he said gently, gesturing to the table. Then he closed the door and waited behind a screen while she put on a dressing gown.

The examination was quick but thorough, punctuated with inquiries about heartburn and bloating. Was sleep difficult? Did the baby move at certain times? If so, for how long? And finally the big question: Why had she waited so long to come in? She was well into her last trimester.

"Work," she told him. But that was a lie. The real reason was because she'd quietly hoped the pregnancy would take care of itself. End as these things sometimes do. In the 1950s, abortion was out of the question. Coincidentally, so was having a baby out of wedlock.

"You're also a scientist, is that right?" he asked from the other end of her body.

"Yes."

"And Hastings kept you on. They must be more progressive than I thought."

"They didn't," she said. "I'm freelancing."

"A freelance scientist. I've never heard of such a thing. How does that work?"

She sighed. "Not very well."

Registering the tone in her voice, he finished up quickly, tapping her belly here and there as if she were a cantaloupe.

"Everything looks shipshape," he said as he stripped off his gloves. And when she didn't smile or say anything in return, he said in a low voice, "For the baby at least. I'm sure this has been enormously difficult for you."

It was the first time someone had acknowledged her situation, and the shock of it caught in her throat. She felt a cache of tears threatening escape just behind her eyes.

"I'm sorry," he said gently, studying her face the way a meteorologist might watch a storm develop. "Please know you can talk to me. Rower to rower. It's all confidential."

She looked away. She didn't really know him. Worse, she wasn't sure, despite his assurances, that her feelings were allowable. She'd come to believe she was the only woman on earth who'd planned to remain childless. "If I'm being perfectly honest," she finally said, her voice heavy with guilt, "I don't think I can do this. I was not planning on being a mother."

"Not every woman wants to be a mother," he agreed, surprising her. "More to the point, not every woman should be." He grimaced as if thinking of someone in particular. "Still, I'm surprised by how many women sign up for motherhood considering how difficult pregnancy can be—morning sickness, stretch marks, death. Again, you're fine," he added quickly, taking in her horrified face. "It's just that we tend to treat pregnancy as the most common condition in the world—as ordinary as stubbing a toe—when the truth is, it's like getting hit by a truck. Although obviously a truck causes less damage." He cleared his throat, then made a note in her file. "What I mean to say is, the exercise is helping. Although I'm not sure how you erg properly at this stage. Pulling into the sternum would be problematic. What about *The Jack LaLanne Show*? Ever watch him?"

At the mention of Jack LaLanne's name, Elizabeth's face fell.

"Not a fan," he said. "No problem. Just the erg, then."

"I only kept on with it," she offered in a low voice, "because it exhausts me to the point where I can sometimes sleep. But also because I thought it might, well—"

"I understand," he said, cutting her off and looking both ways as if making sure no one else could hear. "Look, I'm not one of those people who believe a woman should have to—" He stopped abruptly. "Nor do I believe that—" He stopped again. "A single woman . . . a widow . . . it's . . . Never mind," he said as he reached for her file. "But the truth is, that erg probably made you stronger; made the baby stronger for that matter. More blood to the brain, better circulation. Have you noticed it has a calming effect on the baby? Probably all that back and forth."

She shrugged.

"How far are you erging?"

"Ten thousand meters."

"Every day?"

"Sometimes more."

"Mother of god," he whistled. "I've always thought pregnant women developed an extra capacity for suffering, but ten thousand meters? Sometimes *more*? That's—that's—actually, I don't know what that is." He looked at her with concern. "Do you have someone to lean on? A friend or relative—your mother—someone like that? Infants are hard work."

She hesitated. It was embarrassing to admit that she had no

one. She'd only gone to see Dr. Mason because Calvin had always insisted rowers enjoyed some sort of special bond.

"Anyone?" he repeated.

"I have a dog."

"I like it," Mason said. "A dog can be tremendously helpful. Protective, empathetic, intelligent. What kind of dog—he, she?"

"He—"

"Wait, I think I remember your dog. Three O'clock, something like that? Ugly as sin?"

"He's—"

"A dog and an erg," he said, making a note in her file. "Okay. Excellent."

He clicked his pen again, then set her file aside. "Now, as soon as you're able—let's say in a year—I want to see you back at the boathouse. My boat's been looking for the right two seat and something tells me you're it. You'll have to arrange for a sitter, though. No babies in the boat. We have plenty of those as it is."

Elizabeth reached for her jacket. "That's very kind, Dr. Mason," she said, assuming he was only trying to be nice, "but according to you I'm about to get hit by a truck."

"An accident from which you'll recover," he corrected. "Look, I have an impeccable memory when it comes to rows, and I very much remember ours. They were good. Very good."

"Because of Calvin."

Dr. Mason looked surprised. "No, Miss Zott. Not just because of Evans. It takes all eight to row well. *All* eight. Anyway, back to the business at hand. I'm starting to feel a bit better about your situation. I know you've been through quite a shock with Evans's passing, and then this," he added, pointing to her belly. "But things will be fine. Maybe even better than fine. A dog, an erg, two seat. Excellent."

Then he took both of her hands in his and gave them a cheerful squeeze, and although his words hadn't made complete sense, compared to everything else she'd heard up to that point, they were the first that finally made some.

CHAPTER 16

Labor

"Library?" Elizabeth asked Six-Thirty about five weeks later. "I've got an appointment with Dr. Mason later today and I'd like to return these books first. I'm thinking you might enjoy *Moby-Dick*. It's a story about how humans continually underestimate other life-forms. At their peril."

In addition to the receptive learning technique, Elizabeth had been reading aloud to him, long ago replacing simple children's books with far weightier texts. "Reading aloud promotes brain development," she'd told him, quoting a research study she'd read. "It also speeds vocabulary accumulation." It seemed to be working because, according to her notebook, he now knew 391 words.

"You're a very smart dog," she'd told him just yesterday, and he longed to agree, but the truth was, he still didn't understand what "smart" meant. The word seemed to have as many definitions as there were species, and yet humans—with the exception of Elizabeth—seemed to only recognize "smart" if and when it played by their own rules. "Dolphins are smart," they'd say. "But cows aren't." This seemed partly based on the fact that cows didn't do tricks. In Six-Thirty's view that made cows smarter, not dumber. But again, what did he know?

Three hundred ninety-one words, according to Elizabeth. But really, only 390.

Worse, he'd just learned that English wasn't the only human language. Elizabeth revealed that there were hundreds, maybe thousands of others, and that no human spoke them all. In fact, most people spoke only one—maybe two—unless they were something called Swiss and spoke eight. No wonder people didn't understand animals. They could barely understand each other.

At least she realized he would not be able to draw. Drawing seemed to be the way young children preferred to communicate, and he admired their efforts even if their results fell short of the mark. Not a day went by when he didn't witness little fingers earnestly pressing their chunky chalks into the sidewalk, their impossible houses and primitive stick figures filling the cement with a story no one understood but themselves.

"What a pretty picture!" he heard a mother say earlier that week as she looked down on her child's ugly, violent scribble. Human parents, he'd noted, had a tendency to lie to their children.

"It's a puppy," her child said, her hands covered in chalk.

"And such a pretty puppy!" the mother rejoined.

"*No,*" the child said, "it's not pretty. The puppy's dead. It got *killed*!" Which Six-Thirty, after a second, closer look, found disturbingly accurate.

"It is *not* a dead puppy," the mother said sternly. "It is a *very* happy puppy, and it is *eating* a bowl of ice cream." At which point the frustrated child flung the chalk across the grass and stomped off for the swings.

He retrieved it. A gift for the creature.

They walked the five blocks together, Elizabeth in a shirtdress that strained at her bump, striding as if going off to war. On her back was a bright red satchel stuffed with books; on his, bike messenger panniers repurposed for all the extra books her satchel could not hold.

"I'm starving," she said aloud as they walked, the air heavy with November. "I could eat a horse. I've been monitoring my urine, analyzing my hair proteins, and . . ."

This was true. She'd been tracking her urine's glucose levels, noting the amino acid chain of her hair's keratin, and analyzing her body's temperature in their lab for the last two months. It wasn't clear to Six-Thirty what any of it meant, but he was relieved to see her taking more interest in their creature—more scientific interest at least. Her only practical preparation had been the purchase of thick white cloth squares and several dangerous-looking pins. She'd also purchased three tiny outfits that looked like sacks.

"It sounds fairly straightforward," she told him as they strode down the street. "I'll experience prelabor, then labor. We've still got two weeks to go, Six-Thirty, but I think it's good to think about these things now. The important thing to remember," she said, "is that when the time comes, we stay calm."

But Six-Thirty was not calm. Her water had broken several hours earlier. She hadn't noticed because she'd expelled only a modest amount of moisture, but he'd noticed because he was a dog. The scent was unmistakable. As for her hunger pains, they weren't hunger pains; they were prelabor contractions. As they neared the library's front door, the creature decided to make things a bit clearer.

"Oh," Elizabeth moaned, doubling over. "Oh my goddddd."

Thirteen hours later, Dr. Mason held the infant up for an exhausted Elizabeth to see.

"That's a big one," he said, looking at the baby as if he'd just reeled in a catch. "Definitely a rower. Don't quote me, but I think she'll row port." He looked down at Elizabeth. "Good job, Miss

Zott. And you did it all without anesthesia. I told you all that erging would come in handy. She's got great lungs." He peered at the baby's tiny hands as if imagining future calluses. "You'll both be with us for a few days. I'll swing by your room tomorrow. In the meantime, rest."

But worried about Six-Thirty, Elizabeth checked herself out the very next morning.

"Absolutely *not*," the head nurse said. "Completely against protocol. Dr. Mason will have a fit."

"Tell him I need to erg," she said. "He'll approve."

"Erg?" the nurse practically shouted as Elizabeth dialed for a cab. "What is *erg*?"

Thirty minutes later, Elizabeth walked up the driveway, the baby tucked snugly against her chest, her heart pounding with relief at the sight of Six-Thirty, panniers still on, sitting like a sentry at the front door.

Oh my god, Six-Thirty panted, *oh my god oh my god you're alive you're alive oh my god I was so worried.*

She bent down and showed him the bundle.

The creature was—sniff—*a girl!*

"It's a girl," Elizabeth told him, smiling.

Hello, Creature! It's me! Six-Thirty! I've been worried sick!

"I'm so sorry," she said, unlocking the door. "You must be starving. It's"—she consulted her watch—"nine twenty-two. You haven't eaten in more than twenty-four hours."

Six-Thirty wagged his tail in excitement. Just as some families give their children names starting with the same letter (Agatha, Alfred) and others prefer the rhyme (Molly, Polly) his family went by the clock. He was named Six-Thirty to commemorate the exact time they'd become a family. And now he knew what the creature would be called.

Hello, Nine Twenty-Two! he communicated. *Welcome to life on the outside! How was the trip? Please, come in, come in! I've got chalk!*

As the three of them bustled through the door, a strange joy filled the air. For the first time since Calvin's death, it felt as if they'd turned a corner.

Until ten minutes later when the creature started to cry and everything fell apart.

CHAPTER 17

Harriet Sloane

"What's *wrong?*" Elizabeth begged for the millionth time. "Just TELL me!"

But the baby, who'd been crying nonstop for weeks, refused to be specific.

Even Six-Thirty was flummoxed. *But I told you about your father,* he communicated. *We talked about this.* But still the creature wailed.

Elizabeth paced the small bungalow at two a.m., bouncing the bundle up and down, her arms stiff like a rusted robot until she ran into a stack of books and almost tripped. "Dammit," she cried, mashing the baby against her chest in a protective move. In her new-mother stupor, the floor had become a convenient dumping ground for everything: tiny socks, unsecured diaper pins, old banana peels, unread newspapers. "How can someone this small cause all this?" she cried. In response, the baby placed its tiny mouth against Elizabeth's ear, took a deep breath, and roared back the answer.

"Please," Elizabeth whispered, sinking into a chair. "Please, please, please *stop.*" She nestled her daughter in the crook of her arm, nudged the bottle's nipple against her doll lips, and although she'd refused it five times before, the little thing latched on voraciously as if she knew her ignorant mother would get there in the end. Elizabeth held her breath as if the smallest intake of air might cause the thing to go off again. The baby was a ticking time bomb. One false move and it was over.

Dr. Mason had warned her that infants were hard work, but this wasn't work: it was indenture. The tiny tyrant was no less demanding than Nero; no less insane than King Ludwig. And the crying. It made her feel inadequate. Worse, it raised the possibility that her daughter might not like her. Already.

Elizabeth closed her eyes and saw her own mother, a cigarette stuck to her bottom lip, her ashes landing in the casserole Elizabeth had just taken out of the oven. Yes. Not liking one's mother from the very start was entirely possible.

Beyond that, there was the repetitiveness—the feeding, the bathing, the changing, the calming, the wiping, the burping, the soothing, the pacing; in short, the volume. Many things were repetitive—erging, metronomes, fireworks—but all of those things usually ended within an hour. This could go on for years.

And when the baby slept, *which was never,* there was still more work to be done: laundry, bottle prep, sanitizing, meals—plus the constant rereading of Dr. Spock's *The Common Sense Book of Baby and Child Care.* There was so much to do she couldn't even make a to-do list because making a list was just one more thing to do. Plus, she still had all of her other work to do.

Hastings. She glanced in worry across the room at an untouched foot-high pile of notebooks and research papers, the larger stacks work from her colleagues. When she'd been in labor, she told Dr. Mason she didn't want anesthesia. "It's because I'm a scientist," she'd lied. "I want to be fully conscious during the procedure." But the real reason: she couldn't afford it.

From below came a small sigh of contentment and Elizabeth looked down surprised to find her daughter asleep. She froze, not wanting to disturb the baby's slumber. She studied the flushed face, the pouty lips, the slim blond eyebrows.

An hour went by, and with it, all circulation in her arm. She stared in wonder as the child moved her lips, as if trying to explain.

Two more hours went by.

Get up, she told herself. *Move.* She leaned forward, gently propelling both of them out of the chair, then walked without a single misstep to the bedroom. She lay down, carefully placing the still-sleeping infant beside her. She closed her eyes. She exhaled. Then she slept heavily, dreamlessly, until the baby awoke.

Which, according to her clock, was approximately five minutes later.

"This a good time?" Dr. Boryweitz asked at seven a.m. as she opened the door. He tipped his head and moved past her, picking his way through the war zone to the sofa.

"No."

"Well, but this isn't really work," he explained. "Just a quick question. Anyway, I wanted to drop by and see how it's going. I heard you had the baby." He took in her unwashed hair, her misbuttoned blouse, her still-swollen abdomen. He unlatched his briefcase and took out a wrapped gift. "Congratulations," he said.

"You . . you got me a . . . gift?"

"Just a small thing."

"Do you have children, Dr. Boryweitz?"

His eyes slid left. He didn't reply.

She opened the box to find a plastic pacifier and a small stuffed rabbit. "Thank you," she said, suddenly feeling glad he'd dropped by. He was the first adult she'd talked to in weeks. "Very thoughtful."

"You're very welcome," he said clumsily. "I hope he—she—enjoys it."

"She."

She as in banshee, Six-Thirty explained.

Boryweitz reached into his briefcase to pull out a sheaf of papers.

"I haven't slept, Dr. Boryweitz," Elizabeth apologized. "This really isn't a good time."

"Miss Zott," Boryweitz pleaded, his eyes downcast. "I've got a meeting with Donatti in two hours." He removed some bills from his wallet. *"Please."*

The sight of the cash made her hesitate. She hadn't had any income for a month.

"Ten minutes," she said, taking the cash. "The baby is only dozing." But he needed a full hour. After he left, and surprised to find the baby still sleeping, she made her way to her lab, determined to work, but without meaning to, she slid to the floor as if it were a mattress, her head craning toward a textbook as if it were a pillow. In moments she was sound asleep.

Calvin was in her dream. He was reading a book on nuclear magnetic resonance. She was reading *Madame Bovary* aloud to Six-Thirty. She'd just finished telling Six-Thirty that fiction was problematic. People were always insisting they knew what it meant, even if the writer hadn't meant that at all, and even if what they thought it meant had no actual meaning. "Bovary's a great example," she said. "Here, where Emma licks her fingers? Some believe it signifies carnal lust; others think she just really liked the chicken. As for what Flaubert actually meant? No one cares."

At this point Calvin looked up from his book and said, "I don't remember there being any chicken in *Madame Bovary*." But before Elizabeth could reply, there came an insistent *tap tap tap tap tap tap,* like an industrious woodpecker, followed by a "Miss Zott?," followed by more *tap-tap-tap-tap-tap*-ing, then another "Miss Zott?," followed by a strange little hiccuppy wail, which made Calvin jump up and run out of the room.

"Miss *Zott,*" the voice said again. It was louder.

Elizabeth awoke to find a large gray-haired woman in a rayon dress and thick brown socks looming in her laboratory.

"It's me, Miss Zott. Mrs. Sloane. I peeked in and saw you slumped on the floor. I knocked and knocked but you didn't respond, so I pushed open the door. I wanted to make sure you're all right. *Are* you all right? Maybe I should call a doctor."

"S-Sloane."

The woman bent down and studied Elizabeth's face. "No, I think you're all right. Your baby is crying. Shall I go get it? I'll go get it." She left, returning a moment later. "Oh, look at it," she said, rocking the small bundle back and forth. "What's the devil's name?"

"Mad. M-Madeline," Elizabeth said as she pushed off from the floor.

"Madeline," Mrs. Sloane said. "A girl. Well that's nice. I've been wanting to drop by. Ever since you brought your little Satan home, I've told myself, *Go by and check on her.* But you seem to have a constant stream of visitors. In fact, I saw one leave not long ago. I didn't want to intrude."

The woman held Madeline's bottom up to her nose, took a deep sniff, then laid her on the table, and, swiping a clean diaper from the nearby drying rack, changed the writhing infant like a cowboy roping a calf. "I know it can't be easy for you, Miss Zott, without Mr. Evans I mean. I'm very sorry for your loss, by the way. I know it's a bit late to say so, but better late than never. Mr. Evans was a good man."

"You knew . . . Calvin?" Elizabeth asked, still foggy. "H-How?"

"Miss Zott," she said pointedly. "I'm your neighbor. Across the street? In the little blue house?"

"Oh, oh, yes, of course," Elizabeth said, reddening, realizing she'd never spoken to Mrs. Sloane before. A few waves from the driveway; that had been it. "I'm sorry, Mrs. Sloane, of course I know you. Please forgive me—I'm tired. I must have fallen asleep on the floor. I can't believe I did that; it's a first."

"Well, it won't be the last," Mrs. Sloane said, suddenly noticing that the kitchen was not really a kitchen at all. She got up and holding Madeline in the crook of one arm like a football, gave herself a tour. "You're a new mother and you're all alone and you're exhausted and you can barely think and—what the hell is *this*?" She pointed at a large silver object.

"A centrifuge," Elizabeth said. "And no, I'm fine, really." She attempted to sit up straight.

"No one's fine with a newborn, Miss Zott. The little gremlin will suck the life right out of you. Look at you—you've got the death row look. Let me make you some coffee." She started toward the stove but was stopped by the fume hood. "For the love of god," she said, "what *the hell* happened to this kitchen?"

"I'll make it," Elizabeth said. As Mrs. Sloane watched, Elizabeth drifted to the stainless-steel counter, where she picked up a jug of distilled water and poured it into a flask, plugging the flask with a stopper outfitted with a tube wriggling from its top. Next, she clipped the flask onto one of two metal stands that stood between two Bunsen burners and struck a strange metal gadget that sparked like flint striking steel. A flame appeared; the water began to heat. Reaching up to a shelf, she grabbed a sack labeled "$C_8H_{10}N_4O_2$," dumped some into a mortar, ground it with a pestle, overturned the resulting dirtlike substance onto a strange little scale, then dumped the scale's contents into a 6- x 6-inch piece of cheesecloth and tied the small bundle off. Stuffing the cheesecloth into a larger beaker, she attached it to the second metal stand, clamping the tube coming out of the first flask into the large beaker's bottom. As the water in the flask started to bubble, Mrs. Sloane, her jaw practically on the floor, watched as the water forced its way up the tube and into the beaker. Soon the smaller flask was almost empty and Elizabeth shut off the Bunsen burner. She stirred the contents of the beaker with a glass rod. Then the brown liquid did the strangest thing: it rose up like a poltergeist and returned to the original flask.

"Cream and sugar?" Elizabeth asked as she removed the stopper from the flask and started to pour.

"Mother of *god,*" Mrs. Sloane said as Elizabeth placed a cup of coffee in front of her. "Have you never heard of Folger's?" But as soon as she took a sip she said no more. She'd never had coffee like this before. It was heaven. She could drink it all day.

"So how have you found it so far?" Mrs. Sloane asked. "Motherhood."

Elizabeth swallowed hard.

"I see you've got the bible," Mrs. Sloane said, noting Dr. Spock's book on the table.

"I bought it for the title," Elizabeth admitted. "*Common Sense Book of Baby and Child Care.* There seems to be so much nonsense about how one raises a baby—so much overcomplication."

Mrs. Sloane studied Elizabeth's face. A strange remark coming from a woman who just added twenty extra steps to making a cup of coffee. "Funny, isn't it?" Mrs. Sloane said. "A man writes a book about things of which he has absolutely no firsthand knowledge—childbirth and its aftermath, I mean—and yet: boom. Bestseller. My suspicion? His wife wrote the whole thing, then put his name on it. A man's name gives it more authority, don't you think?"

"No," Elizabeth said.

"Agreed."

They both took another sip of coffee.

"Hello there, Six-Thirty," she said, extending her free hand. He went to her.

"You know Six-Thirty?"

"Miss *Zott.* I live just there—across the street! I often see him out and about. By the way, there's a leash law in effect—"

At the word "leash," Madeline opened her tiny mouth and let loose a bloodcurdling cry.

"Oh Jesus Mary mother of god!" Mrs. Sloane swore as she leapt up, Madeline still in her arms. "That is *truly* hideous, child!" She looked into the small red face and bounced the bundle around the laboratory, her voice raised above the noise. "Years ago, when I was a new mother, Mr. Sloane was away on business and a horrible man broke into the house and said if I didn't give him all our money, he'd take the baby. I hadn't slept or showered in four days, hadn't combed my hair for at least a week, hadn't sat down in I don't know how long. So I said, 'You want the baby? Here.'" She shifted Madeline to the other arm. "Never seen a grown man run so fast." She glanced around the room uncertainly. "Do you have some fancy way of fixing a bottle too, or can I make it like normal?"

"I've got one ready," Elizabeth said, retrieving a bottle from a small pan of warm water.

"Newborns are horrible," Mrs. Sloane said, clutching at the fake pearls around her neck as Elizabeth took Madeline from her. "I thought you had some help; otherwise I would have come earlier. You've had so many, well, so many *men* dropping by at the oddest hours." She cleared her throat.

"It's work," Elizabeth said as she coaxed Madeline to take the bottle.

"Whatever you want to call it," Mrs. Sloane said.

"I'm a scientist," Elizabeth said.

"I thought Mr. Evans was the scientist."

"I'm one, too."

"Of course, you are." She clapped her hands together. "All right, then. I'll get going. But now you know—whenever you need a spare pair of hands, I'm across the street." She wrote her phone number in thick pencil directly on the kitchen wall just above the phone. "Mr. Sloane retired last year and he's at home all the time now, so don't think you'll be interrupting anything because you won't; in fact, you'll be doing me a favor. Understood?" She bent down to retrieve something from her shopping bag. "I'll just leave this here," she said, removing a foil-wrapped casserole. "I'm not saying it's good, but you need to eat."

"Mrs. Sloane," Elizabeth said, realizing she did not want to be alone. "You seem to know a lot about babies."

"As much as anyone can ever know," she agreed. "They're self-ish little sadists. The question is, why anyone has more than one."

"How many did you have?"

"Four. What are you trying to say, Miss Zott? Are you worried about something in particular?"

"Well," Elizabeth said, trying to keep her voice from wavering, "it's . . . it's just that . . ."

"Just say it," Sloane instructed. "Boom. Out."

"I'm a terrible mother," she said in a rush. "It's not just the way you found me asleep on the job, it's many things—or rather, everything."

"Be more specific."

"Well, for instance, Dr. Spock says I'm supposed to put her on a schedule, so I made one, but she won't follow it."

Harriet Sloane snorted.

"And I'm not having any of those moments you're supposed to have—you know, the moments—"

"I don't—"

"The blissful moments—"

"Women's magazine rot," Sloane interrupted. "You need to steer clear of that stuff. It's complete fiction."

"But the feelings I'm having—I . . . I don't think they're normal. I never wanted to have children," she said, "and now I have one and I'm ashamed to say I've been ready to give her away at least twice now."

Mrs. Sloane stopped at the back door.

"Please," Elizabeth begged. "Don't think badly of me—"

"Wait," Sloane said, as if she'd misheard. "You've wanted to give her away . . . twice?" Then she shook her head and laughed in a way that made Elizabeth shrink.

"It's not funny."

"Twice? Really? Twenty times would still make you an amateur."

Elizabeth looked away.

"Hells bells," huffed Mrs. Sloane sympathetically. "You're in the midst of the toughest job in the world. Did your mother never tell you?"

And at the mention of her mother, Sloane noticed the young woman's shoulders tense.

"Okay," she said in a softer tone. "Never mind. Just try not to worry so much. You're doing fine, Miss Zott. It'll get better."

"What if it doesn't?" Elizabeth said desperately. "What if . . . what if it gets worse?"

Although she wasn't the type to touch people, Mrs. Sloane found herself leaving the sanctuary of the door to press down lightly on the young woman's shoulders. "It gets better," she said. "What's your name, Miss Zott?"

"Elizabeth."

Mrs. Sloane lifted her hands. "Well, Elizabeth, I'm Harriet."

And then there was an awkward silence, as if by sharing their names, they'd each revealed more than they'd planned.

"Before I go, Elizabeth, can I offer just one bit of advice?" Harriet began. "Actually no, I won't. I hate getting advice, especially unsolicited advice." She turned a ruddy color. "Do you hate advice givers? I do. They have a way of making one feel inadequate. And the advice is usually lousy."

"Go on," Elizabeth urged.

Harriet hesitated, then pursed her lips side to side. "Well, fine. Maybe it's not really advice anyway. It's more like a tip."

Elizabeth looked back expectantly.

"Take a moment for yourself," Harriet said. "Every day."

"A moment."

"A moment where *you* are your own priority. Just you. Not your baby, not your work, not your dead Mr. Evans, not your filthy house, not anything. Just you. Elizabeth Zott. Whatever you need, whatever you want, whatever you seek, reconnect with it in that moment." She gave a sharp tug to her fake pearls. "Then recommit."

And although Harriet didn't mention she'd never followed this advice herself—that she'd actually only read it in one of those

ridiculous women's magazines—she wanted to believe that someday she would recommit to her goal. To be in love. *Real* love.
Then she opened the back door and gave a small nod and pulled
the door closed behind her. And as if on cue, Madeline began
to cry.

CHAPTER 18

Legally Mad

Harriet Sloane had never been pretty, but she'd known pretty people and they always seemed to attract trouble. They were either loved for being pretty or hated for exactly the same reason. When Calvin Evans began dating Elizabeth Zott, Harriet assumed pretty was why. But when she first spied on them from her perch in her living room, their curtains obligingly parted to give her an unobstructed view into their living room, she had to rethink her assumption.

To her it seemed Calvin and Elizabeth had enjoyed a strange relationship—almost supernatural—like identical twins separated at birth who accidentally stumble upon each other in a foxhole and despite death all around, are amazed to discover that not only do they look alike and share a serious allergy to clams, but neither liked Dean Martin. "Really?" she imagined Calvin and Elizabeth saying to each other all the time. "Me, too!"

It hadn't been that way with her and the now-retired Mr. Sloane. The only excitement had come at the beginning but it had worn off like cheap nail polish. She'd found him bold because he had a tattoo and seemed not to notice that her ankles were thick and her hair was thin. In retrospect, that should have been a clue—that he didn't notice her—because then maybe she would have realized he was never going to notice her.

She couldn't remember how soon into their marriage she began to realize she wasn't in love with him, nor he with her, but it was probably somewhere between the way he pronounced drawer "joor" and the way his thicket of body hair constantly detached itself like seeds from a dandelion head, blanketing their home.

Yes, living with Mr. Sloane was revolting, but Harriet was not completely repelled by his physical defects—she shed herself. Rather, it was his low-grade stupidity she abhorred—his dull, opinionated, know-nothing charmless complexion; his ignorance, bigotry, vulgarity, insensitivity; and above all, his wholly undeserved faith in himself. Like most stupid people, Mr. Sloane wasn't smart enough to know just how stupid he was.

When Elizabeth Zott moved in with Calvin Evans, Mr. Sloane took instant notice. He talked about her constantly, his comments lewd and low like a mangy hyena. "Would you look at that," he'd say, staring out the window at the young woman getting in her car while rubbing his naked belly in a circular motion, dispersing tiny black curls to every corner of the room. "Yeah."

Whenever this happened, Harriet left the room. She knew she should be used to it by now, his desire for other women. It was on their honeymoon that he'd first masturbated to girlie magazines right next to her in bed. She'd gone along with it because what else was she supposed to do? Besides, she'd been told it was normal. Healthy, even. But as the magazines got raunchier, the habit grew, and now here she was, fifty-five years old, neatening his sticky stack of periodicals with a stone in her heart.

That was the other revolting thing about him. Like so many undesirable men, Mr. Sloane truly believed other women found him attractive. Harriet had no idea where that specific brand of self-confidence came from. Because while stupid people may not know they're stupid because they're stupid, surely unattractive people must know they're unattractive because of mirrors.

Not that there was anything wrong with being unattractive. She was unattractive and she knew it. She also knew that Calvin Evans was unattractive, and the sloppy dog Elizabeth brought home one day was unattractive, and there was a good chance Elizabeth's future baby would be unattractive, too. But none of them were—or would ever be—ugly. Only Mr. Sloane was ugly, and that was because he was unattractive on the inside. In reality, the only physically beautiful thing on the entire block was Elizabeth herself, and Harriet had avoided her for that very reason. Like she'd said, pretty people were trouble.

But then Mr. Evans had died and those ridiculous men with their self-important briefcases kept stopping by Elizabeth's house, and she realized that she might have picked up some of Mr. Sloane's judgmental ways. That's why she'd gone that day to check on Elizabeth. Because while she was stuck forever being Mrs. Sloane—she was a Catholic—she never wanted to turn into a Mr. Sloane. And besides, she knew what newborns were like.

Call me, she begged, peeking through her curtains at the house across the street. *Call me. Call me. Call me.*

On the other side of the street, Elizabeth had picked up the phone to dial Harriet Sloane at least a dozen times in the last four days, but each time she'd failed to complete the call. She'd always thought herself a capable human being, but suddenly, based solely on the small amount of time she'd spent in Harriet's presence, she realized she was not.

She stood at the window and looked across the street. A sort of desperation gripped her. She'd had a baby and would be raising it to adulthood. My god—*adulthood.* From across the room, Madeline announced it was feeding time.

"But you just ate," Elizabeth reminded her.

"WELL I DON'T REMEMBER," Madeline screamed back,

formally initiating the least fun game in the world: Guess What
I Want Now.

She had another problem: every time Elizabeth looked into
her daughter's eyes, Calvin looked back. It was unnerving. The
truth was, she was still mad at Calvin—the way he'd lied to her
about her research funding, the way his sperm defied the con-
traceptive odds, the way he'd run outdoors when everyone else
ran indoors in ballet slippers. She knew being mad at him was
unfair, but grief is like that: arbitrary. Anyway, no one else knew
how mad she was; she'd kept it to herself. Well, except during
labor, when she *might* have shouted some regrettable things, her
fingernails *possibly* digging into some unknown person's forearm
as the bigger contractions took hold. She remembered someone
besides herself shrieking and swearing. It seemed strange and
unprofessional.

So, sometime after it was all over, when a nurse came in with
a stack of papers demanding to know something—how she felt?—
she decided to tell her.

"Mad."

"Mad?" the nurse had asked.

"Yes, *mad*," Elizabeth had answered. Because she was.

"Are you sure?" the nurse had asked.

"Of course I'm sure!"

And the nurse, who was tired of tending to women who were
never at their best—this one had practically engraved her name
on her arm during labor—wrote "Mad" on the birth certificate
and stalked out.

So there it was: the baby's legal name was Mad. Mad Zott.

Elizabeth only discovered the issue a few days later at home
when she'd stumbled across the birth certificate in a jumble of
hospital paperwork still lumped on the kitchen table. "What's
this?" she'd said, looking at the fancy calligraphed certificate
in astonishment. "Mad Zott? For god's sake! Did I take off that
much skin?"

She immediately set about to rename the baby, but there was a problem. She'd originally believed the right name would present itself the moment she saw her daughter's face, but it hadn't.

Now, standing in her laboratory, looking down at the small lump who lay sleeping in a large basket lined with blankets, she studied her child's features. "Suzanne?" she said cautiously. "Suzanne Zott?" But it didn't feel right. "Lisa? Lisa Zott? Zelda Zott?" Nothing. "Helen Zott?" she tried. "Fiona Zott. Marie Zott?" Still nothing. She placed her hands on her hips, as if bracing herself. "*Mad* Zott," she finally ventured.

The baby's eyes flew open.

From his station beneath the table, Six-Thirty exhaled. He'd spent enough time on a playground to understand one could not name a child just *anything,* especially when the baby's name had only come about from misunderstanding or, in Elizabeth's case, payback. In his opinion, names mattered more than the gender, more than tradition, more than whatever sounded nice. A name *defined* a person—or in his case, a dog. It was a personal flag one waved the rest of one's life; it had to be right. Like his name, which he'd had to wait more than a year to receive. Six-Thirty. Did it get any better than that?

"Mad Zott," he heard Elizabeth whisper. "Dear god."

Six-Thirty got up and padded off to the bedroom. Unbeknownst to Elizabeth, he'd been stashing biscuits under the bed for months, a practice he'd started just after Calvin died. It wasn't because he feared Elizabeth might forget to feed him, but rather because he'd made his own important chemical discovery. When faced with a serious problem, he'd found it helped to eat.

Mad, he considered, chewing a biscuit. *Madge. Mary. Monica.* He withdrew another biscuit, crunching loudly. He was very fond of his biscuits—yet another triumph from the kitchens of Elizabeth Zott. It made him think, *Why not name the baby after something in the kitchen? Pot. Pot Zott. Or from the lab? Beaker. Beaker Zott. Or maybe something that actually meant chemistry—something like, well, Chem? But Kim. Like Kim Novak, his favorite actress from* The Man with the Golden Arm. *Kim Zott.*

No. Kim was too short.

And then he thought, *What about Madeline?* Elizabeth had read him *Remembrance of Things Past*—he couldn't really recommend it—but he had understood that one part. The part about the madeleine. The biscuit. *Madeline Zott? Why not?*

"What do you think of the name 'Madeline,'" Elizabeth asked him after finding Proust inexplicably propped open on her nightstand.

He looked back at her, his face blank.

The only problem was, getting Mad's name changed to Madeline required a trip to city hall, and once there, a form that demanded a marriage certificate and several other details Elizabeth wasn't very excited to share. "You know what?" Elizabeth said, meeting Six-Thirty on the stairs just outside the building. "We'll just keep this between ourselves. She's legally Mad, but we'll call her Madeline and no one will be the wiser."

Legally Mad, Six-Thirty thought. *What could possibly go wrong?*

The other thing about Mad: she got really mad when the Hastings people dropped by. "Colicky," Dr. Spock would have diagnosed. But Elizabeth thought it might be that the baby was a good judge of character. Which worried her. Because what, then, would she think of her own mother's character? A woman who didn't speak to her family, who'd refused to marry a man she deeply loved, who'd gotten fired from her job, who spent her days teaching her dog words? Would she seem selfish or crazy or both?

She wasn't sure, but she had a feeling that the woman across the street would know. Elizabeth wasn't one for church, but there was something holy about Harriet Sloane. She was like a practical priest, someone to whom one could confess things—fears, hopes, mistakes—and expect in return, not a simpleton's recipe for prayers and beads, or a psychologist's standard "And how does that make you feel?" runaround, but actual wisdom. How to get on with the business at hand. How to survive.

She picked up the phone, unaware that Harriet's binoculars were already confirming the dialing pattern from her front window.

"Hello?" Harriet answered casually as she forced her binoculars back between the sofa cushions. "You've reached the Sloane residence."

"Harriet. This is Elizabeth Zott."

"Be right over."

CHAPTER 19

December 1956

The biggest benefit in being the child of a scientist? Low safety bar.

As soon as Mad could walk, Elizabeth encouraged her to touch, taste, toss, bounce, burn, rip, spill, shake, mix, splatter, sniff, and lick nearly everything she encountered.

"Mad!" Harriet shouted every morning as she let herself in. "Put that down!"

"Down!" Mad agreed, flinging a half-filled coffee cup across the room.

"No!" shouted Harriet.

"No!" agreed Mad.

As Harriet fetched the mop, Madeline teetered into the living room, picking up this, discarding that, her grubby little hands automatically reaching for the too-sharp, too-hot, too-toxic, the things most parents keep out of reach on purpose—in short, the best things. Nevertheless, she lived.

It was because of Six-Thirty. He was always there, sniffing out danger, blocking light sockets, positioning himself beneath the bookshelf so when she scaled it—which she did nearly every day—he would be the cushion that broke her fall. He'd failed once to protect someone he loved. He would not fail again.

"Elizabeth," Harriet scolded her. "You can't just let Mad do whatever she wants."

"You're absolutely right, Harriet," Elizabeth said without taking her eyes off three test tubes. "You'll notice I've moved the knives."

"*Elizabeth,*" Harriet implored. "You have to watch her. I found her crawling into the washing machine yesterday."

"Don't worry," Elizabeth said, still staring at the test tubes. "I never start a load without checking first."

Yet despite her constant state of alarm, Harriet could not dispute that Mad seemed to be growing in ways her children never had. Even more unusual: the mother-daughter relationship had a symmetry Harriet could not ignore. The child learned from the mother, but the mother also learned from the child. It was like a mutual adoration society—you could see it in the way Mad looked at Elizabeth when she was being read to, the way she crowed when her mother whispered in her ear, the way Elizabeth beamed when the child combined baking soda with vinegar, the way they constantly shared whatever they were thinking and doing—chemistry, babble, drool—sometimes using a sort of secret language that felt to Harriet just a bit exclusionary. One could not—should not—be one's child's friend, she'd warned Elizabeth. She'd read that in one of her magazines.

She watched as Elizabeth popped Mad up onto her lap, then held her close to the bubbling test tubes. The child's eyes filled with wonder. What had Elizabeth called her teaching method? Experiential learning?

"Children are sponges," Elizabeth explained the previous week as Harriet chided her for reading aloud to Madeline from *On the Origin of Species*. "I'm not about to allow Mad to dry out early."

"Dry," Mad shouted. "Dry, dry, dry!"

"But surely she can't understand a word of what Darwin wrote," Harriet argued. "At the very least, couldn't you read her the abridged version?" Harriet only ever read abridged versions. *Reader's Digest* was her favorite publication for that very reason—they cut big boring books down to a chewable size like St. Joseph aspirin. She once overheard a woman in the park saying she wished *Reader's Digest* would condense the Bible, and Harriet found herself thinking, *Yes—and marriages.*

"I don't believe in abridgments," Elizabeth said. "Anyway, I think Mad and Six-Thirty enjoy it."

That was the other thing—Elizabeth read to Six-Thirty, too. Harriet was fond of Six-Thirty; in fact, sometimes she felt like she and the dog shared similar worries about Elizabeth's *que será, será* approach to parenting.

"I wish you could talk to her," Harriet told him more than once. "She'd listen to you."

Six-Thirty looked back at her, exhaling. Elizabeth *did* listen to him—obviously communication was not limited to conversation. Still, he sensed that most people did not listen to their dogs. This was called ignoring. Or wait, no. Ignorance. He'd just learned that one. By the way and not to brag, but his word count was up to 497.

The only person besides Elizabeth who didn't seem to under-estimate what a dog understood, or what it meant to be a working mother, was Dr. Mason. As threatened, he dropped by her home about a year after the delivery, ostensibly to see how things were going, but more obviously to remind her about his boat.

"Hello, Miss Zott," he said as she opened the door at seven fif-teen a.m., astonished to see him there, in his rowing kit, his crew cut damp from a hard row in the morning fog. "How are things? Not to make this about me, but I had the most godawful row this morning." He stepped in and walked past her, casually fighting his way upstream through the litter of babyhood until making it to the lab, where he found Mad contemplating her escape from her high chair.

"Well there she is!" he beamed. "All grown up and still alive. Excellent." He noted a pile of freshly washed diapers, grabbed one, and began to fold. "I can't stay long, but I was in the neighborhood and thought I'd check in." He leaned down to take a better look at Mad. "My golly, she's a big one. I guess we can thank Evans for that. How goes the parenting?" But before Elizabeth could answer, he picked up Dr. Spock's baby book. "Spock's a decent source of information. He's a rower, you know. Won a gold medal in the Olympics in 1924."

"Dr. Mason," Elizabeth said, surprised at how glad she was to see him as she took in the smell of ocean on his clothes. "It's nice of you to drop by, but—"

"Don't worry, I can't stay long; I'm on call. I promised my wife I'd watch the kids this morning. Just wanted to see how things are going. You look tired, Miss Zott. What about help? Do you have someone?"

"My neighbor drops by."

"Excellent. Proximity is critical. And what about you—how are you taking care of yourself?"

"What do you mean?"

"Still exercising?"

"Well, I—"

"Erging?"

"A lit—"

"Good. Where is it? The erg." He went to the next room. "Oh my lord," she heard him say. "Evans was a sadist."

"Dr. Mason?" she called, drawing him back to the lab. "It's nice to see you, but I've got a meeting here in thirty minutes and I have a lot to—"

"Sorry," he said, popping back in. "I don't usually do this—drop in on patients postdelivery. To be honest, I never see any of my patients again unless they decide to swell the ranks."

"I'm honored," she said. "But like I said, I'm—"

"Busy," he finished for her. He went over to the sink and started to wash the dishes. "So," he said, "you've got the baby, the

erg, your freelance work, your research." He ticked off her com-
mitments, lifting his soapy hands as he ran his eyes around the
room. "This is a decent lab by the way."

"Thank you."

"Did Evans—"

"No."

"Then—"

"I built it. During my pregnancy."

He shook his head in wonder.

"I had help," she said, gesturing to Six-Thirty, who stood by
Mad's chair like a sentry waiting for food to drop.

"Ah, yes, there he is. Dogs are enormously helpful. My wife
and I found our dog was a sort of a child trial run," he said, examining a pan. "Brillo pad?"

"To your left."

"Speaking of trial runs," he said, adding more soap. "It's
time."

"Time?"

"Time to row. It's been a year already."

She laughed. "That's funny."

He turned to look at her, his hands dripping water on the
floor. "What's funny?"

Now it was Elizabeth's turn to look confused.

"We have an opening. Two seat. It would work for us to have
you back as soon as possible. Next week at the latest."

"What? No. I'm—"

"Tired? Busy? Probably going to argue you don't have time."

"Because I don't."

"Who does? Being an adult is overrated, don't you think?" he
said. "Just as you solve one problem, ten more pull up."

"Up!" Madeline shouted.

"The only decent thing I learned in the marines was the value
of making my bed every morning. But a chilly splash of water in
the face off starboard, just before dawn? It fixes things."

Elizabeth took a sip of coffee as Mason prattled on. She was
well aware that she needed fixing. She'd reached a new stage in
her grief: from mourning the man she'd fallen in love with, to
mourning the father she knew he would have been. She tried
hard not to imagine how high Calvin would have tossed Mad in
the air, how easily he would have plopped her on his shoulders.
Neither of them had wanted children, and Elizabeth still fervently
believed that no woman should be forced to have a baby. Yet here
she was, a single mother, the lead scientist on what had to be the
most unscientific experiment of all time: the raising of another
human being. Every day she found parenthood like taking a test
for which she had not studied. The questions were daunting and
there wasn't nearly enough multiple choice. Occasionally she
woke up damp with sweat, having imagined a knock at the door
and some sort of authority figure with an empty baby-sized basket saying, "We've just reviewed your last parental performance
report and there's really no nice way to put this. You're fired."

"I've tried to get my wife to row for years," Dr. Mason was saying. "I think she'd love it. But she always says no and I have to
assume it's partly because there aren't any other women down at
the boathouse. I'm not crazy, Miss Zott. Women row. You row.
There *are* women's rowing teams."

"Where?"

"Oslo."

"Norway?"

"This one," he said, pointing to Mad. "She's definitely going
to row port. See how she naturally shifts her weight to the right?"

They both looked to Madeline, who was staring at her fingers
as if surprised to find they weren't all the same length. Last night,
when Elizabeth was reading aloud from *Treasure Island,* she'd felt

Mad staring up at her, her lips parted in awe. She looked back down at her daughter, awestruck in a different way. It had been such a long time since anyone had shown her that kind of faith. She felt an avalanche of love for her misinformed child.

"You'd be surprised how much you can tell about a baby at this stage," Mason was saying. "They constantly reveal their future selves in the smallest of ways. This one; she can read a room."

Elizabeth nodded. Last week she'd peeked in on Mad during naptime and found the child sitting up in her crib explaining something in earnest to Six-Thirty. Elizabeth had hung back, watching in wonder as the baby, wobbling back and forth like a bowling pin threatening to topple, waved her hands as she chattered a steady stream of consonants and vowels strung together haphazardly, like laundry on a line, but delivered with the kind of passion that made it clear she was an expert in this area. Six-Thirty stood next to the crib, rapt, his nose stuck between the slats, ears tracking every syllable. Mad paused in midair as if she'd just lost her train of thought, then leaned forward toward the dog and started in again. "Gagagagazozonanowoowoo," she said as if clarifying a point. "Babbadodobabdo."

Having a baby, Elizabeth realized, was a little like living with a visitor from a distant planet. There was a certain amount of give and take as the visitor learned your ways and you learned theirs, but gradually their ways faded and your ways stuck. Which she found regrettable. Because unlike adults, her visitor never tired of even the smallest discovery; always saw the magic in the ordinary. Last month Mad had let out a shriek from the living room, and Elizabeth ruined an hour's worth of work in her rush to her side. "What is it, Mad?" she said, swooping in like a helicopter in a war zone. "What's wrong?"

Mad, wide-eyed, looked back at her as she held up a spoon. *Look at this!* she seemed to say. *It was right here! On the floor!*

"And it's not just exercise," Dr. Mason was saying. "Rowing is a way of life. Am I right?" He was talking to the baby.

"Ite!" shouted Mad, banging on her tray.

"By the way, we have a new coach," he said, turning to Elizabeth. "Very talented. I've told him about you."

"Really? And did you tell him I'm a woman?"

"No!" shouted Mad.

"The point is, Miss Zott," Dr. Mason said, avoiding her question as he grabbed a towel, moistened it, then moved to the high chair, where he used it to clean Mad's sticky hands, "we've been having an ongoing problem with Two Seat. Between you and me, he's a terrible rower, was only ever in the boat because of some old collegiate connections. But that all ended this past weekend when he broke his leg in a ski accident." He tried to hide his delight. "Fractured in three places!"

Madeline stuck out her arms and the doctor lifted her out of the chair.

"I'm sorry to hear that," Elizabeth said. "And I appreciate the vote of confidence. Still, I don't have the experience. I was only in your boat a few times and that was because of Calvin."

"Alv-in," said Mad.

"Of course you have the experience," Dr. Mason said, surprised. "Seriously? Trained by Calvin Evans himself? In a pair? I'd take that kind of expertise over some giant ex-college lackey any day of the week."

"And I'm also busy," she explained again.

"At four thirty in the morning? You'll be back home before this one even knows you've been gone. *Two seat.*" He emphasized the phrase like this was a special deal that wouldn't last. "Remember? We discussed this."

Elizabeth shook her head. Calvin had been the same way—treated rowing as if it naturally superseded everything. She remembered a morning in particular when some of the other rowers in a different boat were expressing surprise that their five seat hadn't shown up. The coxswain called him at home, discov-

ering that Five Seat had a high fever. "Okay, but you're still coming, right?" he demanded.

"Miss Zott," Dr. Mason said, "I don't mean to put you on the
spot, but the truth is, we need you. I know I only rowed with
you those few times, but I know what I felt. Plus, getting back in
a boat will make *you* feel so much better. We *all*," he said, thinking of his row that morning, "will feel so much better. Ask your
neighbor. See if she won't watch the baby."

"At four thirty in the morning?"

"This is what is so unsung about rowing," Dr. Mason said,
turning to leave. "It happens at a time when no one's really that
busy."

"I'll do it," Harriet said.

"You can't be serious," Elizabeth said.

"It'll be fun," Harriet said as if everyone agreed getting up
in the middle of the night was fun. But really it was because of
Mr. Sloane. He'd been drinking more and swearing more and the
only way she knew how to deal with it was to stay away. "Anyway, it's only three mornings a week."

"It's just a tryout. I may not pass muster."

"You'll be fine," Harriet said. "You'll pass with flying colors."

But as Elizabeth wended her way through the boathouse two days
later, small pods of drowsy rowers glancing at her in surprise, she
began to feel that Harriet's faith and Dr. Mason's needs were both
exaggerated.

"Good morning," she said to rowers at random. "Hello."

"What's she doing here?" she heard someone whisper.

"Jesus," said another.

"Miss Zott," Dr. Mason called from the far end of the boathouse. "Over here."

She plotted a path through the labyrinth of bodies to a disheveled group of men who looked as if they'd just received some very bad news.

"Elizabeth Zott," she said firmly, holding out her hand. No one took it.

"Zott will be rowing two seat today," Mason said. "Bill broke his leg."

Silence.

"Coach," Dr. Mason said, turning to a homicidal-looking man. "This is the rower I told you about."

Silence.

"Some of you may remember, she rowed with us before."

Silence.

"Any questions?"

Silence.

"Let's get going then." He tipped his head at the coxswain.

"I think that went well, don't you?" Dr. Mason said later as they walked to their cars. She turned to look at him. When she was in labor and in horrific pain, convinced the baby was snatching her internal organs like suitcases as if to ensure she'd have plenty to wear on the outside, she screamed so violently the bed frame shook. Once the contraction passed, she'd opened her eyes to see Dr. Mason leaning over her. *See?* he'd said. *Not so bad, right?*

She fiddled with her car keys. "I think the coxswain and coach would disagree."

"Oh that," he said, waving it off with his hand. "Normal. I thought you knew. New rower gets blamed for everything. You mostly rowed with Evans—you don't really understand the finer points of rowing culture. Just give it a few rows; you'll see."

She hoped he was being honest, because the truth was, she'd loved being out on the water again. She felt exhausted, but in a good way.

"What I find interesting about rowing," Dr. Mason was saying, "is that it's always done backwards. It's almost as if the

sport itself is trying to teach us not to get ahead of ourselves."
He opened his car door. "Actually, when you think about it,
rowing is almost exactly like raising kids. Both require patience,
endurance, strength, and commitment. And neither allow us to
see where we're going—only where we've been. I find that very
reassuring, don't you? Except for the flip-outs—of course. I could
really do with fewer flip-outs."

"You mean flips."

"Flip-outs," he insisted, getting in his car. "Yesterday one of
my kids hit the other with a shovel."

Chapter 20

Life Story

Although she was only almost four, Mad was already bigger than most five-year-olds and could read better than many sixth graders. But despite these physical and intellectual strides, just like her antisocial mother and grudge-holding father, she had few friends.

"I'm worried it could be a gene mutation," Elizabeth confided to Harriet. "Calvin and I could both be carriers."

"The I-hate-people gene?" Harriet said. "There is one?"

"Shyness," corrected Elizabeth. "Introversion. So guess what: I've enrolled her in kindergarten. The new school year starts Monday and suddenly it made so much sense. Mad needs to be around children—you've said so yourself."

It was true. Harriet had voiced that opinion at least a hundred times in the last few years. Madeline was a precocious child with extraordinary verbal and comprehension abilities, but Harriet wasn't convinced she was gaining in average areas—how to tie shoes, how to play with dolls. The other day she'd suggested they make mud pies and Mad frowned, then wrote 3.1415 with a stick in the dirt. "Done," she'd said.

Besides, if Mad went off to school, what was she, Harriet, supposed to do with her day? She'd grown accustomed to being necessary.

"She's too young," Harriet insisted. "She has to be at least five years old. Better, six."

"They mentioned that," Elizabeth said. "Nevertheless, she's in."

What Elizabeth neglected to say was that it wasn't because Madeline was bright, but rather because Elizabeth had determined the chemical composition of ballpoint pen ink and found a way to alter Madeline's birth certificate. Technically, Mad was far too young to be in kindergarten, but Elizabeth didn't see what a technicality had to do with her daughter's education.

"Woody Elementary," she said, handing Harriet a sheet of paper. "Mrs. Mudford. Room six. I realize she might be a little more advanced than some of the other children, but I doubt she'll be the only one reading Zane Grey, don't you?"

Six-Thirty lifted his head in concern. He wasn't so thrilled to hear this news either. Mad in school? What about *his* job? How could he protect the creature if she was in a classroom?

Elizabeth gathered the coffee cups and took them to the sink. This sudden school enrollment idea wasn't all that sudden. She'd been to the bank several weeks ago to take out a reverse mortgage on the bungalow. They were broke. If Calvin hadn't stuck her name on the deed, a fact she'd only discovered after he died, they'd be on welfare.

The bank manager was grim in his assessment of her situation. "Things will only get worse," he warned. "As soon as your child is old enough, get her in school. Then find a job that actually pays. Or marry rich."

She got back in her car and reviewed her options.

Rob a bank.

Rob a jewelry store.

Or here was a loathsome idea—go back to the place that had robbed her.

Twenty-five minutes later she walked into the Hastings lobby, hands shaking, skin clammy, the body's warning system sounding all alarms. She inhaled, trying to draw in strength. "Dr. Donatti, please," she said to the receptionist.

"Will I like school?" Mad asked, appearing out of nowhere.

"Absolutely," Elizabeth said unconvincingly. "What's that there?" She pointed to a large sheet of black construction paper Madeline was clutching in her right hand.

"My picture," she said, placing it on the table in front of her mother as she leaned up against her. It was another chalk drawing—Madeline preferred chalk over crayons—but because chalk smudged so easily, her drawings often looked blurry, as if her subjects were trying to get off the page. Elizabeth looked down to see a few stick figures, a dog, a lawn mower, a sun, a moon, possibly a car, flowers, a long box. Fire appeared to be destroying the south; rain dominated the north. And there was one other thing: a big swirly white mass right in the middle.

"Well," Elizabeth said, "this is really something. I can tell you've put a lot of work into this."

Mad puffed her cheeks as if her mother didn't know the half of it.

Elizabeth studied the drawing again. She'd been reading Madeline a book about how the Egyptians used the surfaces of sarcophagi to tell the tale of a life lived—its ups, its downs, its ins, its outs—all of it laid out in precise symbology. But as she read, she'd found herself wondering—did the artist ever get distracted? Ink an asp instead of a goat? And if so, did he have to let it stand? Probably. On the other hand, wasn't that the very definition of life? Constant adaptations brought about by a series of never-ending mistakes? Yes, and she should know.

Dr. Donatti had appeared in the lobby ten minutes later. Oddly, he seemed almost relieved to see her. "Miss Zott!" he'd said, giving her a hug as she held her breath, revulsed. "I was just thinking about you!"

Actually, he'd been thinking of nothing *but* Zott.

"Tell me about these people," she said to Mad, pointing at the stick figures.

"That's you and me and Harriet," Mad said. "And Six-Thirty. And that's you rowing," she said, pointing to the boxlike thing, "and that's our lawn mower. And this is fire over here. And these are some more people. That's our car. And the sun comes out, then the moon comes out, and then flowers. Get it?"

"I think so," Elizabeth said. "It's a seasonal story."

"No," Mad said. "It's my life story."

Elizabeth nodded in pretend understanding. A lawn mower?

"And what's this part?" Elizabeth asked, pointing at the swirl that dominated the picture.

"That's the pit of death," Mad said.

Elizabeth eyes widened in worry. "And this?" She pointed at a series of slanty lines. "Rain?"

"Tears," Mad said.

Elizabeth knelt down, her eyes level with Mad's. "Are you sad, honey?"

Mad placed her small, chalky hands on either side of her mother's face. "No. But you are."

After Mad went outside to play, Harriet said something about "out of the mouths of babes," but Elizabeth pretended not to hear. She was already aware that her daughter could read her like a book. She'd noted this before—how Mad could sense exactly those things everyone wanted to hide. "Harriet has never been in love," she'd said out of the blue during dinner last week. "Six-Thirty still feels responsible," she'd sighed at breakfast. "Dr. Mason is sick of vaginas," she'd mentioned at bedtime.

"I'm not sad, Harriet," she lied. "In fact, I have great news. Hastings offered me a job."

"A job?" Harriet said. "But you have a job—one that lets you work, raise Mad, walk Six-Thirty, conduct your research, and row. How many women can say that?"

None, thought Elizabeth, including herself. Her nonstop schedule was killing her, her lack of income threatened her family, her self-esteem had plunged to an all-new low.

"I don't like it," Harriet said, unhappy about the school situation, which would rob her of her purpose. "After the way they treated you and Mr. Evans? It's bad enough that you kowtow to all those idiots who drop by here."

"Science is like anything else," Elizabeth said. "Some are better at it than others."

"That's my point," Harriet said. "Of all disciplines, shouldn't science be able to weed out its own intellectual zeroes? Wasn't that Darwin's deal? That the weak eventually bite the dust?" But she could tell Elizabeth wasn't listening.

"How's the baby?" Donatti had asked, taking her by the arm and leading her to his office. He'd glanced down, surprised to see her fingers were bandaged just as they had been when she'd left.

Zott said something in return, but he was too busy calculating his next move to pay attention. For the last few glorious years, he'd been Zott-Evans-free, and because of it, things had been better. Not in terms of actual breakthroughs, but things were humming along. Even that idiot, Boryweitz, seemed to have acquired a bigger brain. It was almost as if it had taken Evans to die and Zott to leave to allow his other chemists to bloom.

However, there was one major thorn in his side. The fat-cat investor. He was back. Wanted to know what the hell Mr. Zott had been doing with his money all this time. Where were the papers? The findings? The results?

He gazed out the window as Zott nattered on about an unexpected positive ion reaction. God, science was dull. He coughed, trying to disguise his inattention. It was nearly cocktail hour; he could leave soon. He remembered long ago at college—someone had complimented him on his extra-dry martinis. And suddenly it hit him—why not be a bartender? He loved to drink; he was good at it. His libations made other people happy, meaning drunk. Plus, mixology had a ring of science to it. Where was the downside? The paycheck?

Speaking of paychecks, he had no room in his budget to hire Zott—zero. But he had to: he needed her because the investor needed her—or rather the investor needed *him,* Mr. Zott, and his fucking abiogenesis. Seemed to be getting a little frothy about the whole thing, truth be told. He'd been ducking the man's calls for months. Had finally gotten so desperate, he'd asked his team if anyone had done any work that came within ten feet of the topic. Guess who raised his hand? Boryweitz.

The only problem was, Boryweitz couldn't explain his research. That's when Donatti had gotten suspicious and Boryweitz revealed he'd run into Zott and they'd discussed abiogenesis and—how odd was this? They had similar results.

"I want to go on record saying taking a job at Hastings is a big mistake," Harriet said, drying the coffee cups.

"Second time's the charm," Elizabeth insisted.

Off by one, thought Six-Thirty.

CHAPTER 21

E.Z.

The Chemistry Department celebrated Elizabeth's return with a new lab coat.

"It's from all of us," Donatti said. "To show how much we've missed you." Surprised by the gesture, she eagerly accepted it, donning the white jacket amid scattered applause followed by a few loud guffaws. She glanced down at the stitching above the pocket. Where it had once read "E. Zott," it now read only "E.Z."

"Like it?" Dr. Donatti said, winking. "By the way"—he crooked his finger, indicating she should follow him to his office—"a little bird told me you're still pursuing abiogenesis."

Elizabeth drew back. She hadn't told anyone about her research. The only person who might possibly know was Boryweitz, and that was only because the last time he'd been over Mad had woken from a nap, and when she'd returned, she'd found Boryweitz sitting at her desk, going through her files. "What are you *doing*?" she'd asked, shocked.

"Nothing, Miss Zott," he'd said, obviously wounded by her tone.

"I have something coming out myself," said Donatti, settling behind his desk. "It'll be in *Science Journal* soon."

"What's the topic?"

"Nothing earth-shattering," he replied with a shrug. "RNA stuff. You know how it is: have to put something out there every so often or pay the professional price. But I'm interested in yours. When can I read your paper?"

"I have a few things left to focus on," she said. "If I can be allowed to concentrate on just that without distraction for the next six weeks, I should have something for you."

"Concentrate on just *your* work?" he said, surprised. "That seems rather Calvin Evansesque, doesn't it?"

At the mention of Calvin's name, Elizabeth's face froze.

"I'm sure you remember that's not how this department runs," Donatti was saying. "We help one another here. We're a team. Like crew," he mocked. He'd overheard her tell one of the other chemists she was still rowing. Well, maybe if she hadn't *been* rowing, she'd be further on with her own work. Although he'd already gone through the files she'd brought in and he was shocked to realize she was much further along than Boryweitz seemed to realize. The man was an idiot.

"Here," Donatti said, handing her a huge stack of papers. "Start by typing these. Also, we're low on coffee. And talk to each of the fellas—see what kind of support they need."

"Support?" Elizabeth said. "But I'm a chemist, not a lab tech."

"No, you're a lab tech," Donatti said firmly. "You've been out of the game for a while now. Surely you didn't think you could just waltz in here and get your old job back—not after years of thumb twiddling. But here's the deal—work hard and we'll see."

"But this isn't what we discussed."

"*Relax,* Luscious," he drawled. "It's not—"

"*What* did you just call me?"

But before he could answer, his secretary reminded him of a meeting.

"Look," he said, turning back to Elizabeth, "you enjoyed favored status when Evans was here and plenty of people haven't forgiven you for that. This time, though, we'll make sure everyone knows you earned your place. You're a bright girl, Lizzie. It's possible."

"But I was counting on the chemist's paycheck, Dr. Donatti. I can't get by financially as a lab tech. I've got a child to support."

"About that," he said, waving his hand. "I've got some good news. I've asked Hastings to fund your further education."

"Really?" she said, astonished. "Hastings would pay for my PhD?"

Donatti stood up, stretching his arms above his head as if he'd just finished a workout. "No," he said. "What I meant was, I think you might benefit from steno school—dictation. I found a correspondence course for you," he said, handing her a brochure. "The beauty is, you could do it at home in your free time."

Heart rocketing around her chest, Elizabeth returned to her desk, slammed the files down, then headed directly for the ladies room, where she selected the stall farthest from the door and locked herself in. Harriet was right. *What had she done?* But before she could even begin to ponder the question, a banging sound came from the next stall over.

"Hello?" Elizabeth called.

The banging stopped.

"Hello?" Elizabeth tried again. "Is everything all right?"

"Mind your own business," shot a voice.

Elizabeth hesitated, then tried again. "Do you need—"

"Are you deaf? Leave me the hell alone!"

She paused. The voice was familiar. "Miss Frask?" she asked, picturing the Personnel secretary who'd tortured her with Calvin's passing years before. "Is that you, Miss Frask?"

"Who the hell wants to know?" came the belligerent voice.

"Elizabeth Zott. Chemistry."

"Jesus Christ. Zott. Of all people." There was a long moment of silence.

Miss Frask, now age thirty-three, who, for the last four years, had dutifully followed every path promising promotion—from over-selling Hastings's benefits, to spying on specific departments, to authoring an in-house gossip column called "You Heard It Here First"—had still not been promoted. In fact, she was now report-ing to a new hire—a twenty-one-year-old boy fresh out of college with no discernible skills other than making chains out of paper clips. As for Eddie—the geologist she'd slept with to prove she was marriage material—he'd dumped her two years ago for a virgin. Today's latest slap in the face: her new boy-boss had given her a seven-point plan for improvement. Item one: lose twenty pounds.

"So, you really are back," Frask said from her stall. "Like the proverbial bad penny."

"I beg your pardon."

"Bring the dog, too?"

"I did not."

"Turning into a rule follower are we, Zott?"

"My dog is busy in the afternoons." ·

"Your dog is *busy* in the afternoons." Frask rolled her eyes.

"He picks my child up from school."

Frask shifted her position on her seat. That's right—Zott had a kid now.

"Boy? Girl?"

"Girl."

Frask spun the toilet paper roll. "Sorry to hear *that*."

From her stall, Elizabeth studied the floor tiles. She knew exactly what Frask meant. On Mad's first day of school, she watched in horror as the teacher, a puffy-eyed woman with a mal-odorous perm, attempted to pin a pink flower on Mad's blouse. ABCS ARE FUN! it read.

"Can I have a blue flower instead?" Madeline had asked.

"No," the teacher had said. "Blue is for boys and pink is for girls."

"No it isn't," Madeline said.

The teacher, a Mrs. Mudford, shifted her gaze from Madeline to Elizabeth, looking at the too-pretty mother as if to pinpoint the source of the bad attitude. She glanced at Elizabeth's empty ring finger. Bingo.

"So, what brings you back to Hastings?" Frask asked. "Shopping for a new genius?"

"Abiogenesis."

"Oh right," Frask mocked. "Same old song. I'd heard the investor came back, and shazam! Here you are. I'll say one thing for you: you're predictable. At least you're chasing a richer man this time. Although, between us, isn't he a bit old for you?"

"I'm not following."

"Don't be coy."

Elizabeth tightened her jaw. "I wouldn't know how to begin."

Frask thought about this. True. Zott wasn't the coy type. She was obtuse, oblivious, just like that day when she had to be told that Calvin had left her a parting gift—a gift that was (how was this possible?) already in school and being picked up by the dog. Really?

"The man," Frask said, "who gave Hastings a huge grant to fund abiogenesis based on your work? Or rather, the work of Mr. E. Zott."

"What are you talking about?"

"You know very well, Zott. Anyway, the rich man's back, and goodness, *so are you*. I think you might be the only woman at Hastings—out of three thousand employees, mind you—who isn't a secretary. I can't imagine how *that* could have happened. And yet you still tried to pass yourself off as a man. Is there any level to which you won't stoop? By the way, do you know why the institute says we ladies aren't a good investment? It's because we're always running off and having babies. Like *you* did."

"I was *fired*," Elizabeth said, her voice filling with fury.

"Thanks, in part, to women like you," she snapped, "women who pander—"

"I do not pander—"

"Who play along—"

"I do not play along—"

"Who seem to think their self-worth is based on what a man—"

"How dare you—"

"No!" Elizabeth shouted, pounding on the thin steel panel that separated them. "How dare *you, Miss Frask! How dare *you!" She stood up, opened her stall door, strode to the sink, turning the faucet handle with such force it came off in her hand. Water spewed out, soaking her lab coat. "Dammit!" she yelled. "Dammit!"

"Oh Jesus," Frask said, materializing at her side. "Let me." She pushed Elizabeth to the left, then bent down and shut off the water valve under the sink. As she straightened up, the two women faced off.

"I've never pretended to be a man, Frask!" Elizabeth shouted as she blotted her lab coat with a paper towel.

"And I'm not a panderer!"

"I'm a chemist. Not a *woman* chemist. A *chemist*. A damn good one!"

"Well, I'm a personnel expert! An almost-psychologist," Frask shouted.

"*Almost*-psychologist?"

"Shut up."

"No really," Zott said. *"Almost?"*

"I didn't have a chance to finish, okay? What about you? Why aren't you a PhD, Zott?" Frask shot back.

Elizabeth hardened, and without meaning to, revealed a fact about herself that she'd never told anyone other than a police officer. "Because I was sexually violated by my thesis advisor, then kicked out of the doctoral program," she shouted. *"You?"*

Frask looked back, shocked. "Same," she said limply.

CHAPTER 22

The Present

"How was the first day back?" Harriet asked as soon as Elizabeth got home.

"Fine," Elizabeth lied. "Mad," she said, bending over to sweep her daughter into her arms. "How was school? Was it fun? Did you learn something new?"

"No."

"Sure you did," she said. "Tell me."

Madeline put her book down. "Well. Some of the kids are incontinent."

"Good god," said Harriet.

"They were probably just nervous," Elizabeth said, smoothing Madeline's hair. "Starting something new can be difficult."

"Also," Madeline said, "Mrs. Mudford wants to see you." She held out a note.

"Good," Elizabeth said. "That's what proactive teachers do."

"What's proactive?" Madeline asked.

"Trouble," muttered Harriet.

Elizabeth made her way down to Personnel a few weeks later. "Can you give me information on that investor?" Elizabeth asked Miss Frask. "Anything you have."

"Why not," Frask said as she yanked a single slim file folder from accounting stamped CONFIDENTIAL. "I gained two pounds last week."

"Is there more?" Elizabeth asked, looking through the file. "There's nothing in here."

"You know how rich people are, Zott. Private. But why don't we have lunch next week. It'll give me more time to root through the files."

But when the next week came, the only thing Frask brought was a sandwich.

"Couldn't find a thing," Frask admitted. "Which is strange given all the hoopla around his last visit. Probably means he decided to take his money elsewhere; happens all the time. By the way, how's the lab tech job going? Suicidal yet?"

"How did you know about that?" Elizabeth said as a vein on her temple began to throb.

"I'm in Personnel, remember? We know all, see all. Or in my case, knew all, saw all."

"What do you mean?"

"Now I'm the one who's been fired," Frask said matter-of-factly. "I'm out this Friday."

"What? *Why?*"

"Remember my seven-point improvement plan? Lose twenty pounds? I gained seven."

"You can't be fired for gaining weight," Elizabeth said. "That's illegal."

Frask leaned over and squeezed Elizabeth's arm. "Gosh, you know what? I never tire of your naïveté."

"I'm serious," Elizabeth said. "You must fight it, Miss Frask. You can't let them do this."

"Well," Frask said, turning serious, "as a personnel professional, I do always advocate a heart-to-heart with the boss. Point out one's accomplishments; focus on one's future impacts."

"That's it."

"I'm kidding," Frask said. "That never works. Anyway, don't worry—I've already got a bunch of temp typing jobs lined up.

But before I leave, I have a little present for you. Something to make up for all the grief I caused after Mr. Evans died. Why don't you meet me on Friday at the south elevator. Four o'clock. I promise you won't be disappointed."

"Just down this hallway," Frask instructed when Friday afternoon arrived. "Watch where you walk. A bunch of mice escaped from the biology lab." Together she and Elizabeth took the elevator to the basement, then made their way down a long corridor until they reached a door marked NO ADMITTANCE. "Here we are," Frask said cheerfully.

"What is this place?" Elizabeth asked, staring at a row of small steel doors labeled with the numbers one to ninety-nine.

"Storage," said Frask, taking out a set of keys. "You have a car, right? And a big empty trunk?" She spun through the keys until she found number forty-one, inserted it in the lock, and invited Elizabeth to look inside.

Calvin's work. Boxed and sealed.

"We can use this dolly," Frask said, wheeling it over. "It's eight boxes total. But we need to hurry—I have to turn in these keys by five o'clock."

"Is this legal?"

Miss Frask reached for the first box. "Do we care?"

CHAPTER 23

KCTV Studios

ONE MONTH LATER

Walter Pine had been in television from almost the very beginning. He liked the idea of television—the way it promised people an escape from daily life. That's why he'd chosen it—because who didn't want to escape? He did.

But as the years wore on, he began to feel like he was the prisoner permanently assigned to digging the escape tunnel. At the end of the day, as the other prisoners scrambled over him to freedom, he stayed behind with the spoon.

Still, he kept on for the same reason many people keep on: because he was a parent—the lone parent of daughter Amanda, six years old, kindergartner at Woody Elementary, and light of his life. He would do anything for that child. That included taking his daily browbeating from his boss, who recently threatened he'd be out of a job soon if he didn't do something about that empty afternoon programming slot.

Walter took out a handkerchief and blew his nose, looking at the cloth right after, as if to see what his insides were made of.

Phlegm. Not a surprise.

A woman had come to see him a few days back—Elizabeth Zott, mother of . . . he couldn't remember the kid's name. According to Zott, Amanda was causing trouble. No surprise; Mrs. Mudford, her teacher, claimed Amanda was always causing trouble. Which he refused to believe. Yes, Amanda was a bit anxious like he was, a bit overweight like he was, a bit of a people pleaser like he was, but you know what else Amanda was? A *nice* kid. And nice kids, like nice adults, were rare.

You know what else was rare? A woman like Elizabeth Zott. He could not stop thinking about her.

"Finally," Harriet said, wiping her wet hands on her dress as Elizabeth came in through the back door. "I was starting to worry."

"Sorry," she said, trying to keep the rage out of her voice. "Something came up at work." She threw her bag down and collapsed in a chair.

She'd been back at Hastings for two months now and the stress of underemployment was killing her. She knew people in high-stress jobs often longed for a simpler position—something that didn't require heart or brainpower; something that didn't prey on their sagging spirits at three in the morning. But she had learned that underemployment was worse. Not only did her paycheck reflect her lowly status, but her brain hurt from inactivity. And yet despite the fact that her colleagues knew she could run intellectual circles around them, she was expected to rah-rah whatever minor accomplishments they churned out.

But today's accomplishment was not minor. It was major. The latest edition of *Science Journal* was out and Donatti's paper was in it.

"Nothing earth-shattering." That's how Donatti had described his article a few months back. But the work *was* earth-shattering, and she should know. Because it was hers.

She read the article twice just to make sure. The first time, slowly. But the second time she dashed through it until her blood pressure skipped through her veins like an unsecured fire hose. This article was a direct theft from her files. And guess who was listed as a co-contributor.

She lifted her head to see Boryweitz watching her. He turned pale, then hung his head.

"Try to understand!" Boryweitz cried as she slammed the journal down on his desk. "I need this job!"

"We all need our jobs," Elizabeth seethed. "The problem is, you've never done yours."

Boryweitz peered up at her, his lemur eyes begging for mercy, but all he saw was a rogue wave just beginning to crest, its energy unknown, its true power untested. "I'm sorry," he pleaded. "I really am. I had no idea Donatti would go this far. He photo-copied all your files the first day you were back, but I assumed it was to familiarize himself with our work."

"*Our* work?" She managed not to reach out and snap his neck in two. "I'll deal with you later," she promised. Then she turned and marched down the hallway toward Donatti's office, barely breaking stride to shove a meandering microbiologist out of her way.

"You're a liar and a cheat, Donatti," she said, bursting into her boss's office. "And I promise you this: you won't get away with it."

Donatti looked up from his desk. "Zott!" he cried. "Always a pleasure!"

He sat back, taking in her fury with a kind of joy. This would have been the sort of thing Evans would have quit over for sure. If only he were alive to see this—but no, he had to ruin this moment by being dead already.

He listened with half an ear as Zott railed on about his thievery. The investor had called earlier to congratulate Donatti on his work—made some promising noises about sending more money their way. He'd also asked about Zott—whether he'd played any role in the research. Donatti had said no, not really—unfortunately, Mr. Zott had proved to be a bit of a washout; in fact, he'd been demoted. The investor had sighed as if dis-appointed, then asked about Donatti's next steps, abiogenesis-wise. Donatti mucked around with some big words he'd gleaned from other parts of Zott's research, all of which he'd have to ask

Zott about later, *after* she'd calmed the fuck down and remembered she worked for *him*. God, it was hard being a manager. Anyway, whatever he said seemed to satisfy the rich guy.

But then Zott had to go and ruin everything by doing the one thing neither of them could afford for her to do. "Here," she said, plopping her lab key in his coffee. "Keep your damn job." Then she threw her ID tag in the trash, dumped her lab coat in the middle of his desk, and stormed out, taking all those big words with her.

"You got four phone calls," Harriet was saying. "The first was about becoming a Nielsen family. The other three were from a Walter Pine. Pine wants you to call him back. Says it's urgent. Claims you and he had an enjoyable conversation about food—or no, no, I'm sorry, about *lunch,*" she corrected herself, checking her notes again. "Sounded anxious," she said, looking up. "Professionally anxious. Like a well-mannered person, but on edge."

"Walter Pine," Elizabeth said, gritting her teeth, "is Amanda Pine's father. I drove to his office a few days back to talk with him about the lunch issue."

"How did the talk go?"

"It was more of a confrontation."

"Violent, I hope."

"Mom?" a voice said, appearing in the doorway.

"Hi, bunny," Elizabeth said, attempting to sound calm as she encircled her gangly child with one arm. "How was school?"

"I made a clove hitch knot," Madeline said, holding up a rope. "For show-and-tell."

"Did everyone enjoy it?"

"No."

"That's okay," Elizabeth said, pulling her close. "People don't always like what we like."

"No one ever likes my show-and-tell stuff."

"Little bastards," muttered Harriet.

"They liked that arrowhead you brought in."

"No."

"Well, next week why not try the periodic table? That's always a crowd pleaser."

"Or you could try my bowie knife," Harriet suggested. "Let them know where you stand."

"When's dinner?" Madeline said. "I'm hungry."

"I put one of your casseroles in the oven," Harriet said to Elizabeth as she heaved herself toward the door. "I need to go feed the beast. Call Pine back."

"You *called* Amanda Pine?" Madeline gasped.

"Her father," Elizabeth said. "I told you. I visited him three days ago and got the entire lunch business straightened out. I think he understood our position, and I am certain Amanda will not be stealing your lunch ever again. Stealing is *wrong*," she snapped, thinking of Donatti and his article. *"Wrong!"* Both Madeline and Harriet jumped.

"She . . . she brings a lunch, Mom," Madeline said carefully. "But it's not normal."

"That's not our problem."

Madeline looked at her mother as if she was missing the point.

"You need to eat your own lunch, bunny," Elizabeth said more quietly. "To grow up tall."

"But I'm *already* tall," Madeline complained. "Too tall."

"One can never be too tall," Harriet said.

"Robert Wadlow *died* from being too tall," Madeline said, tapping the cover of *The Guinness Book of Records*.

"But that was a pituitary gland disorder, Mad," Elizabeth said.

"Nine feet tall!" Madeline emphasized.

"Poor man," Harriet said. "Where does someone like that shop?"

"Height *kills*," Madeline said.

"Yes, but everything kills eventually," Harriet said. "That's why everyone ends up dead, sweetheart." But when she noticed

Elizabeth's mouth drop and Madeline slump, she instantly regretted her words. She opened the back door. "I'll see you tomorrow
morning before rowing," she said to Elizabeth. "And I'll see you,
Mad," she said to the little girl, "when you get up."

This was the schedule she and Elizabeth had worked out ever
since Elizabeth had returned to work. Harriet took Mad to school,
Six-Thirty picked Mad up from school, Harriet watched her until
Elizabeth got home. "Oh, I almost forgot." She extracted a slip of
paper from her pocket. "You got another note." She gave Elizabeth a meaningful look. "From you-know-who."

Mrs. Mudford.

Elizabeth already knew Mudford didn't approve of Madeline.
She did not approve of the way Mad could read, or the way she
could kick a ball, or the way she knew a complicated series of
nautical knots—a skill she practiced frequently, including in the
dark, in the rain, without help, just in case.

"Just in case of what, Mad?" Elizabeth had asked her once,
finding the child huddled outside at night covered in a tarp, rain
coming in from every direction, a piece of rope in her hands.

Mad had looked up at her mother, surprised. Wasn't it obvious
that "just in case" wasn't an option but rather the *only* option? Life
required preparedness; just ask her dead father.

Although, honestly, if she'd been able to ask her dead father
anything it would have been how he'd felt the first time he saw
her mother. Was it love at first sight?

His ex-colleagues too still had questions for Calvin—like how
he managed to win so many awards when he never seemed to be
doing anything. And what about sex with Elizabeth Zott? She
seemed like she'd be frigid—was she? Even Madeline's teacher,
Mrs. Mudford, had questions for the long-gone Calvin Evans.

But obviously asking Madeline's father anything was out of the question, not just because he was dead, but because in 1959, fathers had nothing to do with their children's education.

Amanda Pine's father was the exception, but that was only because there was no longer a Mrs. Pine. She'd left him (and quite rightly, Mudford believed), followed by a loud and public divorce where she claimed the much older Walter Pine was not fit to be a father, much less a husband. There'd been an embarrassing sexual connotation to the whole thing; Mrs. Mudford didn't like to think of the specifics. But because of it, Mrs. Walter Pine ended up with everything Walter Pine had, including Amanda, whom, as it turned out, she hadn't actually wanted. And who could blame her? Amanda wasn't the easiest child. Thus Amanda went back to Walter, and Walter came to school, where Mrs. Mudford was forced to listen to his poor excuses regarding the contents of Amanda's highly unusual lunch boxes.

Still, while conferences with Walter Pine were irritating, they paled in comparison to the sessions she had with Zott. Wasn't it just her luck that the two parents she liked least she saw the most? Although admittedly, that's how it always was. Child behavior problems started at home. Still, if she had to choose between Amanda Pine, lunch thief, and Madeline Zott, inappropriate question asker, she'd take Amanda any day.

"Madeline asks inappropriate questions?" Elizabeth said, alarmed, during their last meeting.

"Yes, she does," Mrs. Mudford said sharply, plucking lint from her sleeve like a spider attacking its prey. "For instance, yesterday during circle time, we were discussing Ralph's pet turtle, and Madeline interrupted to ask how she might become a freedom fighter in Nashville."

Elizabeth paused as if trying to understand the underlying issue. "She shouldn't have interrupted," she finally said. "I'll speak to her."

Mrs. Mudford clicked her teeth. "You misunderstand me, Mrs. Zott. Children interrupt; that I can deal with. What I can't deal with is a child who wants to change the discussion to civil rights. This is kindergarten, not *The Huntley-Brinkley Report*. Furthermore," she added, "your daughter recently complained to our librarian that she was unable to find any Norman Mailer on our bookshelves. Apparently, she tried to put in a request for *The Naked and the Dead*." The teacher raised one eyebrow, her eyes zeroing in on the E.Z. machine-stitched above the breast pocket in a slutty-looking cursive.

"She's an early reader," Elizabeth said. "I may have forgotten to mention that."

The teacher folded her hands together, then leaned forward threateningly. *"Norman. Mailer."*

Back in the kitchen, Elizabeth unfolded the note Harriet had given her. On it screamed two words in Mudford's handwriting. *VLADIMIR. NABOKOV.*

She placed a serving of baked spaghetti Bolognese on Madeline's plate. "Other than show-and-tell, did you have a good day?" She'd stopped asking Mad if she'd learned anything at school. There was no point.

"I don't like school."

"Why?"

Madeline looked up from her plate suspiciously. "No one likes school."

From his position beneath the table, Six-Thirty exhaled. Well, there it was: the creature didn't like school, and since he and the creature agreed on everything, now he didn't like school either.

"Did you like school, Mom?" Mad asked.

"Well," said Elizabeth, "we moved a lot, so sometimes there

weren't schools for me to go to. But I went to the library. Still, I always believed going to a real school could be lots of fun."

"Like when you went to UCLA?"

A sudden sharp vision of Dr. Meyers floated in front of her. "No."

Madeline cocked her head to the side. "Are you okay, Mom?"

Without realizing it, Elizabeth had covered her face with her hands. "I'm just tired, bunny," she said as the words slipped out between her fingers.

Madeline laid down her fork and studied her mother's stricken posture. "Did something happen, Mom?" she asked. "At work?"

From behind her fingers, Elizabeth considered her young daughter's question.

"Are we poor?" Madeline asked, as if that question naturally followed the former.

Elizabeth took her hands away. "What makes you say that, honey?"

"Tommy Dixon says we're poor."

"Who's Tommy Dixon?" she asked sharply.

"A boy at school."

"What *else* did this Tommy Dixon—"

"Was Dad poor?"

Elizabeth flinched.

The answer to Mad's question lay in one of the boxes she and Frask had stolen from Hastings. At the very bottom of box number three lay an accordion folder labeled "Rowing." When she first spied it, Elizabeth naturally assumed it would be filled with newspaper clippings recording the glorious wins of his Cambridge boat. But no; it was stuffed with Calvin's post-Cambridge employment offers.

She'd skimmed the offers jealously—chairs at major universities, directorships at pharmaceutical companies, major stakes in privately held concerns. She'd sifted through the stack until she found the Hastings offer. There it was: the promise of a private lab—although all the other places had guaranteed that, too. The only thing that made the Hastings offer stand out from the others? A salary so low it was insulting. She glanced down at the signature. Donatti.

As she jammed the letters back in, she wondered why he'd even labeled this folder "Rowing"—there wasn't anything rowing-like about it. Until she noticed two quick penciled notations at the top of each offer: distance to a rowing club and area precipitation. She returned to the Hastings offer letter—yes, the computations were there, too. But there was one other thing: a big, thick circle drawn around the return address.

Commons, California.

"If Dad was famous, then he must have been rich, right?" Mad said, twirling her spaghetti around her fork.

"No, honey. Not all famous people are rich."

"Why not? Did they mess up?"

She thought back to the offers. Calvin had accepted the lowest one. Who does that?

"Tommy Dixon says it's easy to get rich. You paint rocks yellow, then say it's gold."

"Tommy Dixon is what we call a flimflam man," Elizabeth said. "Someone who schemes to get what they want through illegal means." Like Donatti, she thought, her jaw locking in place.

She thought back to another folder she'd found in Calvin's boxes, this one full of letters from people just like Tommy Dixon—wackos, get-rich-quick investors—but also a wide assortment of fake family members, each of whom desperately wanted Calvin's help: a half sister, a long-lost uncle, a sad mother, a cousin twice removed.

She'd skimmed the fake family letters quickly, surprised at how similar they were. Each claimed a biological connection, each provided a memory from an age he wouldn't be able to remember, each wanted money. The only exception was Sad Mother. While she, too, claimed a biological connection, instead of asking for money, she insisted she wanted to give it. *To help your research,* she claimed. Sad Mother had written to Calvin at least five times, imploring him to respond. It was really rather heartless, Elizabeth thought, the way Sad Mother persisted. Even Long-Lost Uncle had called it quits after two. *They told me you were dead,* Sad Mother had written over and over again. Really? Then why had she, like all the others, only written to Calvin *after* he'd become famous? Elizabeth assumed her ploy was to hook him, then steal his research. And why did she think this? Because it had just happened to her.

"I don't get it," Mad said, shoving a mushroom to the side of her plate. "If you're smart and you work hard, doesn't that mean you make more money?"

"Not always. Still, I'm sure your dad could have earned more money," Elizabeth said. "It's just that he made a different choice. Money isn't everything."

Mad looked back, dubious.

What Elizabeth didn't tell Mad was that she knew very well why Calvin had eagerly accepted Donatti's ridiculous offer. But his reason was so short-sighted—so *dumb*—she hesitated to share it. She wanted Mad to think of her father as a rational man who made smart decisions. This proved just the opposite.

She found it in a folder labeled "Wakely," which contained a series of letters between Calvin and a would-be theologian. The two men were pen pals; it was clear they'd never met face-to-face. But their typed exchanges were fascinating and numerous, and lucky for her, the folder included Calvin's carbon copy replies. This was something she knew about Calvin: he made copies of everything.

Wakely, who was attending Harvard Divinity School at the same time Calvin was at Cambridge, seemed to be struggling with his faith based on science in general, and on Calvin's research in particular. According to his letters, he'd attended a symposium where Calvin had spoken briefly and, based on that, had decided to write to him.

"Dear Mr. Evans, I wanted to get in touch with you after your brief appearance at the science symposium in Boston last week. I'd hoped to speak with you about your recent article, 'The Spontaneous Generation of Complex Organic Molecules,'" Wakely had written in the first letter. "Specifically, I wanted to ask: Don't you think it's possible to believe in both God *and* science?"

"Sure," Calvin had written back. "It's called intellectual dishonesty."

Although Calvin's flippancy had a tendency to annoy a lot of people, it didn't seem to faze the young Wakely. He wrote back immediately.

"But surely you'd agree that the field of chemistry could not exist unless and until it was created by a chemist—a *master* chemist," Wakely argued in his next letter. "In the same way that a painting cannot exist until it is created by an artist."

"I deal in evidence-based truths, not conjecture," Calvin replied just as quickly. "So no, your master chemist theory is bullshit. By the way, I notice you're at Harvard. Are you a rower? I row for Cambridge. Full-ride rowing scholarship."

"Not a rower," Wakely wrote back. "Although I love the water. I'm a surfer. I grew up in Commons, California. Ever been to California? If not, you should go. Commons is beautiful. Best weather in the world. They row there, too."

Elizabeth sat back on her heels. She remembered how vigorously Calvin had circled Hastings's return address in the offer letter. *Commons, California.* So he'd accepted Donatti's insulting offer, not to further his career, but to row? Thanks to a one-line

weather report from a religious surfer? *Best weather in the world.*
Really? She moved on to the next letter.

"Did you always want to be a minister?" Calvin asked.

"I come from a long line of ministers," Wakely answered
back. "It's in my blood."

"Blood doesn't work that way," Calvin corrected. "By the
way, I've been meaning to ask: Why do you think so many people
believe in texts written thousands of years ago? And why does it
seem the more supernatural, unprovable, improbable, and ancient
the source of these texts, the more people believe them?"

"Humans need reassurance," Wakely wrote back. "They
need to know others survived the hard times. And, unlike other
species, which do a better job of learning from their mistakes,
humans require constant threats and reminders to be nice. You
know how we say, 'People never learn?' It's because they never
do. But religious texts try to keep them on track."

"But isn't there more solace in science?" Calvin responded.
"In things we can prove and therefore work to *im*prove? I just
don't understand how anyone thinks anything written ages ago
by drunk people is even remotely believable. And I'm not making
a moral judgment here: those people had to drink, the water was
bad. Still, I ask myself how their wild stories—bushes burning,
bread dropping from heaven—seem reasonable, especially when
compared to evidence-based science. There isn't a person alive
who would opt for Rasputin's bloodletting techniques over the
cutting-edge therapies at Sloan Kettering. And yet so many insist
we believe these stories and then have the audacity to insist others
believe them, too."

"You make a fair point, Evans," Wakely wrote back. "But
people need to believe in something bigger than themselves."

"Why?" Calvin pressed. "What's wrong with believing in
ourselves? Anyway, if stories must be used, why not rely on a
fable or fairy tale? Aren't they just as valid a vehicle for teaching

morality? Except maybe better? Because no one has to pretend to believe that the fables and tales are true?"

Although he didn't admit to it, Wakely found himself agreeing. No one had to pray to Snow White or fear the wrath of Rumpelstiltskin to understand the message. The stories were short, memorable, and covered all the bases of love, pride, folly, and forgiveness. Their rules were bite-sized: Don't be a jerk. Don't hurt other people or animals. Share what you have with others less fortunate. In other words, be nice. He decided to change the topic.

"Okay, Evans," he wrote, referring to a previous letter, "I take your very *literal* point about how ministering can't, technically, be in my blood, but we Wakelys become ministers just like cobblers' sons become shoemakers. I'll confess: I've always been attracted to biology, but that would never fly in my family. Maybe I'm just trying to please my father. Isn't that what we all do in the end? What about you? Was your father a scientist? Are you trying to please him? If so, I'd say you succeeded."

"I HATE MY FATHER," Calvin typed in all capital letters in what would prove to be their final exchange. "I HOPE HE'S DEAD."

I hate my father; I hope he's dead. Elizabeth read it again, stunned. But Calvin's father *was* dead—hit by a train at least two decades earlier. Why would he have written such a thing? And why had Calvin and Wakely stopped corresponding? The last letter was dated nearly ten years ago.

"Mom," Mad said. "Mom! Are you listening? Are we poor?"

"Honey," Elizabeth said, trying to stave off a nervous breakdown—*had she really quit her job?* "I've had a long day," she said. "Please. Just eat your dinner."

"But, Mom—"

They were interrupted by the jangle of the telephone. Mad jumped from her chair.

"Don't answer it, Mad."

"Might be important."

"We're eating dinner."

"Hello?" Mad said. "Mad Zott speaking."

"Honey," Elizabeth said, taking the phone. "We don't give out private information on the telephone, remember? Hello?" she said into the mouthpiece. "With whom am I speaking?"

"Mrs. Zott?" a voice said. "Mrs. Elizabeth Zott? It's Walter Pine, Mrs. Zott. We met earlier this week."

Elizabeth sighed. "Oh. Yes, Mr. Pine."

"I've been trying to reach you all day. Perhaps your house-keeper neglected to give you my messages."

"She is not a housekeeper and she did not neglect to give me your messages."

"Oh," he said, embarrassed. "I see. I'm sorry. I hope I'm not disturbing you. Do you have a moment? Is this a good time?"

"No."

"I'll be quick, then," he said, not wanting to lose her. "And again, Mrs. Zott, I've rectified the lunch situation. It's all fixed; Amanda will only be eating her own lunch from now on, again my apologies. But now I'm calling for another reason—a business reason."

He went on to remind her he was a producer of local after-noon TV programming. "KCTV," he said proudly, even though he wasn't. "And I've been thinking of changing my lineup a bit—adding a cooking show. Trying to spice things up, you might say," he continued, taking a stab at humor, something he normally didn't do but did now because Elizabeth Zott made him nervous. As he waited for the polite chuckle that should have come from the other end but didn't, he grew even more anxious. "As a *sea-soned* television producer, I feel the time is *ripe* for such a show."

Again, nothing.

"I've been doing research," he blathered on, "and based on

some very interesting trends, and combined with my personal knowledge of successful afternoon programming, I believe cooking is poised to become a force in afternoon TV."

Elizabeth still offered no reaction, and even if she had, it wouldn't have mattered because none of what Walter said was true.

The truth was, Walter Pine did not conduct research, nor was he aware of any trends. Factually speaking, he had very little personal knowledge of what made afternoon TV successful. As proof, his channel usually hovered near the bottom, ratings-wise. The real situation was this: Walter had an empty programming slot to fill and the advertisers were breathing down his neck to get it filled immediately. A children's clown show had previously filled the now-empty slot, but in the first place, it hadn't been very good, and in the second place, its clown star had been killed in a bar fight, making the show completely dead in the truest sense.

For the last three weeks, he'd been scrambling to find something else to take its place. He'd spent eight hours a day screening promo reels from countless would-be stars—magicians, advice givers, comedians, music instructors, science experts, etiquette mavens, puppeteers. Wading through it all, Walter couldn't believe the drivel other people produced, nor could he believe they had the gall to commit it to film, put it in the mail, and send it to him. Had they no shame? Still, he had to find something fast: his career depended on it. His boss had made that abundantly clear.

On top of work woes, four times this month he'd been summoned in to see Mrs. Mudford, Amanda's kindergarten teacher, who most recently had threatened to report him simply because, in a cloud of exhaustion and depression, he'd inadvertently packed his gin flask where Amanda's milk thermos was supposed to go. He'd also sent a stapler instead of a sandwich, a script instead of a napkin, and some champagne truffles that time they were out of bread.

"Mr. Pine?" Elizabeth said, interrupting his thoughts. "I've had a long day. Is there something you wanted?"

"I want to create a cooking show for afternoon TV," he said in a rush. "And I want you to host. It's obvious to me that you can cook, Mrs. Zott, but I also think you would have a certain appeal." He didn't say it was because she was attractive. Plenty of good-looking people skated by on their looks, but something told him Elizabeth Zott was not one of those people. "This would be a fun show—woman to woman. You'd be singing to your people." And when she didn't respond right away, he added, "Housewives?"

From the other end of the phone, Elizabeth narrowed her eyes. *"I beg your pardon?"*

The tone. Walter should have understood it and hung up right then. But he didn't because he was desperate, and desperate people tend to overlook the most obvious signals. Elizabeth Zott belonged in front of a camera—he was sure of it—plus, she was exactly the kind of woman his boss would go nuts for.

"You're nervous about the audience," he said, "but there's no reason. We use cue cards. All you have to do is read and be yourself." He waited for a response, but when none came, he carried on. "You have presence, Mrs. Zott," he pressed. "You're exactly the kind of person people want to see on TV. You're like a . . ." He tried hard to think of someone like her, but nothing came to mind.

"I'm a scientist," she snapped.

"Right!"

"You're saying the public wants to hear from more scientists."

"Yes," he said. "Who doesn't?" Although he didn't and he was fairly certain no one else did either. "Although this would be a cooking show, you understand."

"Cooking *is* science, Mr. Pine. They're not mutually exclusive."

"Uncanny. I was just about to say that."

From her kitchen table, Elizabeth envisioned her unpaid util-
ity bills. "How much does something like this pay?" she asked.

He named a figure that drew the slightest gasp from her end.
Was she offended or astonished?

"The thing is," he said defensively, "we'd be taking a risk. It's
not like you've been on TV before, correct?" Then he outlined
the basic pilot-series contract, pointing out that the initial term
was six months long. After that, if it wasn't working, that was it.
Finito.

"When would it start?"

"Immediately. We want the cooking show to go live as soon
as possible—within the month."

"You mean a *science* cooking show."

"You said it yourself—they're not mutually exclusive." But
a small bit of doubt regarding her viability as a hostess began to
creep in. Surely, she understood that a cooking show was not
actually science. Didn't she? "We're calling it *Supper at Six*," he
added, emphasizing the word "supper."

On the other end of the line, Elizabeth stared into space. She
absolutely hated the idea—making food on TV for housewives—
but what choice did she have? She turned to look at Six-Thirty
and Mad. They were lying on the floor together. Madeline was
telling him about Tommy Dixon. Six-Thirty bared his teeth.

"Mrs. Zott?" Walter said, wary of the silence coming from
the other end. "Hello? *Mrs. Zott? Are you still there?*"

CHAPTER 24

The Afternoon Depression Zone

"Completely unwearable," Elizabeth said to Walter Pine as she emerged from KCTV's wardrobe room. "Every dress was skin-tight. When your tailor measured me last week, I thought he'd done an accurate job, but perhaps not. He's older. He might need reading glasses."

"Actually," Walter said, shoving his hands in his pockets in an effort to look casual, "the dresses are meant to be snug. Camera adds ten pounds, so we use tight clothing to take it off. Suck it in, slim it down. You won't believe how quickly you'll get used to it."

"I couldn't breathe."

"It's only for thirty minutes. You can breathe as much as you want after."

"With each inhale, our bodies initiate the blood purification process; with each exhale, our lungs release redundant carbon and hydrogen. By compressing any portion of the lungs, we put this process at risk. Clots form. Circulation drops."

"Here's the thing, though," said Walter, trying a different tactic. "I know you don't want to look fat."

"I beg your pardon?"

"On camera—and please don't take this the wrong way—you're a heifer."

Her jaw dropped. "Walter," she stated. "Let me make something very clear to you. I will not wear that clothing."

He clenched his teeth. Was this going to work? As he flailed around for some new way to reason with her, the TV station orchestra down the hall launched into a rehearsal of their latest little ditty. It was the *Supper at Six* theme song—a perky little tune he'd commissioned himself. A cross between a modern cha-cha-cha and a three-alarm fire, it was a toe-tapping tour de force that, just yesterday, his boss had enthusiastically described as Lawrence Welk on amphetamines.

"What on earth is *that?*" she said, gritting her teeth.

Phil Lebensmal, his boss and KCTV's executive producer and station manager, had been very clear when he'd approved the cooking show concept.

"You know what to do," he'd said after meeting Elizabeth Zott. "Big hair, tight dresses, homey set. The sexy-wife-loving-mother every man wants to see at the end of the day. Make it happen."

Walter looked at Phil across the expanse of Phil's ridiculously oversized desk. He didn't like Phil. He was young and successful and clearly better at everything than Walter, but he was also crass. Walter didn't like crass people. They made him feel prudish and self-conscious, as if he were the last remaining member of the Polite People, a now-extinct tribe best known for their decorum and good table manners. He passed his hand across his graying fifty-three-year-old head.

"Here's an interesting twist, Phil. Did I tell you that Mrs. Zott can cook? I mean, *really* cook. She's an actual chemist. Works in a lab with test tubes and things. Even has a master's in chemistry, if you can imagine that. I was thinking we could play up her credentials; give housewives someone to relate to."

"What?" Phil said, surprised. "No, Walter, Zott is not relatable, which is good. People don't want to see themselves on TV, they want to see the people they'll never be on TV. Pretty people, sexy people. You know how this works." He looked at Walter, perturbed.

"Of course, of course," Walter said, "it's just that I thought we might shake things up a bit. Give this show more of a professional feel."

"Professional? This is afternoon TV. You used to run a clown show in this same time slot."

"Yes, that's the unexpected part. Instead of clowns, we'll do something meaningful: Mrs. Zott will teach homemakers how to make a nutritious dinner."

"Meaningful?" Phil snapped. "What are you? Amish? As for nutritious: no. You're killing the show before it even gets started. Look, Walter, it's easy. Tight dresses, suggestive movements—maybe like the way she dons the potholders just so," he demonstrated, as if he were pulling on a pair of satin gloves. "And then there's the cocktail she mixes at the end of every show."

"Cocktail?"

"Isn't that a great idea? I just thought of it."

"I really don't think Mrs. Zott will go for—"

"By the way. What was that thing she said last week—about being unable to solidify helium at absolute zero. Was that supposed to be a joke?"

"Yes," he said. "I'm pretty sure it—"

"Well it wasn't funny."

Phil was right, it hadn't been funny, and worse, Elizabeth hadn't meant it to be funny. She had meant it to be one of the things she might talk about on her show. Which was a problem because no matter how often he explained the show's concept to her, she didn't seem to get it. "These are just normal housewives you'll be talking to," Walter told her. "Just your average Janes." Elizabeth had looked back in a way that scared him.

"There's nothing average about the average housewife," she corrected.

"Walter," Elizabeth was saying after the song had finally finished. "Are you listening? I think I can solve our wardrobe problem in two words. Lab coat."

"No."

"It would give the show a more professional feel."

"No," he said again, thinking of Lebensmal's very clear expectations. "Believe me. No."

"Why not approach this scientifically? I'll wear it for the first week, then we'll review the results."

"This isn't a lab," he explained for the billionth time. "This is a *kitchen*."

"Speaking of the kitchen, how's the set going?"

"It's not quite ready. We're still working on the lighting."

But that wasn't true: the set had been ready for days. From the eyelet curtains at the fake window to the various knickknacks that clogged the counters, it was the ultimate Good Housekeeping kitchen. She would hate it.

"Were you able to get the specialized instruments I need?" she asked. "The Bunsen burner? The oscilloscope?"

"About that," he said. "The thing is, most home cooks won't have that sort of thing. But I was able to round up nearly everything else on your list: utensils, the mixer—"

"Gas stove?"

"Yes."

"Eye wash station, of course."

"Y-yes," he said, thinking of the sink.

"I guess we can always add the Bunsen burner later. It's quite useful."

"I bet."

"What about the work surfaces?"

"The stainless steel you requested was unaffordable."

"Well that's odd," she said. "Nonreactive surfaces are usually quite inexpensive."

Walter nodded as if he were surprised too, but he wasn't. He'd picked out the Formica countertops himself: a fun-filled laminate flecked with shiny gold confetti.

"Look," he said. "I know our goal is about making food that matters—good-tasting, nutritious food. But we want to be careful not to alienate people. We have to make cooking look inviting. You know. Fun."

"Fun?"

"Because otherwise people won't watch us."

"But cooking isn't fun," she explained. "It's serious business."

"Right," he said. "But it could be a little fun, couldn't it?"

Elizabeth frowned. "Not really."

"Right," he said, "but maybe just a little fun. A smidge fun," he said, holding up his forefinger and squeezing it next to his thumb to show just how little. "The thing is, Elizabeth, and you probably already know this, TV is governed by three hard and fast rules."

"You mean rules of decency," she said. "Standards."

"Decency? Standards?" He thought of Lebensmal. "No. I meant actual rules." He used his fingers to count. "Rule one: entertain. Rule two: entertain. Rule three: entertain."

"But I'm not an entertainer. I'm a chemist."

"Right," he said, "but on TV, we need you to be an *entertaining* chemist. And do you know why? I can sum it up in one word. Afternoon."

"Afternoon."

"Afternoon. Just saying the word makes me sleepy. Does it make you sleepy?"

"No."

"Well, maybe that's because you're a scientist. You already know about circadian rhythms."

"Everyone knows about circadian rhythms, Walter. My four-year-old knows about circadian—"

"You mean your five-year-old," he interrupted. "Madeline has to be at least five to be in kindergarten."

Elizabeth waved her hand as if to move on. "You were saying about circadian rhythms."

"Right," he said, "As you well know, humans are biologically programmed to sleep twice a day—a siesta in the afternoon, then eight hours of sleep at night."

She nodded.

"Except most of us skip the siesta because our jobs demand it. And when I say most of us, I really just mean Americans. Mexico doesn't have this problem, nor does France or Italy or any of those other countries that drink even more than we do at lunch. Still, the fact remains: human productivity naturally drops in the afternoon. In TV, this is referred to as the Afternoon Depression Zone. Too late to get anything meaningful done; too early to go home. Doesn't matter if you're a homemaker, a fourth grader, a bricklayer, a businessman—no one is immune. Between the hours of one thirty-one and four forty-four p.m., productive life as we know it ceases to exist. It's a virtual death zone."

Elizabeth raised an eyebrow.

"And although I said it affects everyone," he continued, "it's an especially dangerous time for the homemaker. Because unlike a fourth grader who can put off her homework, or a businessman who can pretend to be listening, the homemaker must force herself to keep going. She has to get the kids down for a nap because if she doesn't, the evening will be hell. She has to mop the floor because if she doesn't, someone could slip on the spilled milk. She has to run to the store because if she doesn't, there will be nothing to eat. By the way," he said, pausing, "have you ever noticed how women always say they need to *run* to the store? Not walk, not go, not stop by. *Run*. That's what I mean. The homemaker is operating at an insane level of hyperproductivity. And even though she's in way over her head, she *still* has to make dinner. It's not sustainable, Elizabeth. She's going to have a heart attack or a stroke, or at the very least be in a foul mood. And it's all because she can't procrastinate like her fourth grader or pretend to be doing something like her husband. She's forced to be productive despite the fact that she's in a potentially fatal time zone—the Afternoon Depression Zone."

"It's classic neurogenic deprivation," Elizabeth said, nodding. "The brain doesn't get the rest it needs, resulting in a drop in executive function and accompanied by an increase in corticosterone levels. Fascinating. But what does this have to do with TV?"

"Everything," he said. "Because the cure for this neuro, uh, deprivation as you call it, is afternoon programming. Unlike morning or evening programming, afternoon programming is designed to let the brain rest. Study the lineup and you'll see it's true: from one thirty p.m. to five p.m., TV is stuffed with kid shows, soap operas, and game shows. Nothing that requires actual brain activity. And it's all by design: because TV executives recognize that between these hours, people are half dead."

Elizabeth envisioned her ex-colleagues at Hastings. They were half dead.

"In a way," Walter continued, "what we're offering is a public service. We're giving people—specifically the overworked housewife—the rest she needs. The children's shows are key here: they're designed to electronically babysit children so the mother has a chance to recuperate before her next act."

"And by act you mean—"

"Making dinner," he said, "which is where you come in. Your program will air at four thirty—exactly the time your audience will be emerging from the Afternoon Depression Zone. It's a tricky time slot. Studies show that most housewives feel the greatest amount of pressure at this time of day. They have much to accomplish in a very short window of time: make dinner, set the table, locate their children—the list is long. But they're still groggy and depressed. That is why this particular time slot comes with such great responsibility. Because whoever speaks to them now must *energize* them. That's why when I tell you that your job is to entertain, I mean it sincerely. You must bring these people back to life, Elizabeth. You must wake them back up."

"But—"

"Remember that day you stormed into my office? It was afternoon. And yet despite the fact that I was in the Afternoon Depression Zone, you woke me up, and I can assure you that is nearly statistically impossible because all I *do* is afternoon programming. But that's how I knew: if you had the power to make me sit up and listen, there is no doubt you can do the same for others. I believe in you, Elizabeth Zott, and I believe in your mission of food that matters—but that's *not* just making dinner. Understand this: you must make it look at least *a little* fun. If I wanted you to put viewers to sleep, I would have slotted you and your hot pads in at two thirty."

Elizabeth thought for a moment. "I guess I hadn't really thought of it that way."

"It's TV science," Walter said. "Hardly anyone knows about it."

She stood silently, weighing his words. "But I'm not entertaining," she said after a few moments. "I'm a scientist."

"Scientists can be entertaining."

"Name one."

"Einstein," Walter shot back. "Who doesn't love Einstein?"

Elizabeth considered his example. "Well. His theory of relativity is riveting."

"See? Exactly!"

"Although it's *also* true that his wife, who was *also* a physicist, was never given credit for—"

"There you go, nailing our audience again. Wives! And how would you wake up these Einsteinian wives? Using TV's time-tested waker-uppers: jokes, clothes, authority—and, of course, food. For instance, when you throw a dinner party, I bet everyone wants to come."

"I've never thrown a dinner party."

"Sure, you have," he said. "I bet you and Mr. Zott throw them all the—"

"There is no Mr. Zott, Walter," Elizabeth interrupted. "I'm unmarried. The truth is, I've never been married."

"Oh," Walter gasped, visibly taken aback. "Well. That is certainly interesting. But would you mind? I hope you won't take this the wrong way, but would you mind never mentioning that to anyone? Specifically to Lebensmal, my boss? Or really—anyone?"

"I loved Madeline's father," she explained, her brow slightly furrowed. "It's just that I couldn't marry him."

"It was an affair," Walter said sympathetically, dropping his voice. "He was stepping out on his wife. Was that it?"

"No," she said, shaking her head. "We loved each other completely. In fact, we'd been living together for—"

"That would be another great thing never to mention," Walter interrupted. "Never."

"—two years. We were soulmates."

"How nice," he said, clearing his throat. "I'm sure it's all in order. But still, that's not the sort of thing we need to tell anyone. Ever. Although I'm sure you had plans to marry him at some point."

"I didn't," she said quietly. "But more to the point, he died." And with those words, her face clouded with despair.

Walter was shocked by her sudden shift in character. She had a way about her—an authority that he knew the camera would love—but she was also fragile. Poor thing. Without thinking twice, he put his arms around her. "I'm deeply sorry," he said, pulling her in.

"So am I," she muffled into his shoulder. "So am I."

He flinched. Such loneliness. He patted her back as he did with Amanda, communicating, as best he could, that he wasn't just sorry for her loss but understood it. Had he ever been in love like that? No. But now he had a very good idea what it looked like.

"I apologize," she said, pulling away, surprised at how much she'd needed that hug.

"It's okay," he said gently. "You've been through a lot."

"Regardless," she said, straightening up, "I should know better than to speak of it. I've already been fired for it once."

For the third time that morning, Walter flinched. When she

said "it," he wasn't sure what she meant. Had she been fired for killing her lover? Or for being an unwed mother? Both explanations were plausible, but he far preferred the second one.

"I killed him," she admitted softly, eliminating his preference. "I insisted he use a leash and he died. Six-Thirty has never been the same."

"That's terrible," Walter said in an even lower voice, because even though he didn't understand what she'd said about the leash or the six thirty time zone, he understood what she'd meant. She'd made a choice and it had ended badly. He'd done the very same thing. And both of their bad choices resulted in small people who now bore the brunt of their parents' poor choices. "I'm so very sorry."

"I'm sorry for you, too," she said, trying to regain her composure. "Your divorce."

"Oh, don't be," he said, waving his hand, embarrassed that his lurch at love could be compared in any way to hers. "It wasn't like your situation. Mine didn't have anything to do with love. Amanda isn't even technically mine in the DNA sense of things," he blurted without meaning to. In fact, he'd only just found out three weeks ago.

His ex-wife had long insinuated that he wasn't Amanda's biological father, but he'd figured she'd only said it to hurt him. Sure, he and Amanda didn't look alike, but plenty of children don't look like their parents. Every time he held Amanda in his arms, he knew she was his; he could sense the deep, permanent biological connection. But his ex-wife's cruel insistence ate at him, and when paternity testing finally became available, he produced a blood sample. Five days later, he knew the truth. He and Amanda were total strangers.

He'd stared at the test results, expecting to feel cheated or devastated or any of the other ways he'd guessed he was supposed to feel, but instead he'd felt completely nonplussed. The results didn't matter at all. Amanda was his daughter and he was her father. He loved her with all his heart. Biology was overrated.

"I'd never planned to be a parent," he told Elizabeth. "But here I am, a devoted father. Life's a mystery, isn't it? People who try and plan it inevitably end up disappointed."

She nodded. She was a planner. She was disappointed.

"Anyway," he continued. "I believe we can make something with *Supper at Six*. But there are some things about TV that you're just going to, well, have to put up with. In terms of the wardrobe, I'll tell the tailor to ease the seams. But in quid pro quo, I'd like you to practice smiling."

She frowned.

"Jack LaLanne smiles when he's doing push-ups," Walter said. "That's the way he makes hard things look fun. Study Jack's style—he's a master."

At the mention of Jack's name, Elizabeth tensed. She hadn't watched Jack LaLanne since Calvin died, and that was partly because she blamed him—yes, she knew it wasn't fair—for Calvin's death. The memory of Calvin coming into the kitchen after Jack's show filled her with a sudden warmth.

"There you go," Walter said.

Elizabeth glanced up at him.

"You were almost smiling."

"Oh," she said. "Well, it was unintentional."

"That's fine. Intentional, nonintentional. Anything will do. Most of mine are forced. Including those at Woody Elementary School, where I'm headed next. I've been summoned by Mrs. Mudford."

"I have too," Elizabeth said, surprised. "I have a conference tomorrow. Does yours concern Amanda's reading list?"

"Reading?" he said, surprised. "They're kindergartners, Elizabeth; they can't read. Anyway, the issue isn't Amanda. It's me. She's suspicious of me because I'm a father raising a daughter alone."

"Why?"

He looked surprised. "Why do you think?"

"*Oh,*" she said, with sudden understanding. "She believes you're sexually deviant."

"I wouldn't have put it so, so . . . blatantly," Walter said, "but yes. It's like wearing a badge that says 'Hello! I'm a pedophile—and I babysit!'"

"I guess we're both suspect, then," Elizabeth said. "Calvin and I had sex nearly every day—completely normal for our youth and activity level—but because we weren't married . . ."

"Ah," Walter said, paling. "Well—"

"As if marriage has anything to do with sexuality—"

"Ah—"

"There were times," she explained matter-of-factly, "that I would wake up in the middle of the night filled with desire—I'm sure that's happened to you—but Calvin was in the middle of a REM cycle, so I didn't disturb him. But then I mentioned it later and he was practically apoplectic. 'No, Elizabeth,' he said, 'always wake me up. REM cycle or no REM cycle. Do not hesitate.' It wasn't until I did more reading on testosterone that I better understood the male sex drive—"

"Speaking of drive," Walter interrupted, his face scarlet. "I wanted to remind you to park in the north lot."

"The north lot," she said, her hands on her hips. "That's the one off to the left as I pull in?"

"Exactly."

"Anyway," she continued. "I'm sorry that Mudford has implied you're anything other than a loving father. I very much doubt she's read the Kinsey Reports."

"The Kinsey—"

"Because if she had, she'd actually understand that you and I are the opposite of sexual deviants. You and I are—"

"*Normal* parents?" he rushed.

"Loving role models."

"Guardians."

"Kin," she finished.

It was that last word that cemented their odd, tell-all friend-ship, the kind that only arises when a wronged person meets someone who has been similarly wronged and discovers that while it may be the only thing they share, it is more than enough.

"Look," Walter said, marveling that he'd never had such a frank discussion about sex or biology with anyone, including him-self. "About the wardrobe. If the tailor can't make those dresses more breathable, choose something from your closet for now."

"You won't consider the lab coat idea."

"It's more that I want you to be *you,*" he said. "Not a scientist."

She tucked a few stray hairs behind her ears. "But I *am* a sci-entist," she argued. "It's who I am."

"That may be, Elizabeth Zott," he said, not knowing how true this would turn out to be. "But it's only a start."

CHAPTER 25

The Average Jane

In retrospect, he probably should have let her see the set.

As the music started to play—that charming little ditty Walter had paid far too much for and that she already hated—Elizabeth strode out on the stage. He took a short, sharp breath in. She was wearing a drab dress featuring small buttons that ran all the way down to the hem, a stark white multipocketed apron cinched tightly at the waist, and a Timex wristwatch that ticked so loudly, he swore he could hear it over the band's drumbeat. On her head sat a pair of goggles. Just over her left ear, a number-two pencil. In one hand she carried a notebook; in the other, three test tubes. She looked like a cross between a hotel maid and a bomb squad expert.

He watched as she waited for the song to finish, her eyes traveling around the set from one corner to another, lips pressed together, and shoulders tensed in a way that signaled dissatisfaction. As the last note played, she turned toward the cue card, scanned it, then turned away. Setting her notebook and test tubes on the counter, she walked to the sink, her back to the camera, and leaned into the fake window to take in the fake view.

"This is revolting," she said directly into the microphone.

The cameraman turned to look at Walter, his eyes wide.

"Remind her we're live," Walter hissed at him.

LIVE!!! the cameraman's assistant hastily scribbled on a large board, holding it up for her to see.

Elizabeth read the reminder, and then holding up one finger as if to signal that this would only take another second, continued her self-guided tour, stopping to take in the kitchen's carefully curated wall art—a Bless This House needlepoint, a depressed Jesus kneeling in prayer, an amateur painting of ships sailing on a sea—before moving on to crowded countertops, her brows arching in dismay at a sewing basket riddled with safety pins, a Mason jar filled with unwanted buttons, a ball of brown yarn, a chipped candy dish filled with peppermints, and a bread box across which *Our Daily Bread* was scrawled in religious script.

Just yesterday, Walter had given the set designer an A+ for his taste. "I especially love the knickknacks," he'd told him. "They're just right." But today, next to her, they looked like junk. He watched as she paced to the other side of the counter, visibly blanching at the sight of hen and rooster salt and pepper shakers, hostilely eyeing the toaster's knitted pink cozy, recoiling from a strange little ball made entirely of rubber bands. To the left of the ball was a cookie jar molded to look like a fat German woman making pretzels. She stopped abruptly, looking above her head at the large clock hanging on wires, its hands permanently fixed in the six o'clock position. SUPPER AT SIX was printed across its face in glittery type.

"Walter," Elizabeth said, shielding her eyes as she looked out past the bright lights. "Walter, a word, please."

"Commercial, commercial!" Walter hissed to the cameraman as she started to pick her way off the set down to where he was sitting. "Do it now! *Now!*"

"Elizabeth," he said, launching himself out of his chair toward her. "You can't do this! Get back up there! We're live!"

"We are? Well, we can't be. The set doesn't work."

"Everything works, the stove, the sink, it's all been tested, now get back up there," he said, shooing her back with his hands.

"I meant it doesn't work for *me.*"

"Look," he said. "You're nervous. That's why we're taping without a live audience today—to give you a chance to settle in. But you're still *on*—as in *on the air*—and you have a job to do. This is our pilot; things can be tweaked later."

"So, you're saying changes *are* possible," she said, putting her hands back on her hips as she surveyed the set again. "We'll need to make a lot of changes."

"Okay, wait, no," he said, worried. "To be clear, set changes are not possible. What you see represents weeks of solid research by our set designer. This kitchen is exactly what today's woman wants."

"Well I'm a woman, and I don't want this."

"I didn't mean you," Walter said. "I meant the average Jane."

"Average."

"You know what I mean. The normal housewife."

She made a sound like a whale spouting.

"Okay," Walter said in a lower voice, his hand waving fruitlessly at his side. "Okay, okay, look, I understand, but remember, this isn't just *our* show, Elizabeth, it's also the station's show, and since they pay us, it's usually considered good form to do what they ask. You know how this works; you've had a job before."

"But ultimately," she argued, "it's the audience for whom we all work."

"Right," he pleaded. "Sort of. No wait—not really. It's our job to give people what they want even if they don't know they want it. I explained this: it's the afternoon programming model. Half dead, now awake, *you know!*"

"Another ad?" the cameraman whispered.

"Unnecessary," she said quickly. "Sorry everyone. I'm ready now."

"We *are* on the same page, aren't we?" Walter called as she made her way back onstage.

"Yes," Elizabeth said. "You want me to speak to the *average* Jane. The *normal* housewife."

He didn't like the way she said it.

"In five—" the cameraman said.
"Elizabeth," he warned.
"Four—"
"It's all written out for you."
"Three—"
"Just read the cue cards."
"Two—"
"Please," he begged. *"It's a great script!"*
"One . . . and action!"

"Hello," Elizabeth said directly into the camera. "My name is Elizabeth Zott and this is *Supper at Six*."

"So far so good," Walter whispered to himself. *SMILE,* he mimed at her, pulling at the corners of his mouth.

"And welcome to my kitchen," she said sternly as a disappointed Jesus peered over her left shoulder. "Today we're going to have so much—"

She stopped when she got to the word "fun."

An uncomfortable silence followed. The cameraman turned to look at Walter. "Go to commercial again?" he motioned.

"NO," Walter mouthed. "NO! GODDAMMIT. SHE HAS TO DO THIS! GODDAMMIT ELIZABETH," he continued soundlessly as he waved his hands.

But Elizabeth seemed to be in a trance and nothing—not Walter waving his hands, or the cameraman preparing for commercial, or the makeup person mopping her own face with the sponge reserved for Elizabeth's—could break her spell. What was *wrong* with her?

"MUSIC," Walter finally mouthed to the soundman. *"MUSIC."*

But before the music could start, Elizabeth's ticking watch caught her attention and she came back to life. "I'm sorry," she said. "Now, where were we?" She glanced at the cue cards, paused a moment more, and then suddenly pointed at the large clock above her head. "Before I get started, I'd like to advise you to please ignore the clock. It doesn't work."

From the producer's chair, Walter let out a short, sharp exhale.

"I take cooking seriously," Elizabeth continued, completely ignoring the cue cards, "and I know you do, too." Then she pushed the sewing basket off the countertop and into an open drawer. "I also know," she said, looking directly into the few households that had accidentally tuned her in that day, "that your time is precious. Well, so is mine. So let's make a pact, you and I—"

"Mom," a little boy called in a bored way from the TV room in Van Nuys, California, "there's *nothing* on."

"Shut it off, then," the little boy's mother yelled from the kitchen. "I'm busy! Play outside—"

"*Mmoomm . . . Mmoomm . . . ,*" the little boy called again.

"Oh, for heaven's *sake,* Petey," a harried woman said coming into the room, her wet hands holding a half-peeled potato, the baby crying in the high chair in the kitchen, "do I have to do everything for you?" But as she reached to turn Elizabeth off, Elizabeth spoke to her.

"It is my experience that far too many people do not appreciate the work and sacrifice that goes into being a wife, a mother, a woman. Well, I am not one of them. At the end of our thirty minutes together, we *will* have done something worth doing. We *will* have created something that will not go unnoticed. We *will* have made supper. And it *will* matter."

"What's this?" Petey's mother said.

"Dunno," said Petey.

"Now, let's get started," Elizabeth said.

Later, in her dressing room, Rosa, the hairdresser and makeup woman, stopped by to say goodbye. "For the record, I liked the hair pencil."

"For the record?"

"Lebensmal's been screaming at Walter for the last twenty minutes."

"Because of a pencil?"

"Because you didn't follow the script."

"Well, yes. But only because the cue cards were unreadable."

"Oh," Rosa said, visibly relieved. "That was it? The type wasn't big enough?"

"No, no," Elizabeth said. "I meant the cards were misleading."

"Elizabeth," Walter said, appearing at her dressing room door, his face red.

"Anyway," she whispered, "goodbye forever." She gave Elizabeth's arm a little squeeze.

"Hello, Walter," Elizabeth said. "I was just making up a list of a few things we'll need to change right away."

"Don't hello me," he shot back. "What the hell is wrong with you?"

"Why there's nothing wrong with me. I actually thought it went rather well. I admit I stumbled at the beginning, but only because I was in shock. It won't happen again, not after we fix the set."

He stomped across the room and threw himself into a chair. "Elizabeth," he said. "This is a *job*. You have two duties: to smile and read cue cards. That's it. You don't get to have an opinion about the set or the cards."

"I think I do."

"No!"

"Anyway, I couldn't read the cards."

"Nonsense," he said. "We practiced different type sizes, remember? So I *know* you can read the damn cards. Jesus, Elizabeth, Lebensmal's ready to cancel the whole thing. Do you realize you've put both of our jobs in jeopardy?"

"I'm sorry. I'll go speak with him right now."

"Oh no," Walter said quickly. "Not you."

"Why?" she said. "I want to clarify a few things, especially about the set. And as for the cue cards—again, I'm sorry, Walter. I didn't mean I *couldn't* read them; I meant my conscience wouldn't *let* me read them. Because they were awful. Who wrote the script?"

He pursed his lips. "I did."

"Oh," she said, startled. "But those words. They didn't sound like me at all."

"Yes," he said through gritted teeth. "That was *intentional*."

She looked surprised. "I thought you told me to be *me*."

"Not *that* you," he said. "Not the 'this is going to be really, really complicated' you. Not the 'far too many people do not appreciate the work and sacrifice that goes into being a wife, a mother, a woman' you. No one wants to hear that stuff, Elizabeth. You have to be positive, happy, upbeat!"

"But that's not me."

"But it could be you."

Elizabeth reviewed her life to date. "Not a chance."

"Could we *not* argue about this," Walter said, his heart pounding uncomfortably in his chest. "I'm the afternoon programming expert and I've already explained how this all works."

"And I'm the woman," she snapped, "speaking to an all-woman audience."

A secretary appeared in the doorway. "Mr. Pine," she said. "We're getting calls about the show. I'm not sure what to do."

"Jesus mother of god," he said. "Complaints already."

"It's about the shopping list. Some confusion about tomorrow's ingredients. Specifically, CH_3COOH."

"Acetic acid," Elizabeth supplied. "Vinegar—it's four percent acetic acid. I'm sorry—I probably should have written the list in layman's terms."

"You *think*?" Walter said.

"Thanks much," the secretary said, disappearing.

"Where'd the shopping list idea come from anyway?" he demanded. "We never discussed a shopping list—especially not one written in chemical form."

"I know," she said, "it came to me as I was about to walk out on set. I think it's a good idea, don't you?"

Walter sank his head into his hands. It *was* a good idea; he just wasn't willing to admit it. "You can't do this," he said in a muffled voice. "You can't do whatever the hell you want."

"I'm not doing whatever the hell I want," Elizabeth nipped. "If I was doing whatever the hell I wanted, I'd be in a research lab. Look," she said. "If I'm not mistaken, you're experiencing a rise in corticosterone levels—what you call the Afternoon Depression Zone. You should probably eat something."

"Do not," he said stiffly, "lecture *me* on the Afternoon Depression Zone."

For the next few minutes, the two of them sat in the dressing room, one looking at the floor, the other looking at the wall. Not a word passed between them.

"Mr. Pine?" A different secretary poked her head in. "Mr. Lebensmal has a flight to catch, but he wanted me to remind you that you've got the rest of the week to fix 'it.' I'm sorry—I don't know what 'it' is. Says you better make 'it' "—she consulted her notes again—" 'sexy.' " Then she turned pink. "Also, there's this." She handed him a hand-scrawled note Lebensmal had dashed off. *And what about the fucking cocktail?*

"Thanks," Walter said.

"Sorry," she said.

"Mr. Pine," the first secretary said, appearing as the other was leaving. "It's late—I need to go home. But the phones . . ."

"Go on, Paula," he said. "I'll handle it."

"Can I help?" Elizabeth asked.

"You've helped plenty enough today," Walter said. "So, when I say, 'No thank you,' I actually mean *no thank you*."

Then he went out to the secretary's desk, Elizabeth trailing behind, and picked up a phone. "KCTV," he said wearily. "Yeah. Sorry. It's vinegar."

"Vinegar," Elizabeth said into another line.

"Vinegar."
"Vinegar."
"Vinegar."
"Vinegar."

He'd never gotten a single call on the clown show.

CHAPTER 26

The Funeral

"Hello, my name is Elizabeth Zott, and this is *Supper at Six*."

From the producer's chair, Walter squeezed his eyes shut. "Please," he whispered. "Please, please, please." It was the fifteenth day of broadcasting and he was exhausted. Over and over again he'd explained that just as he didn't get to choose the desk he sat behind, neither did she get to choose the kitchen she cooked in. It was nothing personal; sets, like desks, were selected based on research and budgets. But every time he'd made this argument, she'd nod her head as if she understood and then say, "Yes—*but*." And then they'd start all over again. Same with the script. He told her that her job was to *engage* the audience, not bore them. But with all her tiresome chemical asides, she was *so* boring. That's why he'd decided it was finally time to add the live audience. Because he knew real people sitting just twenty feet away would instantly teach her the peril of being dull.

"Welcome to our first live audience show," Elizabeth said.

So far so good.

"Every afternoon, Monday through Friday, we'll make dinner together."

Exactly what he had written.

"Starting with tonight's supper: spinach casserole."

Bronco busted. She was following orders.

"But first we need to clean up our work space." His eyes flew open as she picked up the ball of brown yarn and tossed it into the audience.

No, no, he begged silently. The cameraman glanced back at him as the audience erupted in nervous laughter.

"Anyone need some rubber bands?" she asked, holding up the rubber band ball. Several hands went up, so she tossed that into the audience as well.

Dumbstruck, he gripped the arms of his canvas folding chair.

"I like having room to work," she said. "It reinforces the idea that the work you and I are about to do is important. And today I have a lot to do and could use some help getting even more room. Could anyone use a cookie jar?"

To Walter's horror, almost all the hands went up, and before he knew it, people were milling about the set as Elizabeth encouraged them to take whatever they wanted. In less than a minute, every single item was gone—even the wall art. The only thing that remained was the fake window and the large clock.

"Okay," she said in a serious tone as the audience returned to their seats. "Now let's get started."

Walter cleared his throat. One of the first rules of television, other than to entertain, is to pretend that no matter what happens, it was all part of the plan. This is what TV hosts are trained to do, and this is what Walter, who had never been a host, decided in that moment to try. He sat up in his canvas chair and leaned forward as if he'd orchestrated this total breach of TV conduct himself. But, of course, he hadn't, and everyone knew he hadn't, and they all registered his impotence in their specific ways: the cameraman shook his head, the sound guy sighed, the set designer gave Walter the finger from stage right. Meanwhile, Elizabeth was up onstage hacking at a huge pile of spinach with the biggest knife he'd ever seen.

Lebensmal was going to kill him.

He closed his eyes for a few moments, listening to the stirrings from the studio audience: the seat shifting, the small coughs. From off in the distance, he heard Elizabeth talking about the role potassium and magnesium play in the body. The cue card he'd written for this particular segment had been among his favorites: *Isn't spinach a nice color? Green. It reminds me of springtime.* She'd skipped right over it.

". . . many believe spinach makes us strong because it contains almost as much iron as meat. But the truth is, spinach is high in oxalic acid, which inhibits iron absorption. So when Popeye implies he's getting strong from spinach, don't believe him."

Fantastic. Now she was calling Popeye a liar.

"Still, spinach offers plenty of nutritive value and we'll be talking about that and more," she said, brandishing her knife into the camera, "just after this station break."

Jesus Fucking Christ. He didn't bother to get up.

"Walter," she said at his elbow mere moments later. "What did you think? I took your advice. I engaged the audience."

He turned to look at her, his face wooden.

"It was exactly like you've been saying: *entertain.* Knowing I needed more counter space, I thought of baseball—the way the vendors throw the peanuts at the crowd? And it worked."

"Yes," he said flatly. "And then you invited everyone to help themselves to the home plate, and the bats, and the gloves, and whatever else they could find lying around."

She looked surprised. "You sound mad."

"Thirty seconds, Mrs. Zott," the cameraman said.

"No, no," he said calmly. "I'm not mad. I'm *furious.*"

"But you said to entertain."

"No. What you did was you took things that didn't belong to you and then you gave them away."

"But I *needed* the space."

"On Monday prepare to die," he said. "First me, then you."

She turned away.

"I'm back," he heard her say in an irritated voice as the audience clapped its approval. Thankfully, he heard very little after that, but that was only because his stomach hurt and his heart was pinging about his chest in a way that he hoped indicated something very serious. He closed his eyes to hasten his death—stroke or heart attack, he'd take either one.

He looked up to see Elizabeth waving her arm around the empty kitchen. "Cooking is chemistry," she was saying. "And chemistry is life. Your ability to change everything—including yourself—starts here."

Good god.

His secretary bent down and whispered something about Lebensmal wanting to see him first thing in the morning. He closed his eyes again. *Relax,* he told himself. *Breathe.*

From behind his eyelids, he saw something he did not care to see. It was him at a funeral—*his* funeral—and lots of people in colorful clothing were milling about. He overheard someone—his secretary?—telling the story of how he died. It was a boring story and he didn't like it, but it fit his afternoon programming profile. He listened carefully, hoping to hear news of his life mixed with compliments, but mostly people said things like, "So, what are you doing this weekend?"

From off in the distance, he heard Elizabeth Zott talking about the importance of work. She was sermonizing again, filling the funeralgoers' heads with ideas of self-respect. "Take risks," she was saying. "Don't be afraid to experiment."

Don't be like Walter, she meant.

Weren't people supposed to wear black to funerals?

"Fearlessness in the kitchen translates to fearlessness in life," Zott claimed.

Who'd asked her to give his eulogy anyway? Phil? Rude. And rich considering that the only risk he, Walter Pine, had ever taken—hiring her—was turning out to be the reason for his premature death. Take-risks-don't-be-afraid-to-experiment *my ass,* Zott. Who was dead here?

He continued to hear her voice in the background accompanied by the insistent thwack of a knife. Then after another ten minutes or so came her closing remarks.

"Children, set the table. Your mother needs a moment to herself."

In other words, enough about dead Walter—back to *me*.

The mourners clapped enthusiastically. Time to hit the bar.

There wasn't much after that. Unfortunately, his imagined death was a lot like his life. It occurred to him that "bored to death" might not just be a phrase.

"Mr. Pine?"

"Walter?"

He felt a hand touch his shoulder. "Should I call a doctor?" the first voice asked.

"Maybe," the other voice said.

He opened his eyes to find Zott and Rosa standing next to him.

"We think you may have fainted," Zott said.

"You were slumped over," Rosa added.

"Your pulse is elevated," Elizabeth said, her fingers on his wrist.

"Should I call a doctor?" Rosa asked again.

"Walter, have you eaten? When was the last time you ate?"

"I'm *fine,*" Walter said hoarsely. "Go away." But he didn't feel very good.

"He didn't eat lunch," Rosa said. "Took nothing from the cart. And we know he hasn't had dinner."

"Walter," Elizabeth said, taking charge. "Take this home." She placed a large baking dish in his hands. "It's the spinach casserole I just made. Put it in the oven at three hundred seventy-five degrees for forty minutes. Can you do that?"

"No," he said, sitting up. "I can't. And anyway, Amanda hates spinach, so again, NO." And then realizing he sounded like a petulant child, he turned to the hair and makeup woman (what was her name?) and said, "I'm so sorry to have worried you"—slurring a mixture of possible first names—"but I'm completely fine. You have a nice night, now."

To prove how fine he was, he got up from his chair and walked unsteadily to his office, waiting until he was sure they'd both left the building before he left himself. But when he got to the parking lot, he found the casserole sitting on the hood of his car. *Bake at 375 degrees for forty minutes,* the note said.

When he got home, and only because he was tired, he stuck the damn thing in the oven, and not too long after that, sat down to dinner with his young daughter.

Three bites later, Amanda declared it to be the best thing she'd ever eaten.

CHAPTER 27

All About Me

MAY 1960

"Boys and girls," Mrs. Mudford said the following spring, "we're going to start a new project. It's called All About Me."

Mad took a sharp breath in.

"Please ask your mother to fill this out. It's called a family tree. What she writes on this tree will help you learn about a very important person. Who knows who that person might be? Hint: the answer is in the *title* of our new project, All About Me."

The children sat in a sloppy semicircle at Mrs. Mudford's feet, chins cupped in hands.

"Who wants to guess first," Mudford prodded. "Yes, Tommy," she said.

"Can I go to the bathroom?"

"*May* I, Tommy, and no. School is almost over. You may go in a little bit."

"The president," said Lena.

"*Could it be* the president?" corrected Mrs. Mudford. "And no, that's wrong, Lena."

"Could it be Lassie?" said Amanda.

"No, Amanda. This is a family tree, not a doghouse. We're talking about *people*."

"People are animals," said Madeline.

"No, they aren't, Madeline," Mrs. Mudford huffed. "People are humans."

"What about Yogi Bear?" asked another.

"*Could it be* Yogi Bear?" Mrs. Mudford said irritably. "And of course not. A family tree is not filled with bears, and it is definitely not about TV shows. We're people!"

"But people are animals," Madeline persisted.

"Madeline," Mrs. Mudford said sharply. "That's enough!"

"We're animals?" Tommy said to Madeline, his eyes wide.

"NO! WE ARE NOT!" shouted Mrs. Mudford.

But Tommy had already stuck his fingers into his armpits and started jumping about the classroom yowling like a chimpanzee. "E E!" he called to the other kindergartners, half of whom instantly joined in. "E E O O! E E O O!"

"STOP IT, TOMMY," Mrs. Mudford shouted. "STOP IT ALL OF YOU! UNLESS YOU WANT TO GO TO THE PRINCIPAL'S OFFICE, STOP IT RIGHT NOW!" And the harshness of her voice combined with the threat of a higher authority sent the children back to their positions on the floor. "NOW," she said tersely, "as I was saying, you're going to learn some new things about a very important person. A PERSON," she emphasized, glaring at Madeline. "Now who might this PERSON be?"

No one moved.

"*WHO?*" she commanded.

A few heads shook.

"Well, it's YOU, children," she shouted angrily.

"What? Why?" asked Judy, slightly alarmed. "What did I do wrong?"

"Don't be dense, Judy," Mrs. Mudford said. "For heaven's sake!"

"My mom says she's not giving the school another cent," said a crusty-looking boy named Roger.

"Who said anything about money, Roger!" Mrs. Mudford shrieked.

"Can I see the tree?" asked Madeline.

"*May* I," thundered Mrs. Mudford.

"May I?" asked Madeline.

"NO, YOU MAY NOT," Mrs. Mudford screeched, folding the paper into quarters, as if the mere act of folding would make it Madeline-proof. "This tree is not for *you*, Madeline; it is for your *mother*. Now children," she said, trying to find her way back to control, "organize yourselves into a single-file line. I will pin the paper to your shirts. Then it will be time to go home."

"My mom wants you to stop pinning stuff on me," said Judy. "Says you're making holes in my clothes."

Your mother is a lying whore, Mrs. Mudford wanted to say, but instead she said, "That's fine, Judy. We'll staple yours on instead."

One by one, the children allowed Mrs. Mudford to affix the note to their sweaters and then filed out the door, where, just past the doorjamb, they instantly gained speed like small ponies that had been tethered for hours.

"Not *you*, Madeline," she said. "You stay here."

"Let me get this straight," Harriet said as Mad revealed why she was late. "You had to stay behind because you told your teacher that people are animals? Why did you say such a thing, honey? It's not very nice."

"It isn't?" Madeline said, confused. "But why? We *are* animals."

Harriet wondered to herself if Mad was right—*were* people animals? She wasn't sure. "My point is," she said, "it's sometimes better not to argue. Your teacher deserves your respect and sometimes that means agreeing with her even when you don't. That's how diplomacy works."

"I thought diplomacy meant being nice."

"That's what I mean."

"Even if she's telling us wrong stuff."

"Yes."

Madeline chewed her lower lip.

"You make mistakes sometimes, don't you? And you wouldn't

want someone to correct you in front of a lot of people, would you? Mrs. Mudford was probably just embarrassed."

"She didn't look embarrassed. And this isn't the first time she's given us bad information. Last week she said God created the earth."

"Many people believe that," Harriet said. "There's nothing wrong with believing that."

"You believe that?"

"Why don't we take a look at this note," she said quickly, unpinning the paper from Madeline's sweater.

"It's a family tree project," Madeline said, clunking her lunch box on the counter. "Mom has to fill it in."

"I don't like these things," Harriet muttered as she studied the badly drawn oak, its branches demanding names of relatives— living, lost, dead—one related to the other by marriage, birth, or bad luck. "Nosy little sapsucker. Did it come with a subpoena, too?"

"Should it have?" Madeline asked, awed.

"You know what I think?" Harriet said, folding the note back up. "I think these trees are a poor attempt to feel like you're some-body based on somebody else. Usually comes with an invasion of privacy. Your mother is going to hit the roof. If I were you, I wouldn't show this to her."

"But I don't know any of the answers. I don't know anything about my dad." She thought about the note her mother had left in her lunch box that morning. *The librarian is the most important educator in school. What she doesn't know, she can find out. This is not an opinion; it's a fact. Do not share this fact with Mrs. Mudford.*

But when Madeline had asked her school's librarian if she could point her toward some yearbooks from Cambridge, the librarian frowned, then handed her last month's copy of *Highlights* magazine.

"You know plenty about your father," Harriet said. "For in-stance, you know that your father's parents—your grandparents—

were killed by a train when he was young. And that he went to live with his aunt until she hit a tree. And then he went to live in a boys home—I forget the name but it sounded girlish. And that your father had a godmother of sorts, although godmothers aren't family tree material."

As soon as she'd mentioned the godmother, Harriet wished she'd hadn't. She only knew about the godmother because she was a snoop, and even then, it was obvious she hadn't been a real god-mother, but more of a fairy godmother. And she knew all this because one day, long before he'd even met Elizabeth, Calvin had left for work in a hurry, leaving his front door open, and Harriet, being a good neighbor, had gone over to shut it.

Naturally, because she was the kind of person who always went above and beyond, she'd gone inside to make sure the home hadn't been burglarized. A comprehensive self-guided tour told her that absolutely nothing had happened in the forty-six seconds that had elapsed since Calvin's departure.

Once inside, though, she discovered several things. One, Calvin Evans was some sort of big-deal scientist—he'd been on the cover of a magazine. Two, he was a slob. Three, he'd grown up in Sioux City in a seedy-sounding boys home with religious overtones. She only knew about the boys home because she'd seen a piece of paper wadded up in his trash—a piece of paper that she retrieved because who doesn't, on occasion, accidentally throw away the very thing they actually mean to keep? According to the letter, the home needed money. They'd lost their main donor—someone who'd once ensured the boys were given "sci-entific educational opportunities and healthy outdoor activities." The home was now reaching out to past residents. Could Calvin Evans help? *Say yes! Donate to the All Saints Boys Home today!* His response was in the trash can, too. Basically, it said how dare you, fuck you, you should all be in jail.

"What's a godmother?" Madeline asked.

"A close friend of the family or a relative," Harriet said, pushing the memory away. "Someone who's supposed to look after your spiritual life."

"Do I have one?"

"A godmother?"

"A spiritual life."

"Oh," Harriet said. "I don't know. Do you believe in things you can't see?"

"I like magic tricks."

"I don't," said Harriet. "I don't like being fooled."

"But you believe in God."

"Well. Yes."

"Why?"

"I just do. Most people do."

"My mom doesn't."

"I know," Harriet said, trying to hide her disapproval.

Harriet thought it was wrong not to believe in God. It lacked humility. In her opinion, believing in God was required, like brushing teeth or wearing underwear. Certainly, all decent people believed in God—even indecent people, like her husband, believed in God. God is why they were still married and why their marriage was her burden to bear—because it was given to her by God. God was big on burdens, and He made sure everyone got one. Besides, if you didn't believe in God, you also didn't get to believe in heaven or hell, and she very much wanted to believe in hell because she very much wanted to believe that Mr. Sloane was going there. She stood up. "Where's your rope? I think it's time to work on your knots."

"I know them all already," Mad said.

"Can you do them with your eyes closed?"

"Yes."

"But what about behind your back? Can you do that?"

"Yes."

Harriet pretended to be supportive of Mad's odd hobbies, but the truth was, she wasn't. The child didn't like Barbies or playing jacks—she liked knots, books on war, natural disasters. Yesterday she'd overheard Madeline quizzing the downtown librarian about Krakatoa—when did she think it might next erupt? How would they warn the residents? Approximately how many people would die?

Harriet turned to watch as Madeline stared at the family tree, her large gray eyes taking in the empty branches, her teeth gnawing steadily at the bottom of her lip. Calvin had been a big lip chewer. Could that sort of thing be passed down genetically? She wasn't sure. Harriet had produced four children, each one completely different from the others and wholly different from herself. And now? They were all strangers, each living in a far-off city with lives and children of their own. She wanted to think there was some iron-clad bond that connected her to them for life, but that's not how it worked. Families required constant maintenance.

"Are you hungry?" Harriet asked. "Would you like some cheese?" She reached to the back of the refrigerator as Madeline withdrew a book from her schoolbag. *Five Years with the Congo Cannibals.*

Harriet looked back over her shoulder. "Sweetie, does your teacher know you're reading that?"

"No."

"Keep it that way."

This was another area where she and Elizabeth still did not see eye to eye: reading. Fifteen months ago, Harriet assumed Madeline was just pretending she could read. Children love to imitate their parents. But it was soon obvious that Elizabeth had not only taught Madeline to read but to read highly complex things: newspapers, novels, *Popular Mechanics.*

Harriet considered the possibility that the child was a genius.

Her father had been. But no. It was just that Mad was well taught and that was because of Elizabeth. Elizabeth simply refused to accept limits, not just for herself, but for others. About a year after Mr. Evans had died, Harriet had run across some notes on Elizabeth's desk that appeared to suggest she was trying to teach Six-Thirty a ridiculous number of words. At the time, Harriet chalked it up to temporary insanity—that's what grief is. But then, when Mad was three, she had asked if anyone had seen her yo-yo, and a minute later Six-Thirty dropped it in her lap.

Supper at Six had that same element of impossibility. Elizabeth opened every show by insisting that cooking wasn't easy and that the next thirty minutes might very well be torturous.

"Cooking is not an exact science," Elizabeth had said just yesterday. "The tomato I hold in my hand is different from the one you hold in yours. That's why you must involve yourself with your ingredients. Experiment: taste, touch, smell, look, listen, test, assess." Then she led her viewers through an elaborate description of chemical breakdowns, which, when induced by combining disparate ingredients in heat-specific ways, would result in a complicated mix of enzymatic interactions that would lead to something good to eat. There was a lot of talk about acids and bases and hydrogen ions, some of which, after weeks of hearing it, Harriet was, oddly, beginning to understand.

Throughout the process, Elizabeth, her face serious, told her viewers that they were up for this difficult challenge, that she knew they were capable, resourceful people, and that she believed in them. It was a very strange show. Not exactly entertaining. More like climbing a mountain. Something you felt good about, but only after it was over.

Nevertheless, she and Madeline watched *Supper at Six* together every day, holding their breath, certain each new episode would be the last.

Madeline had opened her book and was now studying an engraving of one man gnawing on the femur of another. "Do people taste good?"

"I don't know," Harriet said as she set a few cubes of cheese down in front of her. "I'm sure it's all in the preparation. Your mother could probably make anyone taste good." *Except for Mr. Sloane,* she thought. *Because he was rotten.*

Madeline nodded her head. "Everybody likes what Mom makes."

"Who's everybody?"

"Kids," Madeline said. "Some of them bring the same lunch as me now."

"Really," Harriet said, surprised. "Leftovers? From the previous night's dinner?"

"Yes."

"Their mothers watch your mom's show?"

"I guess."

"Really?"

"Yes," Madeline emphasized, as if Harriet was slow on the uptake.

Harriet had assumed *Supper at Six* had very few viewers, and Elizabeth had confirmed this by confiding that her six-month trial period was almost up; it had been a battle the entire time; she was fairly certain she would not be renewed.

"But surely you could meet them halfway?" Harriet had asked her, trying not to sound desperate. She loved watching Elizabeth on TV. "Maybe just try to smile."

"Smile?" Elizabeth had said. "Do surgeons smile during appendectomies? No. Would you want them to? No. Cooking, like surgery, requires concentration. Anyway, Phil Lebensmal wants me to act as if the people I'm speaking to are dolts. I won't do it, Harriet, I won't perpetuate the myth that women are incompetent. If they cancel me, so be it. I'll do something else."

But nothing that would pay nearly as well, Harriet thought. Thanks to the TV money, Elizabeth had been true to her word:

she now paid Harriet. It was Harriet's very first paycheck, and she couldn't believe how powerful it made her feel.

"You know I agree," Harriet had said, treading carefully, "but maybe you could only pretend to do what they want. You know, play along."

Elizabeth cocked her head to the side. "Play along?"

"You know what I mean," Harriet said. "You're smart. It might be off-putting to Mr. Pine, or that Lebensmal person. You know how men are."

Elizabeth considered this. No, she did not know how men were. With the exception of Calvin, and her dead brother, John, Dr. Mason, and maybe Walter Pine, she only ever seemed to bring out the worst in men. They either wanted to control her, touch her, dominate her, silence her, correct her, or tell her what to do. She didn't understand why they couldn't just treat her as a fellow human being, as a colleague, a friend, an equal, or even a stranger on the street, someone to whom one is automatically respectful until you find out they've buried a bunch of bodies in the backyard.

Harriet was her only real friend, and they agreed on most things, but on this, they did not. According to Harriet, men were a world apart from women. They required coddling, they had fragile egos, they couldn't allow a woman intelligence or skill if it exceeded their own. "Harriet, that's ridiculous," Elizabeth had argued. "Men and women are both human beings. And as humans, we're by-products of our upbringings, victims of our lackluster educational systems, and choosers of our behaviors. In short, the reduction of women to something *less* than men, and the elevation of men to something *more* than women, is not biological: it's cultural. And it starts with two words: pink and blue. Everything skyrockets out of control from there."

Speaking of lackluster educational systems, just last week she'd been summoned to Mudford's classroom to discuss a related problem: apparently Madeline refused to participate in little girl activities, such as playing house.

"Madeline wants to do things that are more suited to little boys," Mudford had said. "It's not right. You obviously believe a woman's place is in the home, what with your"—she coughed slightly—"*television show.* So talk to her. She wanted to be on safety patrol this week."

"Why was that a problem?"

"Because only boys are on safety patrol. Boys protect girls. Because they're bigger."

"But Madeline is the tallest one in your class."

"Which is another problem," Mudford said. "Her height is making the boys feel bad."

"So no, Harriet," Elizabeth said sharply, coming back to the subject at hand. *"I won't play along."*

Harriet picked some dirt out from beneath a fingernail as Elizabeth harangued about women accepting their subordinate positions as if they were preordained, as if they believed their smaller bodies were a biological indication of smaller brains, as if they were naturally inferior, but charmingly so. Worse, Elizabeth explained, many of these women passed such notions down to their children, using phrases like "Boys will be boys" or "You know how girls are."

"What is wrong with women?" Elizabeth demanded. "Why do they buy into these cultural stereotypes? Worse, why do they perpetuate them? Are they not aware of the dominant female role in the hidden tribes of the Amazon? Is Margaret Mead out of print?" She only stopped when Harriet stood up, indicating she did not wish to be subjected to another unabridged word.

"Harriet. *Harriet,*" Madeline repeated. "Are you listening? Harriet, what happened to her? Did she die, too?"

"Did who die?" Harriet asked distractedly, thinking about

how she'd never read Margaret Mead. Was she the one who wrote *Gone with the Wind*?

"The godmother."

"Oh, her," she said. "I have no idea. And anyway, she—or he—wasn't technically a godmother."

"But you said—"

"It was a *fairy* godmother—someone who gave your dad's home money. That's all I meant. *Fairy* godmother. And she—it could have been a he, by the way—he *or* she gave it to everyone at the home. Not just your dad."

"Who was it?"

"I have no idea. Does it matter? A fairy godmother is just another word for philanthropist. A rich person who gives money to causes—like Andrew Carnegie and his libraries. Although you should know there's a tax break in philanthropy, so it's not completely unselfish. Do you have other homework, Mad? Besides the damn tree?"

"Maybe I could write a letter to Dad's home and ask who the godfather was. Then I could put that name on the tree—maybe as an acorn. Not as a whole branch or anything."

"No. There are *no* acorns on family trees. Also, fairy godmothers—philanthropists—are private people; the home is never going to tell you who ponied up the big bucks. Third, we never say fairy godfathers. The fairy person is always female."

"Because of organized crime?" Madeline asked.

Harriet exhaled loudly in a mixture of wonder and irritation. "*The point is,* fairy godparents don't go on family trees. First because they're not blood, second because they're secretive people. They have to be because otherwise everyone would be hitting them up for cash."

"But keeping secrets is wrong."

"Not always."

"Do you keep secrets?"

"No," Harriet lied.

"Do you think my mom does?"

"No," Harriet said, but now she meant it. How she wished Elizabeth *would* keep a few secrets—or at least opinions—to herself. "Now, let's fill in this tree with a bunch of hodgepodge. Your teacher will never know the difference and then we can watch your mom's show."

"You want me to *lie*?"

"Mad," Harriet said, irritated. "Did I say lie?"

"Do fairies not have blood?"

"Of course, fairies have blood!" Harriet shrieked. She rested a hand on her forehead. "Let's put this on hold for now. Go play outside."

"But—"

"Go throw the ball for Six-Thirty."

"I have to bring a photograph too, Harriet," Madeline added. "Something with the whole family."

From under the table, Six-Thirty rested his head on her bony knee.

"The *whole* family," Madeline emphasized. "That means it has to have my dad in it, too."

"No, it doesn't."

Six-Thirty stood up and made his way to Elizabeth's bedroom.

"If you don't want to throw the ball for Six-Thirty, then take Six-Thirty and go to the library. Your books are overdue. You have just enough time before your mom's show."

"I don't feel like it."

"Well, sometimes we have to do things we don't feel like doing."

"What do you do that you don't feel like doing?"

Harriet closed her eyes. She pictured Mr. Sloane.

CHAPTER 28

Saints

"Madeline," the city librarian said. "What can I help you with today?"

"I need to find an address for a place in Iowa."

"Follow me."

The librarian led Madeline through the warren of the library, pausing briefly to chastise a reader for turning down corners of pages to mark places and another for propping his legs up on an adjacent chair. "This is the Carnegie Library," she whispered angrily. "I can bar you for life."

"Up here, Madeline," she said, leading her to a shelf of phone books. "You said Iowa, correct?" She reached up and pulled down three thick volumes. "Any town in particular?"

"I'm looking for a boys home," Madeline said, "but with a girl's name. That's all I know."

"We'll need more information than that," the librarian said. "Iowa isn't small."

"I'd put my money on Sioux City," came a voice from behind.

"Sioux isn't a girl's name," the librarian said, turning. "It's an Indian name—oh, Reverend, hello. I'm so sorry—I forgot to find that book you wanted. I'll do it now."

"But it could be mistaken as a girl's name, couldn't it?" the

man in the dark robes continued. "Sue versus Sioux? A child
might make that mistake."

"Not this child," the librarian said.

"It's not here," Madeline said fifteen minutes later as her finger
trailed down the "B" column. No Boys Home."

"Oh," the reverend said from across the library table, "I should
have mentioned—sometimes those places are named after saints."

"Why?"

"Because people who take care of other people's children are
saints."

"Why?"

"Because taking care of children is hard."

Madeline rolled her eyes.

"Try Saint Vincent," he said, running his finger just beneath
his clerical collar to let some air in.

"What are you reading?" Madeline asked as she flipped to the
S's in the phone book.

"Religious things," he said. "I'm a minister."

"No, I meant the other thing—that thing," she said, pointing
to a magazine he'd tucked between the pages of scripture.

"Oh," he said embarrassed. "That's just—for fun."

"*Mad* magazine," she read aloud as she yanked it out of
hiding.

"It's humor," the reverend explained, quickly taking it back.

"Can I see it?"

"I don't think your mother would approve."

"Because there are naked pictures?"

"No!" he said. "No, no—it's nothing like that. It's just that
sometimes I need a laugh. There's not much humor in my job."

"Why?"

The reverend hesitated. "Because God isn't very funny, I
guess. Why are you searching for a boys home?"

"It's where my dad grew up. I'm doing a family tree."

"I see," he said, smiling. "Well, a family tree sounds like a lot of fun."

"That's debatable."

"Debatable?"

"It means arguable," Mad said.

"So it does," he said, surprised. "Do you mind me asking? How old are you?"

"I'm not allowed to give out private information."

"Oh," he said, red-faced. "Of course not. Good for you."

Madeline chewed on the end of her eraser.

"Anyway," he said, "it's fun to learn about one's ancestors, isn't it? I think so. What have you got so far?"

"Well," Mad said, swinging her legs under the table, "on my mom's side, her dad is in jail for burning some people up, her mom is in Brazil because of taxes, and her brother is dead."

"Oh—"

"I don't have anything on my dad's side yet. But I'm thinking the people at the boys home are sort of like family."

"In what way?"

"Because they took care of him."

The reverend rubbed the back of his neck. In his experience, these homes were staffed with pedophiles.

"Saints, you called them," she reminded him.

He sighed inwardly. The problem with being a minister was how many times a day he had to lie. This was because people needed constant reassurance that things were okay or were going to be okay instead of the more obvious reality that things were bad and were only going to get worse. He'd been officiating a funeral just last week—one of his congregants had died of lung cancer—and his message to the family, all of whom also smoked like chimneys, was that the man had died, not because of his four-pack-a-day habit, but because God needed him. The family, each inhaling deeply, thanked him for his wisdom.

"But why write to the boys home?" he asked. "Why not just ask your dad?"

"Because he's dead, too." She sighed.

"Good lord!" the reverend said, shaking his head. "I'm very sorry."

"Thank you," Madeline said in a serious way. "Some people think you can't miss what you never had, but I think you can. Do you?"

"Absolutely," he said, touching the back of his neck until he located the small chunk of hair that was slightly too long. When he went to visit a friend in Liverpool, they'd gone to see a brand-new musical group called the Beatles. They were British and they had bangs. It was nearly unheard of for men to have bangs, but he found he liked their look almost as much as he liked their music.

"What are you looking for in there?" she asked him, pointing to his book.

"Inspiration," he said. "Something to move the spirit for Sunday's sermon."

"What about fairy godmothers?" she asked.

"Fairy—"

"My dad's home had a fairy godmother. She gave the home money."

"Oh," he said. "I think you mean a donor. The home may have had several. It takes a lot of money to run those places."

"No," she said. "I mean a fairy godmother. I think you have to be a bit magical to give money to people you don't even know."

The reverend felt another jolt of surprise. "True," he admitted.

"But Harriet says earning a paycheck is better. She doesn't like magic."

"Who's Harriet?"

"My neighbor. She's Catholic. She can't get divorced. Harriet thinks I should fill the family tree with hodgepodge, but I don't want to. It makes me feel like there's something wrong with my family."

"Well," the reverend said carefully, thinking it did very much sound like there was something wrong with the child's family, "Harriet probably only means some things are private."

"You mean secret."

"No, I mean private. For instance, I asked you how old you were and you correctly answered that it was private information. It's not secret; it's just that you don't know me well enough to tell me. But a secret is something we keep because there's a chance that if someone knew our secret, they would use it against us or make us feel bad. Secrets usually involve things we're ashamed of."

"Do you keep secrets?"

"Yes," he admitted. "How about you?"

"Me too," she said.

"I'm pretty sure everyone does," he said. "Especially the people who say they don't. There's no way you go through life without being embarrassed or ashamed about something."

Madeline nodded.

"Anyway, people think they know more about themselves based on these silly branches full of names of people they've never met. For instance, I know someone who's very proud to be a direct descendant of Galileo, and another who can trace her roots back to the *Mayflower*. They both talk about their lineage as if they have a pedigree, but they don't. Your relatives can't make you important or smart. They can't make you *you*."

"What makes me *me*, then?"

"What you choose to do. How you live your life."

"But lots of people don't get to choose how they get to live. Like slaves."

"Well," the reverend said, chagrined by her simple wisdom. "That's true, too."

They sat quietly for a few moments, Madeline skimming her finger down the phone book pages, the reverend considering the purchase of a guitar. "Anyway," he added, "I think family trees aren't a very intelligent way to understand one's roots."

Madeline looked up at him. "A minute ago you said it would be fun to learn about my ancestors."

"Yes," he confessed, "but I was lying," which made both of them laugh. From across the way, the librarian raised her head in warning.

"I'm Reverend Wakely," he whispered, nodding an apology to the frowning librarian. "From First Presbyterian."

"Mad Zott," Madeline said. "Mad—like your magazine."

"Well, Mad," he said carefully, thinking "Mad" must be French for something. "If it's not under Saint Vincent, try Saint Elmo. Or wait—try All Saints. That's what they call places when they can't decide on a single saint."

"All Saints," she said, flipping to the A's. "All, All, All. Wait. Here it is. All Saints Boys Home!" But her excitement was short-lived. "But there's no address. Just a phone number."

"Is that a problem?"

"My mom says you only call long distance if someone dies."

"Well, maybe I could call for you from my office. I have to call long distance all the time. I could say I was helping a member of my congregation."

"You'd be lying again. Do you do that a lot?"

"It would be a *white* lie, Mad," he said, slightly irritated. Would no one ever understand the contradictions of his job? "Or," he said more pointedly, "you could follow Harriet's advice and fill the tree with hodgepodge—which isn't such a bad idea. Because quite often the past belongs only in the past."

"Why?"

"Because the past is the only place it makes sense."

"But my dad isn't in the past. He's still my dad."

"Of course he is," the reverend said, softening. "I just meant—in terms of me calling All Saints—that they might feel more comfortable talking with me because we're both in religion. Like you probably feel more comfortable talking to the kids at school about school things."

Madeline looked surprised. She'd never once felt comfortable talking to the kids at school.

"Or, I know," he said, now wanting to extricate himself from the whole thing. "Ask your mother to call. It's her husband; I'm sure they'd help. They might need proof of the marriage before they'd be willing to give her anything significant—a certificate, something like that—but that should be easy enough."

Madeline froze.

"On second thought," Madeline said, quickly writing two words on a scrap of paper, "here's my dad's name." Then she added her phone number and handed it to him. "How soon can you call?"

The minister glanced down at the name.

"Calvin Evans?" he said, drawing back in surprise.

Back when he'd been at Harvard Divinity School, Wakely audited a chemistry course. His goal: to learn how the enemy camp explained creation so he could refute it. But after a year of chemistry, he found himself in deep water. Thanks to his newly acquired understanding of atoms, matter, elements, and molecules, he now struggled to believe God had created anything. Not heaven, not earth. Not even pizza.

As a fifth-generation minister attending one of the most prestigious divinity schools in the world, this was a huge problem. It wasn't just the familial expectations; it was also science itself. Science insisted on something he rarely encountered in his future line of work: evidence. And in the middle of this evidence was a young man. His name was Calvin Evans.

Evans had come to Harvard to sit on a panel made up of RNA researchers, and Wakely, having nothing better to do on a Saturday night, attended. Evans, who was by far the youngest on the panel, barely said anything. There was a lot of shop talk from the others about how chemical bonds were formed, broken, then re-formed following something called an "effective collision." Frankly, the whole thing was a little boring. Still, one of the panelists continued to drone on about how real change only ever arose through the application of kinetic energy. That's when someone in the audience asked for an example of an ineffective collision—something that lacked energy and never changed, but still had a big effect. Evans had leaned into his microphone. "Religion," he said. Then he got up and left.

The religion comment ate at him so he decided to write to Evans and say so. Much to his surprise, Evans wrote back—and then he wrote back to Evans, and then Evans wrote back to him, and so on. Even though they disagreed, it was clear they liked each other. Which is why, once they'd cleared the hurdles of religion and science, their letters turned personal. It was then they discovered that they were not only the same age but shared two things in common—an almost fanatical love for water-based sports (Calvin was a rower; he was a surfer) and an obsession for sunny weather. In addition, neither had a girlfriend. Neither enjoyed graduate school. Neither was sure what life held after graduation.

But then Wakely had ruined the whole thing by mentioning something about how he was following in his father's footsteps. He wondered if Evans was doing the same. In response, Calvin wrote back in all caps saying that he hated his father and hoped he was dead.

Wakely was shocked. It was obvious that Evans had been badly hurt by his father and, knowing Evans, that his hatred had to be based on the most heartless thing of all. Evidence.

He'd started to write back to Evans several times but couldn't figure out what to say. Him. The minister. The guy currently writing a theology thesis titled "The Need for Consolation in Modern Society." No words.

Their pen-pal relationship ended.

Just after graduation, his father died unexpectedly. He returned to Commons for the funeral and decided to stay. He found a small place by the beach, took over his father's congregation, got out his surfboard.

He'd been there a few years when he finally learned that

Evans was also in Commons. He couldn't believe it. What were the odds? But before he could get up the nerve to reconnect with his famous friend, Evans was killed in a freak accident.

The word went out: someone was needed to officiate the scientist's funeral. Wakely volunteered. He felt compelled to pay his respects to one of the few people he admired; to help in whatever way he could to guide Evans's spirit to a place of peace. Plus, he was curious. Who would be there? Who would grieve the loss of this brilliant man?

The answer: a woman and a dog.

"In case it helps," Madeline added, "tell them my dad was a rower."

Wakely paused, remembering the extra-long casket.

He tried to reconstruct exactly what he'd said to the young woman who stood by the graveside: *I'm sorry for your loss?* Probably. He'd planned to speak with her after the service, but before he'd even finished the closing prayer, she'd walked away, the dog at her heels. He told himself he'd go see her, but he didn't know her name or where she lived, and while it wouldn't have been that difficult to find out, he didn't pursue it. There was something about her that made him feel talking about Evans's soul might just make matters worse.

After the service—for months after—he couldn't get the brevity of Evans's life out of his head. There were so few people who actually did things in the world that mattered—who made discoveries that changed things. Evans had slipped between the cracks of the unknown and explored the universe in a way that theology completely avoided. And for a very short period of time, he felt like he'd been part of it.

Still, that was then and this was now. He was a minister; he didn't need science. What he *did* need were more inventive ways to tell his flock to act like decent people, to stop being so mean to one another, to behave. So, in the end, despite his doubts, he became a reverend, but he continued to think of the remarkable Evans. And now, here was this little girl claiming to be his daughter. God really did move in mysterious ways.

"Just to be clear," he said, "we're talking about Calvin Evans. The one who was killed in a car accident about five years ago."

"It was a leash, but yes."

"Ah," he said. "But here's the tricky part. Calvin Evans didn't have children. In fact, he wasn't—" He hesitated.

"What?"

"Nothing," he said quickly. Obviously, the little girl was illegitimate on top of everything else. "And what's that there?" he asked, pointing to a yellowed newspaper clipping sticking out from her notebook. "More of the assignment?"

"I have to bring in a family photo," she said, retrieving a clipping still damp with dog saliva. She held it out gingerly, the way one might an irreplaceable treasure. "It's the only one we're all in."

He unfolded it carefully. It was an article about Calvin Evans's funeral, and in it was a photograph of the same woman and the dog, their backs to the camera but their devastation clear, watching as the earth swallowed the very casket he had blessed. A wave of depression swept over him.

"But, Mad, how in the world is this a family picture?"

"Well that's my mom," Madeline said, pointing to Elizabeth's back, "and Six-Thirty," she said, pointing at the dog. "And I'm inside my mom, just there," she said, pointing at Elizabeth again, "and my dad is in the box."

Wakely had spent the last seven years of his life consoling people, but there was something about the way this child spoke so matter-of-factly about her loss that depleted him.

"Mad, I need you to understand something," he said, noting, with shock, that his own hands were in the photograph. "Families aren't meant to fit on trees. Maybe because people aren't part of the plant kingdom—we're part of the animal kingdom."

"Exactly," Madeline gasped. "That's *exactly* what I was trying to tell Mrs. Mudford."

"If we were trees," he added, worrying about how much grief this child was going to endure explaining her origins, "we might be a bit wiser. Long life and all that."

And then he realized Calvin Evans hadn't had a very long life and he'd just implied that it was probably because Evans hadn't been very smart. Honestly, he was a terrible minister—the worst.

Madeline seemed to consider this answer, then leaned way across the table. "Wakely," she said in a low voice, "I have to go watch my mom now, but I was wondering. Can you keep a secret?"

"I can," he said, wondering what she meant by watching her mom. Was her mom sick?

She looked at him closely as if trying to determine if he was lying again, then got up from her chair and went to his side and whispered something so vigorously in his ear, his eyes grew wide in wonder. Before he could stop himself, he cupped his hand around her ear and did the same thing. Then they both leaned away from each other in surprise.

"That's not so bad, Wakely," Madeline said. "Really."

But about hers, he couldn't find the words.

CHAPTER 29

Bonding

"My name is Elizabeth Zott, and this is *Supper at Six*."

Hands on her hips, her lips outlined in Brick Red, her thick hair pulled back into a simple French twist secured with a number-two pencil, Elizabeth leveled her gaze and looked directly into the camera.

"Exciting news," she said. "Today we're going to study three different types of chemical bonds: ionic, covalent, and hydrogen. Why learn about bonds? Because when you do you will grasp the very foundation of life. Plus, your cakes will rise."

From homes all over Southern California, women pulled out paper and pencils.

"Ionic is the 'opposites attract' chemical bond," Elizabeth explained as she emerged from behind the counter and began to sketch on an easel. "For instance, let's say you wrote your PhD thesis on free market economics, but your husband rotates tires for a living. You love each other, but he's probably not interested in hearing about the invisible hand. And who can blame him, because you know the invisible hand is libertarian garbage."

She looked out at the audience as various people scribbled notes, several of which read "Invisible hand: libertarian garbage."

"The point is, you and your husband are completely different and yet you still have a strong connection. That's fine. It's also ionic." She paused, lifting the sheet of paper over the top of the easel to reveal a fresh page of newsprint.

"Or perhaps your marriage is more of a covalent bond," she said, sketching a new structural formula. "And if so, lucky you, because that means you both have strengths that, when combined, create something even better. For example, when hydrogen and oxygen combine, what do we get? Water—or H_2O as it's more commonly known. In many respects, the covalent bond is not unlike a party—one that's made better thanks to the pie you made and the wine he brought. Unless you don't like parties—I don't—in which case you could also think of the covalent bond as a small European country, say Switzerland. *Alps,* she quickly wrote on the easel, + *a Strong Economy = Everybody Wants to Live There.*

In a living room in La Jolla, California, three children fought over a toy dump truck, its broken axle lying directly adjacent to a skyscraper of ironing that threatened to topple a small woman, her hair in curlers, a small pad of paper in her hands. *Switzerland,* she wrote. *Move.*

"That brings us to the third bond," Elizabeth said, pointing at another set of molecules, "the hydrogen bond—the most fragile, delicate bond of all. I call this the 'love at first sight' bond because both parties are drawn to each other based solely on visual information: you like his smile, he likes your hair. But then you talk and discover he's a closet Nazi and thinks women complain too much. Poof. Just like that the delicate bond is broken. That's the hydrogen bond for you, ladies—a chemical reminder that if things seem too good to be true, they probably are."

She walked back behind the counter and, exchanging the marker for a knife, took a Paul Bunyan swing at a large yellow onion, cleaving it in two. "It's chicken pot pie night," she announced. "Let's get started."

"See?" a woman in Santa Monica demanded as she turned to her sullen seventeen-year-old daughter, the girl's eyeliner so thick, it looked as if planes could land there. "What did I tell you?

Your bond with that boy is hydrogen only. When are you going to wake up and smell the ions?"

"Not this again."

"You could go to college. You could be something!"

"He loves me!"

"He's holding you back!"

"More after this," Elizabeth said as the cameraman indicated a commercial break.

From his producer's chair, Walter Pine slumped. After a massive amount of groveling, he'd managed to get Phil Lebensmal to extend Zott's contract for another six months, but only by agreeing that sexy was in, science was out. The clock, Phil had warned, was really ticking this time. According to him, they'd been getting a lot of complaints. Walter broached the subject with Elizabeth just before the show. "We have to make a few changes," he explained.

She'd listened, nodding her head thoughtfully, as if considering each change carefully. "No," she said.

In addition to that little problem, Amanda had some stupid family tree assignment that demanded a current family photograph *with* mommy, even though mommy was long out of the picture. Worse, it insisted on celebrating the biological relationship between himself and his child, a bond that did not exist and never would. Obviously, he was planning on telling Amanda the truth and soon: that her lousy mother was never coming back and that, technically, he and she weren't related in any way. Adopted children had the right to know. He was waiting for the right moment. Her fortieth birthday.

"Walter," Elizabeth said as she strode toward him. "Have you heard from your insurance people? As you know, tomorrow's show focuses on combustion, and while I continue to believe there's really no significant danger, I— Walter?" She waved her hand in front of his face. "Walter?"

"Sixty seconds, Zott," said the cameraman.

"It wouldn't hurt to have a couple of extra fire extinguishers on hand. Again, I'd prefer the nitrogen propellant over the newer water and foam models, but that's just me; I'm sure either one will do the job. Walter? Are you listening? Respond." She frowned, then turned back to the stage. "I'll catch you next break."

As she made her way back up onstage, Walter turned to watch her mount the steps, her blue trousers—she was wearing *trousers*—belted high on the waist. Who did she think she was? Katharine Hepburn? Lebensmal would go ballistic. He turned, motioning for the makeup woman.

"Yes, Mr. Pine?" said Rosa, her hands full of small sponges. "Did you need something? Zott's face was fine, by the way. She wasn't glistening."

He sighed. "She *never* glistens," he said. "Despite the fact that those lights alone would sear a steak in thirty seconds, she never breaks a sweat. How is that possible?"

"It *is* unusual," Rosa agreed.

"And we're back," he heard Elizabeth say as she pointed both hands at the camera.

"Please be normal," whispered Walter.

"Now," Elizabeth said to her at-home viewers, "I'm confident you used our short break to chop your carrots, celery, and onions into small disparate units, thereby creating the necessary surface area to facilitate the uptake of seasoning, as well as to shorten cooking time. So now things look like this," she said, tipping a pan at the camera. "Next, apply a liberal amount of sodium chloride—"

"Would it kill her to say salt?" Walter hissed. *"Would it?"*

"I like how she uses science-y words," Rosa said. "It makes me feel—I don't know—capable."

"Capable?" he said. *"Capable?* What happened to wanting to feel slim and beautiful? And what the hell is going on with those trousers? Where did those come from?"

"Are you okay, Mr. Pine?" Rosa asked. "Can I get you something?"

"Yes," he said. "Cyanide."

Several more minutes passed as Elizabeth led viewers through the chemical makeup of various other ingredients, explaining, as she added each to the pan, which bonds were being created.

"There," she said, tipping the pan to the camera again. "What do we have now? A mixture, which is a combination of two or more pure substances in which each substance retains its individual chemical properties. In the case of our chicken pot pie, notice how your carrots, peas, onions, and celery are mixed yet remain separate entities. Think about that. A successful chicken pot pie is like a society that functions at a highly efficient level. Call it Sweden. Here every vegetable has its place. No single bit of produce demands to be more important than another. And when you throw in the additional spices—garlic, thyme, pepper, and sodium chloride—you've created a flavor that not only enhances each substance's texture but balances the acidity. Result? Subsidized childcare. Although I'm sure Sweden has its problems, too. Skin cancer at the very least." She took a cue from the cameraman. "We'll be right back after this station identification."

"What was *that*?" Walter gasped. "What did she say?"

"Subsidized childcare," Rosa said as she sponged his forehead. "We should get that on the ballot." She leaned down, taking in a vein pulsing on Walter's forehead. "Listen, why don't I go get you some acetylsalicylic acid. It'll—"

"What did *you* say?" he hissed, batting her sponge away.

"Subsidized childcare."

"No, the other—"

"Acetylsalicylic acid?"

"Aspirin," he demanded hoarsely. "Here at KCTV, we call it *aspirin*. Bayer aspirin. Want to know why? Because Bayer is one of our sponsors. The people who pay our bills. Ring any bells? Say it. *Aspirin*."

"Aspirin," she said. "Back in a flash."

"Walter?" Elizabeth's voice came abruptly from above, causing him to jump.

"Jesus, Elizabeth!" he said. "Must you sneak up on me?"

"I wasn't sneaking. Your eyes were closed."

"I was *thinking.*"

"About the fire extinguishers? So was I. Let's say three. Two will be sufficient, but three should almost completely eradicate any possibility of tragedy. Up to, or slightly beyond, ninety-nine percent."

"My god," he shuddered to himself as he wiped his damp palms on his pants. "Is this a nightmare? Why can't I wake up?"

"You're wondering about the other one percent," Elizabeth said. "Well don't. That tiny amount is mostly act-of-God stuff—earthquakes, tsunamis—things we can't possibly anticipate because the science isn't there yet." She paused, straightening her belt. "Walter, don't you find it interesting that people even use that term 'act of God'? Considering that most want to believe that God is about lambs and love and babies in mangers, and yet this same so-called benevolent being smites innocent people left and right, indicating an anger management problem—maybe even manic depression. In a psychiatric ward, such a patient would be subjected to electroshock therapy. Which I don't favor. Electroshock therapy is still largely unproven. But isn't it interesting that acts of God and electroshock therapy share so much in common? In terms of being violent, cruel—"

"Sixty seconds, Zott."

"—unforgiving, barbarous—"

"Jesus, Elizabeth, please."

"Anyway, let's say three. Every woman should know how to put out a fire. We'll start with the smothering technique, then when that fails, go to nitrogen."

"Forty seconds, Zott."

"And what is with the trousers?" Walter said, his teeth clenched so tightly, the words barely emerged.

"What do you mean?"

"You know what I mean."

"Do you like them? You must. You wear them all the time

and I can see why. They're very comfortable. Don't worry; I plan to give you full credit."

"No! Elizabeth, I *never*—"

"Here's your aspirin, Mr. Pine," Rosa interrupted, appearing at his side. "And Zott—let me take a quick look at your—good, good—turn your face the other way now—good—amazing, really. Okay, you're all set."

"Zott, in ten," called the cameraman.

"Are you sick, Walter?"

"Have you seen the family tree project?" he whispered.

"Eight seconds, Zott."

"You look pale, Walter."

"The *tree*," he barely eked out.

"Free? But I thought you said I couldn't give things away anymore."

Elizabeth climbed back up onstage and turning to the camera said, "And we're back."

"I don't know what you think you gave me," Walter snapped at Rosa, "but it's not working."

"It takes time."

"Which I don't *have*," he said. "Give me the bottle."

"You've already taken the max."

"Oh really?" he snapped, shaking the bottle. "Then explain why there are still some in here."

"Now pour your version of Sweden," Elizabeth was saying, "into the starch, lipid, and protein molecule configuration you rolled out earlier—your piecrust—the one whose chemical bonds were enabled using the water molecule, H_2O, and through which you created the perfect marriage of stability and structure." She paused, her now-floured hands pointing at a piecrust filled with vegetables and chicken.

"Stability and structure," she repeated, looking out at the studio audience. "Chemistry is inseparable from life—by its very definition, chemistry *is* life. But like your pie, life requires a strong base. In your home, you are that base. It is an enormous responsibility, the most undervalued job in the world that, nonetheless, holds everything together."

Several women in the studio audience nodded vigorously.

"Take a moment now to admire your experiment," Elizabeth continued. "You've used the elegance of chemical bonding to construct a crust that will both house and enhance the flavor of your constituents. Consider your filling one more time, then ask yourself: What does Sweden want? Citric acid? Maybe. Sodium chloride? Probably. Adjust. When you're satisfied, lay your second crust on top like a blanket, crimping the edges to create a seal. Then make a few short slashes across the top, creating a vent. The purpose of the vent is to give the water molecule the space it needs to convert to steam and escape. Without that vent, your pie is Mount Vesuvius. To protect your villagers from certain death, always slash."

She picked up a knife and made three short slits on top. "There," she said. "Now pop it in your oven at three hundred seventy-five degrees Fahrenheit. Bake for approximately forty-five minutes." She looked up at the clock.

"It looks like we have a little extra time," she said. "Perhaps I could take a question from the studio audience." She looked at the cameraman, who held a finger up to his throat as if to slit it. "NO, NO, NO," he mouthed.

"Hello," she said, pointing at a woman in the front row, her glasses perched atop a stiff hairdo, her thick legs swathed in support hose.

"I'm Mrs. George Fillis from Kernville," the woman said nervously as she stood up, "and I'm thirty-eight years old. I just wanted to say how much I enjoy your show. I . . I can't believe how much I've learned. I know I'm not the brightest bulb," she said, her face pink with shame, "that's what my husband always says—and yet last week when you said osmosis was the movement of a less concentrated solvent through a semipermeable membrane to another more concentrated solvent, I found myself wondering if . . . well . . ."

"Go on."

"Well, if my leg edema might not be a by-product of faulty hydraulic conductivity combined with an irregular osmotic reflection coefficient of plasma proteins. What do you think?"

"A very detailed diagnosis, Mrs. Fillis," Elizabeth said. "What kind of medicine do you practice?"

"Oh," the woman stumbled, "no, I'm not a doctor. I'm just a housewife."

"There isn't a woman in the world who is *just* a housewife," Elizabeth said. "What else do you do?"

"Nothing. A few hobbies. I like to read medical journals."

"Interesting. What else?"

"Sewing."

"Clothes?"

"Bodies."

"Wound closures?"

"Yes. I have five boys. They're always tearing holes in themselves."

"And when you were their age you envisioned yourself becoming—"

"A loving wife and mother."

"No, seriously—"

"An open-heart surgeon," the woman said before she could stop herself.

The room filled with a thick silence, the weight of her ridiculous dream hanging like too-wet laundry on a windless day. Open-heart surgery? For a moment it seemed as if the entire world was waiting for the laughter that should follow. But then from one end of the audience came a single unexpected clap— immediately followed by another—and then another—and then ten more—and then twenty more—and soon everyone in the audience was on their feet and someone called out, "Dr. Fillis, heart surgeon," and the clapping became thunderous.

"No, no," the woman insisted above the noise. "I was only kidding. I can't actually do that. Anyway, it's too late."

"It's never too late," Elizabeth insisted.

"But I couldn't. Can't."

"Why."

"Because it's hard."

"And raising five boys isn't?"

The woman touched her fingertips to the small beads of sweat dotting her forehead. "But where would someone like me even start?"

"The public library," Elizabeth said. "Followed by the MCATs, school, and residency."

The woman suddenly seemed to realize that Elizabeth took her seriously. "You *really* think I could do it?" she said, her voice trembling.

"What's the molecular weight of barium chloride?"

"208.23."

"You'll be fine."

"But my husband—"

"Is a lucky man. By the way, it's Free Day, Mrs. Fillis," Elizabeth said, "something my producer just invented. To show our support for your fearless future, you'll be taking home my chicken pot pie. Come on up and get it."

Amid roaring applause, Elizabeth handed the now-determined-looking Mrs. Fillis the foil-covered pie. "We're officially out of time," Elizabeth said. "But I hope you'll tune in tomorrow as we explore the world of kitchen conflagrations."

Then she looked right through the camera lens, and almost as if she divined it, directly into the astonished faces of Mrs. George Fillis's five children sprawled in front of the TV in Kernville, their eyes open wide, their mouths agape, as if they had just seen their mother for the very first time.

"Boys, set the table," Elizabeth commanded. "Your mother needs a moment to herself."

CHAPTER 30

99 Percent

"Mad," Elizabeth began carefully a week later, "Mrs. Mudford called me at work today. Something about an inappropriate family photo?"

Madeline took a sudden interest in a scab on her knee.

"And attached to this photo was a family tree," Elizabeth said gently. "In which you claim to be a direct descendant of"—she paused, consulting a list—"Nefertiti, Sojourner Truth, and Amelia Earhart. Does that sound familiar?"

Madeline looked up innocently. "Not really."

"And the tree includes an acorn labeled 'Fairy Godmother.'"

"Huh."

"And at the bottom someone wrote, 'Humans are animals.' That was underlined three times. And then it says, 'Inside, humans are genetically ninety-nine percent the same.'"

Madeline looked up at the ceiling.

"Ninety-nine percent?" Elizabeth said.

"What?" Madeline said.

"That's inaccurate."

"But—"

"In science, accuracy matters."

"But—"

"The fact is, it can be as high as ninety-nine point nine percent. Ninety-nine *point nine*." Then she stopped and wrapped her arms around her daughter. "It's my fault, sweetheart. With the exception of pi, we really haven't covered decimals yet."

"Sorry to intrude," Harriet called as she let herself in the back door. "Phone messages. Forgot to leave them." She plunked a list down in front of Elizabeth and turned to go.

"Harriet," Elizabeth said, scanning the list. "Who's this one? The reverend from First Presbyterian?"

Madeline's hair rose on her arms.

"It sounded like one of those church drum-up-the-business calls. He asked for Mad. Probably working from a bad list. Anyway, this is the one I wanted to make sure you saw," she said, tapping the list. "The *LA Times*."

"They've been calling at work, too," Elizabeth said. "They want an interview."

"An interview!"

"You're gonna be in the newspaper again?" Mad said, worried. Her family had been in the newspaper twice: once when her father died, and once when her father's gravestone was blown to bits by a stray bullet. Not a great track record.

"No, Mad," Elizabeth said. "The person who wants to interview me isn't even a science reporter; he writes for the women's page. He's already told me he has no interest in talking about chemistry, just dinner. Clearly, he doesn't understand you can't separate the two. And I suspect he also wants to ask questions about our family, even though our family is none of his business."

"Why not?" Madeline asked. "What's *wrong* with our family?"

From under the table, Six-Thirty lifted his head. He hated that Mad thought there might be something wrong with their family. As for Nefertiti and the others, it wasn't just Mad's wishful thinking—it was accurate in one critical sense: all humans shared a common ancestor. How could Mudford not know this? He was a dog and even *he* knew this. By the way and in case anyone was interested, he'd just learned a new word: "diary." It was a place where one wrote vicious things about one's family and friends and hoped to god they never saw. With "diary" his word count was now up to 648.

"See you both in the morning," Harriet called, slamming the door behind her.

"What's wrong with our family, Mom?" Madeline repeated.

"Nothing," Elizabeth said sharply, clearing the table. "Six-Thirty, help me with the fume hood. I want to try cleaning the dishes using a hydrocarbon vapor."

"Tell me about Dad."

"I've told you everything, sweetheart," she said, her face suddenly lit with affection. "He was a brilliant, honest, loving man. A great rower and gifted chemist. He was tall and gray eyed, like you, and he had very large hands. His parents died in an unfortunate collision with a train, and his aunt hit a tree. He went to live in a boys home, where . . ." She paused, her blue-and-white-checked dress swaying at her calves as she reconsidered her dishwashing experiment. "Do me a favor, Mad, and put on this oxygen mask. And Six-Thirty, let me help you with your goggles. There," she said, adjusting everyone's straps. "Anyway, then your father went on to Cambridge where he—"

"Oys ome," Mad attempted through the mask.

"We've been over this, honey. I don't know much about the boys home. Your father didn't like to talk about it. It was private."

"Pri-ate? Or se-ret?" she attempted through the mask.

"Private," her mother said firmly. "Sometimes bad things happen. This is a fact of life. In terms of the boys home, your father did not talk about it because I suspect he knew dwelling on it would not change it. He was raised without a family, without parents he could count on, without the protection and love every child is entitled to. But he persevered. Often the best way to deal with the bad," she said, feeling for her pencil, "is to turn it on end—use it as a strength, refuse to allow the bad thing to define you. *Fight* it."

The way she said it—like a warrior—made Madeline worry. "Have bad things happened to you too, Mom?" she tried to ask. "Besides dad dying?" But the dish cleaning experiment was in full swing, and her question was lost in the cocoon of the mask and the ringing of the phone.

"Yes, Walter," Elizabeth said a moment later.

"I hope I'm not disturbing anything—"

"Not at all," she said, despite an unusual humming in the background. "How can I help?"

"Well, I was calling about two things. The first is the family tree assignment. I was just wondering—"

"Yes," she confirmed. "We're in trouble."

"Us too," he said miserably. "She seemed to know the names I put on the branches were complete fabrications. Is that what you did, too?"

"No," Elizabeth said. "Mad made a math error."

He paused, not understanding.

"I have to see Mudford tomorrow," she continued. "By the way, I wasn't sure if you'd heard, but both girls have been assigned to her classroom again in the fall. She's teaching first grade, and when I say 'teaching' of course I'm being ironic. I've already registered a complaint."

"Lord," Walter sighed.

"What's the second thing, Walter?"

"It's Phil," he said. "He's, uh . . . he's not . . . happy."

"Nor am I," Elizabeth said. "How did he ever become executive producer? He lacks vision, leadership, and manners. And the way he treats the women at the station is contemptible."

"Well," Walter said, thinking how, when discussing Elizabeth a few weeks back, Lebensmal had actually spat at him. "I agree that he can be a bit of a character."

"That's not character, Walter. That's degradation. I'm going to register a complaint with the board."

Walter shook his head. *Again with the complaints.* "Elizabeth, Phil's *on* the board."

"Well, someone needs to be made aware of his behavior."

"Surely," Walter said with a sigh, "surely you know by now that the world is filled with Phils. Our best bet is to try and get along. Make the best of a bad situation. Why can't you just do that?"

She tried to think of a good reason to make the best of Phil Lebensmal. No—she couldn't come up with a single thing.

"Look, I have an idea," he continued. "Phil's been courting a new potential sponsor—a soup manufacturer. He wants you to use the soup on your show, like in a casserole. Do that—attract a big sponsor—and I think he'll cut us some slack."

"A soup manufacturer? I only work with fresh ingredients."

"Can you at least *try* to meet me halfway?" he begged. "It's one can of soup. Think of the others—all the people who work on your show. We all have families to feed, Elizabeth; we all need to keep our jobs."

From her end of the phone came silence, as if she were weighing his words. "I'd like to meet with Phil face-to-face," she said. "Clear the air."

"*No,*" Walter emphasized. "Not that. Never that."

She exhaled sharply. "Fine. Today is Monday. Bring the can in on Thursday. I'll see what I can do."

But the week steadily got worse. The next day—Tuesday—Mudford's tree assignment revelations were the talk of the school: Madeline had been born out of wedlock; Amanda didn't have a mother; Tommy Dixon's father was an alcoholic. Not that any of the children themselves cared about these facts, but Mudford, her mean eyes wet with excitement, ate up the data like a hungry virus, then fed it to the other mothers, who spread it around school like frosting.

On Wednesday, someone surreptitiously shoved a sheet of paper listing the compensation of every KCTV employee under Elizabeth's door. Elizabeth stared at the figures. She made a third of what the sports guy did? A guy who was on the air less than three minutes a day and whose only skill involved reading scores? Worse, apparently there was something called "profit-sharing" at KCTV. But only the male employees had been invited to take part.

But it was the way Harriet looked when she arrived on Thursday morning that made Elizabeth rage.

She'd just finished tucking a note into Madeline's lunch box—*Matter can neither be created nor destroyed, but it can be rearranged. In other words, don't sit next to Tommy Dixon*—when Harriet sat down at the table, and despite the darkness of the morning, did not remove her sunglasses.

"Harriet?" Elizabeth said, instantly alarmed.

In a voice that was trying very hard to make it seem like it was no big deal, Harriet explained that Mr. Sloane had been out of sorts last night. She'd tossed some of his girlie magazines, the Dodgers had lost, he didn't approve of the way Elizabeth encouraged that woman to be a heart surgeon. He winged an empty beer bottle at her and she'd fallen back like a target at a shooting range.

"I'm calling the police," Elizabeth said, reaching for the phone.

"No," Harriet said, resting her hand on Elizabeth's arm. "They won't do anything and I refuse to give him that satisfaction. Besides, I belted him with my purse."

"I'm going over there right now," Elizabeth said. "He needs to understand this sort of behavior will not be tolerated." She stood up. "I'll get my baseball bat."

"No. If you attack him, the police will be all over you, not him."

Elizabeth thought about this. Harriet was right. Her jaw

tensed and she felt the too-familiar rage from her own police encounter years ago. *No statement of regret, then?* She reached back and felt for her pencil.

"I can take care of myself. He doesn't scare me, Elizabeth; he disgusts me. There's a difference."

Elizabeth knew this feeling exactly. She bent down and put her arms around Harriet. Despite their friendship, the two women rarely touched. "There's nothing I wouldn't do for you," Elizabeth said, pulling her close. "You *know* that, don't you?"

Harriet, surprised, looked up at Elizabeth, tears forming. "Well me, too. Ditto." Then the older woman finally pulled away. "It'll be okay," Harriet promised, wiping her face. "Just let it go."

But Elizabeth was not the type of person who let things go. When she pulled out of the driveway five minutes later, she'd already formulated a plan.

"Hello, viewers," Elizabeth said three hours later. "And welcome back. See this?" She held a soup can close to the camera. "It's a real time-saver."

From his producer's chair, Walter gasped in gratitude. She was using the soup!

"That's because it's full of chemicals," she said, tossing it with a clunk into a nearby garbage can. "Feed enough of it to your loved ones and they'll eventually die off, saving you tons of time since you won't have to feed them anymore."

The cameraman turned to look at Walter, confused. Walter glanced down at his watch as if he'd forgotten an important appointment, then got up and walked out, making his way directly to the parking lot, where he got in his car and drove home.

"Luckily, there are much faster ways to kill off your loved ones," she continued, walking to her easel, where a selection of mushroom drawings was on display, "and mushrooms are an excellent place to start. If it were me, I'd opt for the *Amanita phalloides,*" she said, tapping one of the drawings, "also known as the death cap mushroom. Not only does its poison withstand high heat, making it a go-to ingredient for a benign-looking casserole, but it very much resembles its nontoxic cousin, the straw mushroom. So if someone dies and there's an inquiry, you can easily play the dumb housewife and plead mistaken mushroom identity."

Phil Lebensmal looked up from his desk at one of the screens in his TV-littered office. What did she just say?

"The great thing about poisonous mushrooms," she continued, "is how easily they adapt to different forms. If not a casserole, why not try a stuffed mushroom? Something you can share with your next-door neighbor—the one who goes out of his way to make life miserable for his wife. He's already got one foot in the grave. Why not help him with the other?"

At this, someone in the audience let out a whoop of unexpected laughter and a clap. Meanwhile, the camera also managed to capture several pair of hands carefully writing down the words *Amanita phalloides.*

"Of course, I'm only kidding about poisoning your loved ones," Elizabeth said. "I'm sure your husbands and children are all wonderful human beings who always go out of their way to tell you how much they appreciate your hard work. Or, in the unlikely event that you work outside the home, that your fair-minded boss ensures you're paid the same wage as your male counterpart." This also got even more laughs and claps, all of which followed her as she walked back behind the counter. "It's broccoli-*mushroom* casserole night," she said, holding up a basket of—maybe?—straw mushrooms. "Let's get started."

It's fair to say no one in California touched their dinners that night.

"Zott," Rosa, the makeup woman, said on her way out. "Lebensmal wants to see you at seven."

"Seven?" Elizabeth blanched. "Obviously the man has no

children. By the way, have you seen Walter? I think he's mad at me."

"He left early," Rosa said. "Look, I don't think you should go see Lebensmal by yourself. I'll come with you."

"I'm fine, Rosa."

"Maybe you should call Walter first. He never lets any of us meet with Lebensmal alone."

"I know," Elizabeth said. "Don't worry."

Rosa hesitated, looking at the clock.

"Go home. It's not a big deal."

"At least call Walter first," Rosa said. "Let him know." She turned to gather her things. "By the way, I loved tonight's show. It was funny."

Elizabeth looked up, her eyebrows raised. "Funny?"

A few minutes before seven, after finishing her notes for tomorrow's show, Elizabeth hefted her large bag to her shoulder and walked the empty hallways of KCTV to Lebensmal's office. She knocked twice, then let herself in. "You wanted to see me, Phil?"

Lebensmal was sitting behind an enormous desk covered with stacks of papers and half-eaten food, four huge televisions broadcasting loud reruns in a ghostly black and white, the air stale with cigarette smoke. One set was airing a soap opera; another, Jack LaLanne; still another a kids' program; and the fourth, *Supper at Six*. She'd never watched her own show before, never once experienced the sound of her own voice coming through a speaker. It was horrible.

"It's about time," Lebensmal said irritably, as he stubbed a cigarette into a decorative cut-glass bowl. He pointed to a chair indicating that Elizabeth should sit, then huffed to the door and slammed it shut, pressing the lock button.

"I was told seven," she said.

"Did I tell you to speak?" he snapped.

From the left she heard herself explain the interaction of heat and fructose. She cocked her head toward the set. Had she gotten the pH right? Yes, she had.

"Do you know who I am?" he demanded from across the room. But the blaring TVs muddled his words.

"Do I know about . . . *yams?*"

"I said," he spoke louder this time, as he returned to his desk, *"do you know who I am?"*

"You are Phil LEBENSMAL," Elizabeth said loudly. "Would you mind if I turned the TVs off? It's hard to hear."

"Don't sass me!" he said. "When I say do you know who I am, I mean *do you know who I am?*"

For a moment she looked confused. "Again, you are Phil Lebensmal. But if you like, we could double-check your driver's license."

His eyes narrowed.

"Waist bends!" shouted Jack LaLanne.

"Dance party!" laughed a clown.

"I never loved you," confessed a nurse.

"Acidic pH levels," she heard herself say.

"I am *Mister* Lebensmal, executive producer of—"

"I'm sorry, Phil," she said, gesturing at the television speaker closest to her, "but I really can't—" She reached for the volume control.

"DO NOT," he boomed, "TOUCH MY TELEVISONS!"

He rose, picking up a stack of file folders, and marched across the room, planting himself in front of her, his legs spread wide like a tripod.

"You know what these are?" he said, wagging the folders in her face.

"File folders."

"Don't get smart with me. They're *Supper at Six* audience viewer questionnaires. Ad sales figures. Nielsen ratings."

"Really?" she said. "I'd love to take—" But before she could take a look, he snatched them away.

"As if you'd even know how to interpret the findings," he

said sharply. "As if you have *any* idea what any of this means." He slapped the folders against his thigh, then strode back to his desk. "I've let this nonsense go on far too long. Walter has failed to rein you in but I won't. If you want to keep your job, you will wear what I choose, mix the cocktails I want, and make dinner using normal words. You will also—"

He stopped in midsentence, put off by her reaction—or rather, nonreaction. It was the way she sat in her chair. Like a parent waiting for her child to finish his tantrum.

"On second thought," he spat impulsively, "you're fired!" And when she still didn't react, he got up and stomped over to the four TVs and switched them all off, breaking two knobs in the process. "EVERYONE IS FIRED!" he bellowed. "You, Pine, and anyone and everyone who has had even the smallest role in aiding and abetting your crap. You're all OUT!" Breathing hard, he went back to his desk and flung himself in his chair, awaiting the only two reactions from her that could or should inevitably follow: crying or apologies, preferably both.

Elizabeth nodded in the now-quiet room as she smoothed the front of her trousers. "You're firing me because of tonight's poison mushroom episode. As well as any other person associated with the show."

"That's *right,*" he emphasized, unable to hide his surprise that his threat had not impressed her. "Everyone's out and it's because of *you.* Jobs lost. All because of you. *Done.*" He sat back and waited for her to grovel.

"So to clarify," she said, "I'm being fired because I won't wear your clothes and smile into your camera, but also because—is this correct?—I don't know 'who you are.' And to further make your point, you're firing everyone associated with *Supper at Six* even though these people also work on four or five other shows for which they'd suddenly be in absentia. Meaning that those other shows will also be affected to the point where they will not be able to air."

Frustrated by her obvious logic, Phil tensed. "I can have those positions filled in twenty-four hours," he said, snapping his fingers. "Less."

"And this is your final decision, despite the show's success."

"*Yes,* it's my final decision," he said. "And *no,* the show is *not* a success—that's the point." He picked up the folders again and waved them. "Complaints pour in every day—about you, your opinions . . . your *science.* Our sponsors are threatening to walk. That soup manufacturer—they'll probably sue us."

"Sponsors," she said, tapping her fingertips together as if glad for the reminder. "I've been meaning to speak with you about them. Acid reflux tablets? Aspirin? Products like these seem to imply the show's dinners aren't going to sit well."

"Because they don't," Phil shot back. He'd already crunched more than ten antacid tablets in the last two hours and his insides were still in an uproar.

"As for the complaints," she acknowledged. "We've had a few. But they're nothing compared to the letters of support. Which I didn't expect. I have a history of not fitting in, Phil, but I'm starting to think that not fitting in is why the show works."

"The show does not work," he insisted. "It's a disaster!" What was happening here? Why did she keep talking as if she wasn't fired?

"Feeling like one doesn't fit is a horrible feeling," she continued, unruffled. "Humans naturally want to belong—it's part of our biology. But our society makes us feel that we're never good enough to belong. Do you know what I mean, Phil? Because we measure ourselves against useless yardsticks of sex, race, religion, politics, schools. Even height and weight—"

"*What?*"

"In contrast, *Supper at Six* focuses on our commonalities—our chemistries. So even though our viewers may find themselves locked into a learned societal behavior—say, the old 'men are like this, women are like that' type of thing—the show encourages them to think beyond that cultural simplicity. To think sensibly. Like a scientist."

Phil heaved back in his chair, unfamiliar with the sensation of losing.

"That's why you want to fire me. Because you want a show that reinforces societal norms. That limits an individual's capacity. I completely understand."

Phil's temple began to throb. Hands shaking, he reached for a pack of Marlboros, tapped one out, and lit it. For a moment all was quiet as he inhaled deeply, the radiant end emitting the smallest crackle, like a doll's campfire. As he exhaled, he studied her face. He got up abruptly, his body vibrating with frustration, and strode over to a sideboard littered with important-looking amber whiskeys and bourbons. Grabbing one, he tipped it into a thick-walled shot glass until the liquid hit the rim and threatened to spill over. He threw it down his throat and poured another, then turned to look at her. "There's a pecking order here," he said. "And it's about time you learned how that works."

She looked back at him, nonplussed. "I want to go on record saying that Walter Pine has been absolutely tireless in his efforts to get me to follow your suggestions. This is despite the fact that he, too, believes the show could and *should* be more. He shouldn't be punished for my actions. He's a good man, a loyal employee."

At the mention of Walter, Lebensmal set down his glass and took another drag off his cigarette. He didn't like anyone who questioned his authority, but he could not and would not tolerate a woman doing so. With his pinstriped suit jacket parted at the waist, he locked his eyes on her, then slowly started to undo his belt. "I probably should have done this from the very beginning," he said, snaking the belt from its loops. "Establish the ground rules. But in your case, let's just consider this part of your exit interview."

Elizabeth pressed her forearms down on the armchair. In a steady voice she said, "I would advise you not to get any closer, Phil."

He looked at her meanly. "You really don't seem to understand who's in charge here, do you? But you will." Then he glanced down, successfully freeing the button and unzipping his pants. Removing himself, he stumbled over to her, his genitals bobbing limply just inches from her face.

She shook her head in wonder. She had no idea why men believed women found male genitalia impressive or scary. She bent over and reached into her bag.

"I know who I am!" he shouted thickly, thrusting himself at her. "The question is, who the *hell* do you think you are?"

"I'm Elizabeth Zott," she said calmly, withdrawing a freshly sharpened fourteen-inch chef's knife. But she wasn't sure he'd heard. He'd fainted dead away.

CHAPTER 31

The Get-Well Card

It was a heart attack. Not a massive one, but in 1960, most people didn't survive even minor heart attacks. The man was lucky to be alive. The doctors said he'd remain hospitalized for three weeks, followed by complete home bed rest for at least a year. Work was out of the question.

"*You* were the one who called the ambulance?" Walter gasped. "You were *there*?" It was the next day and Walter had just heard the news.

"I was," Elizabeth said.

"And he was—what? On the floor? Clutching his heart? Gasping?"

"Not exactly."

"Well then *what*?" Walter said, spreading his arms in frustration as Elizabeth and the makeup woman exchanged glances. "What *happened*?"

"Why don't I come back later," Rosa said quickly as she packed up her case. Before she left, she gave Elizabeth's shoulder a small squeeze. "Always an honor, Zott. An absolute honor."

Walter watched this whole interaction, his eyebrows raised in panic. "You saved Phil's life," he said nervously as the door clicked shut, "I get that. But what happened exactly? Don't leave anything out, start with why you were there in the first place. After seven p.m.? That makes no sense. Tell me. Omit nothing."

Elizabeth swiveled her chair to face Walter. She reached for her number-two pencil, removing it from her bun and securing it in behind her left ear, then picked up her coffee cup and took a sip. "He asked for a meeting," she said. "Said it couldn't wait."

"A *meeting*?" he said, horrified. "But I've said—you know—we've *talked* about this. You are never to meet with Phil on your own. It's not that I don't think you can't handle yourself; it's just that I'm your producer and I think it's always better if—" He took out a handkerchief and held it to his forehead. "Elizabeth," he said, dropping his voice. "Between you and me, Phil Lebensmal is not a good man—do you know what I mean? He's not trustworthy. He has a way of dealing with problems that—"

"He fired me."

Walter blanched.

"And you as well."

"Jesus!"

"He fired everyone who works on the show."

"No!"

"He said you failed to rein me in."

Walter turned an ashy gray. "You have to understand," he said, clenching his handkerchief. "You know how I feel about Phil; you know I don't agree with everything he says. *Have* I reined you in? Don't make me laugh. *Have* I forced you to wear those ridiculous outfits? Not once. *Have* I begged you to read the cheery cue cards? Well yes, but only because I wrote them." He threw his hands up in the air. "Look, Phil gave me two weeks— two weeks to find an appropriate way to make him see that your outrageous way of doing things actually works—that you get more fan mail, more calls, more people lining up for your studio audience than all of the other shows combined, and for those reasons alone, you should stay. But you know I can't just waltz in there and say, 'Phil you're wrong and she's right.' That's suicide. No. Dealing with Phil means stroking his ego, using the angles, saying what he wants to hear. You *know* what I mean. When you held up that can of soup, I thought we'd cinched it. Until you told everyone it was poison."

"Because it is."

"Look," Walter said. "I live in the real world, and in that world, we say and do things in order to keep our stupid jobs. Do you have any idea how much crap I've endured in the last year? Plus, did you even know this? Our sponsors are about to walk."

"Phil told you that."

"Yes, and here's a news flash. It doesn't matter how many warm and fuzzy letters *you* get—if the sponsors say, 'We hate Zott,' that's it. And Phil's research says they hate you." He shoved his handkerchief back in his pocket, then got up and filled a Dixie Cup with water, awaiting the glug from the gallon jug, an unpleasant sound that always reminded him of his ulcer. "Look," he said, his hand on his abdomen. "We should keep this between ourselves until I can figure something out. How many people know? Just you and me, right?"

"I told everyone on the show."

"No."

"I think it's safe to say the entire building knows by now."

"No," he repeated, planting his palm to his forehead. "Dammit, Elizabeth, what were you thinking? Don't you know how being fired works? Step one: never tell anyone the truth—claim you won the lottery, inherited a cattle ranch in Wyoming, got a huge offer in New York, that sort of thing. Step two: drink to excess until you figure out what to do. Jesus. It's like you're not familiar with TV's tribal ways!"

Elizabeth took another sip of coffee. "Do you want to hear what happened or not?"

"There's more?" he said anxiously. "What? He's going to repossess our cars, too?"

She looked at him straight on, her normally lineless forehead slightly furrowed, and just like that his attention turned from himself to her. He felt uneasy. He'd completely overlooked the most critical component of her meeting with Phil. She'd met with him alone.

"Tell me," he said, feeling as if he might vomit. "Please tell me."

Were most men like Phil? In Walter's opinion, no. But did most men *do* anything about men like Phil, himself included? No. Sure, maybe that seemed shameful or cowardly, but, honestly, what *could* anyone actually do? You didn't pick a fight with a man like Phil. To avoid these outcomes, you simply did what you were told. Everyone knew it and everyone did it. But Elizabeth wasn't everyone. He put a trembling hand to his forehead, hating every bone in his spineless body. "Did he try something? Did you have to fight him off?" he whispered.

She sat up in her chair, the light of her makeup mirror providing an extra aura of fortitude. He studied her face with fear, thinking this was probably the same way Joan of Arc looked right before they lit the match.

"He tried."

"God!" Walter shouted, crushing his Dixie Cup in one hand. "God, no!"

"Walter, relax. He failed."

Walter hesitated. "Because of the heart attack," he said, relieved. "Of course! What uncanny timing. The heart attack. Thank the Lord!"

She looked at him quizzically, then reached down into her bag, the same bag she'd taken to Phil's office the previous night.

"I wouldn't thank the Lord," she said, pulling that same fourteen-inch chef's knife out of her bag.

He gasped. Like most cooks, Elizabeth insisted on using her own knives. She brought them in each morning and took them home each evening. Everyone knew this. Everyone except Phil.

"I didn't touch him," she explained. "He just keeled over."

"Jesus—" Walter whispered.

"I called an ambulance, but you know how traffic is at that

time of day. Took forever. So while I waited, I made good use of my time. Here. Take a look." She handed him the folders Lebensmal had waved at her. "Syndication offers," she said as he registered obvious surprise at the contents. "Did you know that we've been syndicated in the state of New York for the last three months? Also, some interesting new sponsorship offers. Despite what Phil told you, sponsors are falling all over themselves to be part of our show. Like this one," she said, tapping an ad for the RCA Victor company.

Walter kept his eyes down, staring at the stack. He motioned for Elizabeth to hand him her coffee cup, and when she did, he downed it.

"Sorry," he finally managed. "It's just that it's all so overwhelming."

She glanced impatiently at the wall clock.

"I can't believe we're fired," he continued. "I mean, we have a hit show on our hands and *we're fired*?"

Elizabeth looked at him with concern. "No, Walter," she said slowly. "We're *not* fired. We're in charge."

Four days later, Walter sat behind Phil's old desk, the room swept clean of ashtrays, the Persian rug gone, the phone buttons ablaze with important calls.

"Walter, just make the changes you know need to be made," she said, reminding him that he was acting executive producer. And when he balked at the responsibility, she simplified the job description. "Just do what you know is right, Walter. It's not that hard, is it? Then tell others to do the same."

It wasn't quite as easy as she made it sound—the only management style he knew was intimidation and manipulation; that's how *he'd* always been managed. But she seemed to believe—god, she was so naïve!—that employees were more productive when they felt respected.

"Stop flailing, Walter," she said as they stood outside Woody Elementary awaiting yet another conference with Mudford. "Take the helm. Steer. When in doubt, pretend."

Pretend. *That* he could do. Within days, he'd made a series of deals, syndicating *Supper at Six* from one coast to the other. Then he negotiated a new set of sponsorships that could double KCTV's bottom line. Finally, before he could chicken out, he called a station-wide meeting to update everyone on Phil's cardiovascular condition, including Elizabeth's role in saving his life, and how, despite the "incident," he very much hoped everyone would continue to enjoy their meaningful work at KCTV. Out of all those things, Phil's heart attack got the loudest applause.

"I asked our graphic artist to create this get-well greeting," he said, holding up a gigantic card featuring a caricature of Phil making a winning touchdown. But instead of clutching a normal football, Phil was clutching his heart, which now that Walter thought about it, maybe wasn't the best choice. "Please take the time to sign your name," Walter said. "And if you'd like, add a personal note."

Later that day, when the card was delivered to him for his own signature, he glanced at the well-wishes. Most were the standard "Feel better!" but a few were a bit darker.

Fuck you, Lebensmal.

I wouldn't have called an ambulance.

Die already.

He recognized the handwriting on the last one—one of Phil's secretaries.

Even though he knew he couldn't possibly be the only one who'd hated the boss, he'd had no idea what a large club he belonged to. It was validating, sure, but also gut-wrenching.

Because as a producer, he was part of Phil's management team, and that meant he was responsible for pushing Phil's agenda while ignoring those who ultimately paid the price for it. He reached for a pen and, for the fourth time that day, followed Elizabeth Zott's simple advice: do what was right.

MAY YOU NEVER *RECOVER,* he wrote in huge letters across the middle. Then he stuffed the card in an enormous envelope, put it in the out basket, and made a solemn promise. Things had to change. He would start with himself.

CHAPTER 32

Medium Rare

"Does Mom know?" Mad asked as Harriet bustled her into her Chrysler. It was well into the new school year, and as promised, she'd gotten Mudford for her teacher again. That's why Harriet thought she could miss a day. Or twenty.

"Good gravy, no!" Harriet said as she adjusted the rearview mirror. "If she knew, would we be doing this?"

"But won't she be mad?"

"Only if she finds out."

"You did a pretty good job on her signature," Mad said, examining the note Harriet had written to get Mad out of school. "Except for the E and the Z."

"Well," Harriet said, irritated, "aren't I lucky the school doesn't employ forensic handwriting experts."

"You really are," Mad agreed.

"Here's the plan," Harriet said, ignoring her. "We stand in line like everybody else, and once in, make a beeline for the back row. No one ever goes for the back row. We want to sit there because should something go wrong, we'll be right next to the emergency exit."

"But the emergency exit is *only* to be used for emergencies," Mad said.

"Yes, well, if your mother spies us, that qualifies as an emergency."

"But the doors will be armed."

"Yes—another bonus. Should we have to make a quick exit, the noise will distract her."

"Are you *sure* we should be doing this, Harriet?" Mad said. "Mom says a TV studio isn't safe."

"Nonsense."

"She says it's—"

"Mad, it's safe. It's an environment for learning. Your mother teaches cooking on TV, doesn't she?"

"She teaches chemistry," Madeline corrected.

"What kind of danger could we possibly encounter?"

Madeline looked out the window. "Excess radioactivity," she said.

Harriet exhaled loudly. The child was turning into her mother. Normally this sort of thing happened later in life, but Mad was way ahead of schedule. She thought about Mad being all grown up. *If I've told you once, I've told you a thousand times,* she'd shout at her own child. *Never leave a Bunsen burner unattended!*

"We're here!" Mad suddenly erupted as the studio parking lot came into view. "KCTV! Oh boy!" And then her face fell. "But, Harriet, look at the line."

"I'll be damned," Harriet swore as she took in the mass of humanity snaking around the parking lot. There were hundreds of people, mostly women with purses sitting heavily on sweaty forearms, but also a few dozen men with suit jackets dangling from two fingers. Everyone used a makeshift fan—maps, hats, newspapers.

"Are they all here for Mom's show?" Madeline said, awestruck.

"No, honey, they tape lots of shows here."

"Excuse me, ma'am," a parking lot attendant said, signaling Harriet to stop. He leaned in on Madeline's side, "but didn't you see the sign? Lot's full."

"All right, then, where should I park?"

"Are you here for *Supper at Six*?"

"Yes."

"I'm sorry to hafta tell you, then—you won't get in," he said, gesturing at the long line. "These people, most of them are here for nothing. People start lining up at four a.m. Most of the studio audience has been selected already."

"What?" Harriet exclaimed. "I had no idea."

"Show's popular," the man said.

Harriet hesitated. "But I took this child out of school for this."

"Sorry, grandma," he said. Then he leaned farther into the car. "Sorry to you too, kid. I turn away a lot of people every day. Not a fun job, believe me. People yell at me all the time."

"My mom wouldn't like that," Mad said. "She wouldn't like anyone yelling at anyone."

"Your mom sounds sweet," the man said. "But could you move it? I got a lot more people to turn away."

"Okay," Mad said. "But could you do me a quick favor? Could you write your name in my notebook? I'll tell my mom how hard it is out here for you."

"Mad," Harriet hissed.

"You want my autograph?" He laughed. "Well that's a first." And before Harriet could stop him, he took the notebook from Mad and wrote *Seymour Browne,* careful to use the lines in her school notebook that showed just how high the tall letters should be and just how small the small letters should be. Then he closed the notebook, the two words on the cover jolting him like a loose electrical wire.

"Madeline *Zott?*" he read incredulously.

The studio was dark and cool, with thick cords running from one end to the other and huge cameras on either side, each primed to swivel and record what the lights from above illuminated.

"Here we are," Walter Pine's secretary said, ushering Madeline and Harriet to a pair of suddenly vacant seats in the front row. "Best seats in the house."

"Actually," Harriet said, "would you mind? We kind of had our hearts set on sitting in the back."

"Oh gosh no," the woman said. "Mr. Pine would kill me."

"Someone's going to die," Harriet murmured.

"I like these seats," Madeline said, sitting down.

"Seeing a show live is very different from watching it at home," the secretary explained. "You're not just seeing the show anymore—you're part of it. And the lights—they change everything. I guarantee, this is the place to sit."

"It's just that we don't want to distract Elizabeth Zott," Harriet said, trying again. "Don't want to make her nervous."

"Zott, nervous?" The secretary laughed. "That's funny. Anyway, she can't see the audience. The set lighting blinds her."

"You're *sure*?" Harriet said.

"Sure as death and taxes."

"Everyone dies," Mad pointed out. "But not everyone pays their taxes."

"Aren't you a precocious little thing," the secretary said, her voice suddenly irritated. But before Madeline could offer some statistics on tax evasion, the quartet launched into the *Supper at Six* theme song and the secretary disappeared into the ether. From off to the left, Madeline watched as Walter Pine settled into a cloth-backed chair. He gave a nod, then a camera rolled into position, then a man wearing headphones gave a thumbs-up. As the song reached its final measures, a familiar figure strode like a president to the podium, her head held high, posture erect, hair aglow under the bright lights.

Madeline had seen her mother in a thousand different ways—first thing in the morning, last thing at night, leaning away from a Bunsen burner, peering into a microscope, facing off with Mrs. Mudford, frowning into a powder-filled compact, coming out of the shower, gathering her in her arms. But she had never seen her mother like this—never, ever like this. *Mom!* she thought, her heart swelling with pride. *Mommy!*

"Hello," Elizabeth said. "My name is Elizabeth Zott, and this is *Supper at Six*."

The secretary was right. There was something about the lights, the way they revealed things that the grainy black and white at home could not.

"It's steak night," Elizabeth said, "which means we'll be exploring the chemical composition of meat, specifically focusing on the difference between 'bound water' and 'free water' because—and this may surprise you," she said, picking up a large slab of top sirloin, "—meat is about seventy-two percent water."

"Like lettuce," Harriet whispered.

"Obviously not like lettuce," Elizabeth said, "which contains far more water—up to ninety-six percent. Why is water important? Because it's the most common molecule in our bodies: sixty percent of our composition. While our bodies can go without food for up to three weeks, without water, we're dead in three days. Four days max."

From the audience came a murmur of distress.

"Which is why," Elizabeth said, "when you think about fueling your body, think water first. But now, back to meat." She picked up a large, sleek knife, and while demonstrating how to butterfly a hunk of meat, launched into the steak's vitamin content, explaining not only what the body did with its iron, zinc, and B-vitamins, but why protein was critical to one's growth. She then explained what percentage of the water in the muscle tissue existed as free molecules, ending with what she obviously thought were exciting definitions of free and bound water.

Throughout her explanation, the studio audience remained rapt—no coughing, no whispering, no crossing and uncrossing of legs. If there was one sound, it was only the occasional scratching of pen on paper as people took notes.

"Time for station identification," Elizabeth said, acknowledging a cue from the cameraman. "Stay with us, won't you?" Then she put the knife down and strode off the set, pausing briefly as the makeup woman pressed a sponge to her forehead and patted down a few loose hairs.

Madeline turned to take in the audience. They sat nervously, impatient for Elizabeth Zott to reappear. She felt a small pang of jealousy. She suddenly realized she had to share her mother with a lot of other people. She didn't like it.

"After you've rubbed your steak with a halved clove of fresh garlic," Elizabeth said a few minutes later, "sprinkle both sides of the meat with sodium chloride and piperine. Then, when you notice the butter foaming"—she pointed to a hot cast-iron skillet— "place the steak in the pan. Be sure and wait until the butter foams. Foam indicates that the butter's water content has boiled away. This is critical. Because now the steak can cook in lipids rather than absorb H_2O."

As the steak sizzled, she removed an envelope from her apron pocket. "While that's cooking, I wanted to share with you all a letter I received from Nanette Harrison in Long Beach. Nanette writes, 'Dear Mrs. Zott, I'm a vegetarian. It's not for religious reasons—it's just that I don't think it's very nice to eat living things. My husband says the body needs meat and I'm being stupid, but I just hate thinking an animal has given up its life for me. Jesus did that and look what happened to him. Sincerely yours, Mrs. Nanette Harrison, Long Beach, California.'

"Nanette, you've brought up an interesting point," Elizabeth said. "What we eat has consequences for other living things. However, plants are living things too, and yet we rarely consider that they are still alive even as we chop them to bits, crush them with our molars, force them down our esophagi, and then digest them in our stomachs filled with hydrochloric acid. In short, I applaud you, Nanette. You think before you eat. But make no mistake, you're still actively taking life to sustain your own.

There is no way around this. As for Jesus, no comment." She turned and, jabbing the steak out of the pan, the dripping juices a bloody red, looked directly into the camera. "And now a word from our sponsor."

Harriet and Madeline turned to look at each other, their eyes wide. "Sometimes I ask myself: *How* is this show popular?" Harriet whispered.

"Excuse me, ladies." The secretary was back. "Mr. Pine asked if he might have a quick word?" She phrased it as a question even though it wasn't. "Follow me?" She spirited them away from the stage and down a corridor until they reached an office where Walter Pine was pacing back and forth. Four TVs were lined up against the wall, all airing *Supper at Six.*

"Hello, Madeline," he said. "I'm delighted to see you, but also surprised. Shouldn't you be in school?"

Mad tipped her head to the side. "Hi, Mr. Pine." She pointed at Harriet. "This is Harriet. It was her idea. She forged the note."

Harriet threw her a look.

"Walter Pine," Walter said, taking Harriet's hand. "At long last. Very pleased to meet you, Harriet . . . Sloane, correct? I've heard nothing but good things. But," he said, his voice dropping, "what were you two thinking? If she finds out you're here—"

"I know," Harriet said. "For the record, we asked to sit in the back."

"Amanda wanted to come too," Mad said, "but Harriet didn't want to compound the crime. Forgery is a felony, but kidnapping—"

"How thoughtful of you, Mrs. Sloane," he interrupted. "Although just so you both know, if it were up to me, you would always be welcome. Still, it's not up to me. Your mother," he said, turning to Madeline, "is only trying to protect you."

"From radioactivity?"

He hesitated. "You're a very smart little girl, Madeline, so when I tell you your mom is trying to protect you from celebrity, I'm betting you'll know what I mean."

"I don't."

"It means that she wants to protect your privacy. To protect you from all the things people say and think about someone who is in the public eye. Someone who is famous."

"How famous *is* my mom?"

"Since syndication," Walter said, touching his fingertips to his forehead, "she's a bit more well-known. Because now people in places like Chicago and Boston and Denver can watch your mommy, too."

"Chop the rosemary," Elizabeth was saying quietly in the background, "with the sharpest knife you have. This minimizes damage to the plant and avoids excess electrolyte leakage."

"Why is being famous bad?" Madeline asked.

"I wouldn't say it's bad," Walter said. "It's just that it comes with some surprises and not all of them are good. Sometimes people want to believe they know a celebrity like your mom on a personal level. This makes them feel important. But to do this, they have to make up stories about your mom, and not all the stories are very nice. Your mom is just trying to make sure no one makes up a story about you."

"People are making up stories about my mom?" Madeline said, alarmed. It had to be the lights—the way they made her mother look invincible. That's what the audience needed to see: a woman who both demanded respect and got it—even if her mother had problems like everybody else. Mad guessed it was a bit like her pretending she couldn't read very well. You did what you did to get by.

"Don't worry," Walter said, placing his hand on her bony shoulder. "If there's one person who can handle herself, it's your mother. Very few will try to take on Elizabeth Zott. All she's trying to do is make sure they don't try to take advantage of you. Do you understand? That goes for you too, Mrs. Sloane," he said, turning to look at Harriet. "You spend more time around Elizabeth than most; I'm sure your friends would love to hear you tell all."

"I don't have a lot of friends," Harriet said. "And even if I did, I know better."

"Smart woman," Walter said. "I don't have a lot of friends either."

Actually, he thought to himself, he only had one: Elizabeth Zott. And she wasn't just a friend, she was his best friend. He'd never told her she was, but she was. Yes, there were plenty of people who would argue that a man and woman couldn't really be friends. They were wrong. He and Elizabeth discussed everything, intimate things—death, sex, and children. Plus, they had each other's backs like friends do, even laughed together like friends do. Granted, Elizabeth wasn't a big laugher. Still, despite the show's growing popularity, she seemed more depressed than ever.

"So," Walter said, "why don't we get you out of here before your mom sees us and we all fry in stomach acid."

"But why do you think my mom's so popular?" Madeline asked, still wishing she didn't have to share her.

"Because she says exactly what she thinks," Walter said. "Which is very rare. But also because the food she makes is very, very good. And because everyone seems to want to learn chemistry. Oddly."

"But why is saying what you think so rare?"

"Because there are consequences," Harriet said.

"Huge consequences," Walter agreed.

From a TV in the corner Elizabeth said, "It looks like we have time today to take a question from our studio audience. Yes—you there, in the lavender dress."

A woman stood up, beaming. "Yes, hello, my name is Edna Flattistein and I'm from China Lake? I just want to say, I love the show, and I especially loved what you said about being grateful for food, and I just wondered if you have a favorite grace you recite before each meal, to thank our Lord and Savior for the bounty! I'd love to hear it! Thank you!"

Elizabeth shielded her eyes as if to get a better look at Edna.

"Hello, Edna," she said, "and thanks for your question. The answer is no; I don't have a favorite grace. In fact, I don't say grace at all."

Standing in the office, both Walter and Harriet paled.

"Please," Walter whispered. "Don't say it."

"Because I'm an atheist," Elizabeth said matter-of-factly.

"Thar she blows," Harriet said.

"In other words, I don't believe in God," added Elizabeth as the audience gasped.

"Wait. Is that rare?" Madeline piped up. "Is not believing in God one of those *rare* things?"

"But I do believe in the people who made the food possible," Elizabeth continued. "The farmers, the pickers, the truckers, the grocery store shelf stockers. But most of all, I believe in you, Edna. Because you made the meal that nourishes your family. Because of you, a new generation flourishes. Because of you, others live."

She paused, checking the clock, then turned directly to the camera. "That's all we have time for today. I hope you'll join me tomorrow as we explore the fascinating world of temperature and how it affects flavor." Then she cocked her head slightly to the left, almost as if she were considering whether she'd gone too far or not far enough. "Children, set the table," she said with extra resolution. "Your mother needs a moment to herself."

And within a few seconds, Walter's phone began to ring and did not stop.

CHAPTER 33

Faith

In 1960, people did not go on television and say they didn't believe in God and expect to be on television much longer. As proof, Walter's phone was soon filled with threats from sponsors and viewers who wanted Elizabeth Zott fired, jailed, and/or stoned to death. The latter came from self-proclaimed people of God—the same God that preached tolerance and forgiveness.

"Goddammit, Elizabeth," Walter said, having slipped Harriet and Madeline out the side door ten minutes earlier. "Some things are just better left unsaid!" They were sitting in Elizabeth's dressing room, her yellow-checked apron still wound firmly around her narrow waist. "You have every right to believe what you want to believe, but you shouldn't force your belief on others, especially not on national television."

"How did I force my belief on others?" she asked, surprised.

"You know what I mean."

"Edna Flattistein asked me a direct question and I answered it. I'm glad she feels she can express her belief in God and I welcome her right to do so. But I should be extended the same courtesy. Plenty of people don't believe in God. Some believe in astrology or tarot cards. Harriet believes if you blow on dice, you'll get better numbers at Yahtzee."

"I think we both know," Walter said through gritted teeth, "that God is just a bit different from Yahtzee."

"Agreed," Elizabeth said. "Yahtzee is fun."

"We're going to pay for this," Walter warned.

"Come on, Walter," she said. "Have a little faith."

Faith—that was supposed to be Reverend Wakely's area of expertise, but today he was having trouble finding his. After spending
hours consoling a whiney congregant who blamed everyone for
everything, he returned to his office, wanting to be alone. But
instead, he found his part-time typist, Miss Frask, at his desk,
using his typewriter, plodding along at thirty words per minute,
her eyes glued to his office's television set.

"Take a good look at this tomato," he heard a vaguely
familiar-looking woman on the television say, a pencil sticking
out from behind her head. "You might not believe you have anything in common with this fruit, but you do. DNA. Up to sixty
percent. Now turn and look at the person next to you. Does she
look familiar? She may or may not. Still, you and she share even
more: ninety-nine point nine percent of your DNA—as you
each do with every other human on earth." She set the tomato
down and held up a photograph of Rosa Parks. "That's why I
stand with our leaders of the civil rights movement, including
the very brave Rosa Parks. Discrimination based on skin color
is not only scientifically ludicrous, it's also a sign of profound
ignorance."

"Miss Frask?" Wakely said.

"Hold on, Rev," she said, holding up a finger. "It's almost over.
Here's your sermon." She yanked a sheet out of the typewriter.

"One would think the ignorant would die off sooner," Elizabeth continued. "But Darwin overlooked the fact that the ignorant rarely forget to eat."

"What *is* this?"

"*Supper at Six*. You've never heard of *Supper at Six*?"

"I have time for a question," Elizabeth was saying, "Yes, you
there in the—"

"Hello, my name is Francine Luftson and I'm from San Diego! And I just want to say, I'm such a fan even if you don't believe in God! I was just wondering: Is there some sort of diet you recommend? I know I need to lose weight, but I really don't want to feel hungry. I do take diet pills every day. Thank you!"

"Thanks, Francine," Elizabeth said. "But I can clearly see that you are not overweight. Therefore, I have to assume you've been unduly influenced by the relentless imagery of the too-thin women that now fill our magazines, destroying your morale and submerging your self-worth. Instead of dieting and taking pills—" She paused. "Can I ask?" she said. "How many people in this audience take diet pills?"

A few nervous hands went up.

Elizabeth waited.

Most of the other hands went up.

"Stop taking those pills," she demanded. "They're amphetamines. They can lead to psychosis."

"But I don't like to exercise," Francine said.

"Maybe you haven't found the right exercise."

"I watch Jack LaLanne."

At the mention of Jack's name, Elizabeth closed her eyes. "What about rowing?" she said, suddenly tired.

"Rowing?"

"Rowing," she repeated, opening her eyes. "It's a brutal form of recreation designed to test every muscle in your body and mind. It takes place before dawn, too often in the rain. It results in thick calluses. It broadens the arms, chest, and thighs. Ribs crack; hands blister. Rowers sometimes ask themselves, 'Why am I doing this?'"

"Jeepers," Francine said, worried. "Rowing sounds awful!"

Elizabeth looked confused. "My point is rowing precludes the need for both diet and pills. It's also good for your soul."

"But I thought you didn't believe in souls."

Elizabeth sighed. She closed her eyes again. Calvin. *Are you actually saying women can't row?*

"I used to work with her," Frask said, switching off the television. "At Hastings, until we both got fired. Seriously—you've never heard of her? Elizabeth Zott. She's syndicated."

"She's a rower, too?" Wakely said, amazed.

"What do you mean, 'too'?" Frask asked. "You know other rowers?"

"Mad," Wakely said, as he took in the enormous dog Madeline had brought with her to the park, "why didn't you tell me your mother was on television?"

"I thought you knew. Everyone knows. Especially now that she doesn't believe in God."

"It's all right not to believe in God," Wakely said. "That's one of the things we mean when we say it's a free country. People are welcome to believe whatever they want as long as their beliefs don't hurt others. Besides, I happen to think science is a form of religion."

Madeline raised one eyebrow.

"Who's this, by the way?" he asked, reaching his hand out for the dog to sniff.

"Six-Thirty," she said as two women walked by chatting loudly.

"Correct me if I'm wrong, Sheila," one of the women was asking, "but didn't she say cast iron requires zero-point-one-one calories of heat to raise the temperature of a single gram of atomic mass by one degree Celsius?"

"That's right, Elaine," the other said. "That's why I'm buying a new skillet."

"I remember him now," Wakely continued after the women had passed. "From your family photograph. What a handsome dog."

Six-Thirty pressed his head into the man's palm. *Good man.*

"Anyway, I bet you think I forgot all about this—so much

time has passed—but I did finally follow up with All Saints. The truth is, I'd called several times after we first spoke, but the bishop was never in. Today, though, I reached his secretary and she said there's no record of a Calvin Evans. Looks like we have the wrong home."

"No," Madeline said. "That's the one. I'm *positive*."

"Mad, I doubt a church secretary would lie."

"Wakely," she said. "Everybody lies."

CHAPTER 34

All Saints

"What's it called again? All Saints?" the bishop repeated in shock. It was 1933, and although he'd been hoping for a new assignment in a wealthy parish soaked in scotch, instead he'd netted a ratty boys home in the middle of Iowa where more than a hundred boys of varying ages in training to become future criminals served as a constant reminder that the next time he made fun of an archbishop he would try not to do it to his face.

"All Saints," the archbishop had said. "The place needs discipline. Just like you."

"The truth is, I'm not good with children," he'd told the archbishop. "Widows, prostitutes—that's where I really shine. What about Chicago?"

"In addition to discipline," the archbishop said, ignoring his plea, "the place needs money. Part of your work there will be to secure long-term funding. Do that and maybe I'll find something better for you in the future."

But the future never seemed to arrive. By the time 1937 rolled around, the bishop still hadn't solved the cash-flow problem. The only productive thing he'd done? Edit his ten-page list of "I hate this place" fury down to five central problems: third-rate priests, starchy food, mildew, pedophiles, and a steady trickle of boys deemed too wild or too hungry to be part of a normal family. They were the kids no one wanted, and the bishop completely understood because he didn't want them either.

They'd been limping along via the usual Catholic means: sherry sales, Bible bookmarks, begging, brownnosing. But what they really needed was exactly what the archbishop had suggested—an endowment. The problem was, rich people tended to endow things the boys home didn't have. Chairs. Scholarships. Memorials. No matter how often he tried to sell the endowment idea, potential donors could identify the fatal flaws right off the bat: "Scholarships?" they'd scoff. The boys home wasn't really a school in the same way a prison isn't really a place to rehabilitate— no one tries to get in. Funding a chair? Same problem—the home didn't have departments, much less department chairs. Memorials? Their wards were too young to die, and anyway, who wanted to memorialize the very children everyone was trying to forget?

So here he was, four years later, still stuck in the middle of cornfields with a bunch of castaway kids. It seemed pretty clear no amount of prayer was going to change that. To pass the time he sometimes ranked the boys by who caused the most trouble, but even that was a waste of time because the same kid always topped the list. Calvin Evans.

"That minister from California called about Calvin Evans again," the secretary said to the now-much-older white-haired bishop, dropping some files on his desk. "I'd already done what you'd said—I told him I'd checked the records and no one by that name had ever been here."

"Good god. Why can't he let us alone?" the bishop said, shoving the files off to the side. "Protestants. They never know when to quit!"

"Who was Calvin Evans anyway?" she asked curiously. "A priest?"

"No," the bishop said, envisioning the boy who was the reason he was *still* in Iowa decades later. "A curse."

After she left, the bishop shook his head, remembering how often Calvin had stood in his office, guilty of yet another infraction— breaking a window, stealing a book, giving a black eye to a priest who was only trying to make him feel loved. Well-meaning couples occasionally came to the boys home to adopt one of the boys, but no one ever showed interest in Calvin. Could you blame them?

But then one day that man, Wilson, had appeared out of thin air. Said he was from the Parker Foundation, a filthy-rich Catholic fund. When the bishop heard someone from the Parker Foundation was in the building, he was certain his ship had finally come in. His heart beat fast as he imagined the size of the donation this man Wilson might propose. He would listen to the offer, then, in a dignified way, push for more.

"Hello, Bishop," Mr. Wilson said, as if he had no time to waste. "I'm looking for a young boy, ten years old, probably tall, blondish hair." He went on to explain that this boy had lost his family via a series of accidents about four years earlier. He had reason to believe the boy was there, at All Saints. The boy had living relatives who'd recently learned of his existence; they wanted him back. "His name is Calvin Evans," he finished, glancing at his watch as if he had another appointment to make. "If a boy of that description is here, I'd like to meet him. Actually, my plan is to take him back with me."

The bishop stared at Wilson, his lips parted in disappointment. Between the time he'd heard that the rich man was in the building and their introductory handshake, he'd already crafted an acceptance speech.

"Is everything all right?" Mr. Wilson asked. "I hate to push, but I have a flight in two hours."

Not a single mention of money. The bishop could feel Chi-

cago slipping away. He took a good long look at Wilson. The
man was tall and arrogant. Just like Calvin.

"Perhaps I could go out and walk among the boys. See if I
can't recognize him on my own."

The bishop turned to the window. Just that morning he'd
caught Calvin washing his hands in the baptismal font. "There's
nothing holy about this water," Calvin informed him. "It's straight
from the tap."

But as eager as he was to get rid of Calvin, his bigger problem—
money—remained. He stared out at the dozen or so wilted gravestones that littered the courtyard. *In Memoriam,* they claimed.

"Bishop?" Wilson was standing. His briefcase was already
dangling from one hand.

The bishop didn't reply. He didn't like the man, or his fancy
clothes, or the way he'd arrived without an appointment. He was
a bishop, for god's sake—where was the respect? He cleared his
throat, stalling for time as he stared at the gravestones of all the
bullied bishops who'd come before him. He could not let the
Parker Foundation with its promise of untold funds get away.

He turned to Wilson. "I have terrible news," he said. "Calvin
Evans is dead."

"By the way, if that annoying minister ever calls here again,"
the old bishop continued to instruct his secretary as she cleared
his coffee cup, "tell him I died. Or wait, no—tell him," he said,
tapping his fingers together, "that you'd learned there was a Calvin Evans in a different home—somewhere like, I don't know,
Poughkeepsie? But the place burned down and all the records
were lost."

"You want me to make something up?" she worried.

"You wouldn't be making something up," he said. "Not
really. Buildings burn down all the time. Hardly anyone takes
building codes seriously."

"But—"

"Just do it," the bishop said. "That minister is wasting our time. Our focus is on fundraising, remember? Money for *our living, breathing* children. You get a money call, I'm in. But this Calvin Evans nonsense—it's a dead end."

Wilson looked as if he must have misheard. "What . . . what did you just say?"

"Calvin recently passed away from pneumonia," the bishop said simply. "Terrible shock. He was such a favorite here." As he spun the tale, he mentioned Calvin's good manners, his Bible class leadership, his love of corn. The more details he gave, the more rigid Wilson became. Fueled by how well the story was going, the bishop went to the filing cabinet to retrieve a photo. "We're using this one for his memorial fund," he said, pointing at a black and white of Calvin, his hands perched at his waist, his torso bent forward, his mouth open wide as if telling someone off. "I love that photo. It just says Calvin to me."

He watched as Wilson stared down at the photograph, silent. The bishop waited for him to ask for some sort of proof. But no—he seemed to be in shock, mournful even.

He'd suddenly wondered if maybe this Mr. Wilson wasn't a so-called long-lost relative. One thing fit—the height. Was Calvin his nephew, maybe? Or no—*his son*? Good god. If that was the case, the man had no idea how much trouble he was saving him. He cleared his throat and allowed a few more minutes for the sad news to sink in.

"Of course, we'll want to endow the memorial fund," Wilson finally said in an unsteady voice. "The Parker Foundation will want to honor the memory of this young boy." He exhaled, which seemed to further deflate him, then reached down and pulled out a checkbook.

"Of course," the bishop said sympathetically. "The Calvin Evans Memorial Fund. A special tribute for a special boy."

"I'll be back in touch with the details of how we'll structure our ongoing contribution, Bishop," Wilson said, struggling, "but in the meantime, please accept this check on behalf of the Parker Foundation. We thank you for all you . . . did."

The bishop had forced himself to take the check without looking at it, but once Wilson was out the door, he laid the slip of paper flat on his desk. Nice chunk of change. And more to come, thanks to his idea to create a memorial fund for someone who wasn't even dead yet. He leaned back in his chair and laced his fingers across his chest. If anyone needed any further proof of God's existence, they need look no further. All Saints: the place where God actually did help those who helped themselves.

After leaving Madeline in the park, Wakely had returned to his office and reluctantly picked up the phone. The only reason he was calling All Saints yet again was to prove to Mad that she was wrong. Not everybody lied. But talk about irony—first he had to lie himself.

"Good afternoon," he said, imitating a British accent upon hearing the secretary's familiar voice. "I'd like to speak to someone in your gifts department. I'm interested in making a sizable donation."

"Oh!" the secretary said brightly. "Let me put you straight through to our bishop."

"I understand you'd like to make a donation," the old bishop said to Wakely a few moments later.

"That's correct," Wakely lied. "My ministry is dedicated to helping—uh—children," he said, picturing Mad's long face. "Orphans, specifically."

But had Calvin Evans been an orphan? Wakely mused to himself. When they were pen pals, Calvin had made it very clear that he did, indeed, have a living parent. *I HATE MY FATHER, I HOPE HE'S DEAD.* Wakely could still see the typing in all caps.

"To be even more specific, I'm looking for the place Calvin Evans grew up."

"Calvin Evans? I'm sorry, but the name doesn't ring any bells."

From the other end of the phone, Wakely paused. The man was lying. He listened to liars every day; he knew. But what were the odds that two men of the cloth would lie to each other at the same time?

"Well, that's too bad," Wakely said carefully. "Because my donation is earmarked for the home where Calvin Evans spent his youth. I'm sure you do wonderful work, but you know how donors can be. Single-minded."

On the other end of the line, the bishop pressed his finger-tips against his eyelids. Yes, he did know how donors could be. The Parker Foundation had made his life a living hell; first with the science books and rowing silliness, then with their outsized reaction when they discovered their endowment was honoring the life of someone who wasn't technically, well, dead. And the way they knew this? Because good old Calvin had managed to rise from the not-really-dead and appear on the cover of some no-name magazine called *Chemistry Today*. And about two seconds later, a woman named Avery Parker was on the phone threaten-ing him with about a hundred different lawsuits.

Who was Avery Parker? The Parker behind the Parker Foundation.

The bishop had never spoken with her before—he'd only ever dealt with Wilson, whom he now gathered was her personal rep-resentative and lawyer. But now that he thought about it, he did remember a sloppy signature that sat next to Wilson's on every single endowment document for the last fifteen years.

"You *lied* to the Parker Foundation?" she'd shouted on the phone. "You pretended Calvin Evans died from pneumonia at age ten just to get an endowment?"

And he thought, *Lady, you have no idea how bad it is here in Iowa.*

"Mrs. Parker," he'd said soothingly. "I understand you're upset. But I swear the Calvin Evans who was here *is* very much dead. Whoever appeared on that cover shares his name, nothing more. It's a very common name."

"No," she insisted. "It was Calvin. I recognized him immediately."

"You'd met Calvin before, then?"

She hesitated. "Well. No."

"I see," he said, using a tone that effectively communicated how ridiculous she was being.

She canceled the endowment five seconds later.

"Ours is a tough business, isn't it Reverend Wakely?" the bishop said. "Donors are slippery fish. But I've got to be honest—we could really use your donation. Even if this Calvin Evans wasn't here, we do have other boys who are just as deserving."

"I'm sure they are," Wakely agreed. "But my hands are tied. I can only give this donation—did I mention it's fifty thousand dollars?—to Calvin Evans's—"

"*Wait,*" the bishop said, his heart beating fast at the mention of such a large sum. "Please try to understand: it's a privacy issue. We don't talk about individuals. Even if that boy had been here, we're really not allowed to say."

"Right," said Wakely. "Still . . ."

The bishop glanced up at the clock. It was almost time for his favorite show, *Supper at Six.* "No, now *wait,*" he barked, not wanting to lose the donation or miss his show. "You've really forced my hand on this one. Between you and me and the wall, yes, this *is* where Calvin Evans grew up."

"Really?" Wakely said, sitting up tall. "You have proof of this?"

"*Of course,* I have proof," the bishop said, affronted, touching his fingertips to all the wrinkles Calvin had given him over the years. "Would we be home to the Calvin Evans Memorial Fund if he hadn't been here?"

Wakely was taken aback. "Excuse me?"

"The Calvin Evans Memorial Fund. We set it up years ago to honor that precious boy who went on to become an amazing young chemist. Any decent library will have tax documents proving its existence. But the Parker Foundation—they endowed it—insisted we never advertise it, and you can probably guess why. It's not like they could afford to fund every home that lost a child."

"Lost a child?" Wakely said. "But Evans was an adult when he died."

"Y-y-yes," the bishop stammered. "Correct. It's just that we still refer to our past residents as children. Because that's when we knew them best—as children. Calvin Evans was a wonderful kid, too. Smart as a whip. Very tall. Now about that donation."

A few days later, Wakely met back up with Madeline in the park. "I have good news and bad news," he said. "You were right. Your dad was at All Saints." He went on to tell her what the bishop had told him: that Calvin Evans had been a "wonderful kid" and "smart as a whip." "They even have a Calvin Evans Memorial Fund," he said. "I confirmed it at the library. It was funded for nearly fifteen years by a place called the Parker Foundation."

She frowned. "Was?"

"The foundation stopped funding it a while ago. That happens sometimes. Priorities change."

"But Wakely, my dad died *six* years ago."

"So?"

"So why would the Parker Foundation fund a memorial for fifteen years? When"—she did a calculation on her fingers—"for the first nine of those years, he wasn't even dead yet?"

"Oh," Wakely said, reddening. He hadn't noticed the date discrepancy. "Well—back then it probably wasn't really a memorial fund, Mad. Maybe more of an honorary fund—he did say it was in *honor* of your dad."

"And if they have this fund, why didn't they say so the first time you called?"

"Privacy issue," he said, repeating what the bishop had told him. At least that made some sense. "Anyway, here's the good part. I looked up the Parker Foundation and discovered it's run by a Mr. Wilson. He lives in Boston." He looked at her expectantly. "Wilson," he repeated. "Otherwise known as your acorn fairy godfather." He sat back on the bench, waiting for a positive response. But when the child said nothing he added, "Wilson sounds like a very noble man."

"He sounds misinformed," Mad said, examining a scab. "Like he's never read *Oliver Twist*."

Mad had a point. But still, Wakely had dedicated a lot of time to this and he'd expected she might be a little more excited. Or at least grateful. Although why did he think that? No one ever expressed gratitude for his work. He was out in the trenches every day comforting people going through their various trials and tribulations, and all he ever heard was the same old tired line: "Why is God punishing me?" Jesus. How the hell should he know?

"Anyway," he said, trying not to sound dejected. "That's the story."

Madeline crossed her arms in disappointment. "Wakely," she said. "Was that supposed to be the good news or the bad news?"

"That was the *good* news," he said pointedly. He had very little experience with children and he was beginning to think he wanted even less. "The only bad news is that while I have an address for Wilson at the Parker Foundation, it's only a post office box."

"What's wrong with that?"

"Rich people use post office boxes to shield themselves from unwanted correspondence. It's like a garbage can for mail." He reached down to his satchel and after some riffling, came up with a slip of paper. Handing it to her he said, "Here it is, the box number. But please, Mad, don't get your hopes up."

"I don't have hopes," Mad explained, studying the address. "I have faith."

He looked at her in surprise. "Well, that's a funny word to hear coming from you."

"How come?"

"Because," he said, "well, you know. Religion is based on faith."

"But you realize," she said carefully, as if not to embarrass him further, "that faith isn't based on religion. Right?"

CHAPTER 35

The Smell of Failure

On Monday morning at four thirty a.m., Elizabeth left her house as she usually did, in the dark, in warm clothes, headed for the boathouse. But as she pulled into the normally empty parking lot, she noticed nearly every space was already taken. She also noticed one other thing. Women. A lot of women. Trudging toward the building in the dark.

"Oh god," she whispered as she pulled her hood over her head and slipped past the small throng, hoping to find Dr. Mason in time to explain. But it was too late. He was sitting at a long table handing out registration forms. He looked up at her, unsmiling.

"Zott."

"You may be wondering what this is all about," she said in a low voice.

"Not really."

"I think what happened," Elizabeth said, "was that one of my viewers asked for a diet tip, and I suggested she start exercising. I may have mentioned rowing."

"May have."

"Possibly."

A woman in line turned to her friend. "The thing I like about rowing already," she said, pointing at a photograph of eight men in a shell, "is that it's all done sitting down."

"See if this jogs your memory," Mason said, handing the next woman in line a pen. "First you described rowing as the worst form of punishment, then you suggested that women all over the nation give it a whirl."

"Well. I don't think those were my *exact* words—"

"They were. I know because I saw your show while I was waiting for a patient to dilate. So did my wife. She never misses."

"I'm sorry, Mason, truly. I never expected—"

"Really?" he snapped. "Because two weeks ago, one of my patients refused to push until you finished explaining the Maillard reaction."

She looked up surprised, then reconsidered. "Well. It *is* a complicated reaction."

"I've been calling you about this since Friday," he said pointedly.

Elizabeth started. He had. He'd called both the studio and home and in her avalanche of things to do she'd neglected to call him back.

"I'm sorry," she said. "I've been so busy."

"Could have used your help in getting this organized."

"Yes."

"Obviously we *won't* be getting on the water today."

"Again, sorry."

"You know what really kills me?" he said, gesturing at a woman doing jumping jacks. "I've been trying to get my wife to row for years. As you know, I believe women have a higher threshold for pain. Still nothing *I* could say could convince her. But one word from Elizabeth Zott—"

The woman doing jumping jacks stopped to give Elizabeth a thumbs-up.

"—and she couldn't get down here fast enough."

"Oh, I see," Elizabeth said slowly as she gave the woman a small nod of approval. "So really, you're glad."

"I—"

"So what you're trying to say is, *Thank you,* Elizabeth."

"No."

"You're very *welcome,* Dr. Mason."

"No."

She glanced back at the woman. "Your wife is getting on the erg."

"Oh god," Mason called. "Betsy, *not* that!"

A similar thing happened at other boathouses across the nation. Women showed up, and some of the clubs encouraged them to join. But that's not to say every club did. Or that everyone who watched Elizabeth's show liked what she had to say.

"GODLESS HEETHEN!" read a hastily scribbled picket sign emblazoned with Elizabeth's likeness and hoisted by a mean-looking woman just outside KCTV Studios.

It was Elizabeth's second parking lot of the morning, and like the first, it was fuller than usual.

"Picketers," Walter said, catching up to her. "This is why we don't say certain things on TV, Elizabeth," he reminded her. "This is why we keep our opinions to *ourselves.*"

"Walter," said Elizabeth, "peaceful protest is a valued form of discourse."

"You call this discourse?" he said, as someone shouted, "BURN IN HELL!"

"They're attention seekers," she said as if speaking from personal experience. "They'll move on eventually."

Still, he worried. She was getting death threats. He'd shared this information with the police and studio security; he'd even called Harriet Sloane and told her. But he hadn't told Elizabeth because he knew she'd take matters into her own hands. Besides, the police had been very reassuring about the threats. "Bunch of harmless kooks" is how they put it.

Across town, hours later in the Zott living room, Six-Thirty found himself worried, too. At the end of Elizabeth's show last Friday, he'd noticed that not everyone was clapping. Today's show, there it was again. A nonclapper.

Anxious, he waited until the creature and Harriet were busy in the lab, then slipped out the back door, jogging four blocks south, then two blocks west, until he was well positioned near the on-ramp. When a flatbed truck slowed to join a line of cars merging onto the freeway, he hopped on.

Obviously, he knew how to find KCTV. Anyone who'd read *The Incredible Journey* would understand how un-incredible it was that dogs could find just about anything. He used to marvel at the needle in the haystack story Elizabeth had once read to him—marvel because what was so hard about finding a needle in a haystack? The scent of high carbon steel wire was unmistakable.

In short, getting to KCTV wasn't hard. Getting inside was.

As he meandered through the parking lot, wending his way between cars, their tail fins and hood ornaments glinting in the unseasonably hot sun, he looked for an entrance.

"Hey there, doggy," a big man in a dark blue uniform said. He was standing in front of an important-looking door. "Where do you think you're going?"

What Six-Thirty wanted to say was *inside,* that, like this man in the blue uniform, he too was in security. But since explaining was out of the question, he opted for acting—the very language of television.

"Oh gosh," the man said as Six-Thirty collapsed in a very convincing heap. "Hold on, boy, I'll get help!" He banged on the door until someone opened it and then hefted Six-Thirty up and carried him into the air-conditioned building. A minute later, Six-Thirty was lapping water from one of Elizabeth's very own mixing bowls.

Say what you want about the human race, their capacity for kindness was what—in Six-Thirty's opinion—put them over the top, species-wise.

"Six-Thirty?"

Elizabeth!

He ran to her in a way that a dog with actual heatstroke never could.

"What the—" began the man in the blue uniform, noting the miracle recovery.

"How did you get in here, Six-Thirty?" Elizabeth said, throwing her arms around him. "How did you find me? This is my dog, Seymour," she told the man in the blue uniform. "It's Six-Thirty."

"Actually, it's five thirty, ma'am, but still blazing out there. Anyway, the dog keeled over so I hauled him in."

"Thank you, Seymour," she gushed. "I really owe you. He must have run all the way here," she said incredulously. "It's nine miles."

"Or maybe he came with your little girl," Seymour suggested. "And the grandma in the Chrysler? Like they did a couple of months back?"

"Wait," said Elizabeth, looking up sharply. *"What?"*

"I can explain," Walter said, holding up his hands as if to ward off a possible attack.

Elizabeth had long ago made it clear that Madeline was never to come to the studio. He had no idea why; Amanda came all the time. But whenever Elizabeth brought it up, he nodded as if he understood and agreed even though he had no clue and couldn't care less.

"It was a homework assignment," he lied. "Watch Your Parent at Work Day." He had no idea why he felt a sudden urge to make up an alibi for Harriet Sloane, but it felt right. "You're busy," he said. "You probably just forgot."

Elizabeth jolted. Maybe she had. Hadn't Mason pointed out exactly the same thing that very morning? "It's just that I don't want my daughter to think of me as a television personality," she explained, rolling up one sleeve. "I don't want her to think that I'm—you know—performing." She pictured her father, her face hardening like cement.

"Don't worry," Walter said dryly. "No one will *ever* mistake what you do for performance."

She leaned forward in earnest. "Thank you."

His secretary came in, carrying a large stack of mail. "I put the things needing immediate attention on top, Mr. Pine," she said. "And I'm not sure you're aware, but there's a big dog in the hallway."

"A what—?"

"He's mine," Elizabeth said quickly. "It's Six-Thirty. He's how I found out about Mad's 'Watch Your Parent at Work Day' visit. Seymour told me—"

Hearing his name, Six-Thirty got up and entered the office, sniffing the air. *Walter Pine. Suffers from low self-esteem.*

Eyes wide, Walter pressed himself back in his chair. The dog was huge. He took a short breath in, then turned his attention to his stack of mail, only half listening as Elizabeth droned on and on about what the thing could do—sit, stay, fetch, probably, god only knows. Dog people were always so relentlessly braggy, so ridiculously proud when it came to their dog's minor accomplishments. But her never-ending discourse gave him the time he needed to ponder how soon he could call Harriet Sloane and get her in on the lie so she could support the story from her end.

"What do you think? You've been wanting to try something new," Elizabeth was saying. "Would it work?"

"Why not?" he said agreeably, having no idea what he'd just agreed to.

"Fantastic," she said. "Then we'll start tomorrow?"

"Sounds great!" he said.

"Hello," Elizabeth said the very next day. "My name is Elizabeth Zott and this is *Supper at Six*. I'd like to introduce you to my dog, Six-Thirty. Say hello to everyone, Six-Thirty." Six-Thirty cocked his head to the side and the audience laughed and clapped, and Walter, who'd only been informed ten minutes ago that not only was a dog in the building again, but that the hairdresser had trimmed his bangs in preparation for his close-up, sank down in his producer's chair and vowed to stop telling lies.

After Six-Thirty had been part of the show for a month, it seemed almost inconceivable that he hadn't been there from the start. Everyone loved him. He'd even started getting his own fan mail.

The only person who still didn't seem thrilled by his presence was Walter. He assumed this was because Walter wasn't a "dog person"—a concept he struggled to understand.

"Thirty seconds before the doors open, Zott," he heard the cameraman say as he positioned himself stage right, thinking of new ways to win Walter over. Last week he'd dropped a ball at Walter's feet, inviting him to play. He didn't like playing fetch himself, found the game pointless. As it turned out, so did Walter.

"All right, let 'em in," someone finally called as the doors opened and grateful viewers, oohing and aahing, found their seats, some pointing at the large clock, its hands still permanently set in the six o'clock position in the same way tourists might point at Mount Rushmore. "There it is," they'd say. "There's the clock."

"And there's the dog!" nearly everyone said. "Look—it's Six-Thirty!"

He didn't understand why Elizabeth didn't like being a star. He loved it.

"The potato's skin," Elizabeth was asserting ten minutes later, "is composed of suberized phellem cells, which make up the outer component of the tuber periderm. They constitute the potato's protection strategy—"

He stood by her side like a Secret Service agent, scanning the audience.

"—proving that even tubers understand that the best defense is a good offense."

The audience was rapt, making it easy to catalogue every face.

"The potato's skin is teeming with glycoalkaloids," she continued, "toxins so indestructible, they can easily survive both cooking and frying. And yet I still use the skin, not only because it's fiber rich, but because it serves as a daily reminder that in potatoes as in life, danger is everywhere. The best strategy is not to fear the danger, but respect it. And then," she added, as she picked up a knife, "deal with it." The camera zoomed in as she expertly excavated a sprouted potato eye. "Always eliminate potato eyes and green spots," she instructed, gouging another potato. "That's where the highest concentration of glycoalkaloids hide."

Six-Thirty studied the audience, looking for one face in particular. Ah, and there she was. The nonclapper.

Elizabeth announced it was time for station identification, then left the stage. He usually followed her, but today he went down into the audience instead, instantly eliciting a few excited claps and cries of "Here, boy!" Walter insisted he not do this—that people might be afraid or allergic—but Six-Thirty did it anyway because he knew it was important to work the crowd, and also because he wanted to get close to the nonclapper.

She was sitting on the end of the fourth row, her faced fixed in thin-lipped disapproval. He knew the type. As others in the row reached out to stroke him, he scanned the woman like an X-ray machine. She was stiff, unforgiving. Truth be told, he felt a little sorry for her. No one turned this mean without having been a victim of the same.

The thin-lipped woman turned to look at him, her expression hard. She reached a cautious hand into her large bag and took out a cigarette, tapping it twice against her thigh.

A smoker. That figured. It was a well-known fact that humans believed they were the most intelligent species on earth, and yet they were the only animals that willingly inhaled carcinogens. He started to turn away, then stopped, picking up a scent just beyond the nicotine. It was faint but familiar. He sniffed again as the *Supper at Six* quartet launched into their "And she's back!" ditty. He glanced again at the nonclapper. She returned her bag to the floor on the edge of the aisle. Her hand shook as she brought the cigarette to her lips.

He lifted his nose in the air. *Nitroglycerin? Not possible.*

"Fill a large pot with H_2O," Elizabeth was saying, back up onstage, "then take your potatoes—"

He sniffed again. *Nitroglycerin. When mishandled, it makes a terrifying noise, like a firework, or*—he swallowed hard, thinking of Calvin—*a backfire.*

"—and place them in your pot on high heat."

"Find it, damn it," he could hear his handler at Camp Pendleton insisting. "Find the fucking bomb!"

"The potato's starch, a long carbohydrate made up of the molecules amylose and amylopectin—"

Nitroglycerin. The smell of failure.

"—as the starch begins to break down—"

It's coming from the nonclapper's handbag.

At Camp Pendleton, the dog was only meant to locate the bomb, not remove it—removal was the handler's job. But occasionally some of the show-offs—the German shepherds—even did that part.

Despite the coolness of the studio, Six-Thirty began to pant. He tried to move forward, but his legs were like water. He stopped. All he had to do, he told himself, was play the game he liked least—fetch—while retrieving the scent he hated most— nitroglycerin. The idea nauseated him.

"What the heck is this?" Seymour Browne said as he spied a ladies handbag, the handle damp, sitting on his security table just inside the door. "Some lady must be worried sick." He unsnapped the purse to look for identification, but as the bag yawned open, he took a sharp breath in and reached for the phone.

"Now stand with your arms crossed," a reporter suggested to Seymour as he put a new flashbulb in his camera. "Look tough—like whoever did this messed with the wrong guy."

Unbelievably, it was that same reporter—the one from the cemetery. Still trying to improve his journalistic odds, he'd recently installed an illegal police radio in his car and today it had finally paid off: someone had found a small bomb in a ladies handbag over at KCTV Studios.

He took notes as Seymour explained that the bag had simply appeared on his table; he had no idea how it got there. He'd opened it to look for identification but instead found a bunch of flyers decrying Elizabeth Zott as a godless Communist and two sticks of dynamite bound together with wires so flimsy, the whole thing looked like a broken toy.

"But why in the world would someone want to bomb KCTV?" the reporter asked. "Don't you mostly do afternoon programming? Soap operas? Clown shows?"

"We have all sorts of shows," Seymour said, running a shaky hand over the top of his head. "But ever since one of our hosts mentioned she doesn't believe in God, we've had some trouble."

"What?" the reporter said incredulously. "*Who* doesn't believe in God? What kind of show are we talking about?"

"Seymour—Seymour!" Walter Pine called as he and a police officer pushed their way through a small throng of worried employees. "Seymour, thank god you're all right. After what you did—you risked your life!"

"I'm fine, Mr. Pine," Seymour said. "And I didn't do anything. Not really."

"Actually, Mr. Browne," the officer said, consulting his notes, "you did. This lady's been on our radar for a while. She's a die-hard McCarthyist, a real nut job. Said she's been sending death threats for months now." He closed his notebook. "Guess she was tired of being ignored."

"*Death threats?*" The reporter perked up. "So this is—what—a news show? Political opinion? Debate?"

"Cooking," Walter said.

"If you hadn't gotten hold of that bag, Mr. Browne, this day might have ended very differently. How'd you do it, anyway?" the officer pressed. "How'd you get the bag without her knowing?"

"That's what I keep telling everyone. I *didn't*," Seymour insisted. "It was just sitting on my table."

"You're being too modest," Walter said, patting him on the back.

"The mark of a true hero," the police officer nodded.

"My editor is going to eat this up," the reporter said.

From a distance, Six-Thirty lay in a corner watching the men, exhausted.

"Just a few more photos and that should—" Out of the corner of his eye the reporter spied Six-Thirty. "Hey," he said. "Don't I know that dog? I know that dog."

"Everyone knows that dog," Seymour said. "He's on the show."

The reporter looked at Walter, confused. "I thought you said this was a cooking show."

"It is."

"A dog on a cooking show? What does the dog *do* exactly?"

Walter hesitated. "Nothing," he admitted. But as the words hung in the air, he suddenly felt awful.

From across the room, Six-Thirty's eyes met his. He wasn't a dog person, but even Walter could see: the mutt was crushed.

CHAPTER 36

Life and Death

"Big news!" Walter said a week later, his body trembling with excitement as he joined Elizabeth, Harriet, Madeline, and Amanda at the table. This had become a regular occurrence—Sunday night dinner in Elizabeth's lab. "*Life* magazine called today. They want to do a cover story!"

"Not interested," Elizabeth said.

"But it's *Life*!"

"They'll want personal details—things that are no one's business. I know how this works."

"Look," Walter said. "We really need this. The death threats have ended, but we could use some positive exposure."

"No."

"You've turned down every single magazine, Elizabeth. You can't keep doing this."

"I'd happily talk with *Chemistry Today*."

"Yes," he said, rolling his eyes. "Fantastic. Not exactly our target audience, but I'm so desperate, I actually called them."

"And?" she said eagerly.

"They said they weren't interested in interviewing some lady who cooks on TV."

Elizabeth stood up and walked out.

"Help me, Harriet," Walter begged as they sat outside on the back step after dinner.

"You shouldn't have called her a TV cook."

"I know, I know. But she shouldn't have told everyone she doesn't believe in God. We're never going to live this down."

The screen door opened. "Harriet?" Amanda interrupted. "Come play."

"In a bit," Harriet said, encircling the little girl with her arm. "Why don't you and Mad build a fort first. Then I'll come."

"Amanda is very fond of you, Harriet," Walter said quietly as his daughter ran back indoors. He managed to stop himself from adding, *As am I.* In the past few months, his repeated visits to the Zott residence meant that he'd seen more and more of Harriet. Each time he left, he found himself thinking of her for hours. She was married—unhappily according to Elizabeth—but so what, she'd still never shown any interest in him, and who could blame her. He was fifty-five years old, going bald, bad at his job, and with a young child who was not even technically his. If there was a textbook called *Least Desirable Traits of Men,* he'd be on the cover.

"Oh?" said Harriet, her neck turning scarlet at the compliment. She fussed with her dress, pulling it low to her socks. "I'll talk to Elizabeth," she promised. "But you should speak with the writer first. Tell him to avoid personal questions. Especially anything relating to Calvin Evans. Keep it focused on Elizabeth—on what *she's* accomplished."

The interview was set for the following week. The reporter, Franklin Roth, an award-winning journalist, was well-known for his ability to gain the trust of even the most recalcitrant stars. As he slipped into his seat in the middle of the *Supper at Six* audience, Elizabeth was already onstage chopping through a large pile of greens. "Many believe protein comes from meat, eggs, and fish," she was saying, "but protein originates in plants, and plants are what the biggest, strongest animals in the world eat." She held up a *National Geographic* magazine featuring a spread on elephants, then went on to explain, in excruciating detail, the metabolic process of the world's largest land animal, asking the camera to zoom in on a photograph of the elephant's feces.

"You can actually see the fiber," she said, tapping the photo.

Roth had seen the show a few times and had found it strangely entertaining, but now, as part of the audience, he found those around him—the audience was 98 percent women—as much a part of the story as Zott was. Everyone seemed to have come armed with a notebook and pencil; a few carried chemistry textbooks. They all paid strict attention like one is supposed to in college lecture halls or church but rarely does.

During one of the advertising breaks he turned to the woman next to him. "If you don't mind me asking," he said politely, showing his credentials, "what is it that you like about the show?"

"Being taken seriously."

"Not the recipes?"

She looked back incredulously. "Sometimes I think," she said slowly, "that if a man were to spend a day being a woman in America, he wouldn't make it past noon."

The woman on the other side of him tapped his knee. "Prepare for a revolt."

After the show, he made his way backstage, where Zott shook his hand and her dog, Six-Thirty, sniffed him like a cop doing a pat-down. After brief introductions, she invited both him and his photographer into her dressing room, where she talked about the show—or rather the chemistry she'd covered on the show. He listened politely, then commented on her trousers—called them a bold choice. She looked at him surprised, then congratulated him on his same bold choice. There was a tone.

As the photographer quietly clicked away, he changed the subject to her hairstyle. She eyed him coldly.

The photographer looked at Roth, worried. He'd been charged with getting at least one photograph of Elizabeth Zott smiling. *Do something,* he motioned to Roth. *Say something funny.*

"Can I ask about that pencil in your hair?" Roth tried again.

"Of course," she said. "It's a number-two pencil. 'Two' signifies the lead hardness, although pencils don't actually contain lead. They contain graphite, which is a carbon allotrope."

"No, I meant why a—"

"A pencil instead of a pen? Because unlike ink, graphite is erasable. People make mistakes, Mr. Roth. A pencil allows one to clear the mistake and move on. Scientists expect mistakes, and because of it, we embrace failure." Then she eyed his pen disapprovingly.

The photographer rolled his eyes.

"Look," Roth said, closing his notepad. "I was under the impression that you'd agreed to this interview, but I can tell that this has been forced upon you. I never interview anyone against their will; I sincerely apologize for our intrusion." Then he turned to the photographer and tipped his head toward the door. They were halfway across the parking lot before Seymour Browne stopped them. "Zott says wait here," he said.

Five minutes later, Roth was riding next to Elizabeth Zott in the front seat of her old blue Plymouth, the dog and the photographer relegated to the back.

"He doesn't bite, does he?" the photographer asked as he crammed himself against the window.

"All dogs have the ability to bite," she said over her shoulder. "Just as all humans have the ability to cause harm. The trick is to act in a reasonable way so that harm becomes unnecessary."

"Was that a *yes?*" he asked, but they were merging onto the freeway and his question was lost in the acceleration of the engine.

"Where are we going?" Roth asked.

"My lab."

But when they pulled up in front of a small brown bungalow in a tired but tidy neighborhood, he thought he must have
misheard.

"I'm afraid I'm the one who now owes you the apology," she
said to Roth as she ushered them inside. "My centrifuge is on the
fritz. But I can still make coffee."

She set to work as the photographer clicked away, Roth's
mouth gaping in wonder as he took in what must have once been
a kitchen. It looked like a cross between an operating room and
a biohazard site.

"It was an unbalanced load," she explained, adding something
about the separation of fluids based on density as she pointed at
a big silver thing. Centrifuge? He had no idea. He reopened his
notepad. She set a plate of cookies in front of him.

"They're cinnamaldehyde," she explained.

He turned to find the dog watching him.

"Six-Thirty is an unusual name for a dog," he said. "What's
it mean?"

"Mean?" She turned toward him as she lit a Bunsen burner,
frowning as if, once again, she didn't understand why he insisted
on asking such basic questions. She then supplied a detailed
description of the Babylonians, who had relied on a sexagesimal
system—counting by sixties, she explained—for both mathemat-
ics and astronomy. "So hopefully that should clear that up," she
said.

Meanwhile, the photographer, whom she'd invited to have a
look around, asked about the contraption in the middle of the living room floor. "The erg?" she said. "It's a rowing machine. I'm
a rower. Many women are."

Roth laid his notepad on the table in the lab and followed
them into the next room, where she demonstrated the rowing
stroke. "An erg is a unit of energy," she'd explained while moving back and forth in a tedious sort of way, the photographer
snapping from multiple angles. "It takes a lot of ergs to row."
Then she'd gotten up and the photographer took several pictures

of her hand calluses before they all returned to the lab, where Roth discovered the dog slobbering on his notes.

That's how the interview went: from one end of dull to the other. He continued to ask his questions and she answered all of them—politely, dutifully, scientifically. In other words, he had nothing.

She placed a cup of coffee in front of him. He wasn't really a coffee drinker—too bitter for his taste—but she'd gone to such extraordinary lengths to make it: flasks, tubes, pipettes, vapors. To be polite, he took a sip. Then he took another.

"Is this really coffee?" he asked, awed.

"Perhaps you'd like to see how Six-Thirty helps me in the lab," she offered. She proceeded to strap some goggles onto the dog, then explained her area of research—abiogenesis, she called it—then spelled it, a-b-i-o, then grabbed his pad and wrote it down in block letters. Meanwhile the photographer snapped shot after shot of Six-Thirty pressing a button that raised and lowered the fume hood.

"I wanted to bring you here," she said to Roth, "because as I want your readers to understand, I'm not really a TV cooking show host. I'm a chemist. For a while, I was trying to solve one of the greatest chemical mysteries of our time."

She went on to explain abiogenesis, her excitement evident as she used precise description to paint a full picture. She was very good at explaining, he realized, had a way of making even dull concepts seem exciting. He took detailed notes as she waved and pointed at various things in her lab, occasionally sharing with him test results and her interpretations, apologizing again for the mal-functioning centrifuge, explaining that a home cyclotron was out of the question, implying that current city zoning laws had kept her from installing some kind of radioactive device. "Politicians don't make it easy, do they?" she said. "Nevertheless, the origin of life. That's what I was after."

"But not anymore?" he asked.

"Not anymore," she said.

Roth twisted on his stool. He'd never had the remotest interest in science—people, that was his gig. But when it came to Elizabeth Zott, getting at who she was over what she did was proving impossible. He suspected there was one way in, but he'd been explicitly warned by Walter Pine not to go down that road—that if he did, the interview would end badly. Nevertheless, Roth decided to chance it. "Tell me about Calvin Evans," he said.

At the mere mention of Calvin's name, Elizabeth whipped around, her eyes filled with disappointment. She gave Roth a good long look—the kind of look one gives to someone who's broken a promise. "So you're more interested in Calvin's work," she said flatly.

The photographer shook his head at Roth and exhaled in a "good going, genius" way. He put his lens cap on in surrender. "I'll be outside," he said, disgusted.

"It's not his work I'm interested in," Roth said. "I wanted to know about your relationship with Evans."

"How is that your business?"

Again, he felt the weight of the dog's eyes on him. *I have mapped and memorized the location of your carotid artery.*

"It's just that there's a lot of chatter about what went on between the two of you."

"Chatter."

"I understand he came from a wealthy background—rower, Cambridge—and that you were," he checked his notes, "a UCLA graduate. Although I notice you weren't an undergrad there. Where did you go? I also learned you were fired from Hastings."

"You've checked my credentials."

"That's part of my job."

"You checked Calvin's too, then."

"Well, no, it wasn't really necessary. He was so famous that—"

She cocked her head in a way he found worrisome.

"Miss Zott," he said. "You're also quite famous—"

"Fame doesn't interest me."

"Don't let the public tell your story for you, Miss Zott," Roth warned. "They have a way of twisting the truth."

"So do reporters," she said, taking the stool next to his. For a moment she seemed on the verge of cooperating, then reconsidered, turning her attention to the wall.

They sat that way for a long time—long enough that the coffee grew cold and even her Timex's tick seemed to lose its enthusiasm. Outside, a horn honked and a woman shouted, "If I've told you once, I've told you a thousand times."

If there's a truism in journalism, it's this: it's only when the reporter stops asking that the subject starts telling. Roth knew this, but that wasn't why he remained silent. Rather, it was because he hated himself. He'd been told not to cross this line and he'd done it anyway. He'd gained her trust, then stomped all over it. He wanted to apologize, but as a writer he already knew words wouldn't work. In true apologies, they seldom do.

Suddenly a siren screamed by and she startled like a deer.

She leaned forward and reopened his notepad for him. "You want to know about Calvin and me?" she said sharply. And then she began to tell him the one thing no one should ever tell a reporter: the bare, naked truth. And he hardly knew what to do with it.

CHAPTER 37

Sold Out

Elizabeth Zott is, without a doubt, the most influential, intelligent person on television today, he wrote from seat 21C on the plane heading back to New York. He paused, then ordered another scotch and water as he looked out on the nothingness below. He was a good writer and a good reporter and the combined skills, mixed with a hearty amount of alcohol, meant he would come up with something—he hoped. Her story was not a happy one, and in his line of work, this was usually a good thing. But in this case, and with this woman—

He drummed his fingers on the airline tray table. As a rule, reporters never want to find themselves in any place other than the middle: unbiased and impervious to emotion. But there he was, somewhere off to the side; more specifically, on *her* side and completely unwilling to see the story any other way. Roth shifted in his seat and downed his new drink in one long swallow.

Dammit. He'd interviewed plenty of others—Walter Pine, Harriet Sloane, a few Hastings people, every crew member of *Supper at Six.* He'd even been given access to the kid, Madeline, who'd wandered into the lab reading—had it really been *The Sound and the Fury*? But he didn't ask the child anything because it felt all wrong, but also because the dog had physically intervened. When Elizabeth was tending to a small cut on Madeline's leg, Six-Thirty turned to him and bared his teeth.

But never mind what the others had said, it was her words that would stay with him the rest of his life.

"Calvin and I were soulmates," she began.

She went on to describe her feelings for the awkward, moody man with an intensity that left him feeling bereft. "You don't need to understand chemistry at an advanced level to appreciate the rarity of our situation," she said. "Calvin and I didn't just click; we collided. Literally, actually—in a theater lobby. He vomited on me. You're familiar with the big bang theory, aren't you?"

She went on to talk about their love affair using words like "expansion," "density," "heat," emphasizing that what underlay their passion was a mutual respect for the other's capabilities. "Do you know how extraordinary that is?" she said. "That a man would treat his lover's work as seriously as his own?"

He took a sharp breath in.

"Obviously I'm a chemist, Mr. Roth," she said, "which on the surface would explain why Calvin was interested in my research. But I've worked with plenty of other chemists and not a single one of them believed I belonged. Except for Calvin and one other." She glowered. "The other being Dr. Donatti, director of Chemistry at Hastings. He not only knew I belonged, he also knew I was onto something. The truth is, he stole my research. Published it and passed it off as his own."

Roth's eyes widened.

"I quit the same day."

"Why didn't you tell the publication?" he said. "Why didn't you demand credit?"

Elizabeth looked at Roth as if he lived on some other planet. "I assume you're kidding."

Roth felt a flush of shame. Of course. Who was going to take a woman's word over the male head of the entire department? If he was being honest with himself, he wasn't even sure he would have.

"I fell in love with Calvin," she was saying, "because he was intelligent and kind, but also because he was the very first man to take me seriously. Imagine if all men took women seriously. Education would change. The workforce would revolutionize. Marriage counselors would go out of business. Do you see my point?"

He did, but he really didn't want to. His wife had recently left him, saying that he didn't respect her job as a housewife and mother. But being a housewife and mother wasn't really a job, was it? More like a role. Anyway, she was gone.

"That's why I wanted to use *Supper at Six* to teach chemistry. Because when women understand chemistry, they begin to understand how things work."

Roth looked confused.

"I'm referring to atoms and molecules, Roth," she explained. "The real rules that govern the physical world. When women understand these basic concepts, they can begin to see the false limits that have been created for them."

"You mean by men."

"I mean by artificial cultural and religious policies that put men in the highly unnatural role of single-sex leadership. Even a basic understanding of chemistry reveals the danger of such a lopsided approach."

"Well," he said, realizing he'd never seen it that way before, "I agree that society leaves much to be desired, but when it comes to religion, I tend to think it humbles us—teaches us our place in the world."

"Really?" she said, surprised. "I think it lets us off the hook. I think it teaches us that nothing is really our fault; that something or someone else is pulling the strings; that ultimately, we're not to blame for the way things are; that to improve things, we should pray. But the truth is, we are very much responsible for the badness in the world. And we have the power to fix it."

"But surely you're not suggesting that humans can fix the universe."

"I'm speaking of fixing *us,* Mr. Roth—our mistakes. Nature

works on a higher intellectual plane. We can learn more, we can go further, but to accomplish this, we must throw open the doors. Too many brilliant minds are kept from scientific research thanks to ignorant biases like gender and race. It infuriates me and it should infuriate you. Science has big problems to solve: famine, disease, extinction. And those who purposefully close the door to others using self-serving, outdated cultural notions are not only dishonest, they're knowingly lazy. Hastings Research Institute is full of them."

Roth stopped writing. This rang a bell. He worked for a well-regarded magazine, yet his new editor had come from *The Hollywood Reporter*—a rag—and he, Roth, despite his Pulitzer, now reported to someone who referred to news as "buzz," who insisted "dirty laundry" was a key part of every story. *Journalism is a for-profit enterprise!* his boss was always reminding him. *People want the sleaze!*

"I'm an atheist, Mr. Roth," she said, sighing heavily. "Actually, a humanist. But I have to admit, some days the human race makes me sick."

She got up, collecting their cups, and set them down near the eye wash station sign. He had the strong feeling that their interview was over, but then she turned back to him.

"As for my undergraduate degree," she said, "I don't have one, nor have I ever claimed I did. My entry into Meyers's graduate program was based solely on self-study. Speaking of Meyers," she said, her voice hard as she removed the pencil from her hair. "There's something you should know." Then she told him the whole story, explaining that she'd had to leave UCLA because when men rape women, they prefer women not to tell.

Roth swallowed hard.

"As for my background, it was my brother who raised me," she continued. "He taught me how to read, he introduced me to the wonders of the library, he tried to shield me from my parents' devotion to money. The day we found John hanging from the shed rafters, my father didn't even wait for the police to arrive. Didn't want to be late for a performance." Her father, she explained, was a doomsday showman now serving twenty-five years to life for killing three people as he performed a miracle, the true miracle being that he hadn't killed more. As for her mother, she hadn't seen her in more than twelve years. Gone for good in Brazil with an all-new family. Avoiding taxes turns out to be a lifetime commitment.

"But I think Calvin's childhood really takes the cake." She went on to explain the death of his parents, then his aunt—the result of which had landed him in a Catholic boys home, where he'd experienced abuse at the hands of priests until he'd grown big enough to stop it. She'd found his old diary buried in the boxes she and Frask had stolen. Although his childish scrawl was often impossible to read, his sorrow sang.

What she didn't tell Roth was that it was within the pages of Calvin's diary that she'd discovered the source of his permanent grudge. *I'm here even though I should not be,* he'd written, as if implying that there'd been an alternative. *And I will never ever forgive that man, him. Never. Not as long as I live.* After reading his correspondence with Wakely, she now understood that this was the father he'd hoped was dead. The one he promised to hate until the day he died. It was a promise he'd kept.

Roth stared down at the table. He'd had a normal upbringing—two parents, no suicides, no murders, not even a single wayward touch by the priest in his parish. And yet he still found plenty to complain about. What was wrong with him? Just as people have a bad habit of dismissing others' problems and tragedies, so too did they have a bad habit of not appreciating what they have. Or had. He missed his wife.

"As for Calvin's death," she said, "I'm one hundred percent responsible." He paled as she went on to describe the accident and the leash and the sirens, and how because of it, she would never hold anyone back in any way, ever again. As she saw it, his death spawned a series of other failures: blindsided by Donatti's theft, she'd given up her research; determined to help her daughter fit in, she'd enrolled her in a school where she did not; worse, she'd become the very person she least wanted to be, a performer like her father. Oh, and also, she'd given Phil Lebensmal a heart attack. "Although I don't actually consider that last one a failure," she said.

"What were you guys talking about in there?" the photographer asked on the way to the airport. "Did I miss anything?"

"Not a thing," Roth lied.

Before he'd gotten in the cab, Roth had already decided he wouldn't reveal what he'd learned. He would write his piece on deadline, to spec, and not a word over. He would write plenty but say nothing. He would tell about her, but not tell *on* her. In other words, he would meet his deadline, and in journalism, that is 99 percent of the law.

Despite what Elizabeth Zott will tell you, Supper at Six *is not just an introduction to chemistry,* he wrote that day on the plane. *It's a thirty-minute, five-day-a-week lesson in life. And not in who we are or what we're made of, but rather, who we're capable of becoming.*

In lieu of any personal information, he wrote a two-thousand-word description of abiogenesis, followed by a five-hundred-word section on how the elephant metabolizes its food.

"This is not a story!" his new editor had written after reading the first draft. "Where's the dirt on Zott?"

"There wasn't any," Roth said.

Just two months later, there she was, on the cover of *Life* magazine, arms folded across her chest, countenance grim, flanked by a headline that read "Why We'll Eat Whatever She Dishes Out." The six-page article included fifteen photographs of Elizabeth in action—on the show, on her erg, in makeup, petting Six-Thirty, in conference with Walter Pine, adjusting her hair. The article opened with Roth's line about her being the most intelligent person on television today, except the editor had swapped out "intelligent" and replaced it with "attractive." It then included a short description of her show's biggest hits—the fire extinguisher episode, the poison mushroom episode, the I-don't-believe-in-God episode, and countless others—ending with his observation that hers was a show of life lessons. But the rest?

"She's the angel of death" was the quote a hungry cub reporter got from Zott's father in the visitation room at Sing Sing. "The devil's spawn. And she's uppity."

The cub reporter had also managed to get a quote from Dr. Meyers at UCLA, who characterized Zott as a "lackluster student more interested in men than molecules," adding that she wasn't nearly as good-looking in person as she was on TV.

"Who?" Donatti had asked when the cub reporter first brought up Zott's employment record. "Zott? Oh wait—you mean Luscious Lizzie? 'Luscious' is what we all called her," he said, "which she used to protest in that way women do when they aren't *actually* protesting." He smiled, proving his point by producing her old lab coat, which still sported her initials, E.Z. "Luscious was a great lab tech—that's a position we have for people who want to be in science but don't have the brains."

The last quote was from Mrs. Mudford. "Women belong in the home, and the fact that Elizabeth Zott is not in the home has proven to be disruptive to her child's well-being. She often exaggerated her child's abilities—the first sign of a status-conscious parent. Naturally, when her daughter was my student, I worked very hard to counter that effect." Mudford's quote was accompanied by, of all things, a copy of Madeline's family tree. *Lies!* Mudford had written across the top. *See me!*

Out of everything in the article, it was the tree that did the most harm. Because on it, Madeline had not only written in Walter as a relative—readers instantly assumed this meant Elizabeth was sleeping with her producer—but had also included a small

drawing of a grandfather in prison stripes, a grandmother eating
tamales in Brazil, a large dog reading *Old Yeller,* an acorn labeled
"Fairy Godmother," a woman named Harriet poisoning her husband, a dead father's tombstone, a kid with a noose around his
neck, as well as some hazy ties to Nefertiti, Sojourner Truth, and
Amelia Earhart.

The magazine sold out in under twenty-four hours.

CHAPTER 38

Brownies

JULY 1961

Some say there's no such thing as bad publicity, and in this case, they were right. *Supper at Six* exploded in popularity.

"Elizabeth," Walter said as she sat facing him in his office, her face stony. "I know you're upset about the article—we all are. But let's look on the bright side. New advertisers are lining up in droves. Several manufacturers are begging to create all-new lines in your name. Pots, knives, all sorts of things!"

She pursed her lips in a way he knew meant trouble.

"Mattel even sent over specs for a girl's chemistry set—"

"A chemistry set?" She perked up slightly.

"Keep in mind, these are just specs," he said carefully, handing her a proposal. "I'm sure some things can—"

" 'Girls!' " she read aloud. " 'Make your very own perfume . . . using science!' " Good god, Walter! And the box is pink? Get these people on the phone right now—I want to tell them where they can stick their plastic vial."

"Elizabeth," he said soothingly, "we don't have to say yes to everything, but there's some potential here for lifelong financial security. Not just for us, but for our girls. We have to think beyond ourselves."

"This isn't thinking, Walter, this is marketing."

"Mr. Pine," a secretary said, "Mr. Roth is on line two."

"Do not," Elizabeth warned, her face still holding the hurt of how she'd been maligned, "take that call."

"Hello," Elizabeth said several weeks later, "my name is Elizabeth Zott, and this is *Supper at Six*."

She stood behind a cutting board, an array of vegetables set before her in a dazzling pile of color. "Tonight's dinner features eggplant," she said, picking up a large purplish vegetable. "Or aubergine, as it's referred to in other parts of the world. Eggplant is highly nutritious, but it can be bitter due to its phenolic compounds. To remove its bitterness—" She stopped abruptly, turning the vegetable over in her hands as if she wasn't at all satisfied. "Let me rephrase. To guard against eggplant's *tendency* toward bitterness—" She stopped again and exhaled loudly. Then she tossed the eggplant aside.

"Forget it," she said. "Life is bitter enough." She turned and opened a cupboard behind her, withdrawing all new ingredients. "New plan," she said. "We're making brownies."

Madeline lay on her stomach in front of the television, her legs crossed in the air behind her. "Looks like we're having brownies again tonight, Harriet. That's five days in a row."

"I make brownies on my bad days," Elizabeth confessed. "I'm not going to pretend that sucrose is an essential ingredient required for our well-being, but I personally feel better when I eat it. Now let's get started."

"Mad," Harriet said over Elizabeth's voice as she applied fresh lipstick and fluffed her hair. "I have to run out for a bit, all right? Don't answer the door or the phone, and don't leave home. I'll be back before your mom gets here. Understand? Mad? Do you hear me?"

"What?"

"See you soon." The door clicked shut behind her.

"Brownies are best when made from either a high-quality cocoa powder or unsweetened baking chocolate," Elizabeth continued. "I prefer Dutch cocoa. It contains a high level of polyphenols, which, as you know, are reducing agents that protect the body against oxidative . . ."

Madeline watched the TV closely as her mother combined the cocoa powder with the melted butter and sugar, whipping the wooden spoon around the bowl with such vigor, it seemed likely the bowl would break. When *Life* hit the stands, she'd been so proud. Her mother—on the cover! But before she could read it, her mother stuffed all of her copies—Harriet's too—in a garbage bag and tossed the heavy bag to the curb. "You are *not* to read this pack of lies," she'd told Madeline. "Do you understand? Under no circumstances."

Madeline nodded. But the next day she went straight to the library and read without stopping, her finger guiding her eyes down the columns. "No," she choked. "No, no, no." Tears spilled all over a photograph of her mother fixing her hair as if that's what she did all day. "My mom's a scientist. A chemist."

She turned her attention back to the television, where her mother was chopping walnuts. "Walnuts contain an unusually high level of vitamin E in the form of gamma-tocopherol," she said. "Proven to protect the heart." Although the way she continued to chop, it seemed clear the walnuts weren't going to make much difference to the damage done to her heart.

From out of nowhere came the doorbell, and Mad jumped. Harriet never let her answer the door anymore, but Harriet wasn't there. She peeked out the window, expecting to see a stranger, but saw Wakely instead.

"Mad," Reverend Wakely said as she opened the door. "I've been so worried."

From the television, Elizabeth Zott was explaining how air was being carried along on the rough surfaces of the sugar crystals and then encased by a film of fat, creating a foam. "When I add the eggs," she said, "their protein will prevent the fat-coated air bubbles from collapsing when heat is applied." She set down the bowl. "We'll be back after this station identification."

"I hope it's all right that I dropped by," Wakely said. "I thought I'd be able to find you at home during your mother's show. Is she really making brownies for dinner?"

"She's having a bad day."

"That *Life* article—I can only imagine. Where's your sitter?"

"Harriet will be back in a bit." She hesitated, knowing this was probably the wrong thing to ask. "Wakely. Want to stay for dinner?"

He paused. If bad days dictated dietary menus, he'd be eating brownies at every meal for life. "I would never intrude like that, Mad. I really did just want to make sure you're okay. I feel terrible that I wasn't able to help you more with that family tree, although I'm proud of what you did. You've defined your family with broad, honest strokes. Family is far more than biology."

"I know."

He glanced around the small room crowded with books, his eyes taking in the erg. "There it is," he said in wonder. "The rowing machine. I saw it in the magazine. Your dad was very handy."

"My *mom* is very handy," she asserted. "My mom turned our kitchen into a—" But before she could show him the lab, from the television Elizabeth announced she was back. "One of the things I like about cooking," she said as she added flour, "is its inherent usefulness. When we make food, we don't just create something good to eat—we create something that provides energy to our cells, something that sustains life. It's very different from what others create. For instance"—she paused, then looked directly into the camera, narrowing her eyes—"magazines."

"Your poor mother," Wakely said, shaking his head.

The back door banged open.

"Harriet?" Mad called.

"No honey, it's me." The voice was weary. "I'm home early."

Wakely froze. "Your mother?"

He wasn't prepared to meet Elizabeth Zott. It was enough just being in the home where Calvin Evans had once lived, but to suddenly meet the woman he'd failed to console at Evans's funeral? The famous atheist TV show host? The person recently gracing the cover of *Life*? No. He had to leave immediately— now, before she saw a grown man alone with her young daughter in an otherwise empty house. My god! What had he been thinking? Could this look any worse?

"Bye," he hissed to Mad, turning to the front door. But before he could open the door, Six-Thirty trotted to his side.

Wakely!

"Mad?" Elizabeth called as she dropped her bags in the lab and wandered into the living room. "Where's—" She stopped. "Oh." She frowned, surprised to see a man wearing a clerical collar gripping her front doorknob.

"Hi, Mommy," Madeline said, attempting to sound casual. "This is Wakely. He's a friend of mine."

"*Reverend* Wakely," Wakely said, reluctantly letting go of the knob as he extended his hand. "First Presbyterian. I'm so very sorry to disturb you, Mrs. Zott," he said in a rush. "So, so very sorry. I'm sure you're tired after your long day, Madeline and I met at the library a while back, and she's right, we're friends, we're—I was just leaving."

"Wakely helped me with the family tree."

"Terrible assignment," he said. "Completely wrongheaded. I very much oppose homework assignments that tread on private family business—but no, I really didn't help at all. I wish I *could* have helped. Calvin Evans was a huge influence in my life—his work—well, it may sound odd seeing the line of work I'm in, but I was an admirer, a fan, even; Evans and I were actually—" He stopped. "Again, I'm so very sorry for your loss—I'm sure it hasn't been—"

Wakely could hear himself running on like a swollen river. The more he babbled the more Elizabeth Zott looked at him in a way that scared him.

"Where's Harriet?" she asked, turning to Madeline.

"Errands."

From the television, Elizabeth Zott said, "I have time to take a question or two."

"Are you really a chemist?" someone asked. "Because *Life* magazine said—"

"*Yes,* I am," she barked. "Does anyone have a real question?"

From her living room, Elizabeth looked panicked. "Shut this off now," she said. But before she could reach the dial, a woman from the studio audience pried, "Isn't it true that your daughter is illegitimate?"

Wakely took two steps toward the television and snapped it off himself. "Ignore that, Mad," he said. "The world is full of ignorance." Then he glanced around as if he wanted to make sure he left nothing behind and said, "I am so very sorry to have disturbed." But as he placed his hand on the front doorknob again, Elizabeth Zott laid a hand on his sleeve.

"Reverend Wakely," she said in the saddest voice he'd ever heard. "We've met before."

"You never told me that," Madeline said as she reached for a second brownie. "Why didn't you tell me you were at my dad's funeral?"

"Because," he said, "I was a bit player, that's all. I very much admired your dad, but it doesn't mean I knew him. I wanted to help—I wanted to find the right words to help your mom with her loss, but I failed. I'd never met your dad, you understand—but I felt like I understood him. That probably sounds pompous," he said, turning to Elizabeth. "I'm sorry."

Throughout dinner, Elizabeth had said very little, but Wakely's confession seemed to touch her in some distant way. She nodded.

"Mad," she said. "Illegitimate means that you were a child born out of wedlock. It means your dad and I weren't married."

"I know what it means," she said. "I just don't know why it's a big deal."

"It's only a big deal to the very stupid," Wakely interjected. "I talk with the stupid all day long, I know the territory. As a minister, I had hoped to put a dent in that type of stupidity—to make people see their actions cause such needless . . . anyway, your mother is absolutely correct when she was quoted in the article saying our society is based largely on myth, that our culture, religion, and politics have a way of distorting the truth. Illegitimacy is but one of those myths. Pay no attention to that word or anyone who uses it."

Elizabeth looked up, surprised. "That didn't make it into the *Life* article."

"What didn't?"

"That part about myth. About the distortion of truth."

It was his turn to look surprised. "Right, not in *Life*. But in Roth's new—" He looked at Mad, as if just now remembering why he'd stopped by. "Oh dear god." He bent down and retrieved an unsealed manila envelope from his satchel and laid it in front of Elizabeth. Three words were written across the front: *Elizabeth Zott. PRIVATE.*

"Mom," Mad said quickly. "Mr. Roth came by a few days ago. I didn't answer the door because I'm not supposed to, but also because it was Roth, and Harriet says Roth is Public Enemy Number One." She paused, hanging her head. "I read his *Life* article," she confessed. "I know you told me not to, but I did and it was awful. Also, I don't know how Roth got my family tree, but he did and it's my fault, and—" Tears rolled down her cheeks.

"Honey," Elizabeth said, her voice dropping as she drew the child onto her lap. "No, of course it's not your fault; none of this is your fault. You didn't do anything wrong."

"Oh yes I did," Mad choked as her mother stroked her hair. "That," she said, pointing to the manila envelope Wakely had placed on the table, "that's from Roth. He left it on the doorstep and I opened it. And even though it said private, I read it. And then I took it to Wakely."

"But Mad, why would you—?" She stopped and looked at Wakely, alarmed. "Wait. You read it, too?"

"I wasn't in when Mad dropped by," Wakely explained, "but my typist told me she'd been there and Mad was very upset. So I confess—I also read the article. Actually, so did my typist—it's quite—"

"My god!" Elizabeth exploded. "What is wrong with you people? Does the word 'private' mean nothing anymore?" She snatched the envelope off the table.

"But Mad," Wakely said, ignoring Elizabeth's ire, "why did it upset you so? At least Mr. Roth is trying to make it right. At least he wrote the truth."

"What do you mean by *truth*?" Elizabeth said. "That man wouldn't know how to—" But as she reached into the envelope and withdrew the contents, she stopped. "Why Their Minds Matter" read the headline of the new piece.

It was an article mock-up—not yet published. Under the headline was a photograph of Elizabeth in her home lab, a goggled Six-Thirty by her side. Surrounding her, a photographic border of other women scientists from around the world in their labs. "The Bias of Science," read the subhead, "and What These Women Are Doing About It."

A note was clipped to the top.

Sorry, Zott. Quit Life. *Still trying to get the truth out, not that anyone wants it. Been rejected from ten scientific publications so far. Off to cover a developing story in a place called Vietnam. Yours, FR.*

As Elizabeth read the new piece, she held her breath. It was all there: her goals, her experiments. And these other women and their work—she felt fortified by their battles, inspired by their progress.

Madeline, however, was crying.

"Honey," Elizabeth said. "I don't understand. Why did this upset you? Mr. Roth did a good job. It's a good article. I'm not mad at you; I'm glad you read it. He wrote something truthful about me and these other women and I very much hope this gets published. Somewhere." She looked at his note again. Rejected by science magazines ten times already? Really?

"I know," Madeline said, swiping her hand under her nose, "but that's why I'm sad, Mom. Because you belong in a lab. But instead you make dinner on TV and . . . and . . . and it's because of *me*."

"No," Elizabeth said gently. "Not true. Every parent has to earn a living. It's part of being an adult."

"But you're not in a lab specifically because of *me*—"

"Again, not true—"

"Yes, it is. Wakely's typist told me."

Elizabeth's mouth dropped open.

"Jesus Christ," Wakely said, covering his face with his hands.

"What?" Elizabeth said. "Who is this typist of yours?"

"I think you might know her," Wakely said.

"Listen to me, Mad," Elizabeth said. "Very closely. I'm still a chemist. A chemist on television."

"No," Mad said sadly. "You're not."

CHAPTER 39

Dear Sirs

It was two days earlier, and Miss Frask was on a roll. Usually she could type around 145 words per minute—fast by any standard—but the world's record was 216 words per minute, and today, Frask, who'd taken three diet pills with coffee, had a feeling she might break it. But just as she entered the home stretch, her fingers pounding the keys, a stopwatch ticking just off to the side, she heard two unexpected words.

"Excuse me."

"Geez Louise!" she shouted, pushing herself away from the desk. She swiveled her head to the left to see a skinny child clutching a manila envelope.

"Hi," the child said.

"What the hell!" Frask gasped.

"Lady, you're fast."

Frask pressed her hand on her heart as if to keep it contained. "Th-thank you," she managed.

"Your pupils are dilated."

"Ex-excuse me?"

"Is Wakely here?"

Frask sat back in her chair, her heart fibrillating, as the child leaned in to scan the contents of the typewriter.

"Do you *mind*?" Frask said.

"I'm calculating," the kid explained. Then she drew back in awe. "Whoa. You're in Stella Pajunas territory."

"H-how would you know who Stella—"

"World's fastest typist. Two hundred sixteen words per—"

Frask's eyes widened.

"—but I interrupted you so we gotta take that into account—"

"Who *are* you?" Frask insisted.

"Lady, you're sweating."

Frask's hand flew to her damp forehead.

"You're at a hundred eighty words per minute. If we round up."

"What's your name?"

"Mad," the kid said.

Frask took in the child's puffy, purplish lips, her long, clumsy limbs. "Evans?" she filled in without thinking.

They looked at each other in equal astonishment.

"Your mom and dad and I used to work together," Frask explained to Mad over a plate of diet cookies. "At Hastings. I was in Personnel and your mom and dad were both in the Chemistry Department. Your dad was very famous—I'm sure you know that. And now your mom is, too."

"Because of *Life,*" the child said, hanging her head.

"No," Frask said firmly. "In spite of it."

"What was my dad like?" Mad asked, taking a small bite of cookie.

"He . . ." Frask hesitated. She realized she had no idea what he'd been like. "He was completely in love with your mother."

Madeline lit up. "Really?"

"And your mother," she continued for the first time without jealousy, "was completely in love with him."

"What else?" Mad asked eagerly.

"They were very happy together. So happy, that before your

dad died, he left your mother a gift. You know what that gift was?" She tipped her head toward Mad. "You."

Madeline rolled her eyes slightly. This was the sort of thing adults said when they were trying to paper over something darker. She'd once heard Wakely tell a librarian that although her cousin, Joyce, had died—dropped dead in the middle of the A&P clutching her heart—Joyce had not suffered. Really? Did anyone ask Joyce?

"And then what happened?"

What happened? Frask thought. *Well, I spread vicious rumors about your mother, which culminated in her firing, which led directly to her state of penury, which led to an eventual return to Hastings, which led to your mother screaming at me in the women's bathroom, which led to the discovery that we'd both been sexually assaulted, which led to our inability to get our PhDs, which led to unfulfilling careers in a company led by a handful of incompetent assholes. That's what happened.*

But instead she said, "Well, your mom decided it would be more fun to stay at home and have you."

Madeline put down her cookie. There it was again. Adults and their on-again, off-again relationship with the truth.

"I don't see how that could be fun," Mad said.

"What do you mean?"

"Wasn't she sad?"

Frask looked away.

"When I'm sad, I don't want to be alone."

"Cookie?" asked Frask half-heartedly.

"Home alone," Madeline continued. "No dad. No work. No friends."

Frask took a sudden interest in a publication called *Our Daily Bread*.

"What really happened?" Mad prodded.

"She was *fired*," Frask said, without considering the effect her words might have. "Fired because she was pregnant with *you*."

Madeline crumpled as if she'd been shot from behind.

"Again, not your fault," Frask reassured the child, who'd been sobbing for the last ten minutes. "Really. You wouldn't have believed how close-minded those people at Hastings were. Complete jerks." Frask, remembering she'd been one of those jerks, ate the rest of the cookies, while Mad, despite her raggedy breath, pointed out that the cookies contained tartrazine, a food coloring additive that had been linked to poor liver and kidney function.

"Anyway," Frask continued, "you're looking at this all wrong. Your mother didn't leave Hastings because of you. She got out *thanks* to you. And then she made the very poor decision to go back, but that's another story."

Madeline heaved a sigh. "I gotta go," she said, blowing her nose while looking at the clock. "Sorry about wrecking your typing test. Would you give this to Wakely?" She held out the unsealed envelope marked *Elizabeth Zott: PRIVATE.*

"I will," Frask promised, giving her a hug. But as soon as the door shut behind her, she ignored the child's instructions and opened the envelope. "Holy hell," she fumed as she read Roth's latest. "Zott really is the real deal."

"Sirs," she typed ferociously, addressing the editors at *Life* magazine thirty seconds later. "I read your ridiculous cover story on Elizabeth Zott and I think your fact-checker should be fired. I know Elizabeth Zott—I used to work with Elizabeth Zott—and I know, for a fact, that everything in this article is a lie. I also used to work with Dr. Donatti. I know what he did at Hastings and I have the documents to back it up."

Her letter went on, listing Elizabeth's accomplishments as a chemist, most of which she discovered only after reading Roth's new article, while highlighting the injustices Zott had faced at Hastings. "Donatti reappropriated her funding," she wrote, "then fired her without cause. I know," she admitted, "because I was part of it—a sin for which I'm currently trying to atone by typing sermons for a living." Then she went on to explain how later,

Donatti not only stole Zott's research but lied to important investors. She finished, asserting that while she knew *Life* would never have the guts to print her letter, she felt she had to write it anyway.

It appeared in the very next issue.

"Elizabeth, read this!" Harriet said excitedly, holding the latest copy of *Life* in her hands. "Women from all over the country have written to *Life* in protest. It's a rebellion—everyone's on your side. There's even one from someone who claims she worked with you at Hastings."

"Not interested."

Having finished her daily lunch box notes to Madeline, Elizabeth closed the lid, then pretended to fuss with a Bunsen burner. For the last few weeks, she'd done her best to keep her head up— ignore the article, she told herself. Carry on. That was the coping strategy that had carried her through suicide, sexual assault, lies, thievery, and catastrophic loss; it would again. Except it hadn't. This time, no matter how high she lifted her head, *Life*'s misrepresentation of who she was beat her back down again. The damage felt permanent, like a brand. She would never outrun it.

Harriet read aloud from the letters. "If it weren't for Elizabeth Zott—"

"Harriet, I said I'm *not* interested," she snapped. What was the point? Her life was over.

"But what about this unpublished piece of Roth's," Harriet said, ignoring Elizabeth's tone. "The science-y one. I had no idea there were other women scientists—besides you and Curie, I mean. I've read the whole thing twice. Found it riveting. Which is saying something because you know. Science."

"It's already been rejected by ten scientific magazines," Elizabeth said in a deadened voice. "Women in science isn't something people have any interest in." She picked up her car keys. "I'll go kiss Mad goodbye, and then I'm off."

"Do me a favor? Try not to wake her this time."

"Harriet," Elizabeth said. "Have I ever?"

After hearing Elizabeth back the Plymouth down the drive, Harriet opened Madeline's lunch box, curious to see what words of wisdom Elizabeth had written this time. *It's not your imagination,* said the note on top. *Most people are awful.*

Harriet pressed her fingertips against her head in worry. She padded around the lab, wiping down counters, the weight of Elizabeth's depression evident in ways she hadn't really registered before. The pile of empty research notebooks, the untouched chemical supplies, the unsharpened pencils. Damn that *Life* magazine, she thought. Despite its name, the magazine had stolen Elizabeth's life—ended it—due in no small part to fraudulent quotes from people like Donatti and Meyers.

"Oh honey," Harriet said as Mad appeared in the doorway. "Did your mom wake you?"

"It's another day."

They sat down together and picked at the breakfast muffins Elizabeth had baked earlier that morning.

"I'm real worried, Harriet," Mad said. "About Mom."

"Well, she's feeling very down, Mad," Harriet said. "But she'll bounce back soon enough. You'll see."

"Are you sure?"

Harriet looked away. No, she wasn't sure. She'd never been less sure of anything in her life. Everyone has a breaking point; she worried that Elizabeth had finally reached hers.

She turned her attention to the latest issue of *Ladies' Home Journal.* "Can You Trust Your Hairdresser?" an article asked. "The Year of the Important Blouse" informed another. Sighing, she reached for another muffin. She'd been the one who'd talked Elizabeth into the *Life* interview. If someone was to blame, it was her.

They sat in silence, Mad picking the paper wrap from her muffin as Harriet replayed Elizabeth's words about how no one had any interest in reading about women in science. It rang true. Or did it?

She cocked her head to the side. "Wait a sec, Mad," she said slowly as an idea came to her. "Wait just a goddamn second."

CHAPTER 40

Normal

"I think about death a lot," Elizabeth confessed to Wakely one chilly November evening.

"Me too," he said.

They sat together on the back step, their voices low. Madeline was just inside watching TV.

"I don't think it's normal."

"Maybe not," he agreed. "But I'm not sure what normal is. Does science recognize normal? How would you define normal?"

"Well," she said. "I guess normal is a little like average."

"I'm not so sure. Normal isn't like weather; you can't expect normal. You can't even make normal. From what I can tell, normal may not exist."

She looked at him sideways. "Strange words coming from someone who finds the Bible normal."

"Not at all," he said. "I can safely say there is not a single normal event in the Bible. Probably one of the reasons it's so popular. Who wants to believe life is exactly how it seems?"

She looked at him curiously. "But you believe those stories. You preach them."

"I believe in a few things," he corrected. "Mostly the things about not giving up hope, not giving in to darkness. As for the word 'preach,' I prefer 'relate.' Anyway, what I believe is irrelevant. What I think is that you feel dead, so you believe you are dead. But you're not dead. You're very much alive. And that puts you in a difficult position."

"What are you saying?"

"You know what I'm saying."

"You're a strange minister."

"No, I'm a terrible minister," he corrected.

She hesitated. "I have a confession to make, Wakely. I've read your letters. The ones you and Calvin wrote to each other. I'm sure they were private, but they were in his belongings and I read them. Years ago."

Wakely turned to look at her. "Evans *kept* them?" He felt a sudden longing for his old friend.

"I don't know if you know this, but you're the reason he took the job at Hastings."

"What?"

"You told him Commons had the best weather."

"I did?"

"You know how Calvin felt about weather. He could have gone a million other places and made a lot more money, but he came here, to Commons. 'Best weather in the world.' I think that's how you phrased it."

Wakely felt the weight of his flippant advice. Because of something he'd said, Evans had come to Commons, then died in Commons. "But the weather is only good later in the day," he explained, as if he had to. "After the morning fog burns off. I can't believe he moved here to row in the sun. There's no sun—not when rowers row."

"You don't have to tell me that."

"I'm responsible," he said, horror-struck, fully recognizing the part he'd played in Calvin's premature death. "It's all my fault."

"No, no." Elizabeth sighed. "I'm the one who bought the leash."

They sat together listening to Madeline sing along with the TV theme song playing in the background. *A horse is a horse, of*

course, of course, and no one can talk to a horse of course, that is, of course,
unless the horse is the famous Mister Ed!

With a start, Wakely remembered the secret Madeline had
whispered in his ear that day in the library. *My dog knows 981
words.* It'd taken him by surprise. Why would a child like Madeline, obsessed with the truth, choose to share such an obvious lie?

As for what he'd told her? It was the worst. *I don't believe in
God.*

She closed her eyes briefly, then cleared her throat. "I had a
brother, Wakely," she said as if confessing a sin. "He died, too."

Wakely's eyebrows furrowed. "A brother? I'm so sorry. When
was this? What happened?"

"It was a long time ago. I was ten. He hanged himself."

"Good *god*," Wakely said, his voice trembling. He suddenly
remembered Madeline's family tree. At the very bottom was a kid
with a noose around his neck.

"I almost died once, myself," she said. "I jumped into a quarry.
I couldn't swim. Still can't."

"What?"

"My brother jumped in right after me. Somehow got me to
the side."

"I see," Wakely said, slowly unraveling her guilt. "Your
brother saved you—so you think you should have been able to
save him. Is that it?"

She turned to looked at him, her face hollow.

"But Elizabeth, you couldn't swim—that's why he jumped in
after you. You have to understand, suicide isn't like that. Suicide
is lot more complicated."

"Wakely," she said. "He didn't know how to swim either."

They stopped talking, Wakely despairing because he didn't know
what to say, Elizabeth depressed because she didn't know what to
do. Six-Thirty pushed through the screen door and pressed himself against Elizabeth.

"You've never forgiven yourself," Wakely finally said. "But it's him you have to forgive. What you need to do is accept."

She made a sad sound, like a tire slowly losing air.

"You're a scientist," he said. "Your job is to question things—to search for answers. But sometimes—and I know this for a fact—there just aren't any. You know that prayer that starts 'God, grant me the serenity to accept the things I can't change'?"

She frowned.

"That's definitely not you."

She cocked her head.

"Chemistry is change and change is the core of your belief system. Which is good because that's what we need more of—people who refuse to accept the status quo, who aren't afraid to take on the unacceptable. But sometimes the unacceptable—your brother's suicide, Calvin's death—is, in fact, permanent, Elizabeth. Things happen. They just do."

"Sometimes I understand why my brother left," she admitted quietly. "After everything that's happened, sometimes I feel like I want out, too."

"I get that," Wakely said, thinking of how damaging the *Life* article was. "Believe me. But that's not really your problem. It's not that you want out."

She turned to look at him, confused.

"It's that you want back *in*."

Chapter 41

Recommit

"Hello," Elizabeth said. "My name is Elizabeth Zott, and this is *Supper at Six*."

From his producer's chair, Walter Pine closed his eyes and thought back to the day they'd met.

She'd stormed past his secretaries in her white lab coat, hair pulled back, voice clear. He remembered feeling stunned by her. Yes, she was attractive, but it was only now that he realized it had little to do with how she looked. No, it was her confidence, the certainty of who she was. She sowed it like a seed until it took root in others.

"I'm starting today's show with an important announcement," she said. "I'm leaving *Supper at Six,* effective immediately."

From the audience came a gasp of disbelief. "What?" people asked one another. "What did she say?"

"This will be my last show," she confirmed.

From a ranch house in Riverside, a woman dropped a carton of eggs on the floor. "You can't be serious!" someone in the third row shouted.

"I'm always serious," Elizabeth said.

A wave of distress filled the studio.

Taken aback, Elizabeth turned to look at Walter. He looked back with an encouraging nod. It was all he could do without falling apart.

She'd driven over to his house last night, unannounced. He almost hadn't answered the door; he'd been entertaining. But when he looked through the peephole and saw her standing there, Mad asleep in the car at the curb, Six-Thirty wedged behind the steering wheel like a getaway driver, he'd thrown open the door in worry.

"Elizabeth," he'd said, his heart pounding. "What's wrong—what happened?"

"It's Elizabeth?" said a worried voice just behind him. "Mother of god, what is it? Is it Mad? Is she hurt?"

"Harriet?" Elizabeth said, drawing back in amazement.

The three of them said nothing for a moment, like in a play when no one can remember the next line. Finally Walter managed, "We were trying to keep this quiet awhile longer," and Harriet blurted, "Until my divorce comes through," and Walter reached for her hand, and Elizabeth cried out in surprise, startling Six-Thirty, who accidentally pressed hard against the horn—repeatedly—which in turn woke up Madeline, then Amanda, then every other person in the neighborhood who'd made the mistake of going to bed early.

Elizabeth remained glued to the doorstep. "I had no idea," she kept saying. "How could I have had no idea? Am I that blind?"

Harriet and Walter looked at each other as if to confirm, well, yes.

"We'll tell you the whole story soon enough," Walter said. "But why are you here? It's nine o'clock." Elizabeth had shown up without an invitation, something she'd never done before. "What's wrong?"

"Everything's fine," Elizabeth said. "It's just that now I feel bad about my reason for being here. Your news is so positive and mine is—"

"What? *What?*"

"Actually," she said, as if amending her response on the spot. "My news is positive, too."

Walter waved his hands impatiently as if to push her along.

"I've . . . I've decided to leave the show."

"What?" Walter gasped.

"Tomorrow," she added.

"No!" Harriet said.

"I'm quitting," she repeated.

It was the tone in her voice, the kind that made it clear that even though hers was a snap decision, she would not be snapping back. Negotiation was futile; there was no use bringing up trivial matters like contracts or unmade fortunes or what was supposed to fill that space if she wasn't in it. Her decision was final, and because of it, Walter started to cry.

Harriet, too, recognized the tone, and proud in that way a mother pretends to be when her child announces she's decided to dedicate her life to something that pays very poorly, she started to cry, too. Using both arms, she drew Walter and Elizabeth in close.

"I've very much enjoyed my time as the host of *Supper at Six,*" Elizabeth continued, looking steadily into the camera, "but I've decided to return to the world of scientific research. I want to take this opportunity to thank you all not only for your viewership," she said, increasing her volume to be heard over the hubbub, "but also for your friendship. We've accomplished a lot together in the last two years. Hundreds of meals, if you can believe that. But supper isn't all we've made, ladies. We've also made history."

She took a step back, surprised, as the audience rose to its feet, roaring its agreement.

"BEFORE I GO," she shouted, "I THOUGHT YOU'D BE INTERESTED TO HEAR—" She held up her hands to quiet the audience. "Does anyone remember a Mrs. George Fillis—the woman who had the audacity to tell us she wanted to become a heart surgeon?" She reached into her apron pocket and pulled out a letter. "I have an update. It seems that Mrs. Fillis has not only completed her premed studies in record time but has also been accepted to medical school. Congratulations Mrs. George—no, I'm sorry—*Marjorie* Fillis. We never doubted you for a second."

With that news, the audience instantly regained its vigor, and Elizabeth, despite her normally serious demeanor, pictured Dr. Fillis scrubbing in and could not help it. She smiled.

"But I'm betting Marjorie would agree," Elizabeth said, raising her voice again, "that the hard part wasn't returning to school, but rather having the courage to do so." She strode to her easel, marker in hand. *CHEMISTRY IS CHANGE,* she wrote.

"Whenever you start doubting yourself," she said, turning back to the audience, "whenever you feel afraid, just remember. Courage is the root of change—and change is what we're chemically designed to do. So when you wake up tomorrow, make this pledge. No more holding yourself back. No more subscribing to others' opinions of what you can and cannot achieve. And no more allowing anyone to pigeonhole you into useless categories of sex, race, economic status, and religion. Do not allow your talents to lie dormant, ladies. Design your own future. When you go home today, ask yourself what *you* will change. And then get started."

From all over the country women leapt from their sofas and pounded on kitchen tables, calling out in a combination of excitement for her words and heartache for her departure.

"Before I GO," she shouted over the din, *"I'd like to thank a very special FRIEND. Her name is HARRIET SLOANE."*

From Elizabeth's living room, Harriet's jaw dropped.

"Harriet," Mad breathed. "You're famous!"

"As you know," Elizabeth continued, again quieting the audience with her hands, "I've always wrapped my shows by telling your children to set the table so that you might have a moment for yourself. 'A moment for yourself'—that was the advice Harriet Sloane gave me the first day I met her, and that is the advice that has resulted in my decision to leave *Supper at Six*. It was Harriet who told me to use that moment to reconnect with my own needs, to identify my true direction, to recommit. And thanks to Harriet, I finally have."

"Holy mother of god," Harriet said, turning pale.

"Boy, Pine is going to kill *you*," Mad said.

"Thank you, Harriet," Elizabeth said. "Thanks to *all* of you," she said nodding at the audience. "And so for the last time, I'd like to ask your children to set the table. And then I'm going to ask each of you to take a moment and recommit. Challenge yourselves, ladies. Use the laws of chemistry and change the status quo."

Again, the audience rose to its feet, and again the clapping was thunderous. But as Elizabeth turned to go, it was obvious the audience was not going anywhere—not without one last directive. Unsure of how to proceed, she looked to Walter. He motioned with his hand as if he had an idea, then scribbled something on a cue card and held it up for her to see. She nodded, then turned back to the camera.

"This concludes your introduction to chemistry," she announced. "Class dismissed."

CHAPTER 42

Personnel

JANUARY 1962

It had been everyone's assumption—everyone being Harriet, Walter, Wakely, Mason, and Elizabeth herself—that she would be flooded with employment offers. Universities, research labs, perhaps even the National Institutes of Health. Despite the mockery *Life* magazine had made of her life, she'd been a prominent personality, a television celebrity.

But it didn't happen. In fact, nothing happened. Not only did she not receive a single call, but her résumés to research concerns were completely ignored. Despite her daytime popularity, the scientific community continued to entertain significant doubt regarding her academic credentials. Dr. Meyers, Dr. Donatti— very important chemists—were quoted in *Life* magazine as having said she wasn't really a scientist. That was all it took.

And thus she was introduced to the other truism of fame: that it was fleeting. The only Elizabeth Zott anyone was interested in was the one who'd worn an apron.

"You could always return to the show," Harriet said as Elizabeth came in through the door with Six-Thirty, her arms full of library books. "You know Walter would put you back on today if you'd let him."

"I know," she said, setting the books down, "but I can't. At least the reruns are doing well. Coffee?" she asked, lighting a Bunsen burner.

"I don't have time. I'm meeting with my attorney. But here," Harriet said, pulling little notes out of her apron pocket. "Dr. Mason wants to talk about new uniforms for the women's team and—are you ready for this?—Hastings called. I almost hung up. Can you imagine? *Hastings*. They have a lot of nerve calling here."

"Who was it?" Elizabeth asked, trying to keep the worry out of her voice. For the last two and a half years, she'd been waiting for Hastings to notice Calvin's boxes were missing.

"The head of Personnel. But don't worry. I told her to go to hell."

"Her?"

Harriet shuffled through the messages. "Here it is. A Miss Frask."

"Frask isn't at Hastings," Elizabeth said, relieved. "She was fired years ago. She types sermons for Wakely."

"Interesting," Harriet said. "Well, she claimed she's head of Personnel at Hastings."

Elizabeth frowned. "She likes to kid."

After Harriet's car pulled out of the driveway, Elizabeth poured herself a cup of coffee, then reached for the phone.

"Miss Frask's office, Miss Finch speaking," said the voice.

"Miss Frask's *office*?" Elizabeth scoffed.

"Excuse me?" came the voice.

Elizabeth hesitated. "I'm sorry," she said, "but who is this?"

"Who is *this*?" demanded the voice.

"Okay, okay," Elizabeth said. "I'll play along. Elizabeth Zott calling for Miss Frask."

"Elizabeth Zott," the person on the other end said. "Good one."

"Is there a problem?" Elizabeth asked.

It was the tone. The woman on the other end recognized it immediately. "Oh," she breathed. "It *is* you. I'm so sorry, Miss Zott. I'm such a fan. It's an honor to connect you. Please hold."

"Zott," came a voice a moment later. "About fucking time!"

"Hello, Frask," Elizabeth said. "Head of Personnel at Hastings? Does Wakely know you're making crank calls?"

"Three things, Zott," Frask said briskly. "One: loved the article. I always knew I'd see you back on the cover of something, but there? Stroke of genius. If you want to reach the choir, it only makes sense to go where they worship."

"What?"

"Two, I love that housekeeper of yours—"

"Harriet is not a housekeeper—"

"—the second I told her I was calling from Hastings, she told me to go to hell. Made my day."

"Frask—"

"Third, I need you to come in as soon as possible—as in today—in the next hour or so if you can swing it. Remember that fat-cat investor? He's back."

"Frask," Elizabeth sighed, "you know I love a good joke, but—"

Frask laughed. "*You* love a joke? Is *that* supposed to be a joke? No, Zott, listen. I'm back at Hastings—in fact I'm top of the heap. That investor of yours saw the letter I wrote to *Life* and contacted me. I'll fill you in on the details later; I don't have time now. I'm cleaning house. God, I love to clean! Can you come or not? Also, and I can't believe I'm saying this, but can you bring the damn dog? The investor wants to meet him."

Harriet entered the law offices of Hanson & Hanson, her hands shaking. For the last thirty years, she'd confessed to her priest that her husband drank and cursed and never himself attended Mass, that he treated her as his own personal slave, that he called her names. And for the last thirty years, the priest had nodded, then explained that while divorce was out of the question, she still had lots of options. For example, she could pray to find ways to become a better wife, she could take a good look at herself and try to understand how she upset him, she could take more care with her appearance.

That's why she'd subscribed to all those women's magazines—because they were bibles of self-improvement and they would show her what to do. But no matter what advice she followed, things between her and Mr. Sloane did not improve. Worse, sometimes the advice backfired—like the time she'd gotten a perm, something the magazine claimed would "make him sit up and take notice," but instead resulted in endless complaints about how terrible she smelled. But then Elizabeth Zott came into her life and she finally realized that maybe what she needed wasn't new clothes or a different hairdo. Maybe what she needed was a career. In magazines.

Was there anyone in the world who knew more about magazines than she did? It wasn't possible. And to prove this point, she knew exactly where to start. With Roth's still unpublished article.

In Harriet's opinion, Roth had made the classic error of article placement—he'd assumed only science magazines would be interested in a piece on women in science. Harriet knew that was wrong. She called him, prepared to present her case, but his answering service relayed that Roth was still in—what was it? Vietnam. So she submitted his article without his permission. Why not? If it was accepted, he'd thank her, and if it wasn't, he wouldn't be any worse off than he was now.

She took the package to the post office to weigh it, added a self-addressed, stamped envelope to ensure a speedy reply, then performed three Hail Marys, two signs of the cross, took one deep breath, and dropped it in the slot.

After two weeks without any response, she felt a twinge of

worry. After four months, the burn of rejection. She tried to face facts. Maybe she didn't know magazines as well as she thought she did. Maybe no one wanted Harriet and her Roth article, just like no one wanted Elizabeth and her abiogenesis.

Or maybe Mr. Sloane, unhappy with Harriet's newfound happiness, had decided to punish her in all new ways. Maybe he threw out her mail.

"Miss Zott," the Hastings receptionist swooned as Elizabeth entered the lobby. "I'll let Miss Frask know you're here." She plugged a cable into the switchboard. *"She's here!"* the woman hissed to someone on the other end. "Would you mind?" She held out a copy of *The Voyage of the Beagle.* "I just started night school."

"Love to," Elizabeth said, signing the cover. "Good for you."

"It's because of you, Miss Zott," the young woman said earnestly. "Also, if it's not too much to ask, could you also autograph my magazine?"

"No," Elizabeth said. "*Life's* dead to me."

"Oh, sorry," the young woman said. "I don't read *Life.* I meant your latest one." She held out a thick, slick publication.

Elizabeth looked down, shocked to see her face staring back at her.

"Why Their Minds Matter" read the cover of *Vogue.*

As they clipped down the hallway, their heels in sharp contrast to the muffled sounds of generators and cooling fans coming from the other laboratories, Frask informed Elizabeth that they were meeting in Calvin's old lab.

"Why *there?*" Elizabeth said.

"The fat cat insisted."

"It's a pleasure, Miss Zott," Wilson said, unfurling his long limbs from the stool. He reached his hand out as Elizabeth took inventory: carefully cut gray hair, sage-colored eyes, pin-striped woolen suit. Six-Thirty, too, gave him a thorough sniff, then turned to Elizabeth. *All clear.*

"I've been wanting to meet you for a very long time," Wilson was saying. "We appreciate your willingness to come in on such short notice."

"We?" Elizabeth asked, surprised.

"He means me," a fiftyish woman said as she emerged from the lab's supply cabinet with a clipboard. She had the kind of hair that had once been blond but was slowly surrendering to age. Like Wilson, she also wore a suit, but hers was bright blue and, despite the careful tailoring, looked less serious, thanks to a cheap daisy brooch pinned to her lapel. "Avery Parker," she said nervously, gripping Elizabeth's hand. "Pleasure."

Six-Thirty, having finished his investigation of Wilson, went to analyze Parker. He sniffed her leg. "Hello, Six-Thirty," she said. She bent over and pressed his head against her thigh. He took an exploratory sniff, then drew his head back in surprise. "He probably smells my dog," she said, drawing him back in. "Bingo's a huge fan of yours," she said, looking down at him. "Loved your work on the show."

What a highly intelligent human being.

"We'll be needing a full inventory from every lab," she said, turning to Frask. "And we'll also need to know what you might need, Miss Zott," she said with a touch of deference, "for your research. Your research here at Hastings, I mean."

"To continue your work on abiogenesis," Wilson interjected. "On your final show you announced your intention to return to your research. What better place than here?"

Elizabeth cocked her head to the side. "I can think of several."

The last time she'd been in this room, Frask was here, too, although at that time Frask was informing her that Calvin's things were gone, Six-Thirty had to go, and Madeline was on the way.

She took in the depressing chalkboard filled with someone else's writing, then looked back at Mr. Wilson. He was draped on Calvin's old stool like a bolt of fabric.

"I really don't want to waste your time," Elizabeth said, "but I don't see myself returning to Hastings. It's personal."

"I can understand," Avery Parker said. "After all that transpired here, who could blame you. Still, I'd like a chance to change your mind."

Elizabeth looked around the lab, her eyes resting on one of Calvin's old signs. KEEP OUT it warned.

"I'm sorry," she said. "You'll be wasting your breath."

Avery Parker looked to Wilson, who in turn looked to Frask.

"Why don't we have some coffee," Frask said, jumping up. "I'll make a fresh pot. And while we're waiting, the Parker Foundation can fill you in on some of their plans." But before she'd gone halfway across the room, the lab door swung open.

"Wilson!" Donatti shouted as if greeting a long-lost friend. "Just heard you were in town." He rushed forward, his hand extended like an overeager salesman. "Dropped everything and came right over. Technically I'm still on vacation, but—" He stopped abruptly, surprised to see a familiar face. "Miss Frask?" he said. "What are you—" Then he swiveled his head toward a frowny-looking older woman holding a clipboard. And just beyond her stood—*what the hell?*—Elizabeth Zott.

"Hello, Dr. Donatti," Avery said, extending her hand just as he dropped his. "It's nice to finally put a face to the name."

"I'm sorry, but you *are* . . . ?" he said condescendingly, while trying to avoid looking at Zott the way one avoids a solar eclipse.

"I'm Avery Parker," she said, pulling her hand back. And when he continued to look confused, she added, "Parker. As in the *Parker* Foundation."

His lips parted in fear.

"I'm sorry to learn we've interrupted your vacation, Dr. Donatti," Avery said. "But the good news is, you're about to have plenty of free time."

Donatti shook his head at her, then turned back to Wilson. "As I said. Had I known you were coming—"

"But we didn't want you to know we were coming," Wilson explained genially. "We wanted to surprise you. Or no, technically I guess this is more of blindside."

"Ex-excuse me?"

"Blindside," Wilson repeated. "You know. Like the way you blindsided us by misappropriating Parker Foundation funds. Or the way you blindsided Miss Zott—or should I say *Mr.* Zott?—when you stole her work."

Across the room, Elizabeth raised her eyebrows in surprise.

"Now look *here,*" Donatti said, jabbing a finger in Zott's general direction. "I don't know what that woman told you, but I can assure you—" He stopped midway. "And why the hell are *you* here?" he demanded, pointing at Frask. "After those ridiculous lies you wrote in your petulant little letter to *Life*? My lawyer wants to sue." He turned to Wilson. "You're probably not aware, Wilson, but we fired Frask years ago. She's got an axe to grind."

"She does," Wilson agreed. "It's a sharp axe, too."

"*Exactly,*" Donatti said.

"I know," Wilson said. "Because I'm her lawyer."

Donatti's eyes bulged.

"Donatti," Avery Parker said as she dug in a bag and pulled out a single sheet of paper. "I hate to be rude, but we're short on time. All we need is a quick signature and then you're free to go." She held out a document headed by two simple words: "Termination Notice."

Donatti, speechless, stared down at the document while Wilson explained that the Parker Foundation had recently acquired a majority share in Hastings. It was Frask's letter in *Life* magazine, Wilson said, that had prompted them to take a closer look—blah, blah, blah—malfeasance—blah, blah, blah—decided to take the whole place over—Donatti could barely listen. *Wasn't this Calvin Evans's old lab?* From somewhere far off in the distance, he heard Wilson droning on about "sloppy management," "faked test results," "plagiarism." God, he needed a drink.

"We're making some cuts," Frask said.

"What do you mean *we*?" Donatti said, snapping back.

"*I'm* making some cuts," Frask said.

"You're a *secretary*," Donatti exhaled, as if he were tired of this charade. "Fired, remember?"

"Frask is our new head of Personnel," Wilson informed him. "We've asked her to find a new director of Chemistry."

"But *I'm* the head of Chemistry," Donatti reminded him.

"We've decided to offer the job to someone else," Avery Parker said. She nodded at Elizabeth.

Elizabeth, surprised, took a step back.

"Out of the *question*!" thundered Donatti.

"I wasn't really asking a question," Avery Parker said, the termination notice hanging limp in her hand. "But if you'd like, we could leave your employment status up to someone who really knows your work." For the second time, she tilted her head in Elizabeth's direction.

All eyes turned to Elizabeth, but she didn't seem to notice; she was already fixated on the sputtering Donatti. Hands on hips, she leaned forward slightly, her eyes narrowed as if peering into a microscope. There were two beats of silence. Then she leaned back as if she'd seen enough.

"Sorry, Donatti," she said, handing him a pen. "You're just not smart enough."

CHAPTER 43

Stillborn

"Very few people surprise me, Mrs. Parker," Elizabeth said as she watched Frask escort Donatti out. "But you have."

Avery Parker nodded. "Good. The offer's sincere. We hope you'll accept. And by the way, it's Miss Parker. I'm not married. Actually," she added, "I've never been married."

"Nor have I," Elizabeth said.

"Yes," Avery Parker said, her voice dropping an octave. "I'm aware."

Elizabeth noted the change in timbre and felt an instant prick of irritation. Thanks to *Life,* the entire world knew Madeline was born out of wedlock, and because of it, she heard that tone all the time.

"I'm not sure how much you know about the Parker Foundation," Wilson began as he wandered around the lab, pausing briefly to read a description on a file folder.

"I know your focus is scientific research," Elizabeth said, turning toward him. "But that your roots were Catholic charities. Churches, choirs, orphanages—" She stopped dead, suddenly acutely aware of that last word. She looked at Wilson more closely.

"Yes, our founders were devoted to Catholic causes; however, our mission is entirely secular. What we do is try to find the best people working on the most critical issues of the day." He set aside the file folder in a way that communicated that it was definitely not one of them. "Seven years ago, when we funded you, you were doing just that—abiogenesis. Whether you know it or not, Miss Zott, you're the reason we came to Hastings in the first place. You and Calvin Evans."

At the mention of Calvin's name, she felt her chest tighten.

"Strange about Evans, isn't it?" Wilson said. "No one seems to have any idea what became of his work."

His casual words hit her like a cyclone. She pulled out a stool and sat down, watching as he poked around the lab like an archeologist, examining a tiny corner of this or that as if it might lead to something much bigger below.

"I know you've already made your position clear," he continued, "but I thought you'd be interested to know we plan to upgrade a lot of the equipment." He pointed to a shelf where an out-of-date distillation apparatus sat unused. As he raised his arm, a shiny cuff link peeked out from under his suit sleeve. "Like that, for instance. That thing looks like it hasn't been touched in years."

But Elizabeth had no reaction. She'd turned to stone.

When Calvin was ten, he'd written about a tall, rich-looking man with shiny cuff links who'd arrived at the boys home in a fancy limo. He seemed to think it was because of this man that the home was given new science books. But instead of being glad for the reading material, Calvin was devastated. *I'm here even though I should not be,* he'd scrawled. *And I will never ever forgive that man, him. Never. Not as long as I live.*

"Mr. Wilson," she said, her voice wooden. "You say your foundation only funds secular projects. Would that include education?"

"Education? Well yes, of course," he said. "We support several universities—"

"No, I mean, have you ever supplied a school with textbooks—"

"On occasion, but—"

"What about an orphanage?"

Wilson stopped short, surprised. His eyes darted to Parker.

In her mind, Elizabeth saw Calvin's letter to Wakely. *I HATE MY FATHER. I HOPE HE'S DEAD.*

"A Catholic boys home," she clarified.

Again, Wilson looked to Parker.

"In Sioux City, Iowa."

A thick silence fell, interrupted only by the sudden whoosh of an exhaust fan.

Elizabeth stared at Wilson, her face unfriendly.

It suddenly seemed clear: the job they were offering her was a ruse. They were there for one reason and one reason only: to claim Calvin's work.

The boxes. They knew about them. Maybe Frask had told them; maybe they'd made an educated guess. In any case, Wilson and Parker had bought Hastings; legally, Calvin's work belonged to them. They were plying her with compliments and promises, hoping that would be enough to coax the boxes out of the woodwork. But if that didn't work, they still had one last card left to play.

Calvin Evans had a blood relative.

"Wilson," Parker said, her voice trembling. "Would you mind? I'd like to speak with Miss Zott alone."

"*No,*" Elizabeth said sharply. "I have questions; I want the truth—"

Parker looked at Wilson, her face deflated. "It's all right, Wilson. I'll join you in a few minutes."

As the door latched closed, Elizabeth turned on Avery Parker. "I know what's going on here," she said. "I *know* why you asked me here today."

"We asked you here to offer you a job," Parker said. "That was our only goal. We're longtime admirers of your work."

Elizabeth searched the woman's face for signs of deceit. "Look," she said in a calmer voice. "I don't have an issue with you. It's Wilson. How long have you known him?"

"We've worked together for nearly thirty years, so I'd say I know him very well."

"Does he have children?"

She gave Elizabeth a peculiar look. "I'm not sure that's any of your business," she said. "But no."

"You're *sure.*"

"Of course I'm sure. He's my lawyer—this is *my* foundation, Miss Zott, but he's the face of it."

"And why is that?" Elizabeth pressed.

Avery Parker looked at her, unblinking. "I'm amazed you have to ask. I may have considerable assets, but like most women in the world, my hands are tied. I can't even write a check unless Wilson cosigns."

"How can that be? It's the *Parker* Foundation," Elizabeth pointed out. "Not the Wilson Foundation."

Parker snorted. "Yes, a foundation I inherited with the proviso that my *husband* make all the financial decisions. As I was unmarried at the time, the board appointed Wilson as trustee. As I'm still unmarried, Wilson continues to hold the reins. You're not the only one who's fought a losing battle, Miss Zott," she said as she stood up, tugging hard on her suit jacket. "Although I'm lucky: Wilson's a decent man."

She turned and walked away as Elizabeth asked another question, but instead of responding, Avery Parker ignored her. *What had she been thinking?* Elizabeth Zott was not interested in returning to Hastings, and maybe, based on her pointed questions about Wilson—not to mention all the *other* issues—it would be better for all if she did not. Distracted, Avery reached up and touched her finger to her cheap daisy brooch. What a foolish woman she'd been. Buying Hastings, coming here, meeting Zott. Yes, she'd always been fascinated by Zott and her research—she'd once dreamed of becoming a scientist herself. But instead, she'd been raised to be one thing and one thing only: nice. Unfortunately, according to both her parents and the Catholic Church, she'd failed at that, too.

"Miss *Parker*—" Elizabeth pressed.

"Miss *Zott*," Avery returned just as emphatically. "I've made a mistake. You don't want to come back to Hastings; fine. I'm not going to beg."

Elizabeth took a short breath in.

"I've been begging my entire life," Parker continued. "I'm sick of it."

Elizabeth brushed a few stray hairs aside. "It's not even me you want," she said hotly. "Isn't that right? You're only here for the boxes."

Avery cocked her head as if she hadn't heard correctly. "Boxes?"

"I understand. You bought Hastings; they belong to you. But this charade—"

"*What* charade?"

"—I want to know about All Saints. I think I have a right to know."

"Excuse me?" Parker said. "You have a right? Let me tell you a little secret about rights. They don't exist."

"They do for the wealthy, Miss Parker," Elizabeth insisted. "Tell me about Wilson. About Wilson and Calvin."

Avery Parker stared back perplexed. "Wilson and Calvin? No, no . . ."

"Again, I think I have a right to know."

Avery pressed her hands down on the counter. "I wasn't planning on doing this today."

"Doing what?"

"I wanted to get to know you first," Avery continued. "I think that's *my* right. To know who *you* are."

Elizabeth crossed her arms. *"Excuse me?"*

Avery reached for the chalkboard eraser. "Look. I . . . I need to tell you a story."

"I'm not interested in stories."

"It involves a seventeen-year-old girl," Avery Parker said, undeterred, "who fell in love with a young man. It's a rather standard story," she said brittlely, "where the young girl got pregnant and her prominent parents, shamed by their daughter's promiscuity, sent her away to a Catholic home for unwed mothers." She turned her back on Elizabeth. "Maybe you've heard of these homes, Miss Zott. They're run like prisons. Filled with young women in the same kind of trouble. They have their babies, then relinquish them. There was an official form to sign and most signed. Those who refused were threatened: they'd have to endure the delivery alone; they might even die. Despite the warning, the seventeen-year-old girl still refused to sign. Kept insisting she had *rights.*" Parker paused, shaking her head as if she still couldn't believe the naïveté.

"True to their word, when her labor started, they put her in a room by herself and locked the door. She stayed there, alone, crying out in pain, for a full day. At some point, the doctor, infuriated by the noise, finally decided he'd had enough. He went in and anesthetized her. When she came to hours later, she was given the grim news. Her baby had been stillborn. Shocked, she asked to see the body, but the doctor said they'd already disposed of it.

"Fast-forward ten years," Avery Parker continued, turning to face Elizabeth, her jaw tight. "A nurse from the unwed mothers home contacts the now-twenty-seven-year-old woman. Wants money for the truth. Tells her the baby didn't die; rather, it, like all the other babies, had been put up for adoption. The only unusual thing: this child's adoptive parents died in a tragic accident, then the child's aunt died. The child was sent to a place called All Saints in Iowa."

Elizabeth froze.

"That was the day," Avery Parker said, her voice turning sad, "the young woman began her quest to find her son." She paused. "My son."

Elizabeth drew back, all the color draining from her face.

"I'm Calvin Evans's biological mother," Avery Parker said slowly, her gray eyes filling with tears. "And with your permission, Miss Zott, I'd very much like to meet my granddaughter."

CHAPTER 44

The Acorn

It was as if all the air had been sucked out of the room. Elizabeth stared at Avery Parker, uncertain how to proceed. This couldn't be true. Calvin's own diary had revealed that his biological mother had died in childbirth.

"Miss Parker," Elizabeth said carefully, as if picking her way across hot coals. "A lot of people have tried to take advantage of Calvin over the years. Many have even pretended to be long-lost family members. Your story is—" She stopped. She thought back to all the letters Calvin had kept. Sad Mother—she'd written to him several times. "If you knew he was in that boys home, why didn't you go get him?"

"I did," Avery Parker said. "Or rather, I sent Wilson. I'm ashamed to admit I wasn't brave enough to go myself." She got up and walked the length of the worktable. "You need to understand. I'd long ago accepted that my child was dead. Now to suddenly learn he was alive? I was afraid to get my hopes up. Like Calvin, I too have been a target for countless scams, including from dozens of people claiming to be *my* so-called relatives. So I sent Wilson," she repeated, looking down at the floor as if reviewing this decision for the fiftieth time. "I sent him to All Saints the very next day."

The vacuum pump started a new cycle, and with it a hissing sound filled the laboratory.

"And—" Elizabeth prodded.

"And," Avery said, "the bishop informed Wilson that Calvin was . . ." She hesitated.

"Was what?" Elizabeth urged. *"What?"*

The older woman's face sagged. "Dead."

Elizabeth sat back, floored. The home needed money, the bishop saw an opportunity, there was a memorial fund. Facts came pouring out of the woman in a dull, lifeless rush.

"Have you ever lost a family member?" Avery suddenly asked in a flat voice.

"My brother."

"Illness?"

"Suicide."

"Oh god," she said. "So you know what it is to feel responsible for someone's death."

Elizabeth tensed. The words fit snugly, like laces knotted twice. "But you didn't kill Calvin," she said with a heavy heart.

"No," Parker said in a voice sick with remorse. "I did something much worse. I buried him."

From the north side of the room, a timer beeped, and Elizabeth, trembling, went to shut it off. She turned to take in the woman standing at the chalkboard. She leaned to the right. Six-Thirty got up and went to Avery. He pressed his head against her thigh. *I know what it's like to fail a loved one.*

"My parents had long funded unwed mothers homes and orphanages," Avery continued, fiddling with the eraser. "They thought this made them good people. And yet thanks to their blind allegiance to the Catholic Church, they managed to make an orphan out of my son." She paused. "I funded my son's memorial before he was dead, Miss Zott," she said, her breath shallow. "I buried him twice."

Elizabeth felt a sudden wave of nausea.

"After Wilson returned from the boys home," Avery continued, "I sank into a deep depression. I'd never had the chance to see my own son, never held him, never heard his voice. Worse, I had to live with the knowledge that he'd suffered. He'd lost me, then his parents, then he ended up in that garbage dump of a boys home. Each of these losses signed, sealed, and delivered in the name of the church." She stopped abruptly, her face reddening. "YOU DON'T BELIEVE IN GOD FOR SCIENTIFIC REASONS, MISS ZOTT?" she suddenly exploded. "WELL, I DON'T BELIEVE IN GOD FOR *PERSONAL* REASONS."

Elizabeth tried to speak but nothing came out.

"The *only* decision I was able to make," Avery Parker said, trying to bring her voice back under control, "was to ensure that all the memorial funds went toward a science education. Biology. Chemistry. Physics. Exercise, too. Calvin's father—his biological father, I mean—was an athlete. A rower. That's why the boys at All Saints learned to row. It was a gesture. In his honor."

Elizabeth saw Calvin. They were in the pair, his face lit by the early morning sun. He was smiling, one hand on the oar, the other reaching for her. "That's how he got to Cambridge," she said as the vision slowly faded away. "On a rowing scholarship."

Avery dropped the eraser. "I had no idea."

Details slowly continued to fall into place, but something still nagged at Elizabeth.

"But . . . but how did you finally find out that Calvin—"

"*Chemistry Today,*" Parker said, slipping onto the stool next to Elizabeth's. "The one with Calvin on the cover. I still remember that day—Wilson came rushing into my office waving it in the air. 'You won't believe this,' he said. I picked up the phone right then and called the bishop. Naturally he insisted it was only a coincidence—'Evans,' he said. 'It's a very common name.' I knew he was lying and I intended to sue—until Wilson convinced me the publicity would not only be ruinous for the foundation but embarrassing for Calvin." She leaned back and took a deep breath before continuing. "I cut off funding immediately. Then I wrote to Calvin—several times. I explained things as best I could, asked to meet him, told him that I wanted to fund his research. I can only imagine what he thought," she said, depressed. "Some lady writing to him out of the blue claiming to be his mother. Or maybe I do because I never heard from him."

Elizabeth started. The Sad Mother letters bloomed again before her eyes, the signature at the bottom of each, radiating a sudden cruel clarity. *Avery Parker.*

"But surely if you'd arranged a meeting. Flown to California—"

Avery's face turned ashen. "Look. It's one thing to pursue a child with vigor. But once that child reaches adulthood, it changes. I decided to move slowly. Give him time to accept the possibility of me, research my foundation, realize I had no reason to delude him. I knew it might take years. I forced myself to be patient. But obviously," she said, "given what happened—" She fixed her gaze on a stack of notebooks. "I was—too patient."

"Oh dear *god,*" Elizabeth said, sinking her head in her hands.

"Still," Parker continued in a monotone, "I followed his career. I thought maybe there'd be a chance, some way to help him. But as it turned out, he didn't need my help. You did."

"But how did you know Calvin and I were even . . ."

"Together?" A wistful smile pulled at the corners of her mouth. "It was all anyone could talk about," Parker said. "From the moment Wilson set foot in Hastings, all he heard were veiled references to Calvin Evans and his scandalous affair. It's one of the reasons why, when Wilson told Donatti he was there to fund abiogenesis, Donatti did his very best to try to steer him elsewhere. The last thing he wanted was for Calvin or anyone associated with Calvin to succeed. And then there was the fact that you were female. Donatti rightly assumed that most donors would not fund a woman."

"But why would you, of all people, put up with that?"

"I'm almost ashamed to admit there was a part of me that enjoyed the position we put him in. He went to such great lengths to convince Wilson you were a man. But Wilson *did* have a plan to meet you without Donatti's knowledge. In fact, he'd booked a flight. But then . . ." Her voice trailed off.

"What?"

"But then Calvin died," she said. "And your work seemed to die with it."

Elizabeth looked as if she'd been slapped. "Miss Parker, I was *fired*."

Avery Parker sighed. "I know that now, thanks to Miss Frask. But at the time I thought you might be trying to move on. You and Calvin never married. I assumed the feelings between you and my son hadn't been mutual. Everyone said he was a very difficult man—that he held grudges. Obviously, I had no idea you were pregnant. You were quoted in the *LA Times* obituary as saying you barely knew him." She took a deep breath in. "By the way, I was there. At his funeral."

Elizabeth's eyes widened.

"Wilson and I stood a few grave sites over. I'd come to bury him for the final time, and to speak with you. But before I could summon the courage, you left. Walked away before the service was even over." She dropped her head in her hands, tears spilling. "As much as I'd wanted to believe someone had loved my son . . ."

With those words, Elizabeth slumped beneath the unrelenting burden of misunderstanding. "I *did* love your son, Miss Parker!" she cried. "With all my heart. I still do." She glanced up at the lab where they'd first met, her face flattened by grief. "Calvin Evans was the best thing that ever happened to me," she choked. "He was the most brilliant, loving man; the kindest, the most interesting—" She stopped. "I'm not sure how else to explain it," she said, her voice beginning to break, "except to say we had chemistry. Actual chemistry. And it was no accident."

And maybe it was finally using the word "accident," but the crushing weight of what she'd lost overtook her and she laid her head on Avery Parker's shoulder and sobbed in a way she never had before.

CHAPTER 45

Supper at Six

Within the lab, time seemed to stop. Six-Thirty lifted his head, watching the two women. The older one's arms surrounded Elizabeth like a protective cocoon, Elizabeth's loss something she seemed to know by heart. Although he would never be a chemist, he was a dog. And as a dog he knew a permanent bond when he saw one.

"I've spent the majority of my life not knowing what happened to my son," Parker said, holding a trembling Elizabeth close. "I have no idea what his adoptive family was like, if the bishop's story was completely false or only partly true. I don't even know what brought him to Hastings. The truth is, I still know very little," she said. "Or did until I checked the foundation's P.O. box and found something unusual buried beneath months of junk mail."

She reached down into her bag and took out a letter.

Elizabeth recognized the handwriting immediately. Madeline.

"Your daughter wrote to Wilson and mentioned her family tree project—the one that appeared in *Life*. She insisted that her father had been raised in a boys home in Sioux City—somehow, she knew Wilson had funded it. She wanted to thank him personally, tell him the Parker Foundation was on her tree. I thought it might be a crank letter, but she had so many details. Adoptions are usually sealed, Miss Zott—a heartless practice—but with

Madeline's information, a private investigator was finally able to ferret out the truth. I have it all here." She reached back into her bag to withdraw a large folder. "Look at this," Parker said, her voice defiant as she extended her own faked death certificate, payback for her non-cooperation at the unwed mothers home. "This is how it all started."

Elizabeth took the certificate in her hands. Madeline had once said Wakely believed some things needed to stay in the past because the past was the only place they made sense. And as it was so often with the things Wakely said, Elizabeth saw the wisdom in it. But there was one last thing she felt Calvin would have wanted her to ask.

"Miss Parker," Elizabeth said carefully, "what became of Calvin's biological father?"

Avery Parker opened the file folder again, handing over yet another death certificate—although this one was real. "He died of tuberculosis," she said. "Before Calvin was even born. I have a picture." She opened her billfold and extracted a weathered photograph.

"But he—" Elizabeth gasped as she took in the young man standing next to a much younger Avery.

"Looks exactly like Calvin? I know." She slid a copy of the old *Chemistry Today* magazine out and placed it next to the photograph. The two women sat side by side as Calvin and his even younger father looked up at them from their separate histories.

"What was he like?"

"Wild," Avery said. "He was a musician or wanted to be. We met by accident. He ran me over with his bike."

"Were you hurt?"

"Yes," she said. "Luckily. Because he lifted me up, put me on his handlebars, told me to hang on, and rushed me to a doctor. Ten stitches later," she said, pointing to an old scar on her forearm, "we were in love. He gave me this brooch," she said, pointing to the lopsided daisy on her lapel. "I still wear it every day." She glanced around at the lab. "I'm sorry about meeting here. In hindsight, I realize this might have caused you some pain. I'm sorry. I just wanted to be in the room where—" She stopped.

"I understand," Elizabeth said. "I really do. And I'm glad we're here together. This is where Calvin and I first met. Right over there," she said, pointing. "I needed beakers, so I stole his."

"That sounds very resourceful," Avery said. "Was it love at first sight?"

"Not exactly," Elizabeth said, remembering how Calvin had demanded that her boss give him a call. "But we ended up having our own happy accident. I'll tell you about it sometime."

"I'd love to hear it," she said. "I wish I could have known him. Perhaps through you, I might." She took a shaky breath, then cleared her throat. "I would very much like to be part of your family, Miss Zott," she said. "I hope that's not too bold."

"Please, call me Elizabeth. And you *are* family, Avery. Madeline understood this a long time ago. It's not Wilson she put on the family tree—it's you."

"I'm not sure what you mean."

"You're the acorn."

Avery, her eyes a watery gray, took in some distant point across the room. "The fairy godmother acorn," she said to herself. *"Me."*

From outside they heard footsteps, then a quick knock. The lab door swung open and Wilson stepped back in. "I'm sorry to intrude," he said cautiously, "but I wanted to make sure everything was—"

"It is," Avery Parker said. "It finally is."

"Thank god," he said, putting his hand to his chest. "In that case, as much as I hate to bring up business, there's a lot that needs your attention, Avery, before we leave tomorrow."

"I'll be right there."

"You're leaving already?" Elizabeth asked, surprised, as Wilson shut the door behind him.

"I'm afraid I must," Avery said. "As I mentioned earlier, I wasn't really planning on telling you any of this—not before we had a chance to get to know each other." Then she added hopefully, "But we'll be back soon, I promise."

"Let's say supper at six, then," Elizabeth said, not wanting her to go. "The home lab. Everyone—you, Wilson, Mad, Sixty-Thirty, me, Harriet, Walter. You'll need to meet Wakely and Mason at some point, too. The whole family."

Avery Parker, her face suddenly familiar with Calvin's smile, turned back and took Elizabeth's hands in her own. "The whole family," she said.

As the door closed behind them, Elizabeth bent down and took Six-Thirty's head in her hands. "Tell me. How soon did you know?"

At two forty-one, he wanted to say. *Which is what I plan to call her.*

But instead he turned and jumped up on the opposite counter and grabbed a fresh notebook. Removing the pencil from her hair, she took it from him, then opened to the first page.

"Abiogenesis," she said. "Let's get started."

ACKNOWLEDGMENTS

Writing is a solo effort, but it takes an army to bring a book to the shelves. I'd like to thank my army:

From Zürich, my pals who read the earliest chapters: Morgane Ghilardi, CS Wilde, Sherida Deeprose, Sarah Nickerson, Meredith Wadley-Suter, Alison Baillie, and John Collette.

My Curtis Brown online writing friends: Tracey Stewart, Anna Marie Ball, Morag Hastie, Al Wright, Debbie Richardson, Sarah Lothian, Denise Turner, Jane Lawrence, Erika Rawnsley, Garret Symth, and Deborah Gasking.

My unbelievably supportive and talented Three-Month Curtis Brown novelists: Lizzie Mary Cullen, Kausar Turabi, Matthew Cunningham, Rosie Oram, Elliot Sweeney, Yasmina Hatem, Simon Hardman Lea, Malika Browne, Melanie Stacey, Neil Daws, Michelle Garrett, Ness Lyons, Ian Shaw, Mark Sapwell, and the brilliant Charlotte Mendelson, who pushed us to be better.

Curtis Brown's Anna Davis for her grace and guidance; the tireless Jack Hadley, Katie Smart, and Jennifer Kerslake for their always-cheery support; Lisa Babalis, who generously read my opening and gave me hope; Sarah Harvey, Katie Harrison, Caoimhe White, and Jodi Fabbri, the best rights management team in the universe; Rosie Pierce, who handles every detail with aplomb; ICM's Jennifer Joel, a reassuring, confident voice when things got complicated; Tia Ikemoto for the helping hand; CB film rights agent Luke Speed, who's probably in some sort of science experiment to see how long a person can go without sleep; and Anna Weguelin, who, I'm pretty sure, doesn't sleep either.

Actually, I'm not sure anyone at Curtis Brown or ICM sleeps.

An extra huge thanks goes to Felicity Blunt at Curtis Brown. A few years back, before I moved to London, I was researching agents and saw an interview Felicity had given, and I remember thinking, *If I could have any agent . . .* And then I did. Thanks, Felicity, for your faith in me, your keen eye, your kindness, your toughness, and your unflagging support. Now that the book is done, please feel free to play with your children.

On the publishing side of things, special thanks to Jane Lawson and Lee Boudreaux, the shrewdest editors a writer could ever hope for, Thomas Tebbe für seine begeisterte Unterstützung, Beci Kelly and Emily Mahon for their eye-catching covers, Maria Carella for the beautiful interior, Cara Reilly for always being on top of things, and Amy Ryan for her gifted copyediting. Thanks also to my publishers, Larry Finlay and Bill Thomas; my talented publicists, Alison Barrow, Elena Hershey, and Michael Goldsmith; the amazing marketing leadership of Vicky Palmer, Lauren Weber, and Lindsay Mandel, and the creative minds of Todd Doughty, Lilly Cox, Sophie MacVeigh, Kristin Fassler, and Erin Merlo. A huge thanks to the patient, eagle-eyed production maven Ellen Feldman, as well as to Lorraine Hyland. Also huge thanks to Tom Chicken, Laura Richetti, Emily Harvey, Laura Garrod, Hana Sparks, Sarah Adams, and the entire sales team. Finally, special thanks to Madeline McIntosh. Your encouragement and support is so very much appreciated.

Researching chemistry is one thing, getting it right is another. To that end, special thanks to Dr. Mary Koto, longtime friend, brilliant biologist, and Eskimo Pie connoisseur, and Dr. Beth Mundy, amazing Seattle chemist and reader, both of whom graciously and meticulously checked the details.

Huge affection and gratitude to all my rowing teammates at

Green Lake and Pocock in Seattle, and extra-special thanks to rower Donya Burns, who once insisted our tired crew "recommit to every stroke." That urging took up permanent residence in my brain and ultimately became the advice Harriet gives Elizabeth.

To the writers who understand how real the struggle is: Joannie Stangeland, poet extraordinaire; Diane Arieff, the most hilarious person on the face of the earth; Sue Monshaw for keeping the faith; and Laura Kasischke, who probably doesn't remember me but her writing advice and encouragement went a very long way. Finally, extra-special thanks to Susan Biskeborn, the most comforting, calming, supportive voice in the writing wilderness. Thanks, Susan, for always knowing what to say and when to say it.

To some people I really wish I could share this with but can't: my parents, lifelong readers, and to Helen Martin, my oldest, dearest friend. I miss you, 86.

And for the three people who were there all the way: Sophie, thanks for getting the whole thing rolling by sending me that link to Curtis Brown in the first place—to say I owe you is the understatement of the year. Also thanks for your constant support and deadpan humor, your empathetic understanding of the bumpy creative process, your publishing insights, and your drop-everything readiness to ask and answer the eternal question: Cookies? Or fairies?

To Zoë, thanks for your kindness on the bad days and your joy on the good ones, also for your scary psycho typo spidey sense, for all the Ellie photos that always make me laugh, and for your highly curated meme selection, which probably belongs in a museum. Despite how much you had on your own plate, you always found time to check in and chat.

And to David, thanks doesn't begin to cover it so I'm putting it in all caps—THANKS. For always being ready to read, for being the better cook, for engaging me in constant debate, and especially for pretending to be unalarmed when you finally discovered just how much I talk to myself during the day. Never in a million years did I imagine so much fun (not to mention the uncanny ability to count down by sevens from three hundred well into the negative numbers in under a minute) could come packaged in one human being. I love and admire you.

Finally, thanks to my dog, Friday, gone but not forgotten, and the ever-stoic 99. I apologize for every time I said to either one of you, "Just let me finish this paragraph—then we'll go."

Bonnie Garmus is a copywriter and creative director who's worked widely in the fields of technology, medicine, and education. She's an open-water swimmer, a rower, and mother to two pretty amazing daughters. Born in California and most recently from Seattle, she currently lives in London with her husband and her dog, 99.